THE
SUBTLE
KNIFE
THE GRAPHIC NOVEL

PHILIP PULLMAN

THE SUBTLE KNIFE

THE GRAPHIC NOVEL

Adapted by Stéphane Melchior,
art by Thomas Gilbert

ALFRED A. KNOPF · NEW YORK

THIS IS A BORZOI BOOK PUBLISHED BY ALFRED A. KNOPF

Visit us on the Web! rhcbooks.com

Educators and librarians, for a variety of teaching tools, visit us at RHTeachersLibrarians.com

Library of Congress Cataloging-in-Publication Data is available upon request.
ISBN 978-0-593-17693-1 (trade) — ISBN 978-0-593-17694-8 (lib. bdg.)
ISBN 978-0-593-17695-5 (ebook) — ISBN 978-0-593-17692-4 (trade pbk.)

MANUFACTURED IN CHINA

January 2022
10 9 8 7 6 5 4 3 2 1
First American Edition

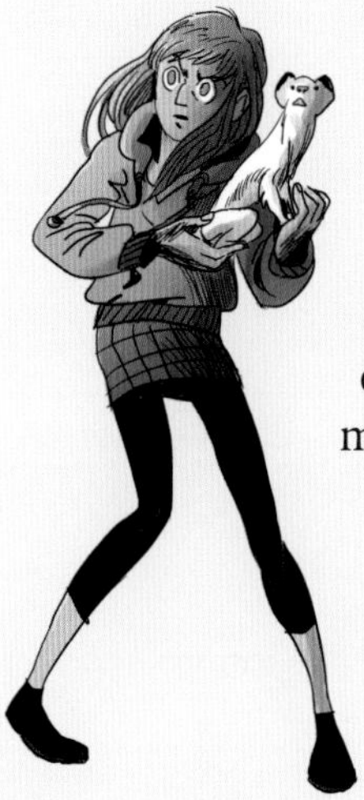

Betrayed by Mrs. Coulter, rejected by Lord Asriel, and devastated by the death of their friend Roger, Lyra and her dæmon cross into the new world. She and Pantalaimon are determined to discover more about Dust. This mysterious substance has been the source of so much consternation, the subject of hideous experiments. But if it is feared and reviled by their enemies, Lyra and Pan feel it must be good, and worthy of protection.

Behind them lie pain and death and fear; ahead of them lie doubt and danger and fathomless mysteries. They'll be on their own in this new world, without their friends the gyptians, the adventurer Lee Scoresby, the witch Serafina Pekkala, and, most of all, the magnificent armored bear Iorek Byrnison. But they have the alethiometer to guide them. And they have each other.

And they are about to discover that they are not the only ones with a destiny. . . .

The word "dæmon," which appears throughout the book, is pronounced like the word "demon."

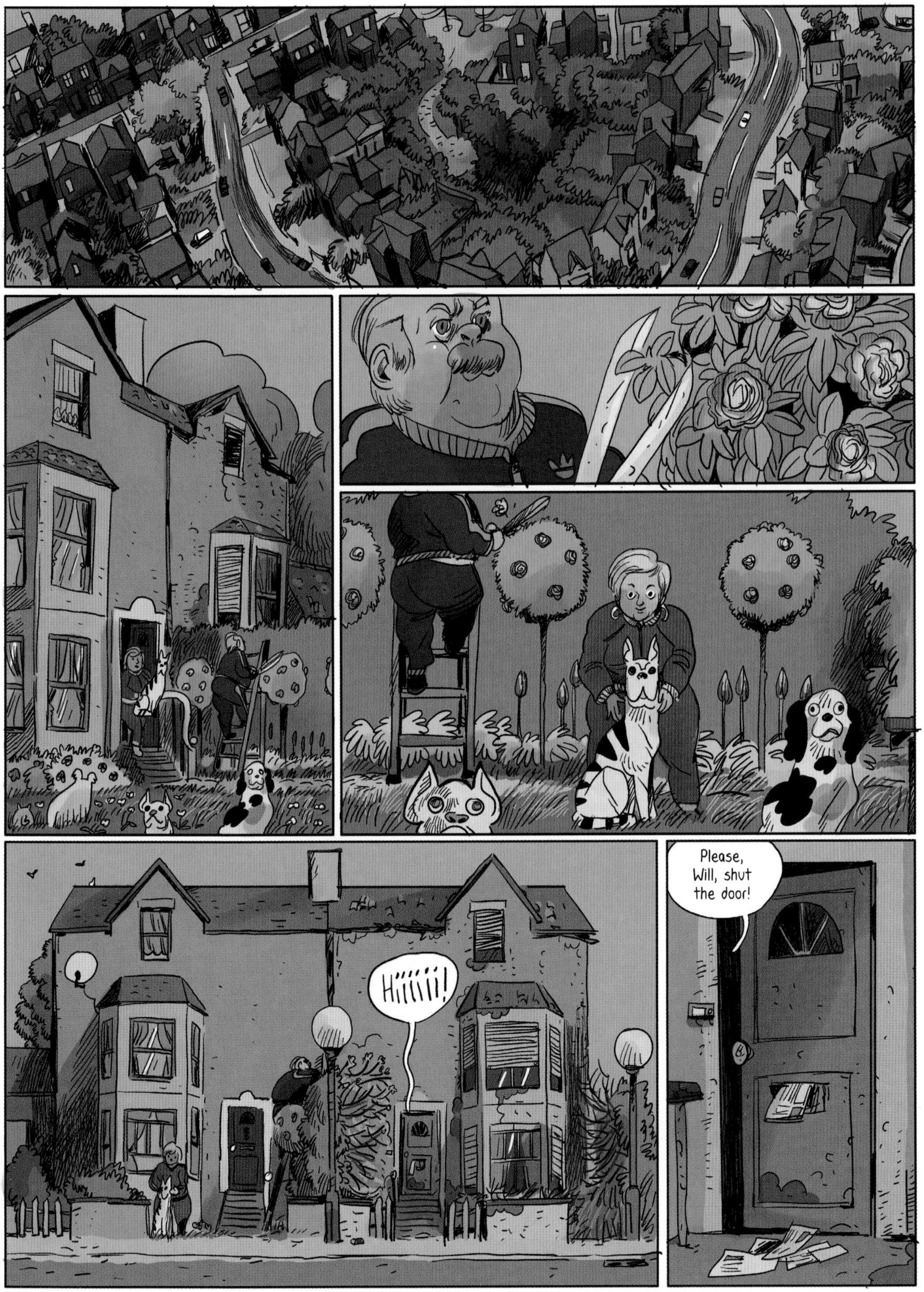
Hiiiiii!
Please, Will, shut the door!

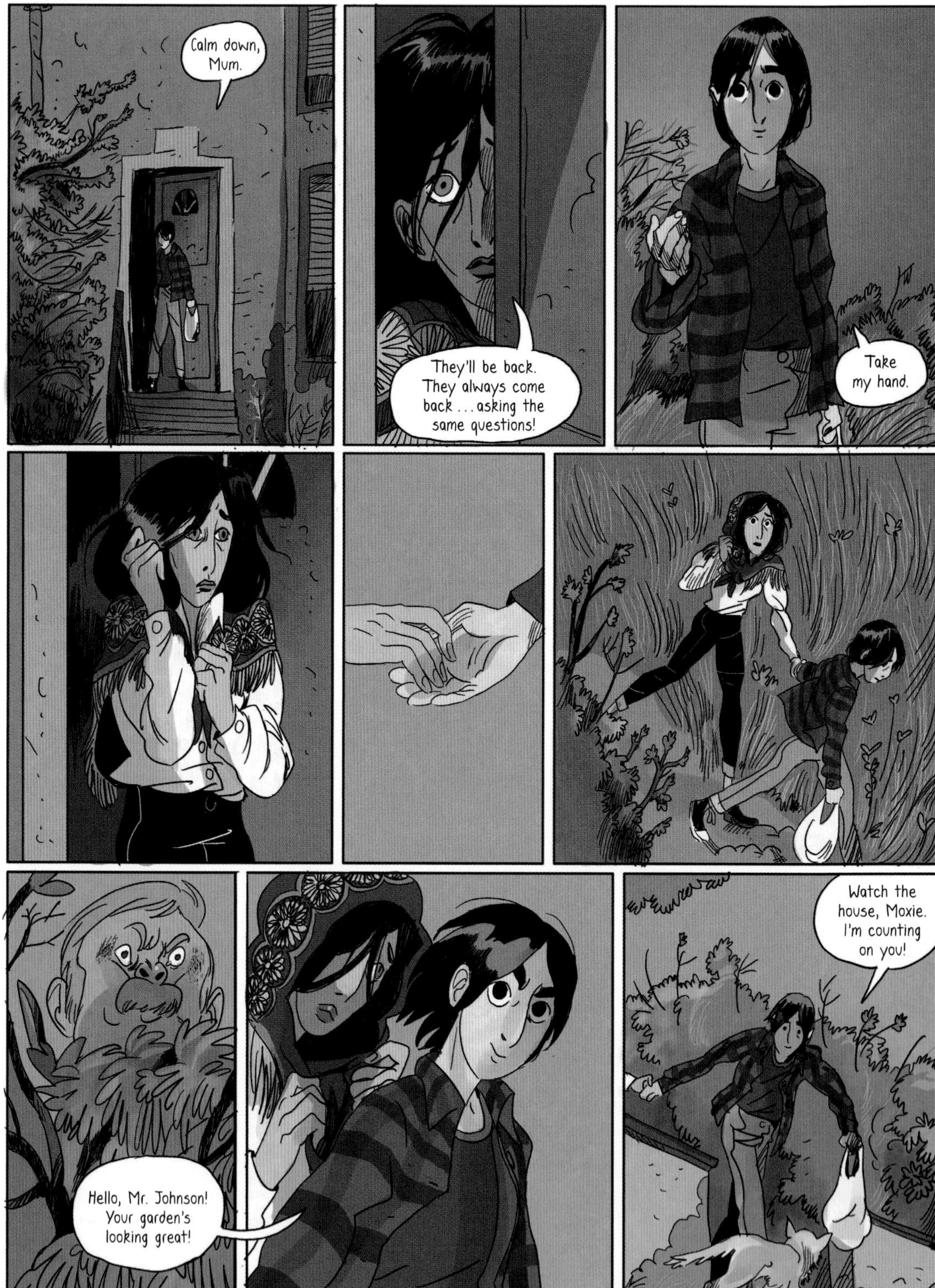
Calm down, Mum.
They'll be back. They always come back . . . asking the same questions!
Take my hand.
Hello, Mr. Johnson! Your garden's looking great!
Watch the house, Moxie. I'm counting on you!

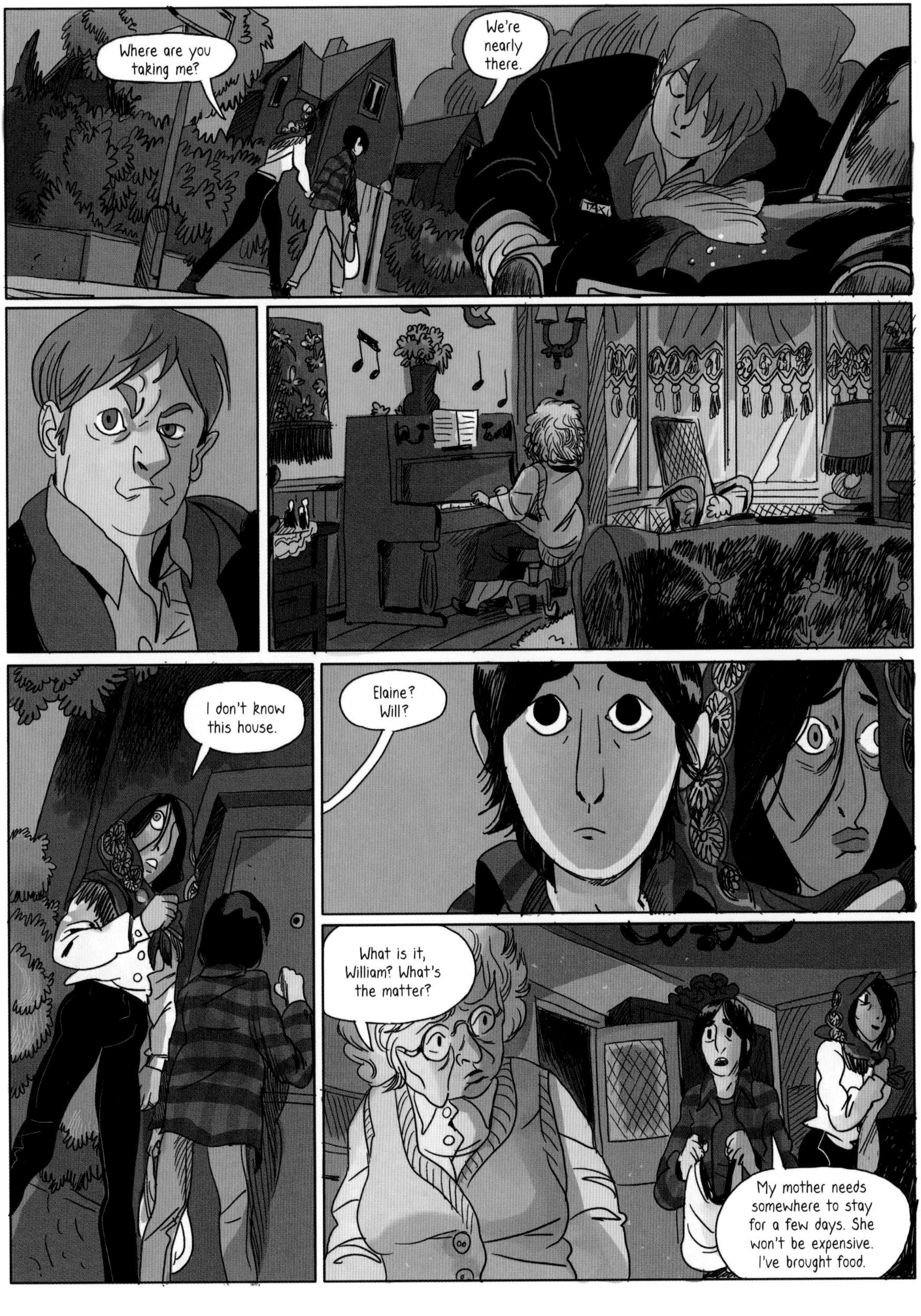
Where are you taking me?
We're nearly there.
I don't know this house.
Elaine? Will?
What is it, William? What's the matter?
My mother needs somewhere to stay for a few days. She won't be expensive. I've brought food.

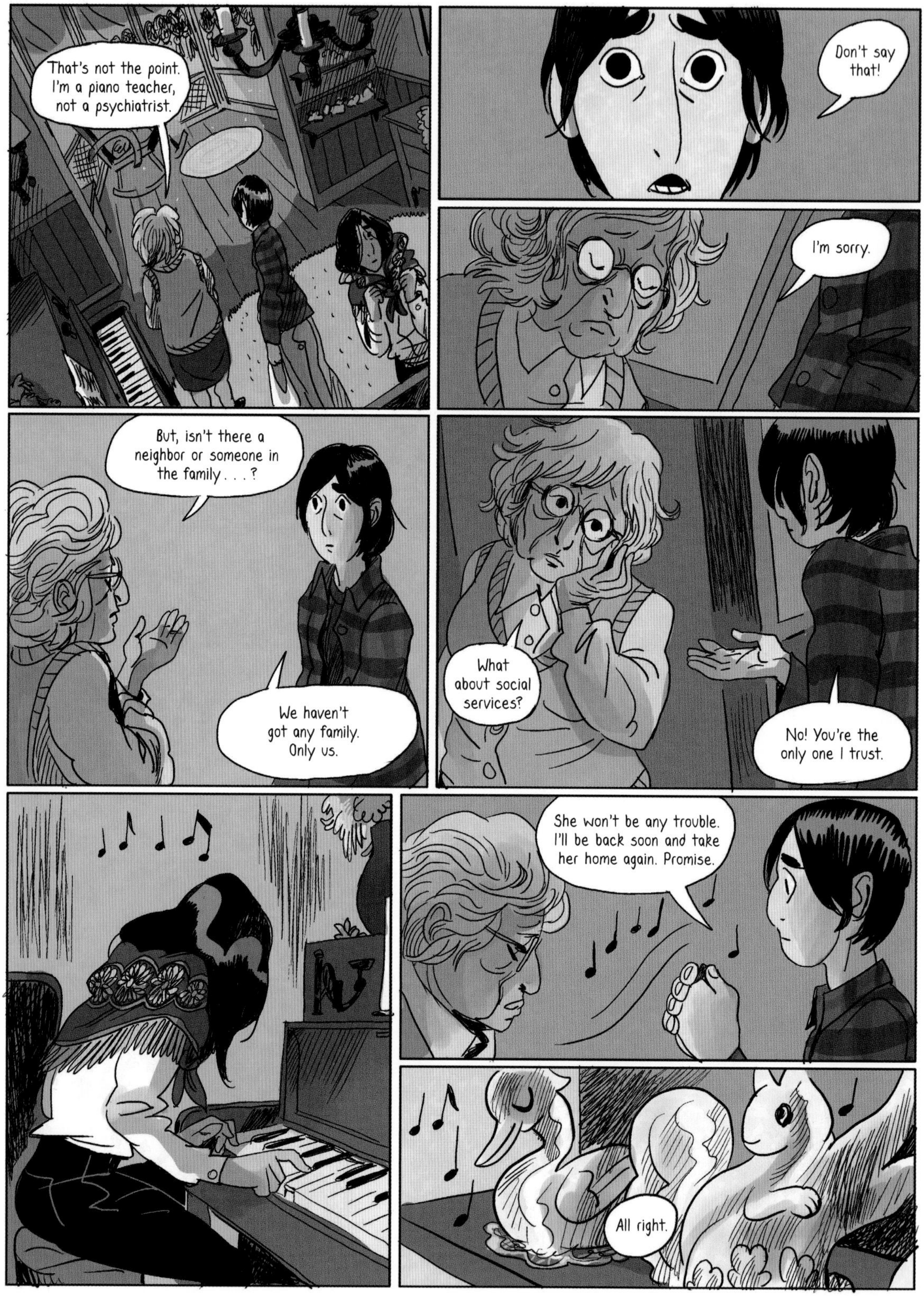
That's not the point. I'm a piano teacher, not a psychiatrist.
Don't say that!
I'm sorry.
But, isn't there a neighbor or someone in the family . . . ?
We haven't got any family. Only us.
What about social services?
No! You're the only one I trust.
She won't be any trouble. I'll be back soon and take her home again. Promise.
All right.

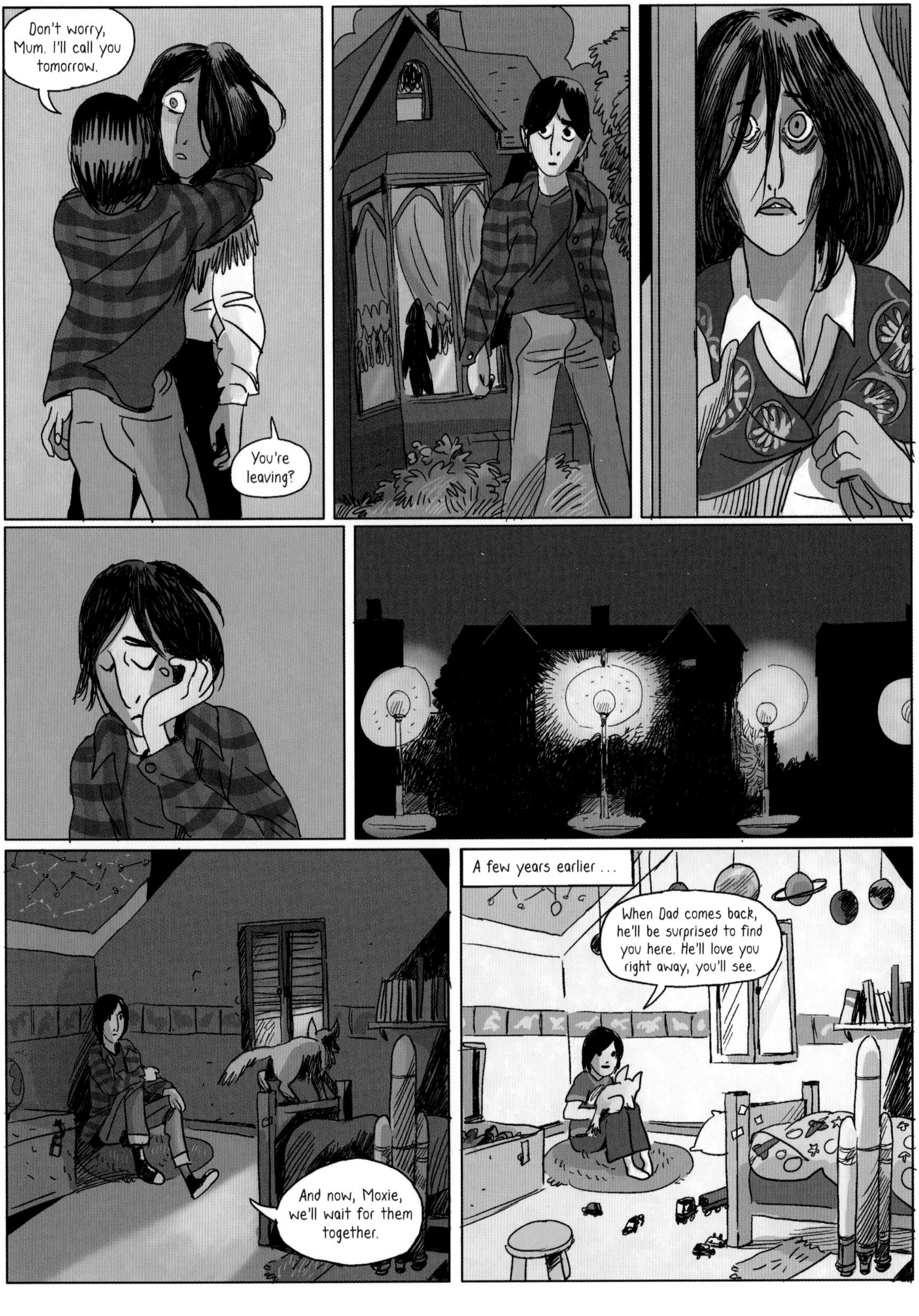
Don't worry, Mum. I'll call you tomorrow.
You're leaving?
A few years earlier . . .
And now, Moxie, we'll wait for them together.
When Dad comes back, he'll be surprised to find you here. He'll love you right away, you'll see.

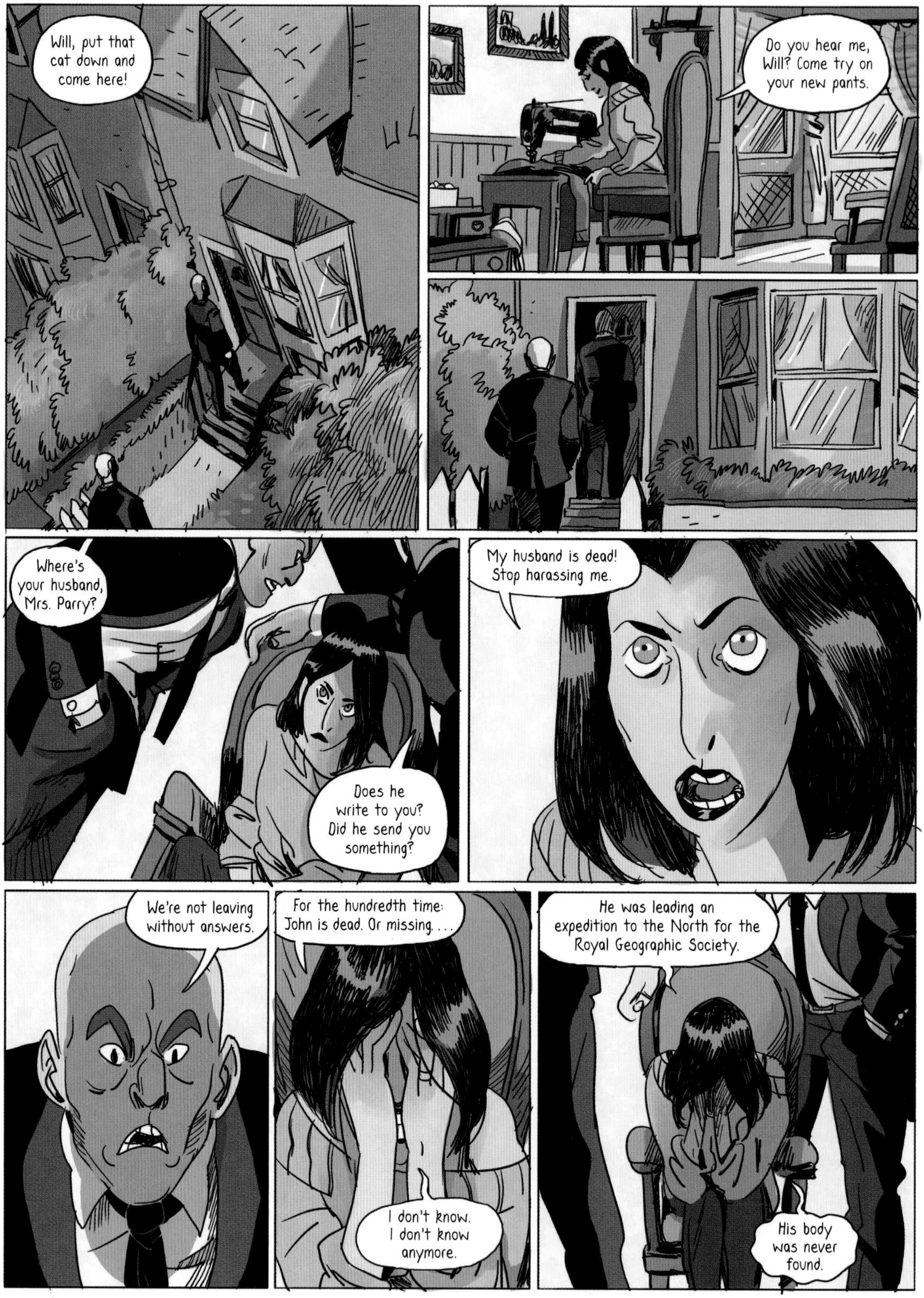
Will, put that cat down and come here!
Do you hear me, Will? Come try on your new pants.
Where's your husband, Mrs. Parry?
Does he write to you? Did he send you something?
My husband is dead! Stop harassing me.
We're not leaving without answers.
For the hundredth time: John is dead. Or missing. . . .
I don't know. I don't know anymore.
He was leading an expedition to the North for the Royal Geographic Society.
His body was never found.

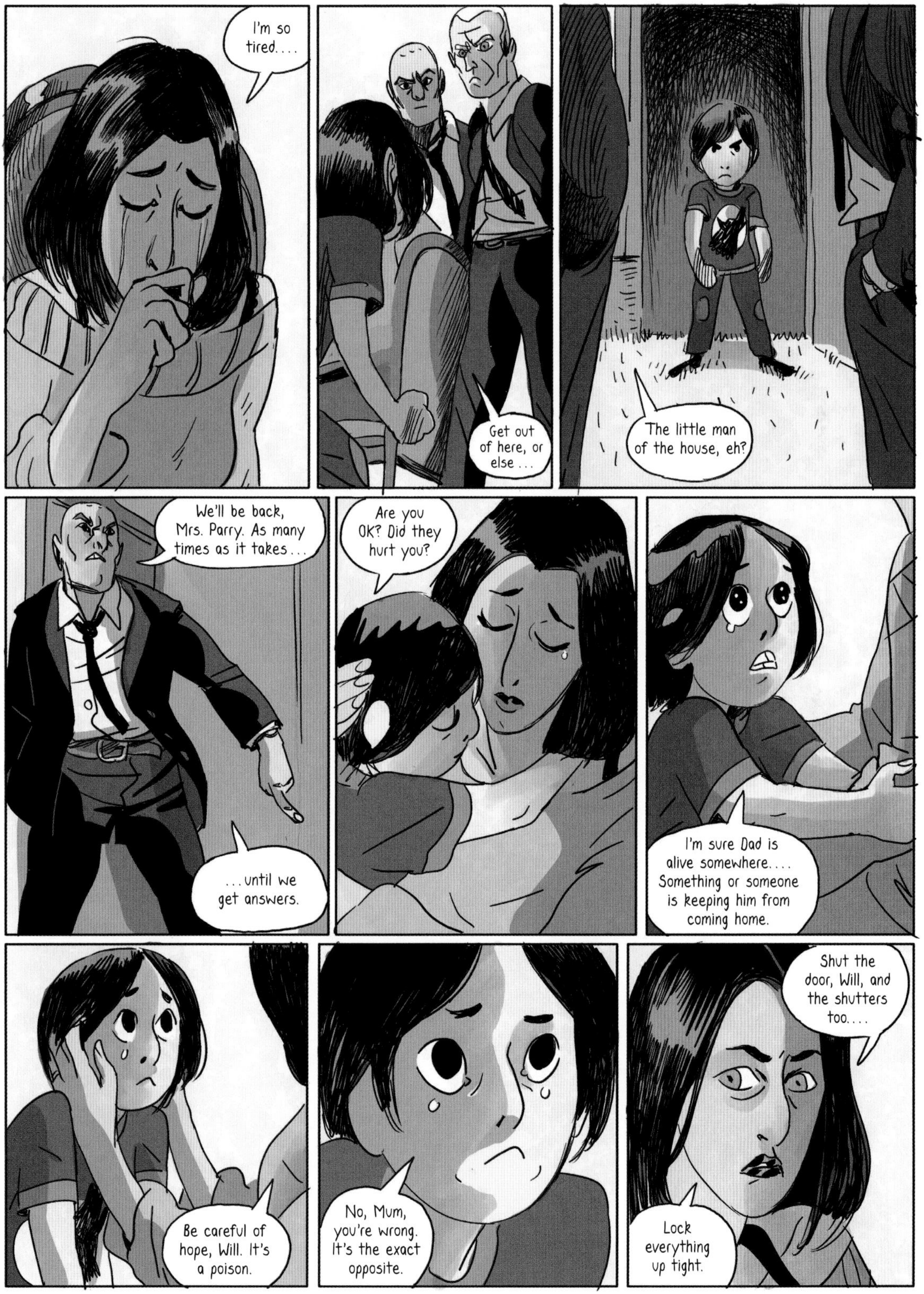
I'm so tired. . . .
Get out of here, or else . . .
The little man of the house, eh?
We'll be back, Mrs. Parry. As many times as it takes . . .
. . . until we get answers.
Are you OK? Did they hurt you?
I'm sure Dad is alive somewhere. . . . Something or someone is keeping him from coming home.
Be careful of hope, Will. It's a poison.
No, Mum, you're wrong. It's the exact opposite.
Shut the door, Will, and the shutters too. . . .
Lock everything up tight.

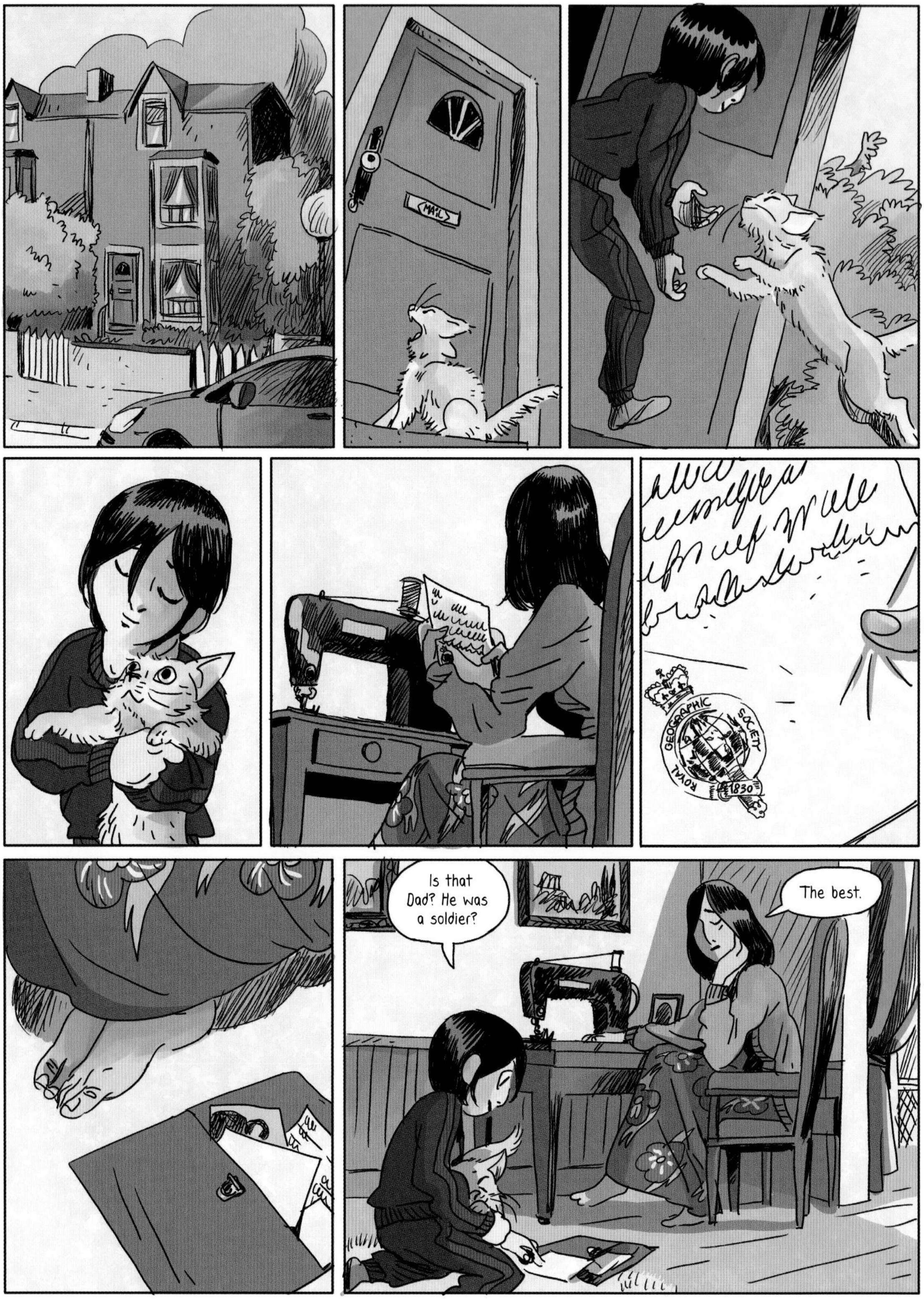
MAIL
ROYAL GEOGRAPHIC SOCIETY
1830
Is that Dad? He was a soldier?
The best.

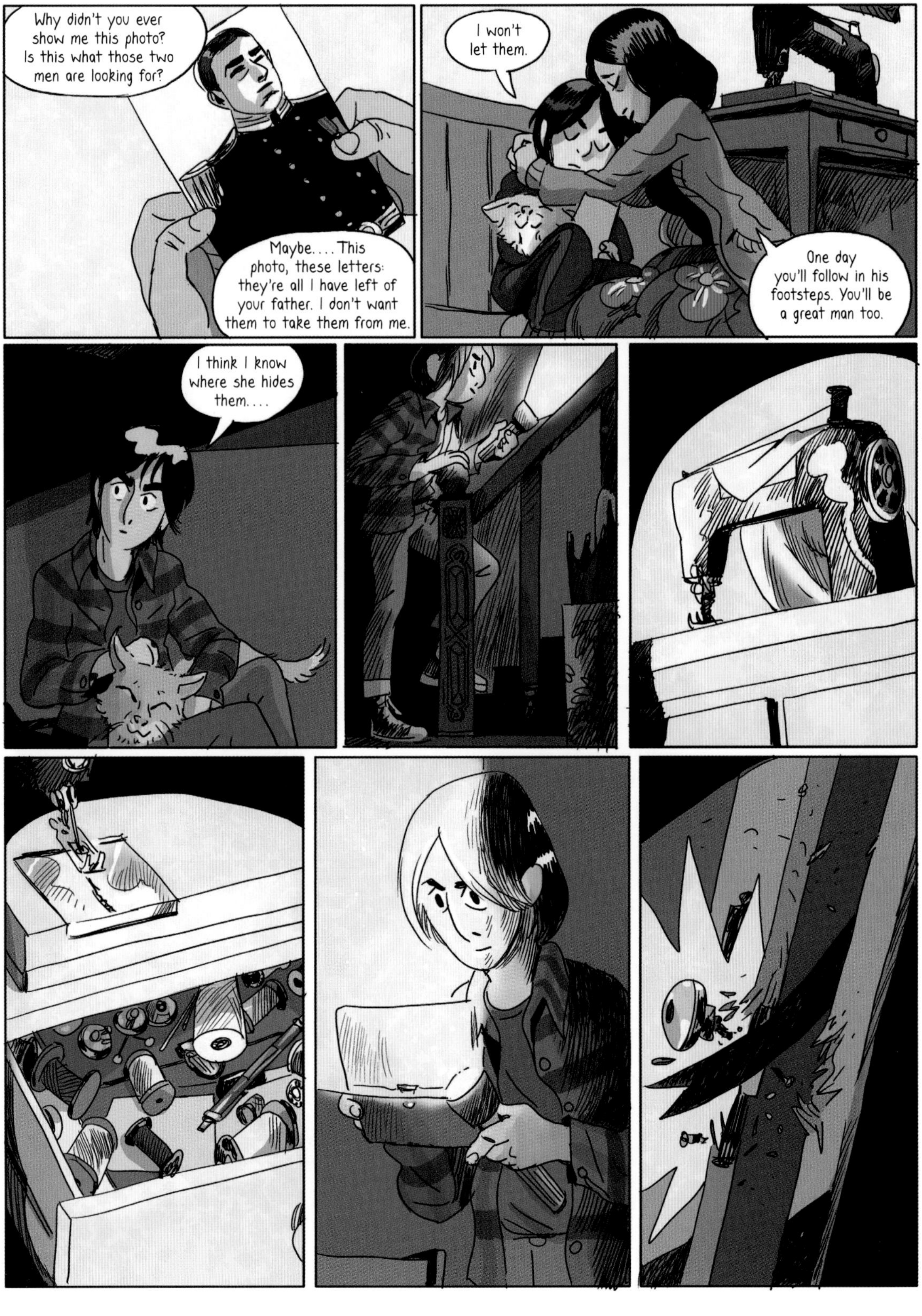
Why didn't you ever show me this photo? Is this what those two men are looking for?
Maybe. . . . This photo, these letters: they're all I have left of your father. I don't want them to take them from me.
I won't let them.
One day you'll follow in his footsteps. You'll be a great man too.
I think I know where she hides them. . . .

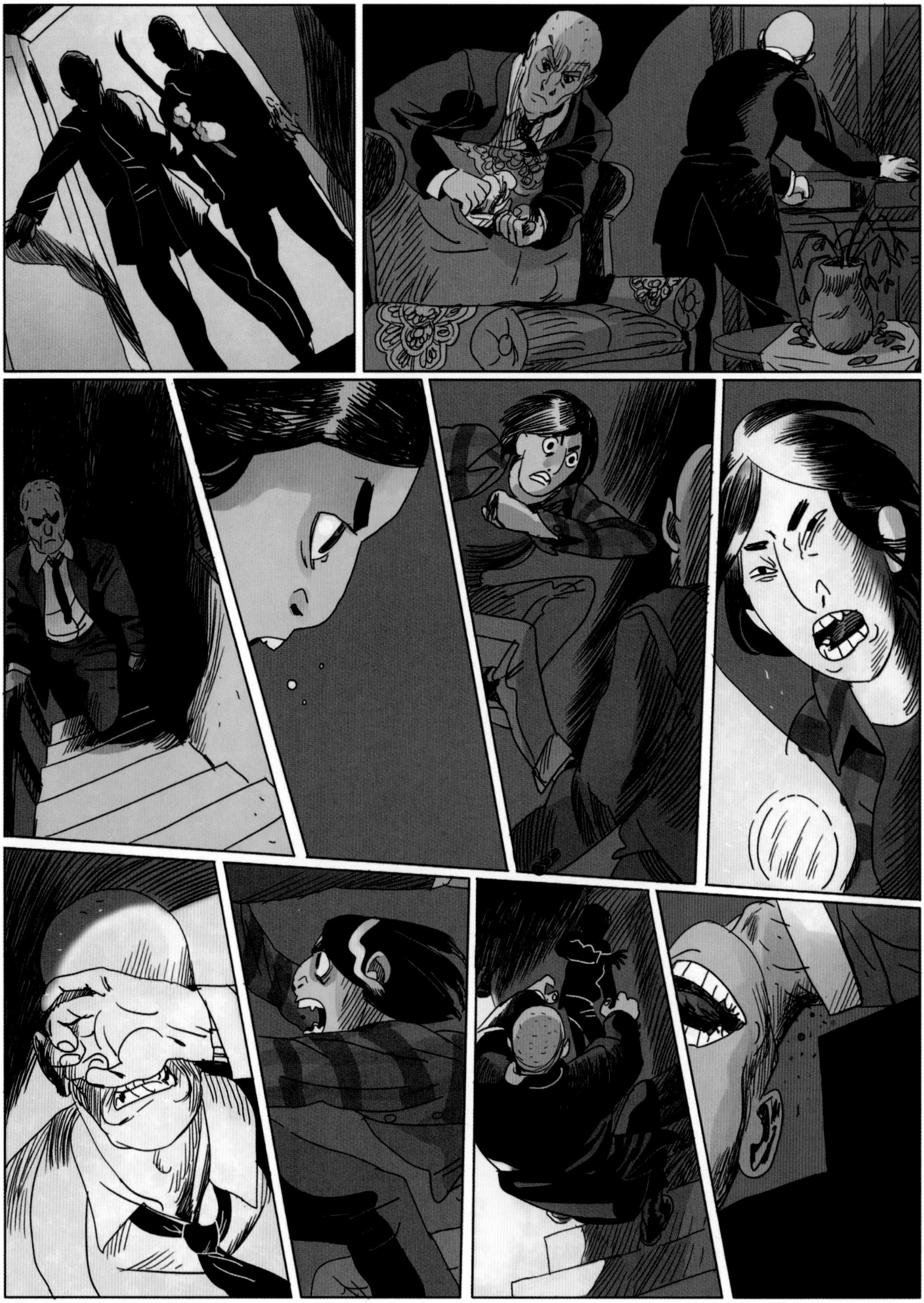

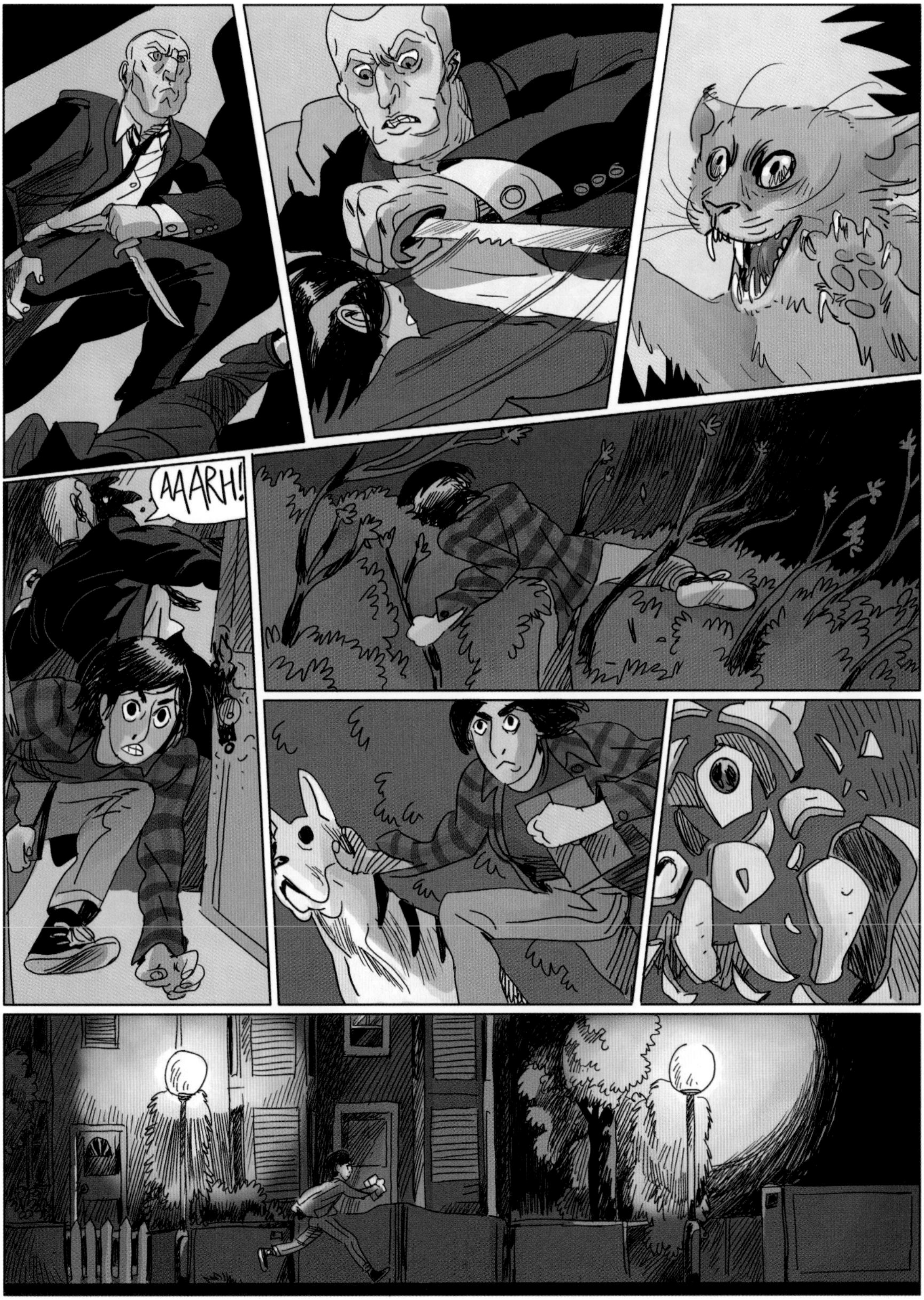
AAARH!

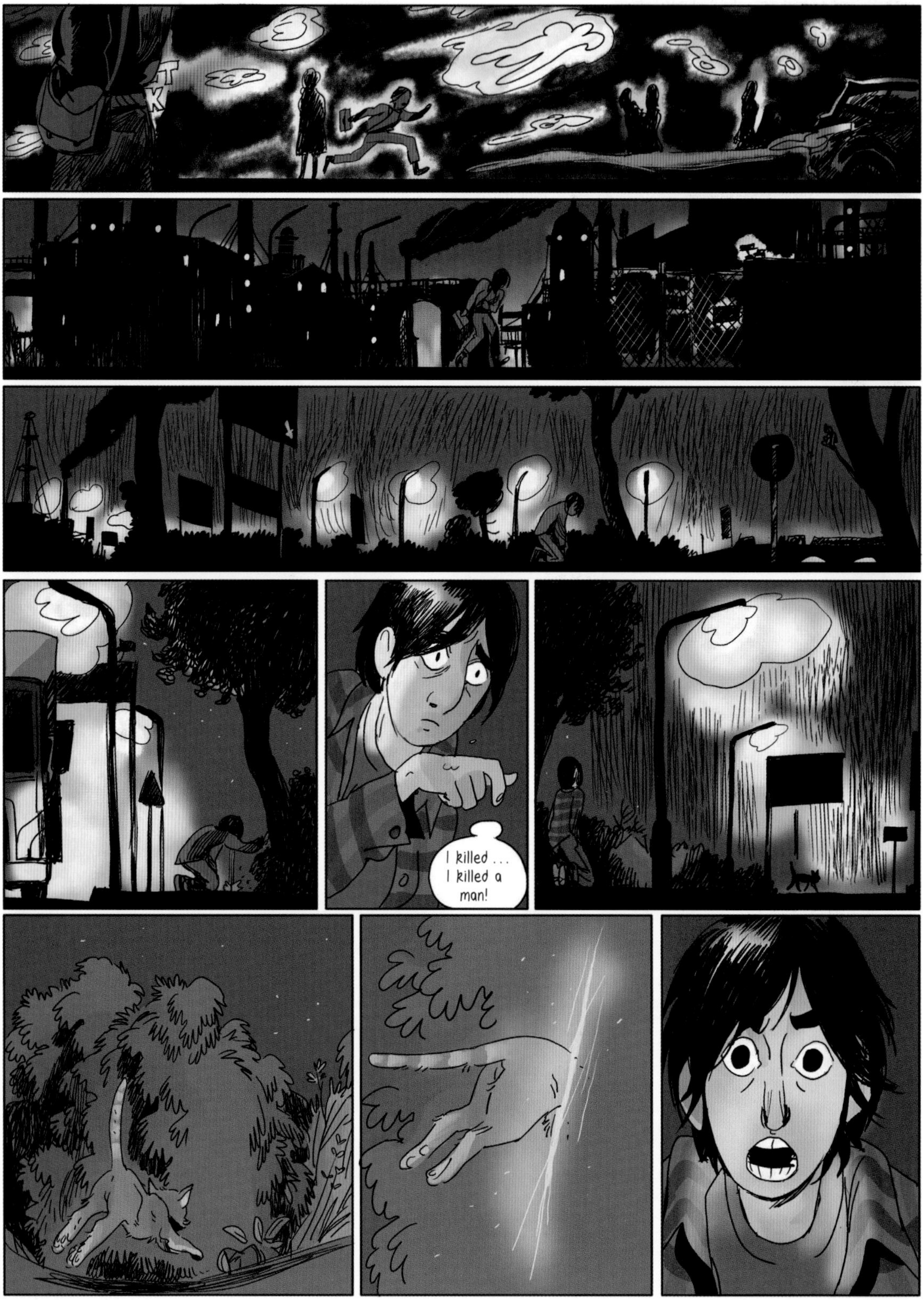
I killed . . . I killed a man!

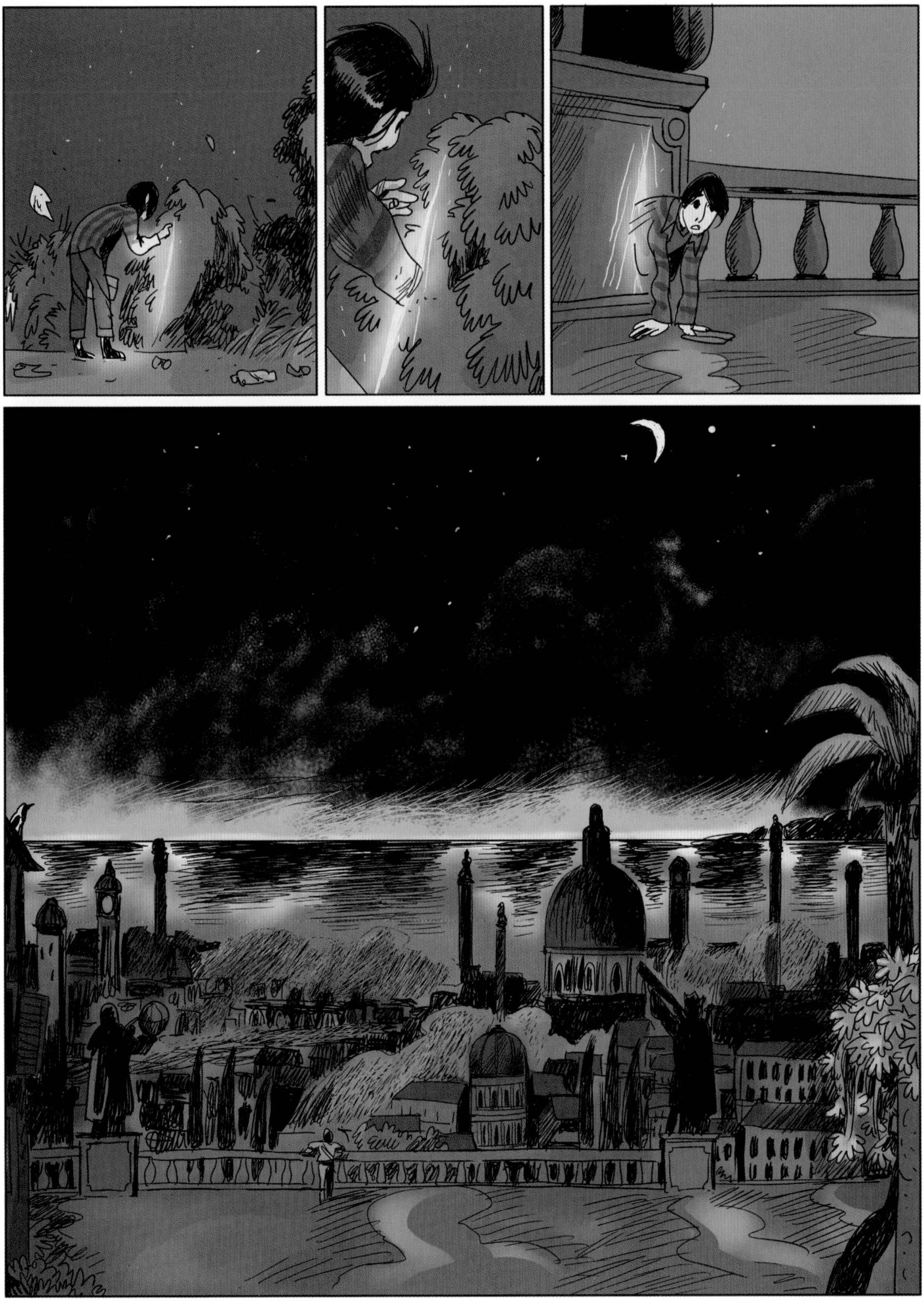

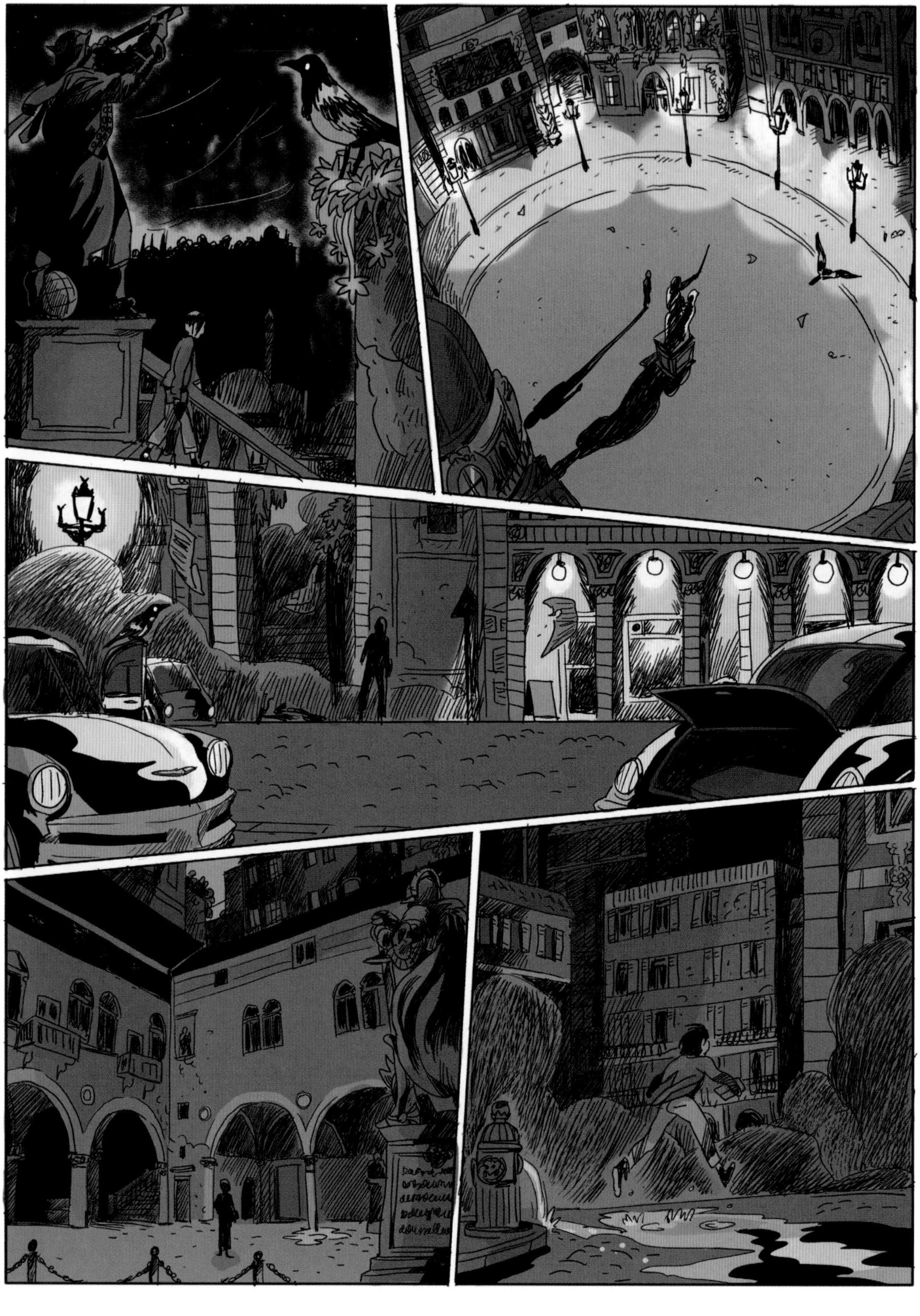

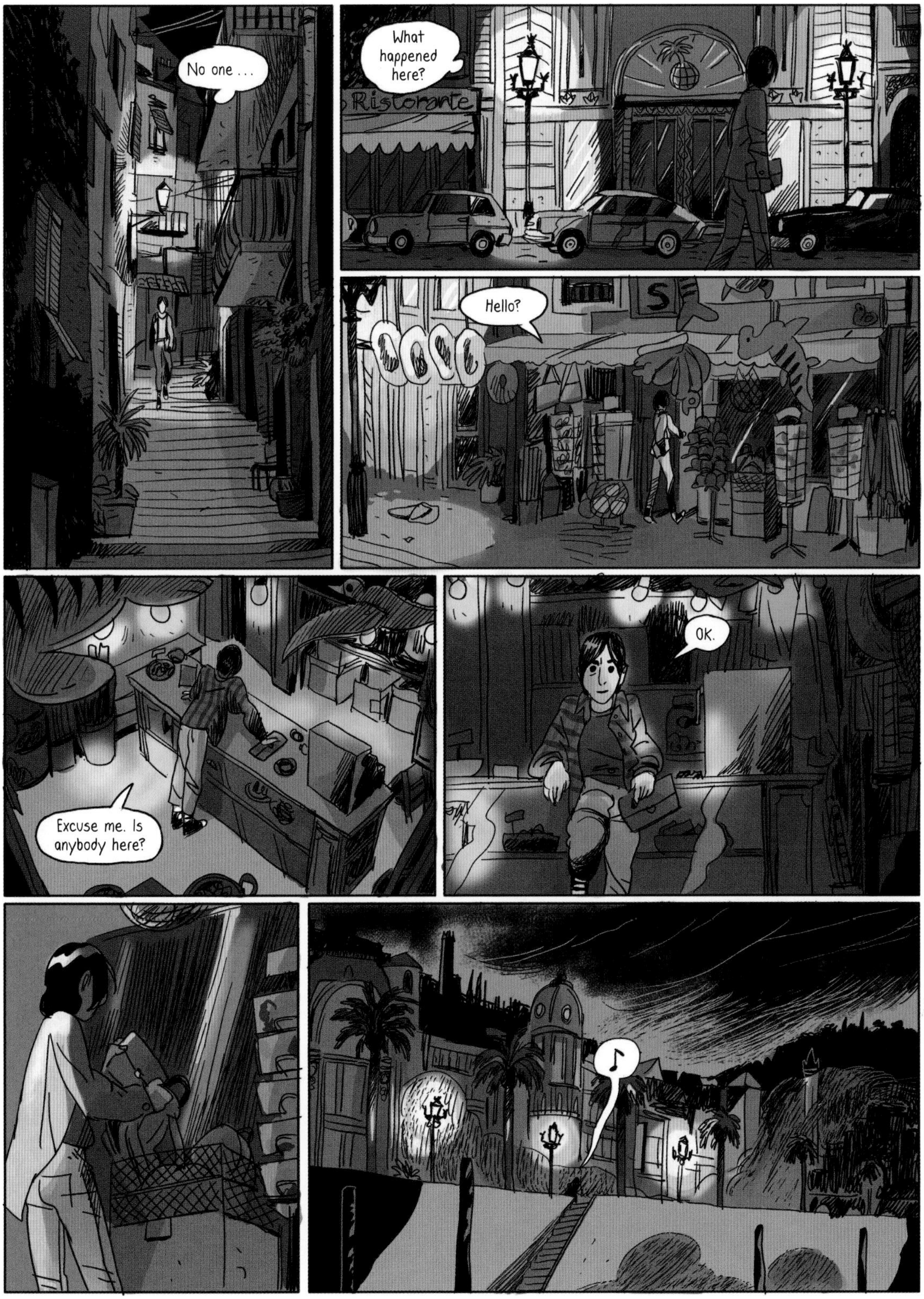
No one . . .
What happened here?
Ristorante
Hello?
Excuse me. Is anybody here?
OK.
♪

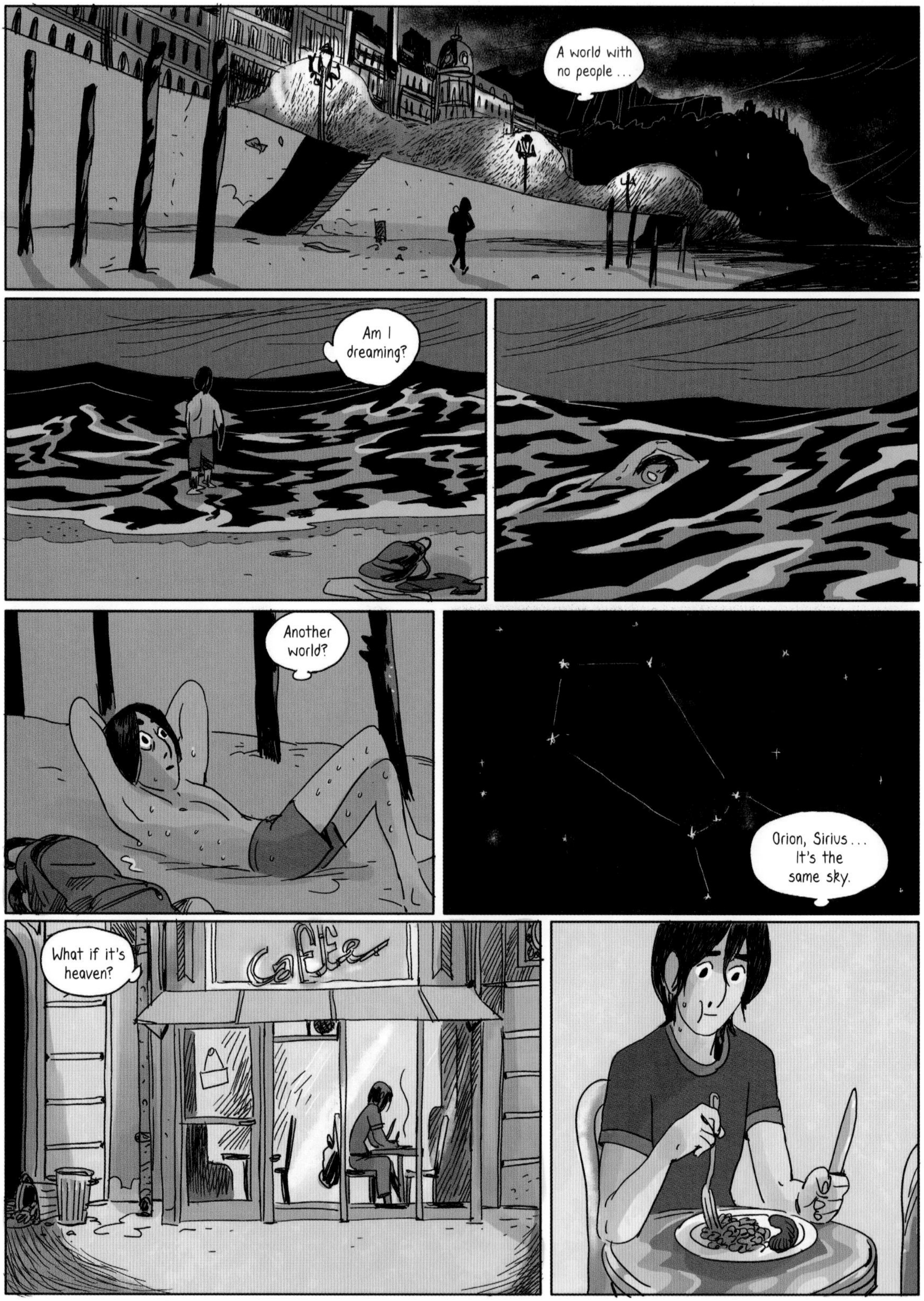
A world with no people . . .
Am I dreaming?
Another world?
Orion, Sirius . . . It's the same sky.
What if it's heaven?
Caffe

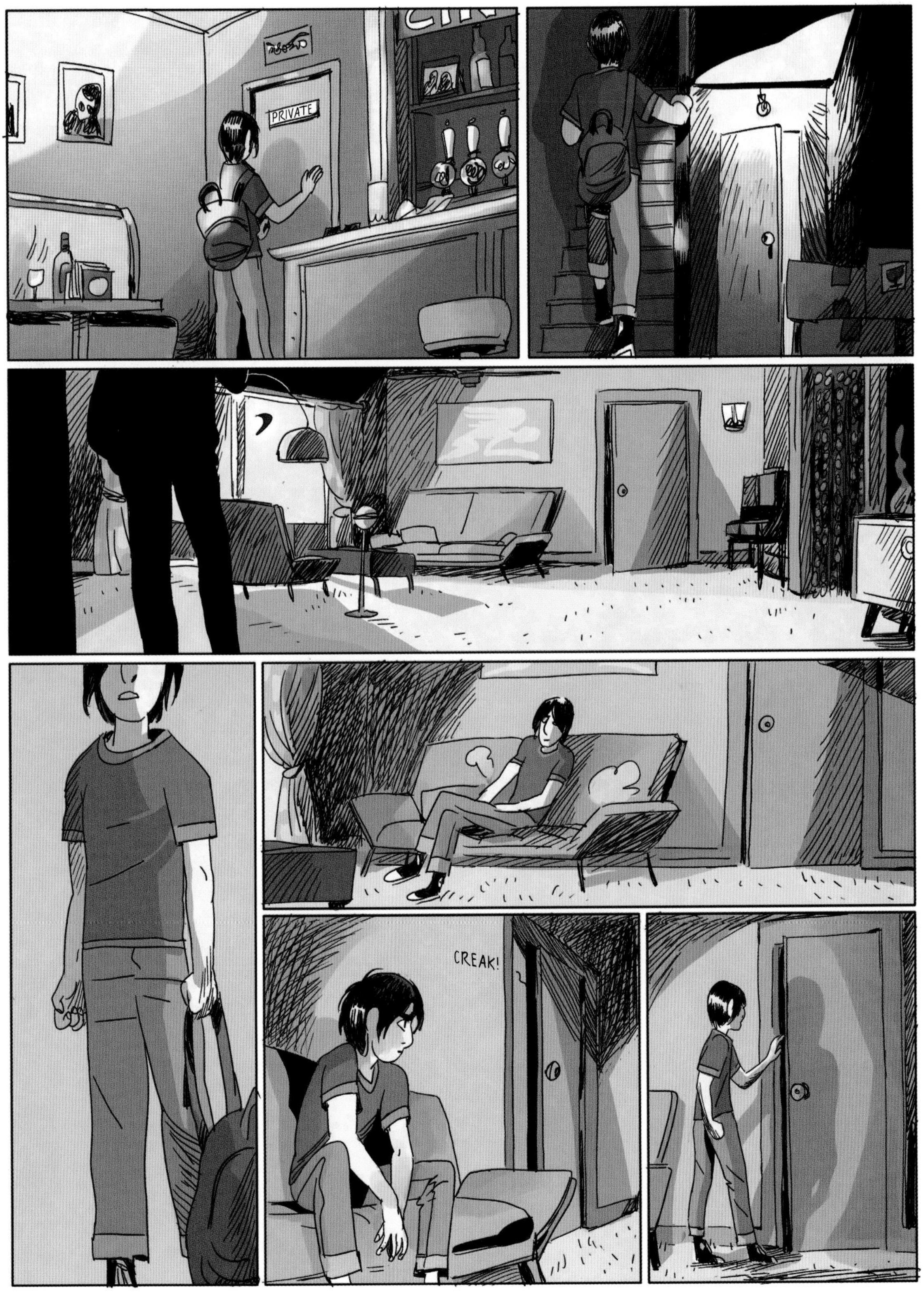
PRIVATE
CREAK!

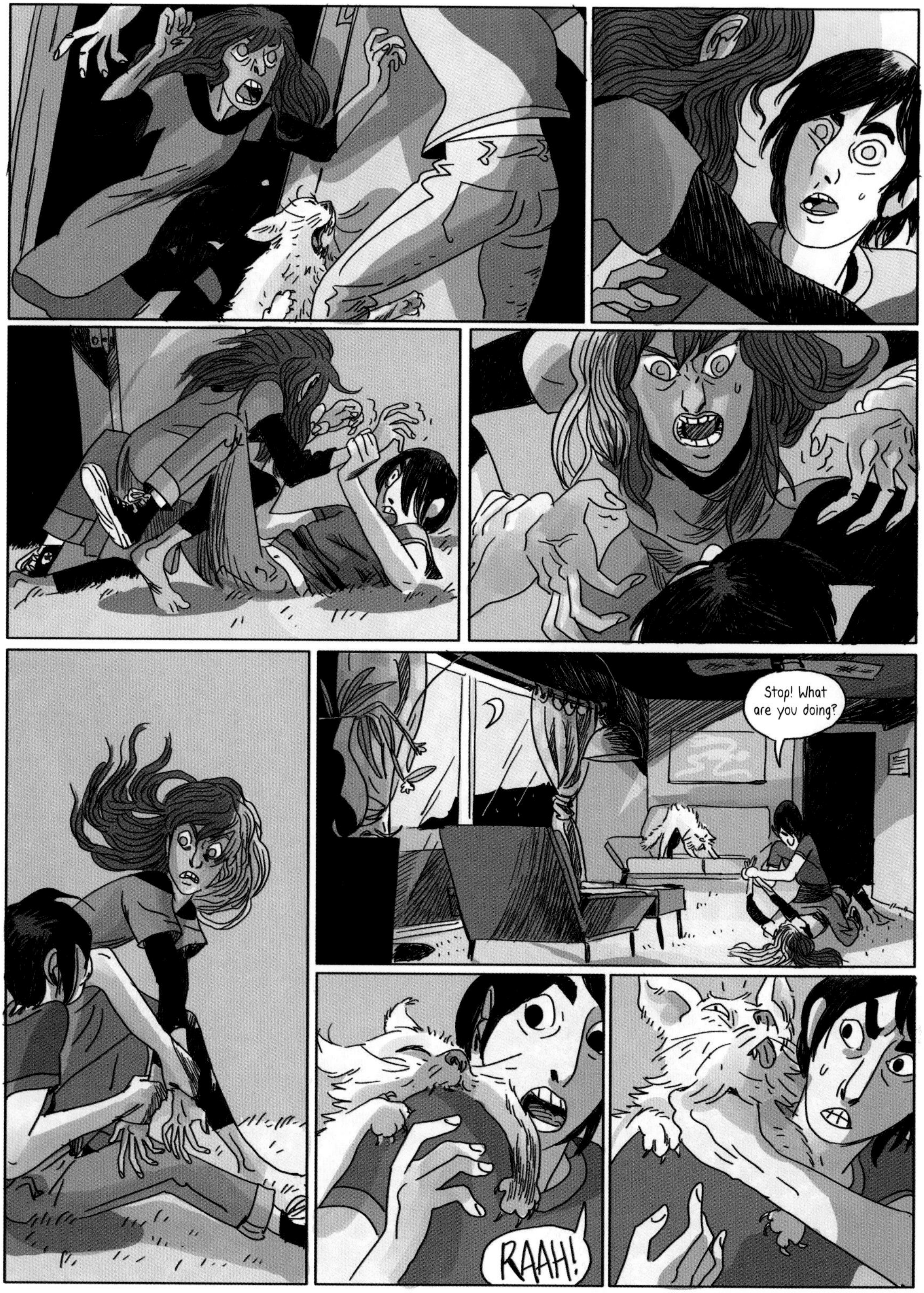
Stop! What are you doing?
RAAH!

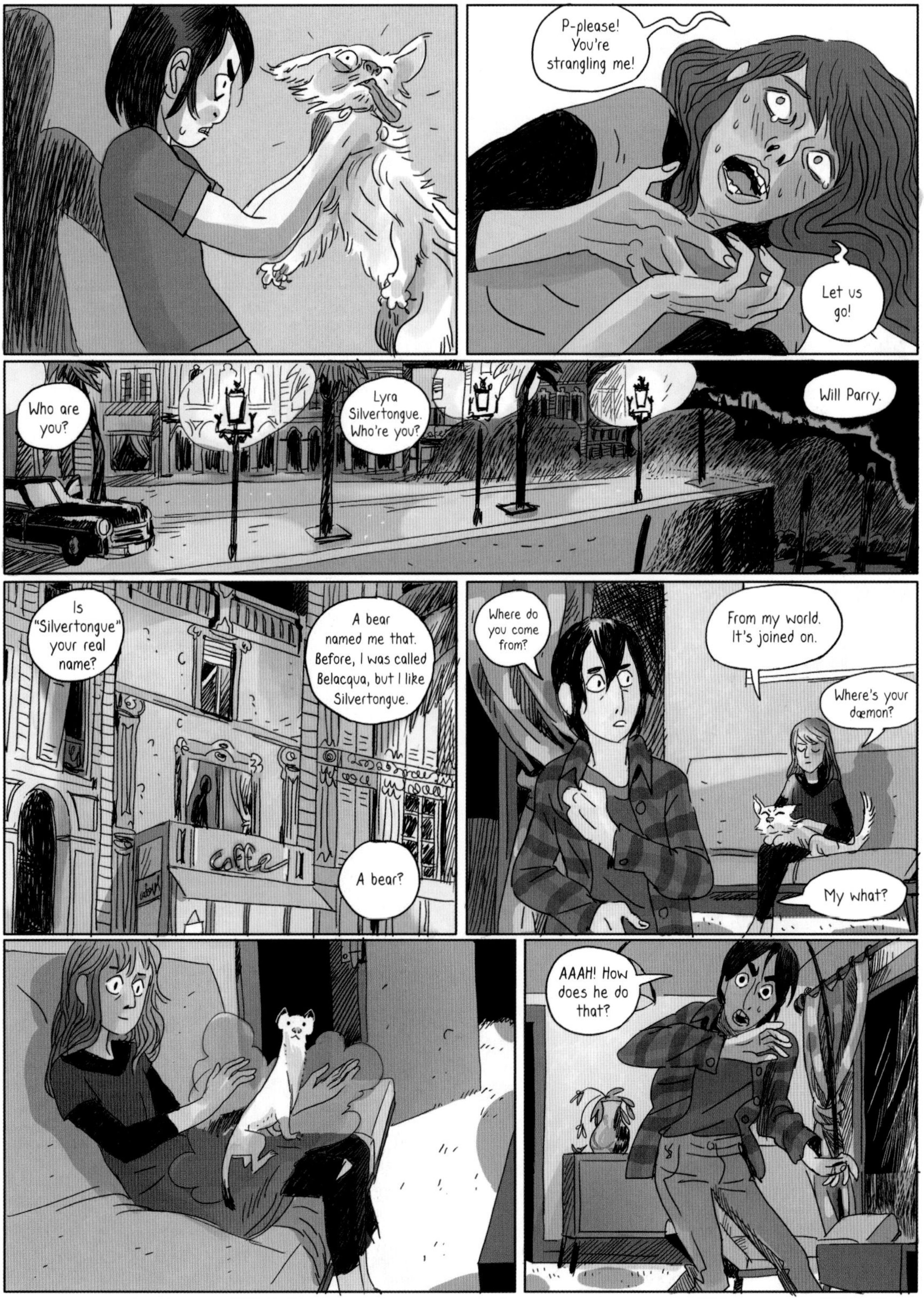
P-please! You're strangling me!
Let us go!
Who are you?
Lyra Silvertongue. Who're you?
Will Parry.
Is "Silvertongue" your real name?
A bear named me that. Before, I was called Belacqua, but I like Silvertongue.
A bear?
Caffe
Where do you come from?
From my world. It's joined on.
Where's your dæmon?
My what?
AAAH! How does he do that?

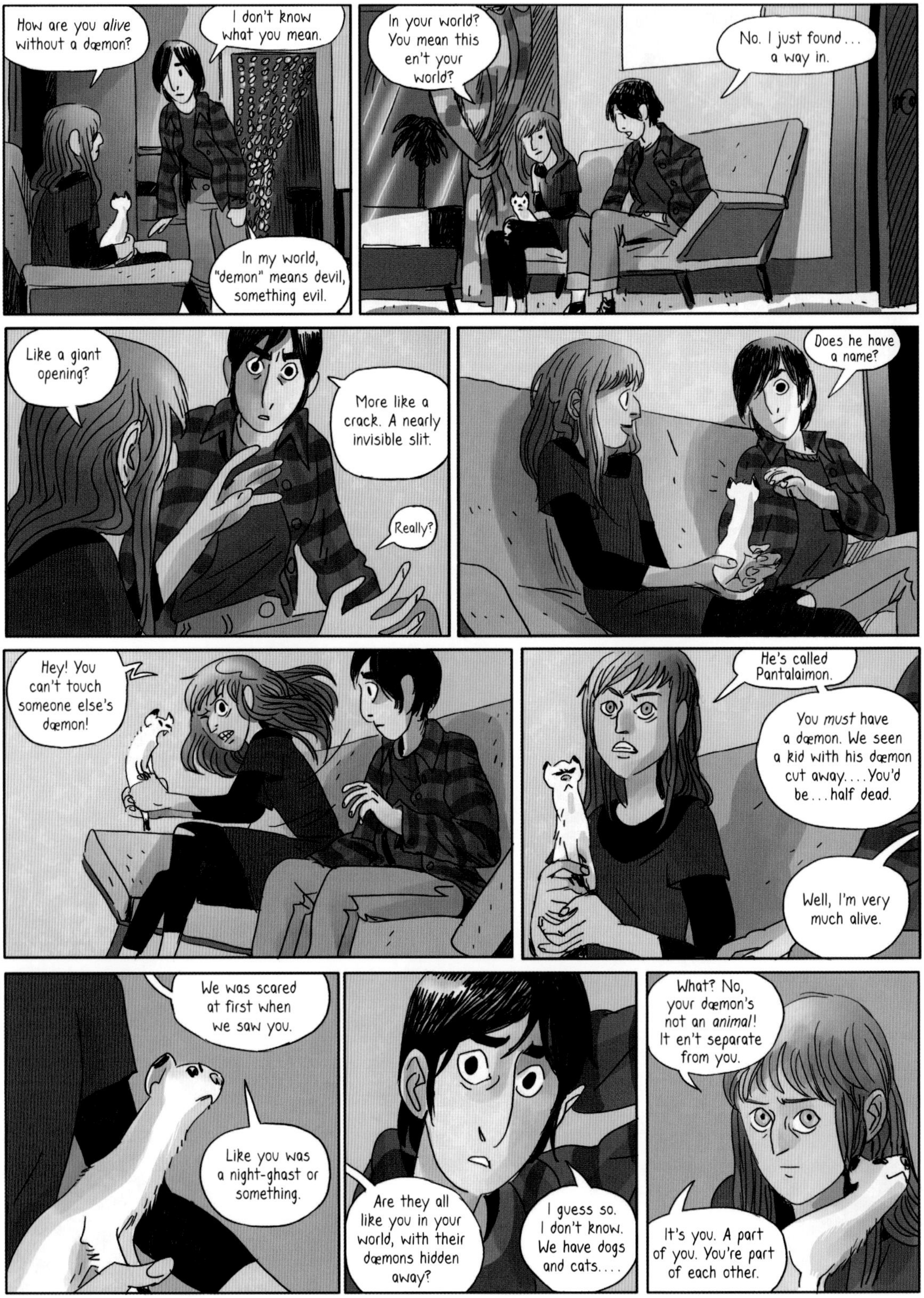
How are you *alive* without a dæmon?
I don't know what you mean.
In my world, "demon" means devil, something evil.
In your world? You mean this en't your world?
No. I just found . . . a way in.
Like a giant opening?
More like a crack. A nearly invisible slit.
Really?
Does he have a name?
Hey! You can't touch someone else's dæmon!
He's called Pantalaimon.
You *must* have a dæmon. We seen a kid with his dæmon cut away. . . . You'd be . . . half dead.
Well, I'm very much alive.
We was scared at first when we saw you.
Like you was a night-ghast or something.
Are they all like you in your world, with their dæmons hidden away?
I guess so. I don't know. We have dogs and cats. . . .
What? No, your dæmon's not an *animal*! It en't separate from you.
It's you. A part of you. You're part of each other.

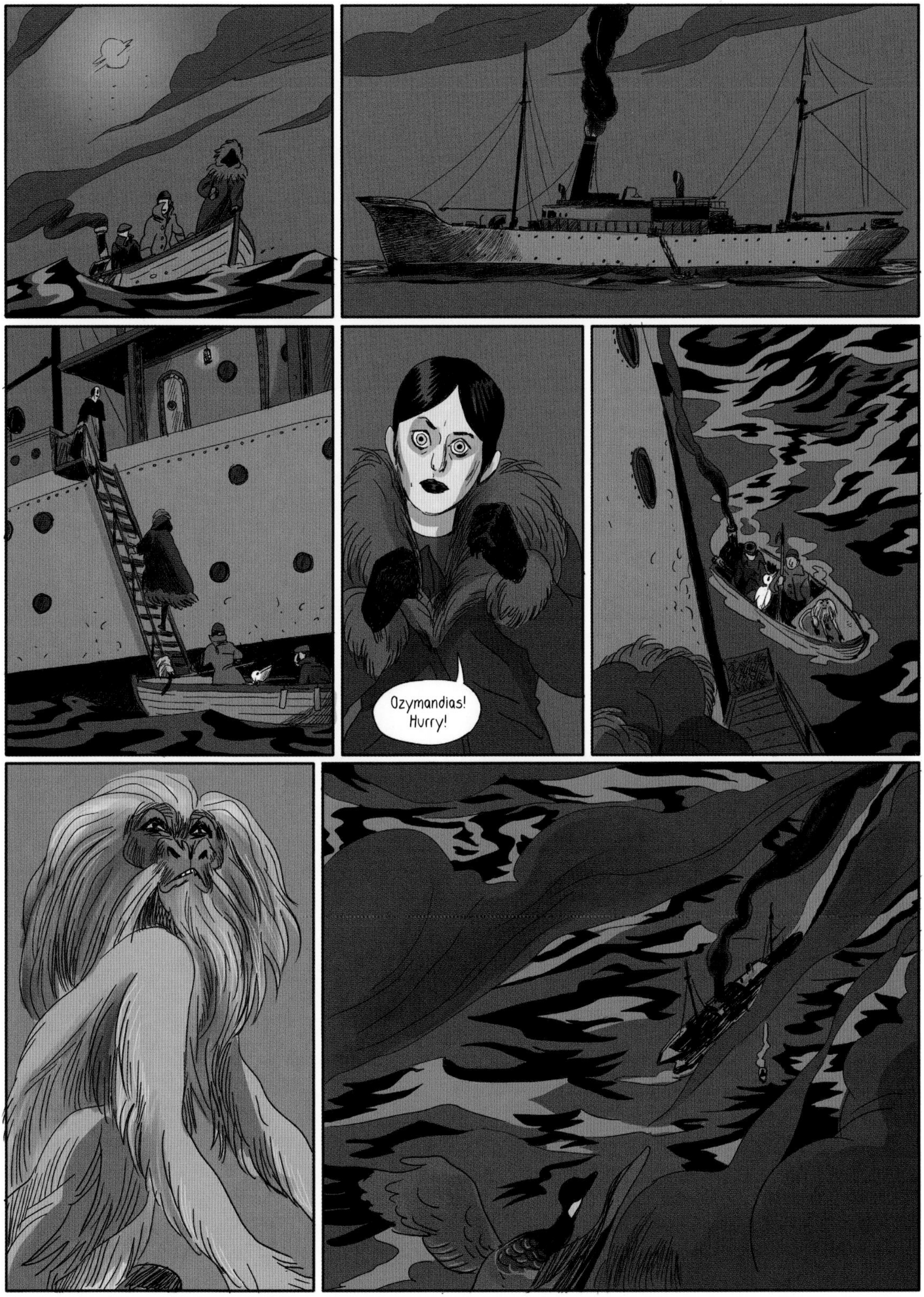
Ozymandias! Hurry!

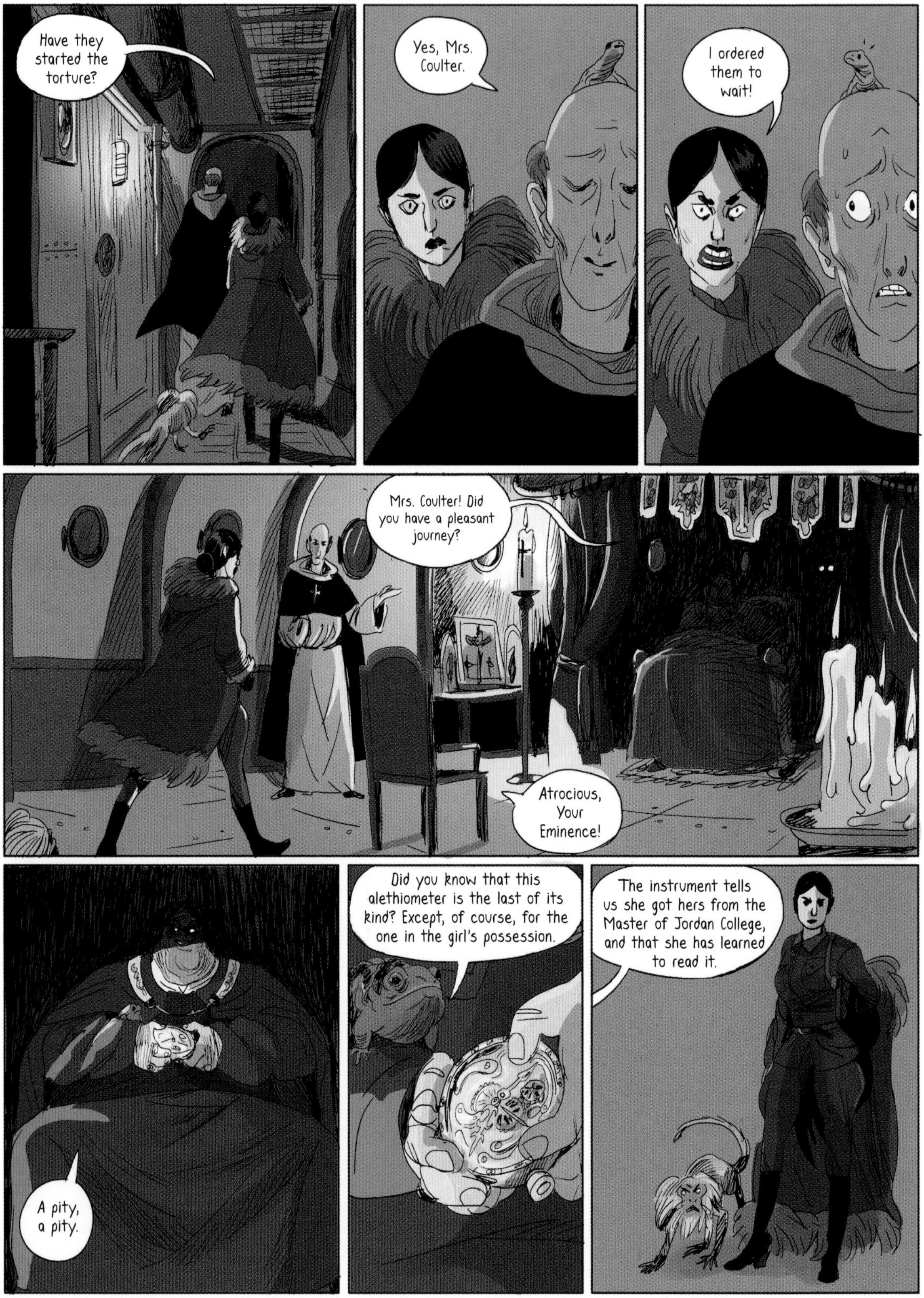
Have they started the torture?
Yes, Mrs. Coulter.
I ordered them to wait!
Mrs. Coulter! Did you have a pleasant journey?
Atrocious, Your Eminence!
A pity, a pity.
Did you know that this alethiometer is the last of its kind? Except, of course, for the one in the girl's possession.
The instrument tells us she got hers from the Master of Jordan College, and that she has learned to read it.

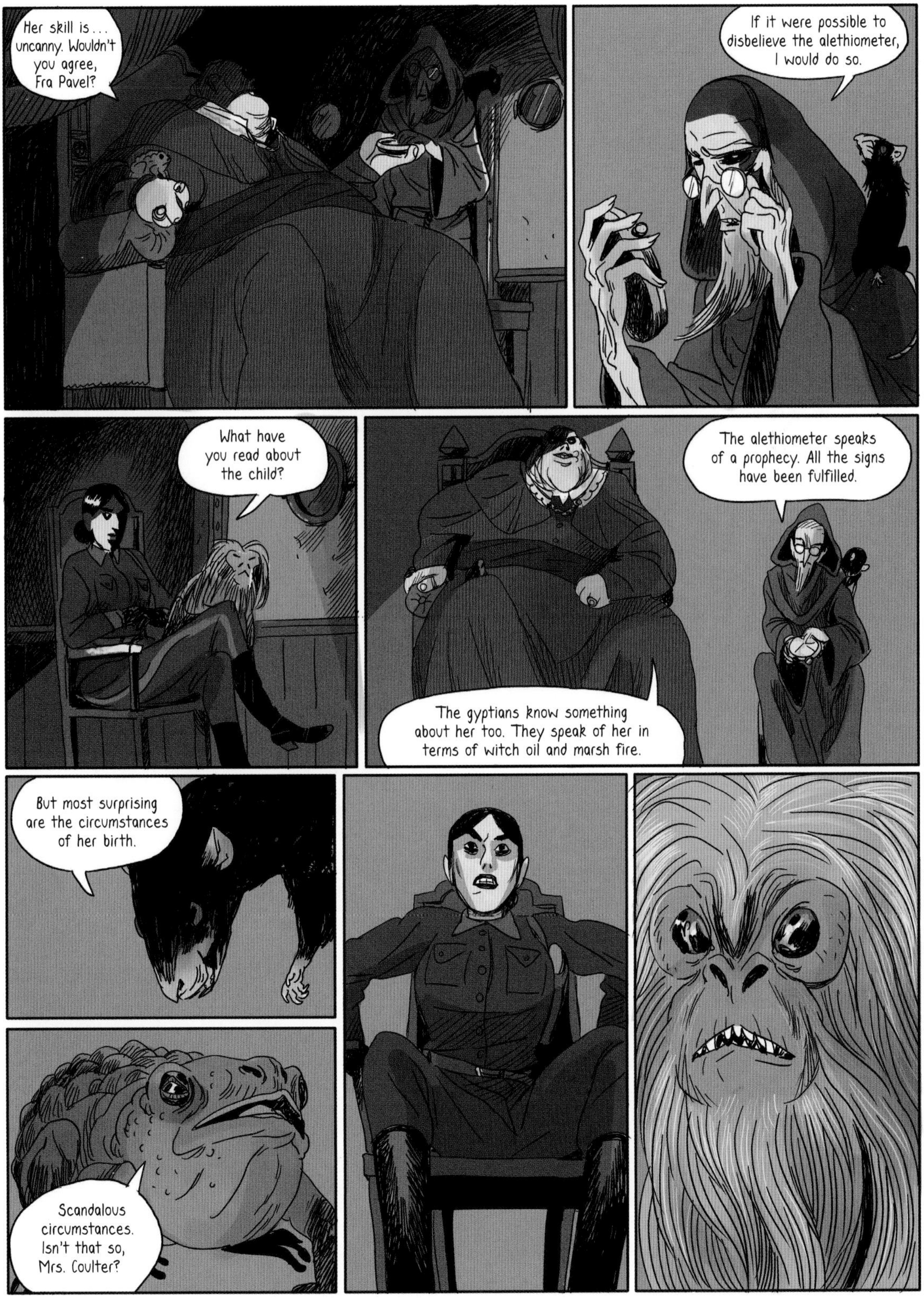
Her skill is . . . uncanny. Wouldn't you agree, Fra Pavel?
If it were possible to disbelieve the alethiometer, I would do so.
What have you read about the child?
The alethiometer speaks of a prophecy. All the signs have been fulfilled.
The gyptians know something about her too. They speak of her in terms of witch oil and marsh fire.
But most surprising are the circumstances of her birth.
Scandalous circumstances. Isn't that so, Mrs. Coulter?

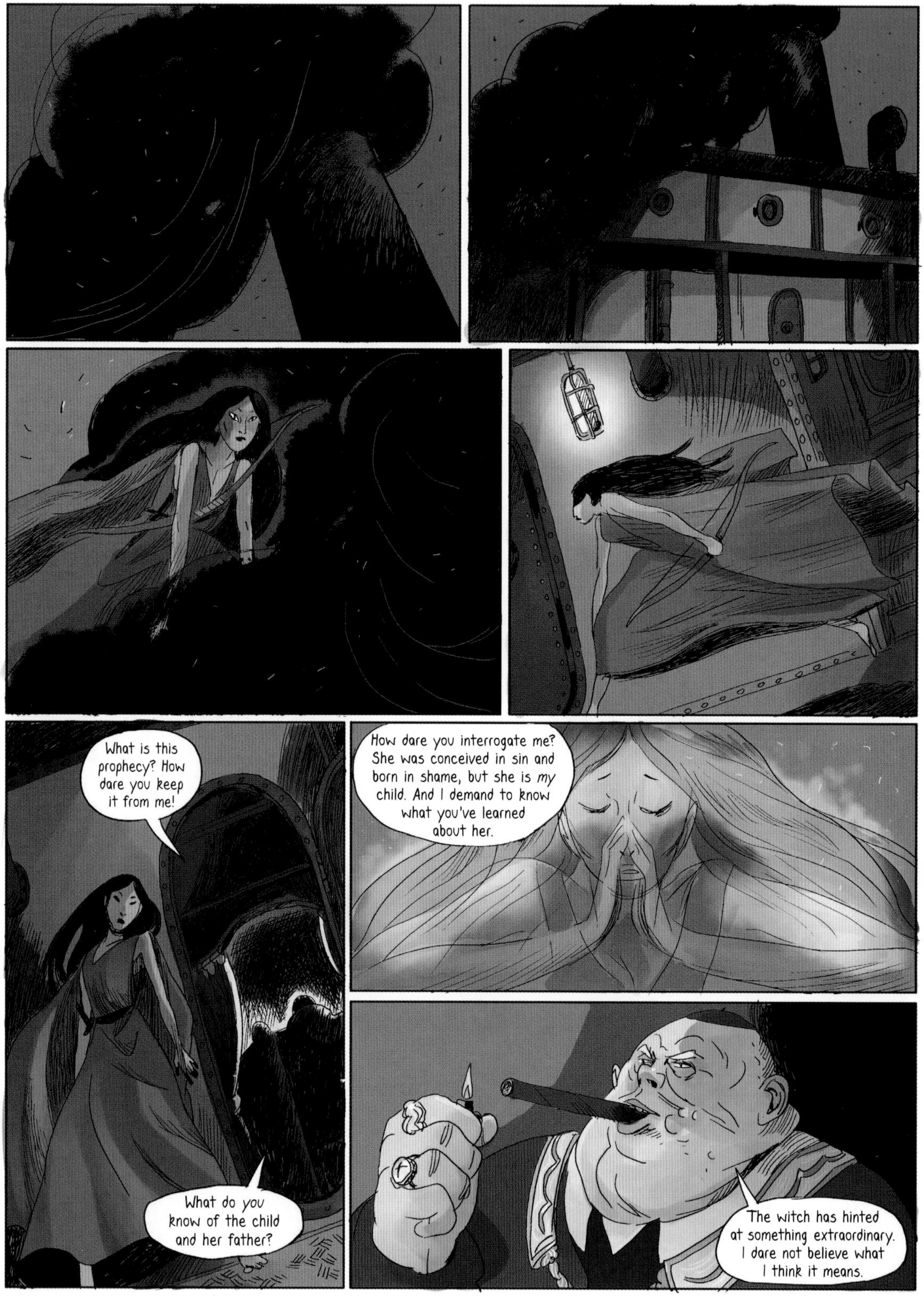
What is this prophecy? How dare you keep it from me!
How dare you interrogate me? She was conceived in sin and born in shame, but she is *my* child. And I demand to know what you've learned about her.
What do *you* know of the child and her father?
The witch has hinted at something extraordinary. I dare not believe what I think it means.

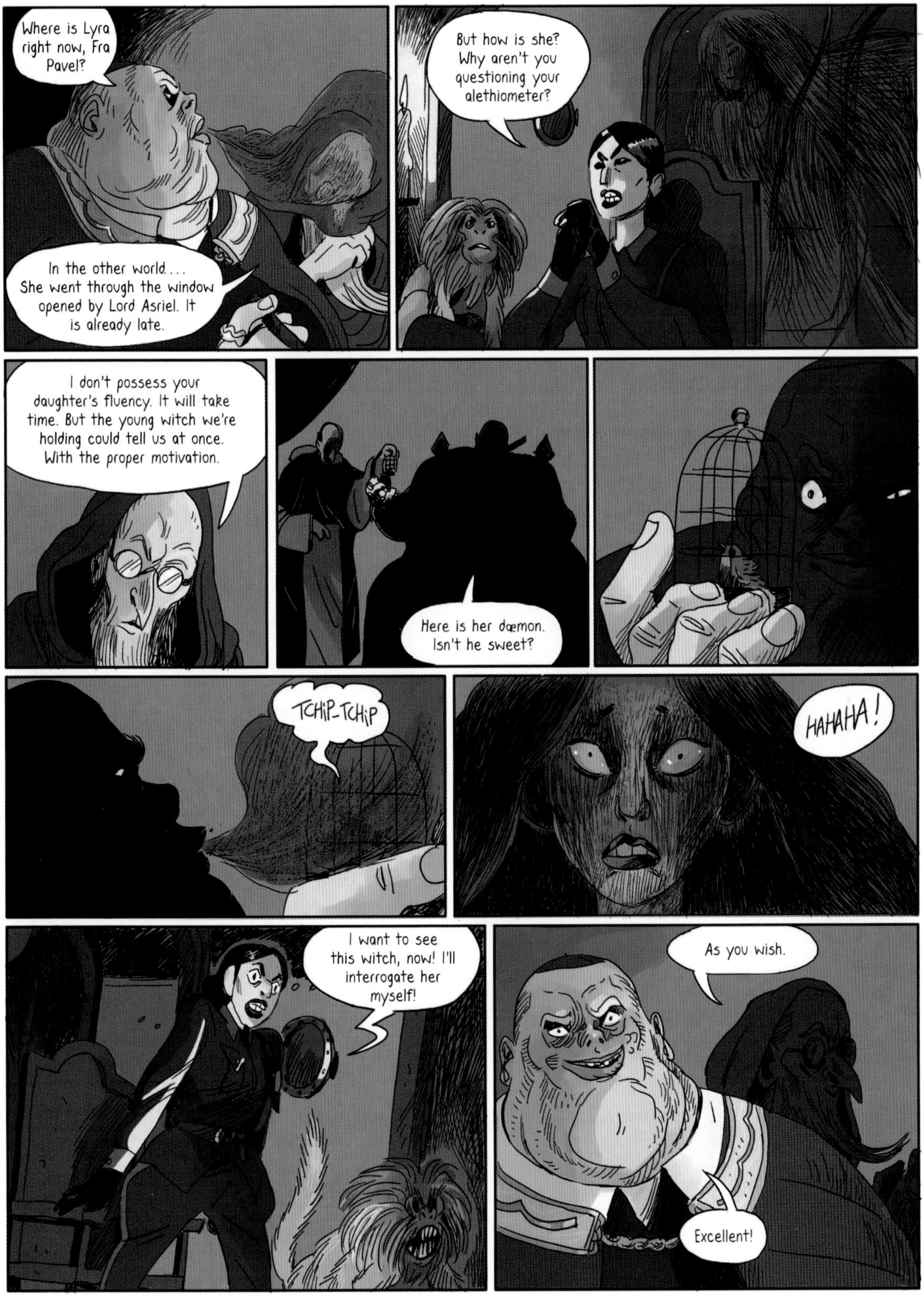
Where is Lyra right now, Fra Pavel?
In the other world. . . . She went through the window opened by Lord Asriel. It is already late.
But how is she? Why aren't you questioning your alethiometer?
I don't possess your daughter's fluency. It will take time. But the young witch we're holding could tell us at once. With the proper motivation.
Here is her dæmon. Isn't he sweet?
TCHIP-TCHIP
HAHAHA!
I want to see this witch, now! I'll interrogate her myself!
As you wish.
Excellent!

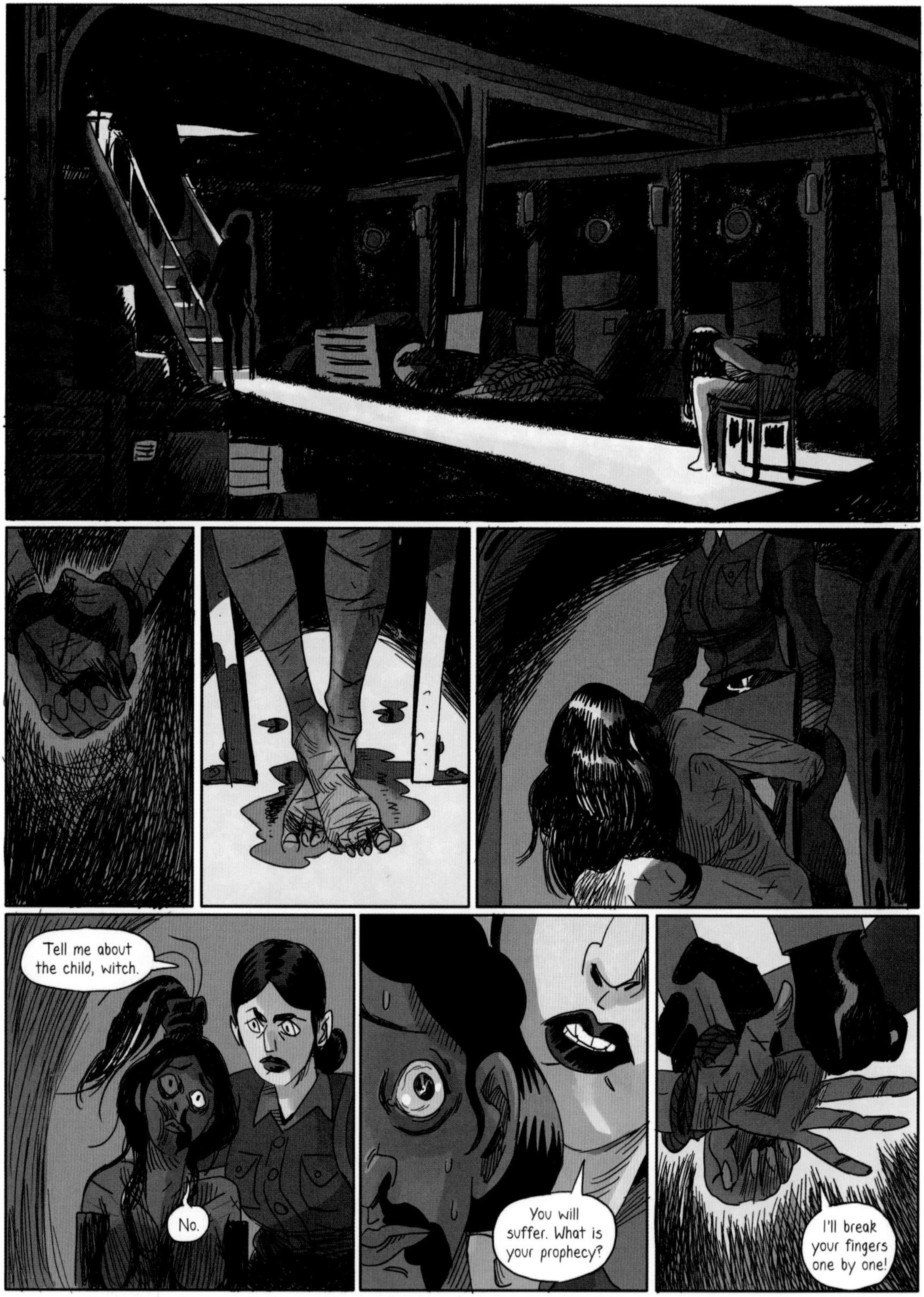
Tell me about the child, witch.
No.
You will suffer. What is your prophecy?
I'll break your fingers one by one!

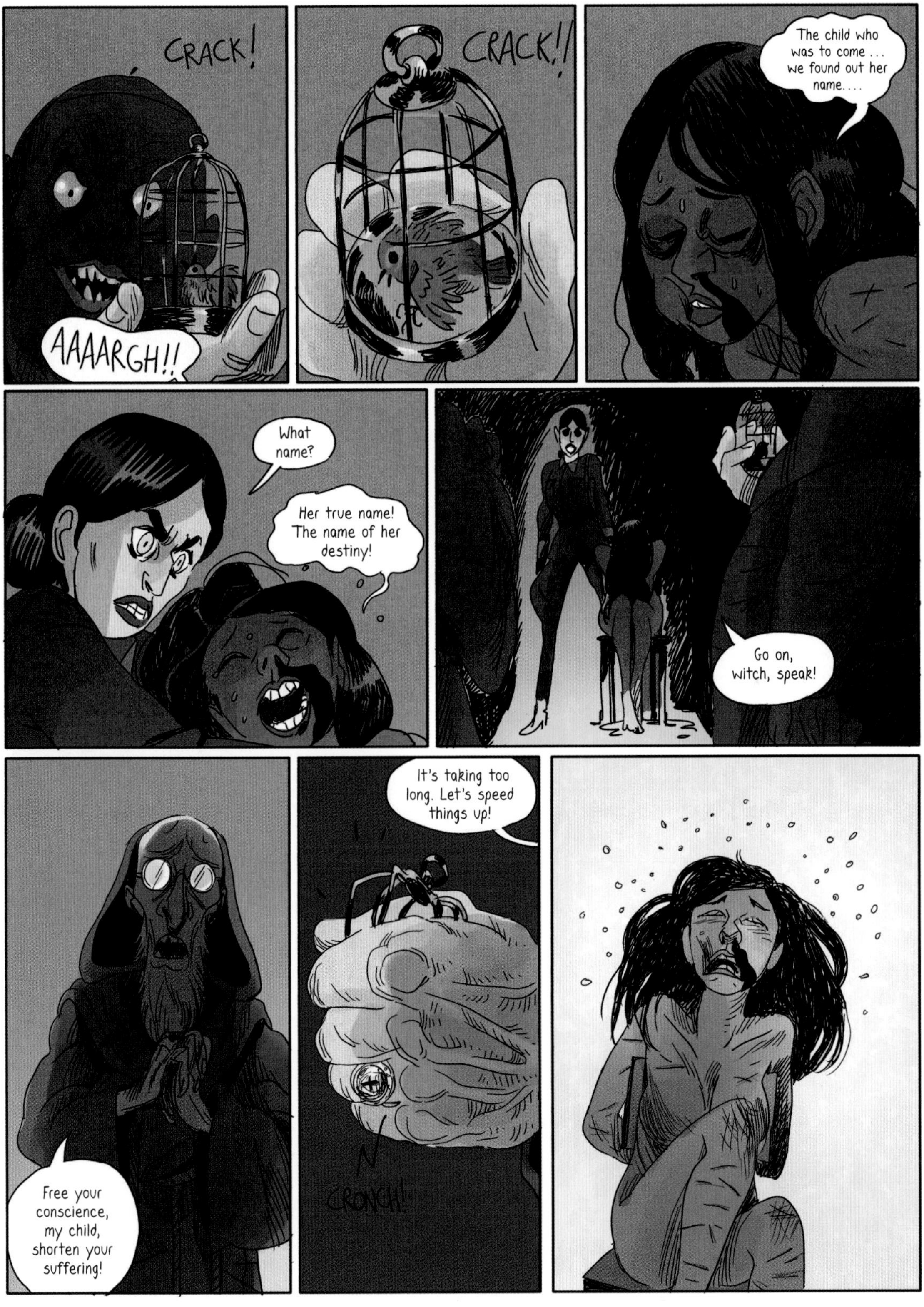
CRACK!
AAAARGH!!
CRACK!!
The child who was to come . . . we found out her name. . . .
What name?
Her true name! The name of her destiny!
Go on, witch, speak!
Free your conscience, my child, shorten your suffering!
It's taking too long. Let's speed things up!
CRONCH!!

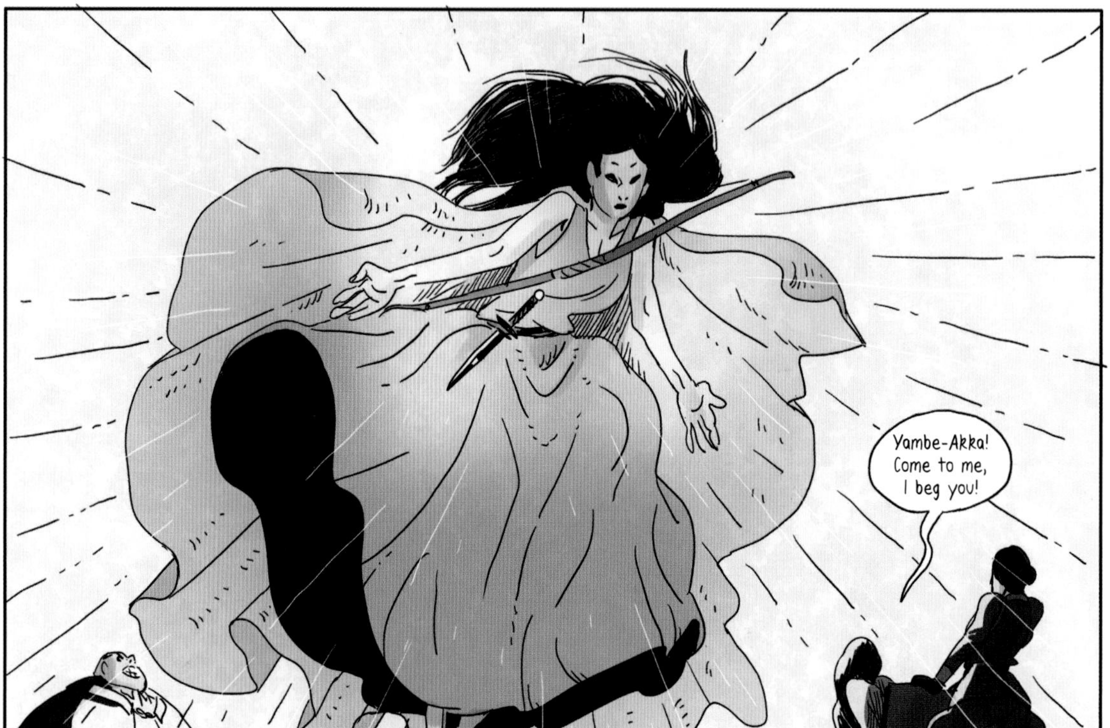

Yambe-Akka! Come to me, I beg you!
Yambe-Akka!
Deliver me!
...Thank you!

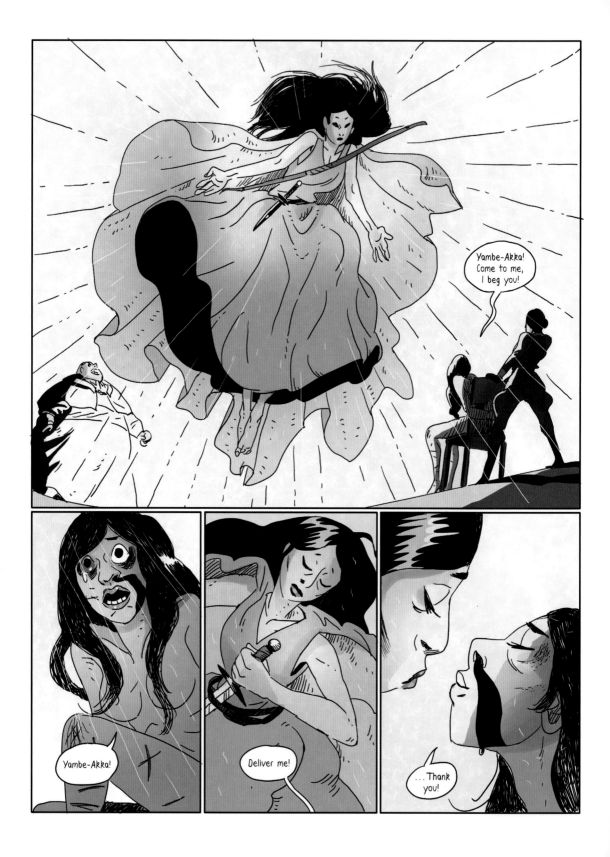

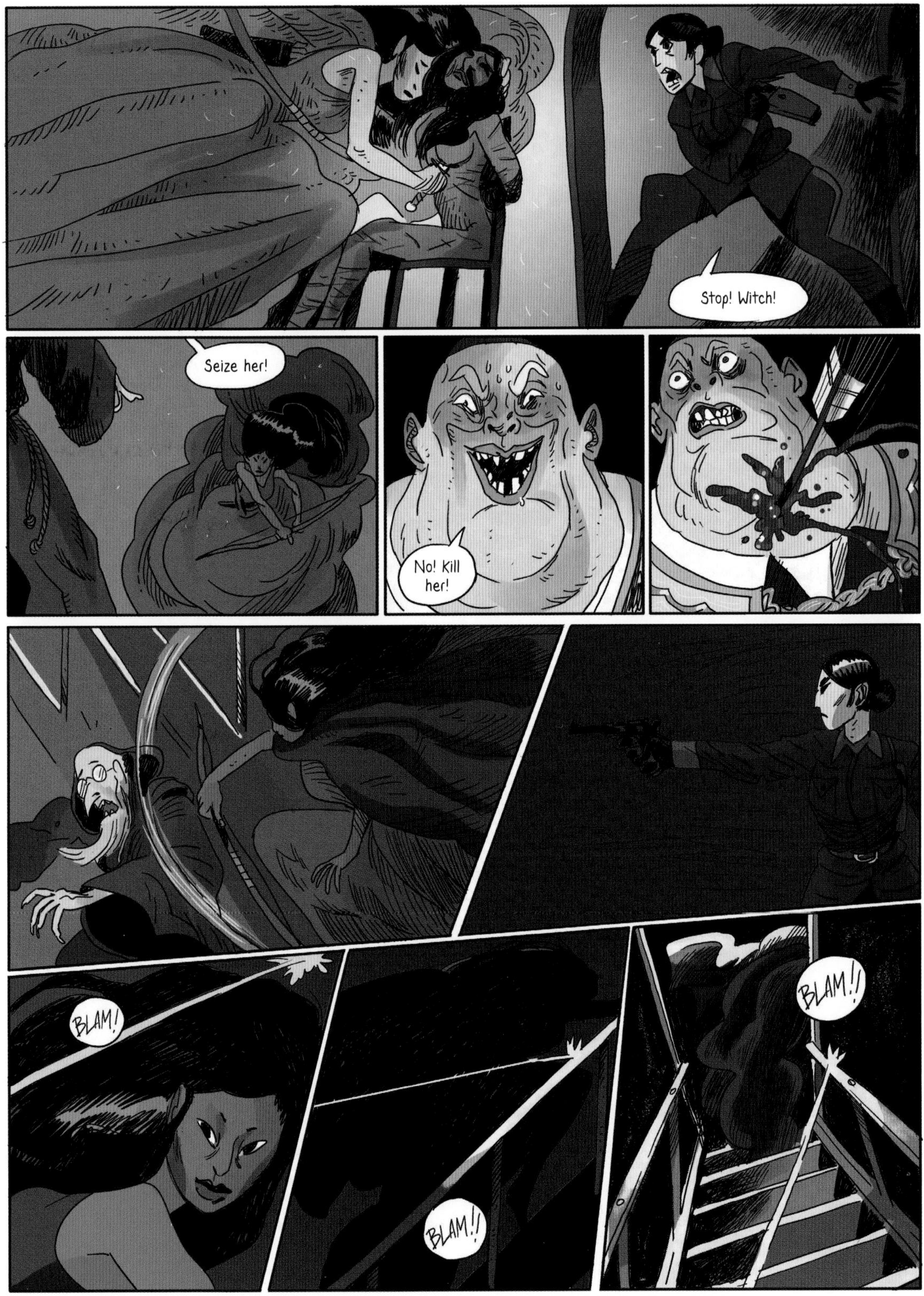
Stop! Witch!
Seize her!
No! Kill her!
BLAM!
BLAM!!
BLAM!!

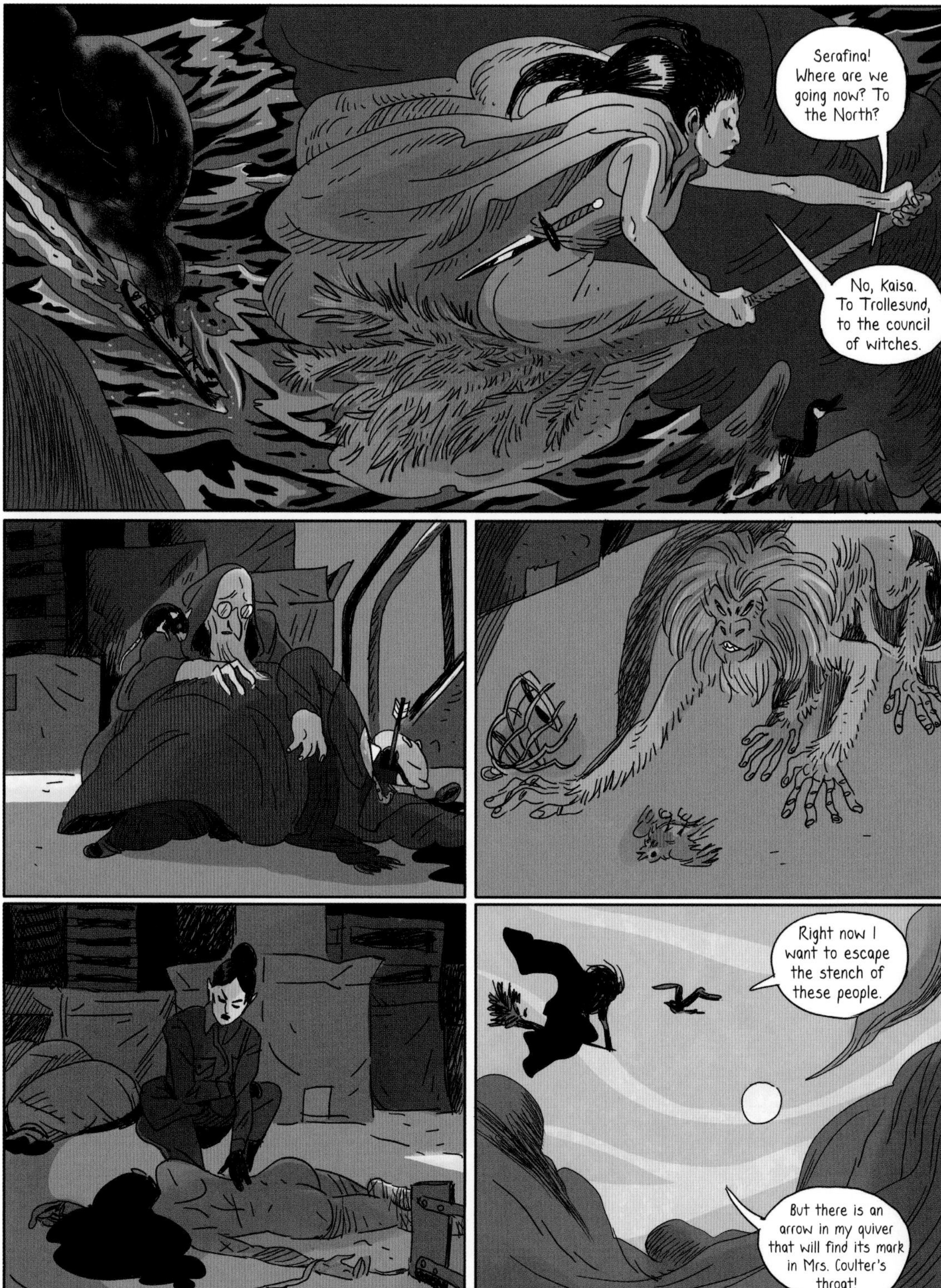
Serafina! Where are we going now? To the North?
No, Kaisa. To Trollesund, to the council of witches.
Right now I want to escape the stench of these people.
But there is an arrow in my quiver that will find its mark in Mrs. Coulter's throat!

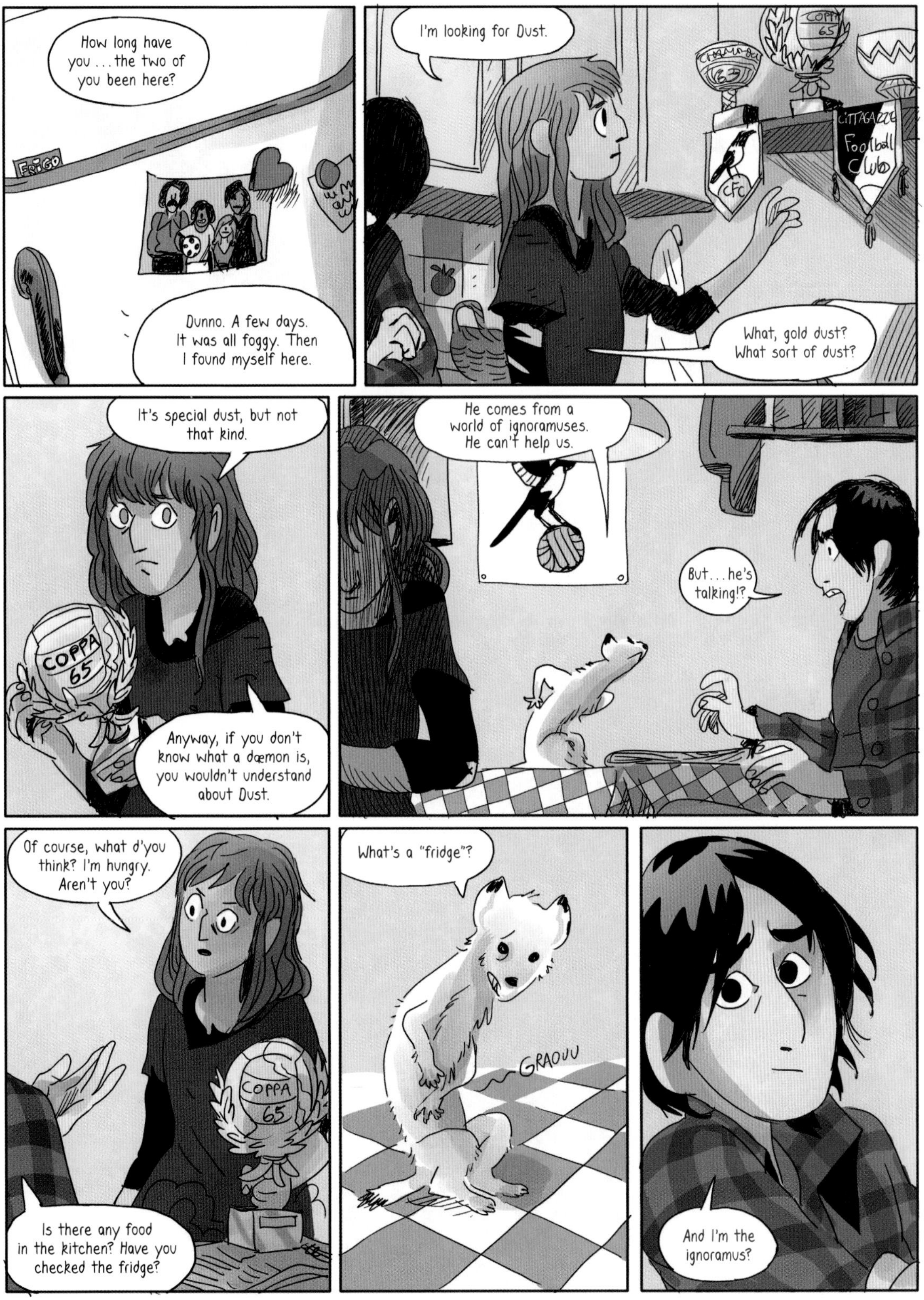
How long have you . . . the two of you been here?
FRIGO
Dunno. A few days. It was all foggy. Then I found myself here.
I'm looking for Dust.
CITTAGAZZE Football Club
CFC
COPPA 65
What, gold dust? What sort of dust?
It's special dust, but not that kind.
COPPA 65
Anyway, if you don't know what a dæmon is, you wouldn't understand about Dust.
He comes from a world of ignoramuses. He can't help us.
But . . . he's talking!?
Of course, what d'you think? I'm hungry. Aren't you?
COPPA 65
Is there any food in the kitchen? Have you checked the fridge?
What's a "fridge"?
GRAOUU
And I'm the ignoramus?

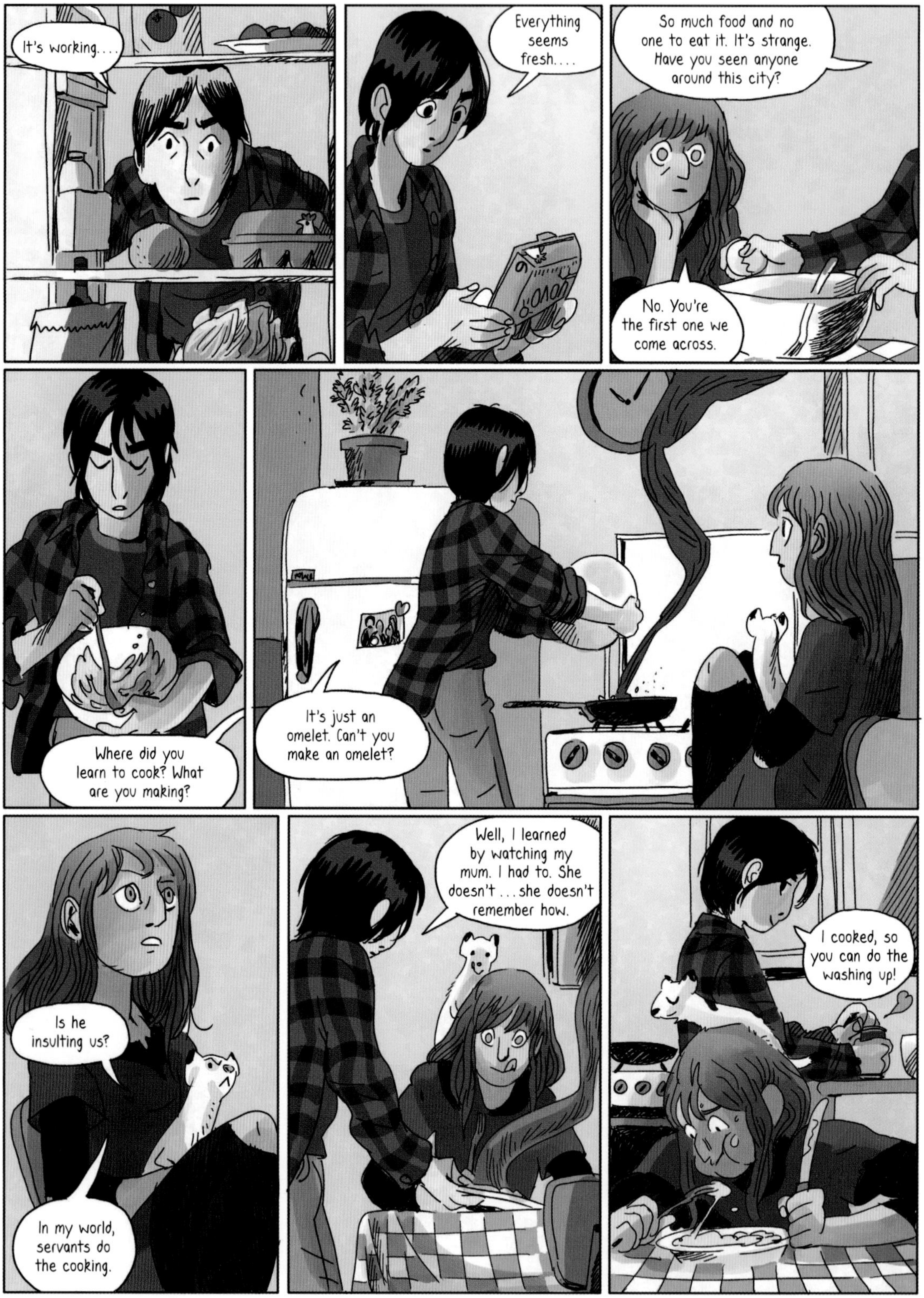
It's working....
Everything seems fresh....
So much food and no one to eat it. It's strange. Have you seen anyone around this city?
No. You're the first one we come across.
Where did you learn to cook? What are you making?
It's just an omelet. Can't you make an omelet?
Is he insulting us?
In my world, servants do the cooking.
Well, I learned by watching my mum. I had to. She doesn't ... she doesn't remember how.
I cooked, so you can do the washing up!

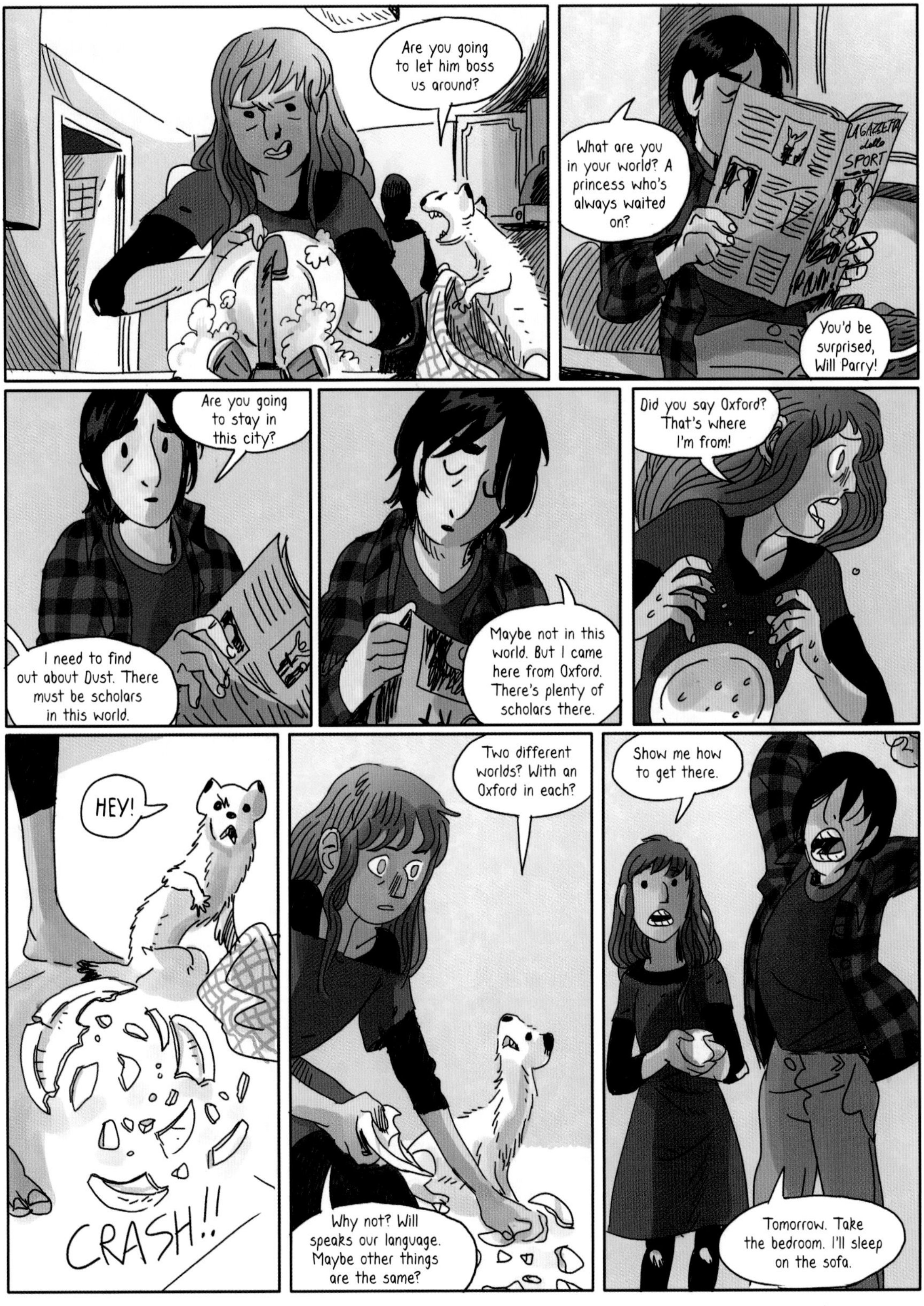
Are you going to let him boss us around?
What are you in your world? A princess who's always waited on?
LA GAZZETTA dello SPORT
You'd be surprised, Will Parry!
Are you going to stay in this city?
I need to find out about Dust. There must be scholars in this world.
Maybe not in this world. But I came here from Oxford. There's plenty of scholars there.
Did you say Oxford? That's where I'm from!
HEY!
CRASH!!
Two different worlds? With an Oxford in each?
Why not? Will speaks our language. Maybe other things are the same?
Show me how to get there.
Tomorrow. Take the bedroom. I'll sleep on the sofa.

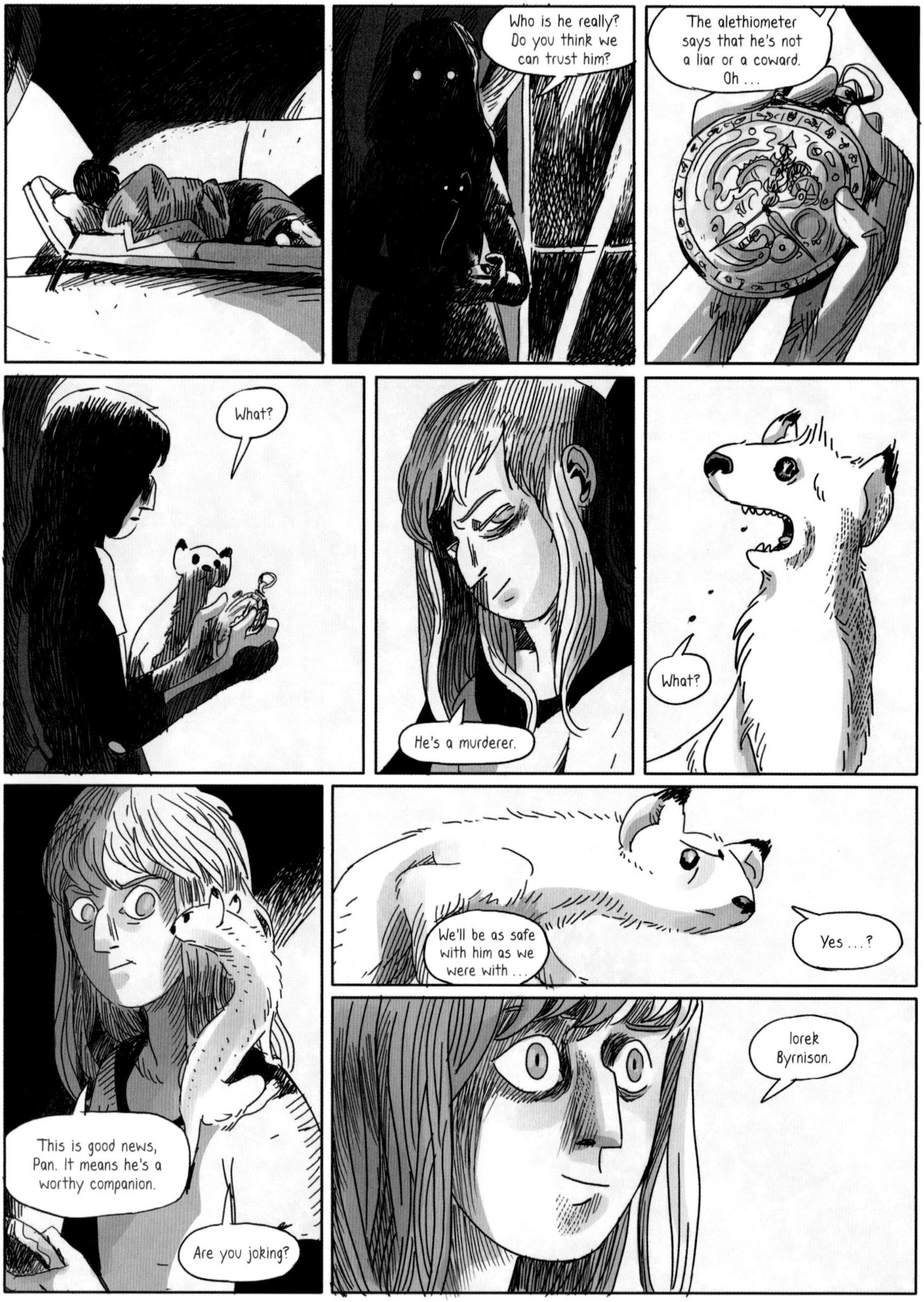
Who is he really? Do you think we can trust him?
The alethiometer says that he's not a liar or a coward. Oh . . .
What?
He's a murderer.
What?
This is good news, Pan. It means he's a worthy companion.
Are you joking?
We'll be as safe with him as we were with . . .
Yes . . . ?
Iorek Byrnison.

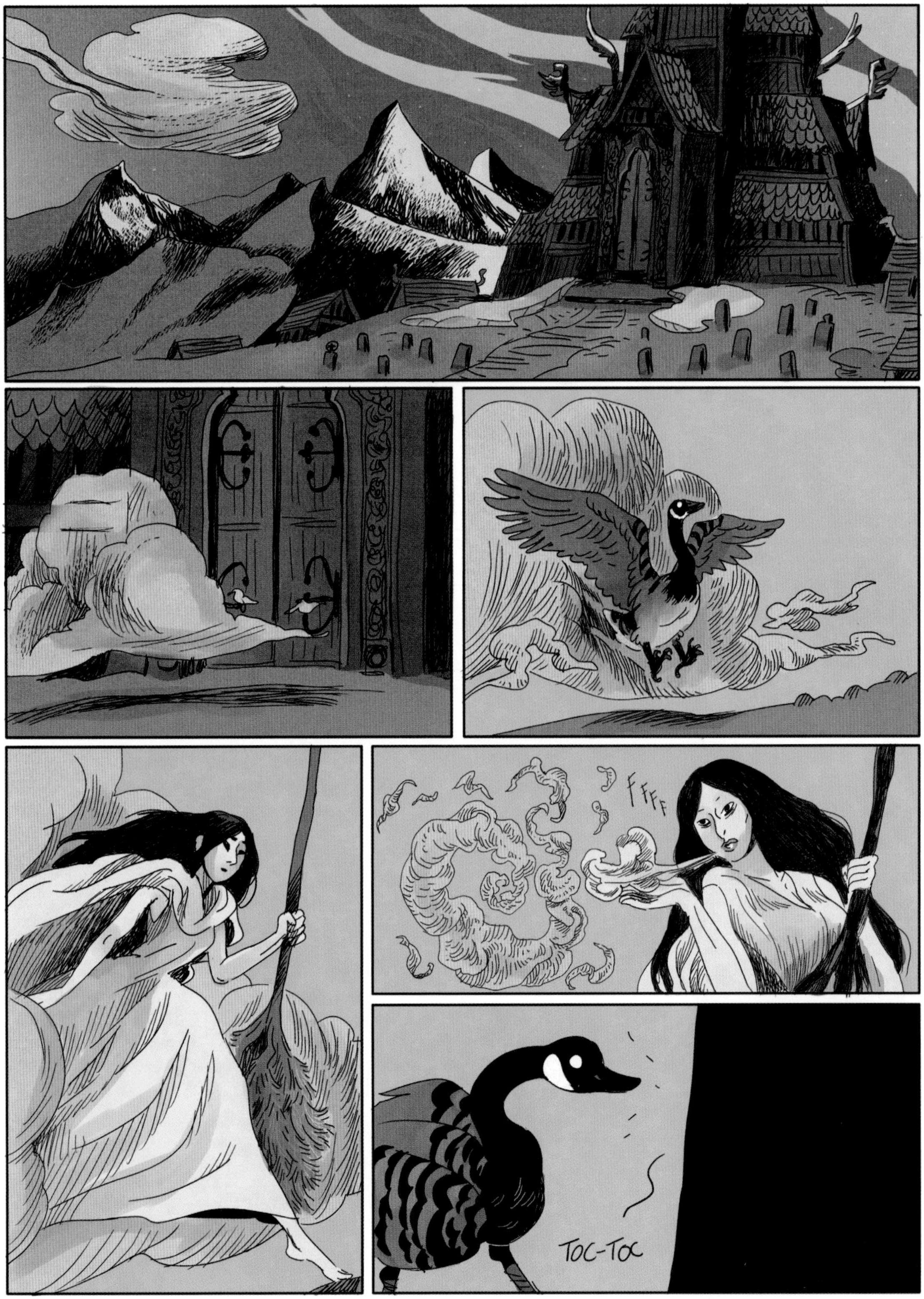
FFFF
TOC-TOC

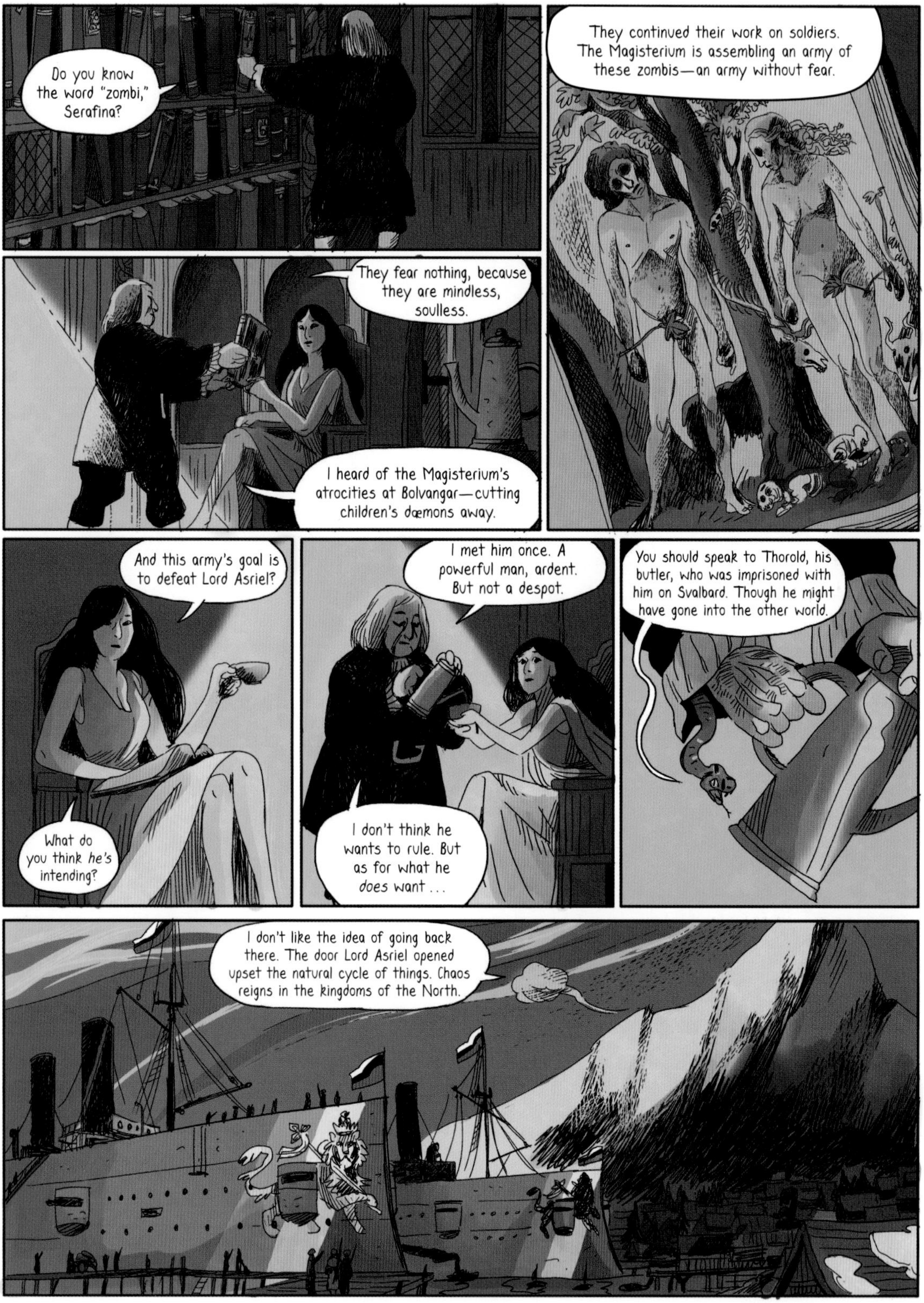
Do you know the word "zombi," Serafina?
They continued their work on soldiers. The Magisterium is assembling an army of these zombis—an army without fear.
They fear nothing, because they are mindless, soulless.
I heard of the Magisterium's atrocities at Bolvangar—cutting children's dæmons away.
And this army's goal is to defeat Lord Asriel?
What do you think *he's* intending?
I met him once. A powerful man, ardent. But not a despot.
I don't think he wants to rule. But as for what he *does* want . . .
You should speak to Thorold, his butler, who was imprisoned with him on Svalbard. Though he might have gone into the other world.
I don't like the idea of going back there. The door Lord Asriel opened upset the natural cycle of things. Chaos reigns in the kingdoms of the North.

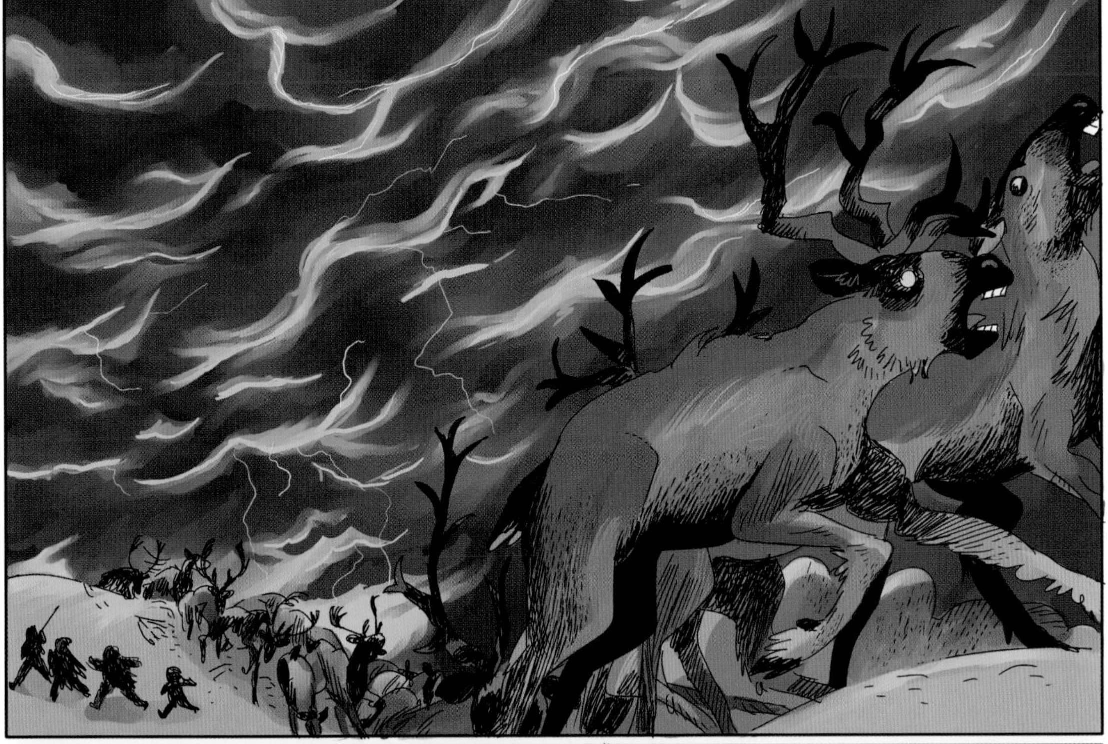

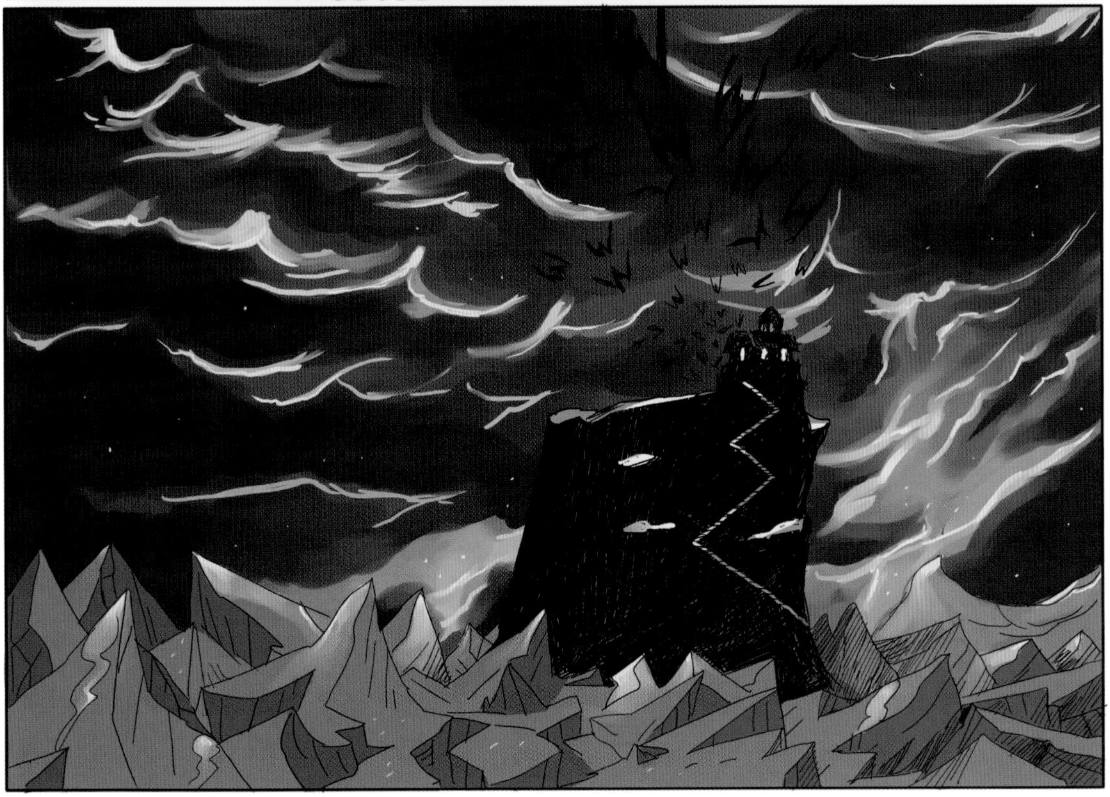

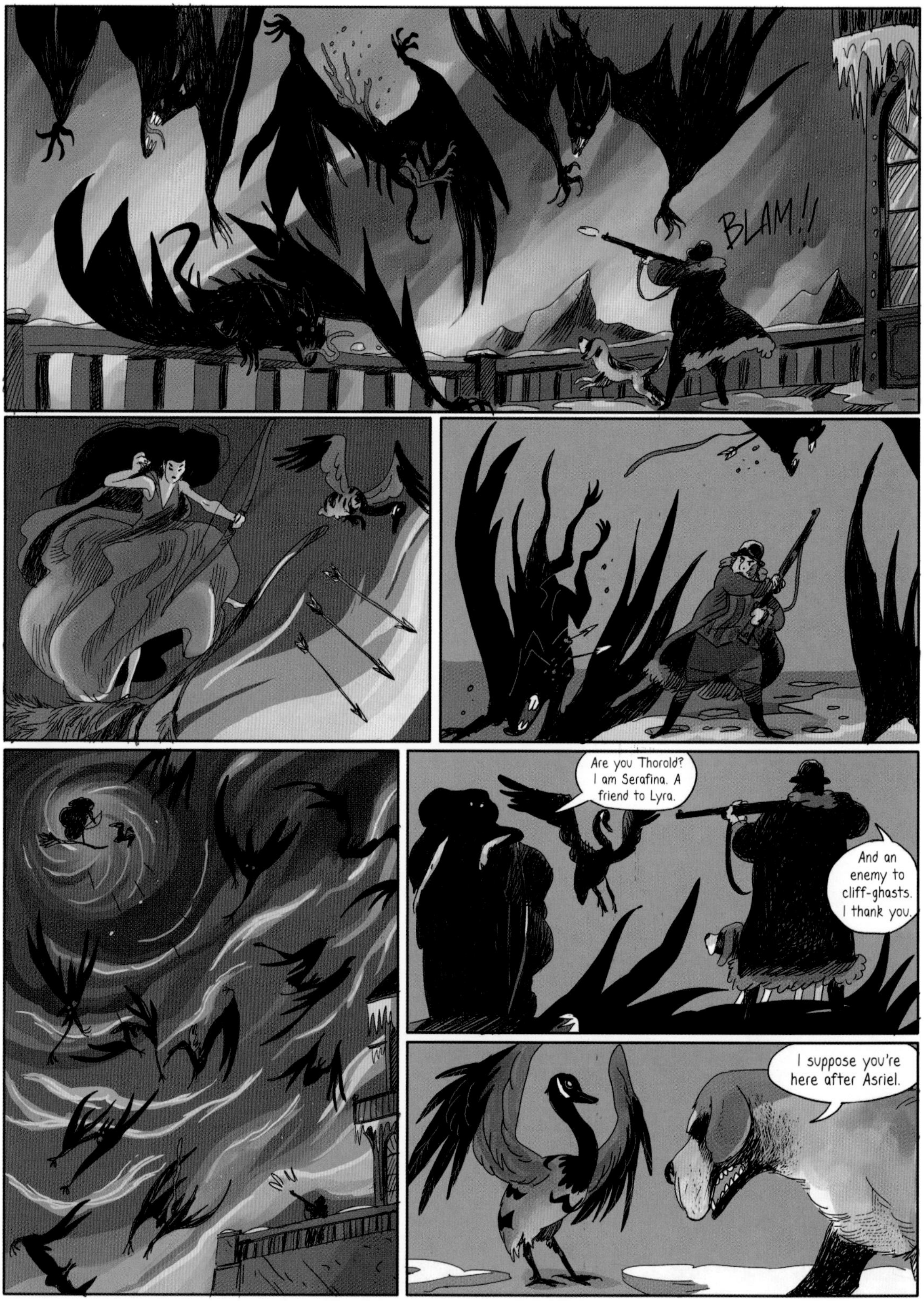
BLAM!!
Are you Thorold? I am Serafina. A friend to Lyra.
And an enemy to cliff-ghasts. I thank you.
I suppose you're here after Asriel.

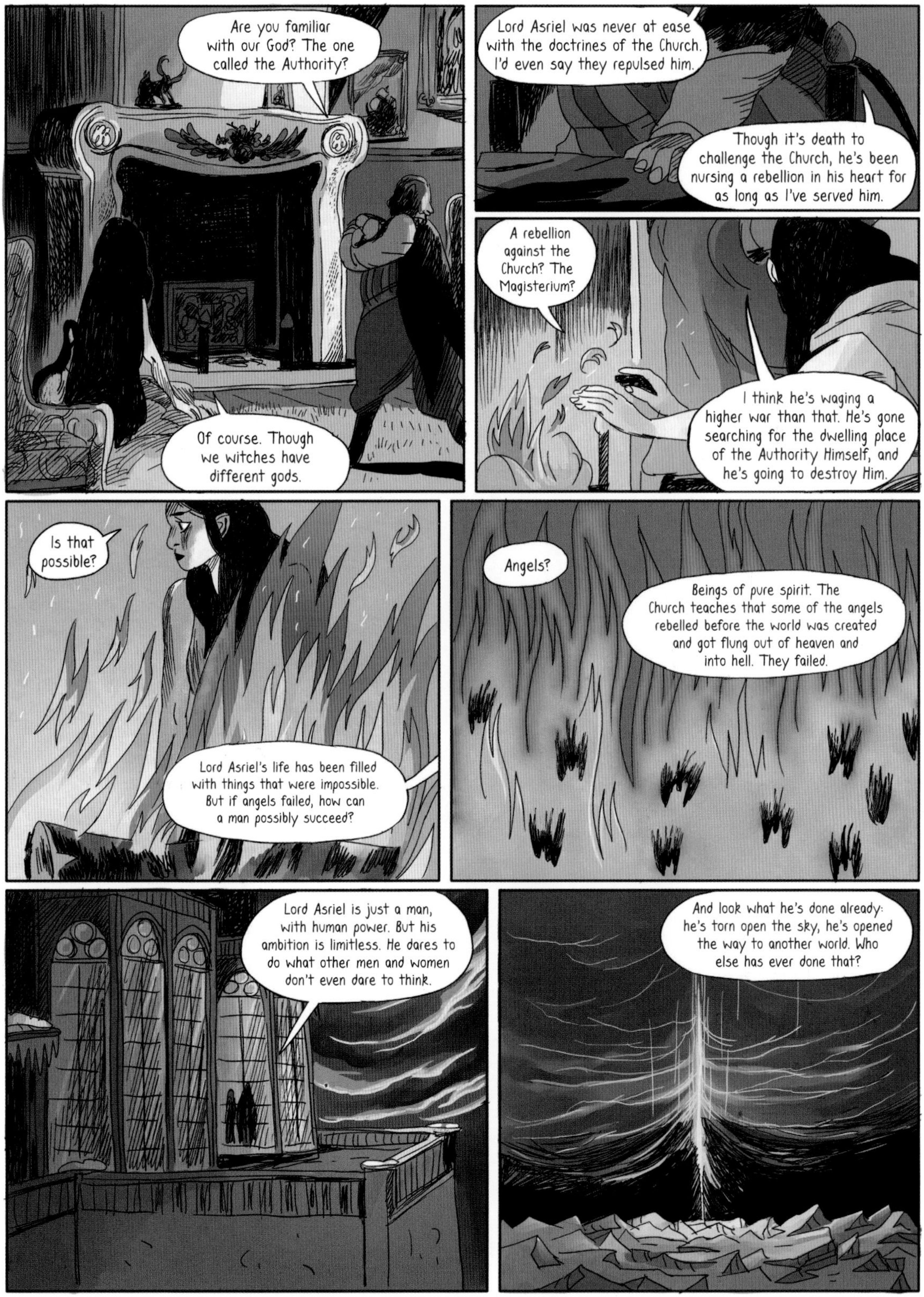
Are you familiar with our God? The one called the Authority?
Of course. Though we witches have different gods.
Lord Asriel was never at ease with the doctrines of the Church. I'd even say they repulsed him.
Though it's death to challenge the Church, he's been nursing a rebellion in his heart for as long as I've served him.
A rebellion against the Church? The Magisterium?
I think he's waging a higher war than that. He's gone searching for the dwelling place of the Authority Himself, and he's going to destroy Him.
Is that possible?
Lord Asriel's life has been filled with things that were impossible. But if angels failed, how can a man possibly succeed?
Angels?
Beings of pure spirit. The Church teaches that some of the angels rebelled before the world was created and got flung out of heaven and into hell. They failed.
Lord Asriel is just a man, with human power. But his ambition is limitless. He dares to do what other men and women don't even dare to think.
And look what he's done already: he's torn open the sky, he's opened the way to another world. Who else has ever done that?

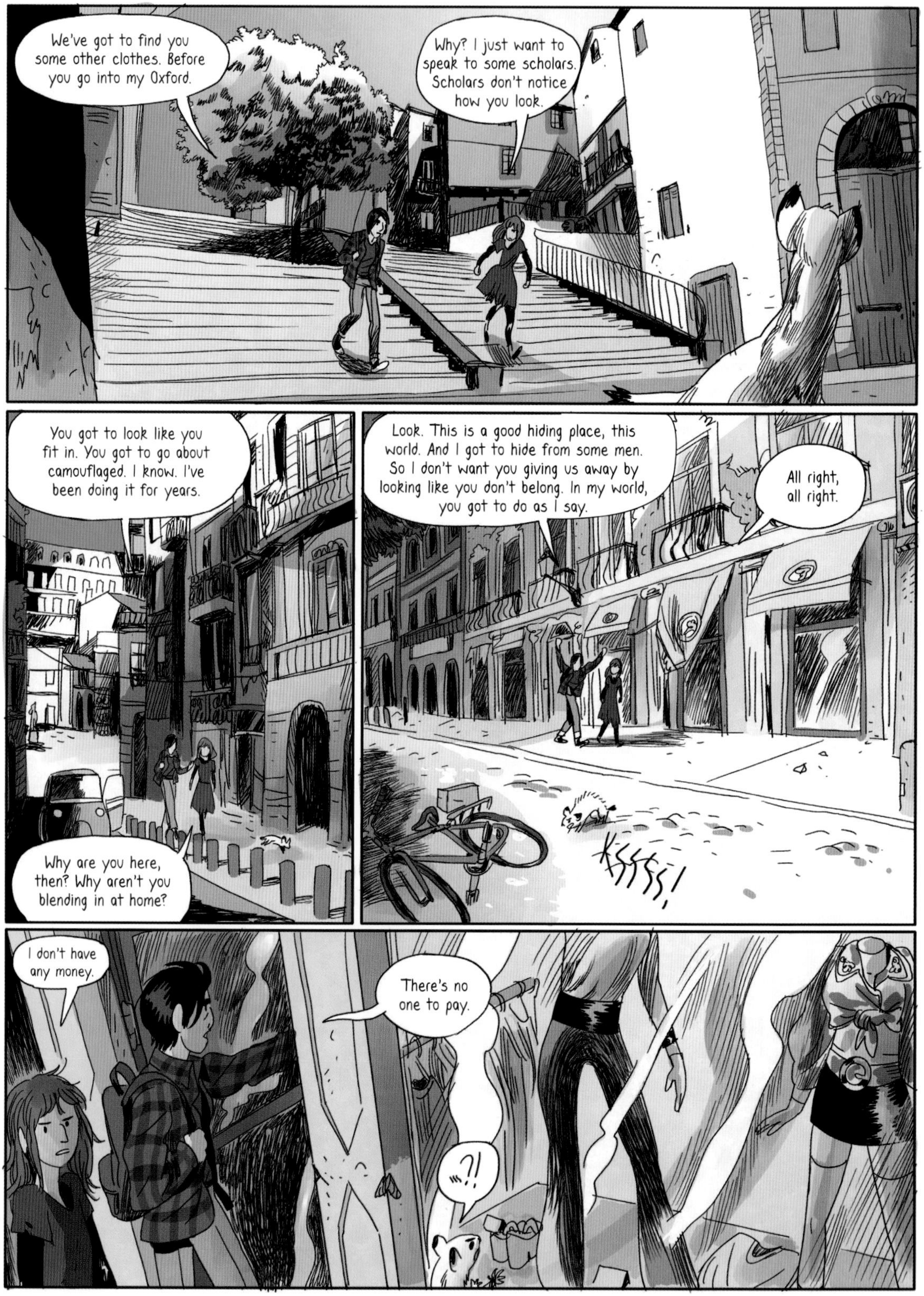
We've got to find you some other clothes. Before you go into my Oxford.
Why? I just want to speak to some scholars. Scholars don't notice how you look.
You got to look like you fit in. You got to go about camouflaged. I know. I've been doing it for years.
Why are you here, then? Why aren't you blending in at home?
Look. This is a good hiding place, this world. And I got to hide from some men. So I don't want you giving us away by looking like you don't belong. In my world, you got to do as I say.
All right, all right.
KSSSS!
I don't have any money.
There's no one to pay.
?!

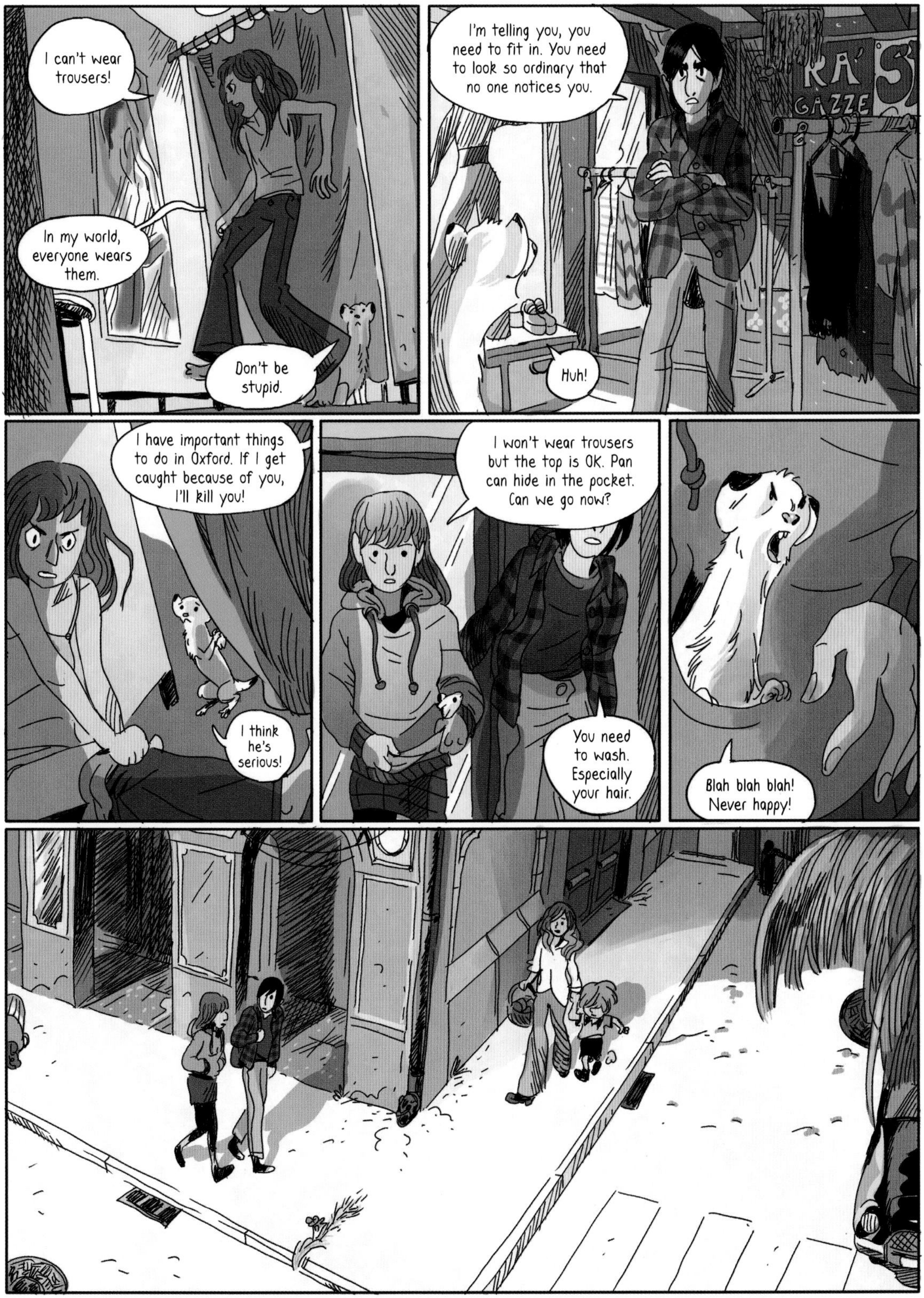
I can't wear trousers!
In my world, everyone wears them.
Don't be stupid.
I'm telling you, you need to fit in. You need to look so ordinary that no one notices you.
Huh!
I have important things to do in Oxford. If I get caught because of you, I'll kill you!
I think he's serious!
I won't wear trousers but the top is OK. Pan can hide in the pocket. Can we go now?
You need to wash. Especially your hair.
Blah blah blah! Never happy!

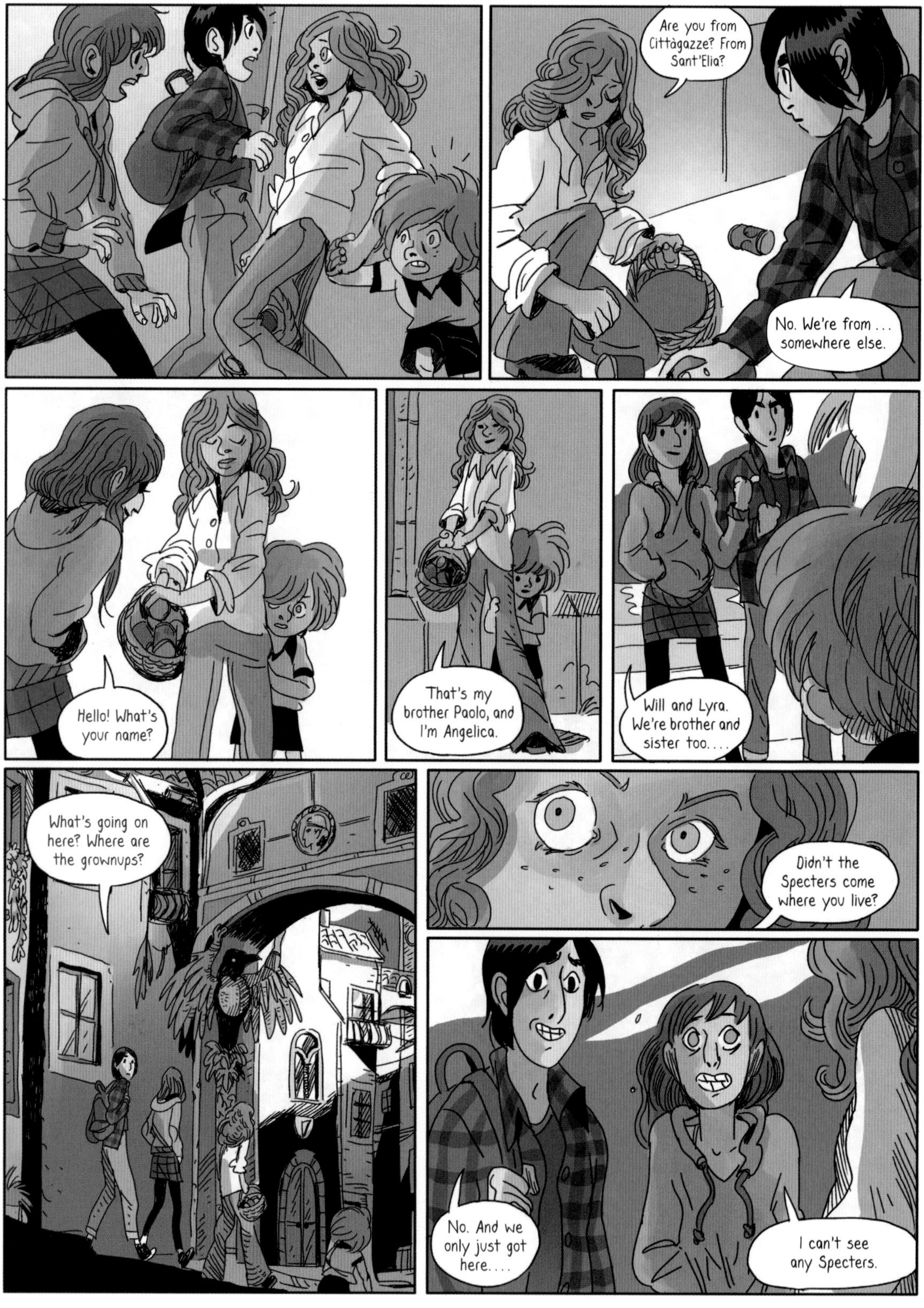

Are you from Cittàgazze? From Sant'Elia?
No. We're from . . . somewhere else.
Hello! What's your name?
That's my brother Paolo, and I'm Angelica.
Will and Lyra. We're brother and sister too. . . .
What's going on here? Where are the grownups?
Didn't the Specters come where you live?
No. And we only just got here. . . .
I can't see any Specters.

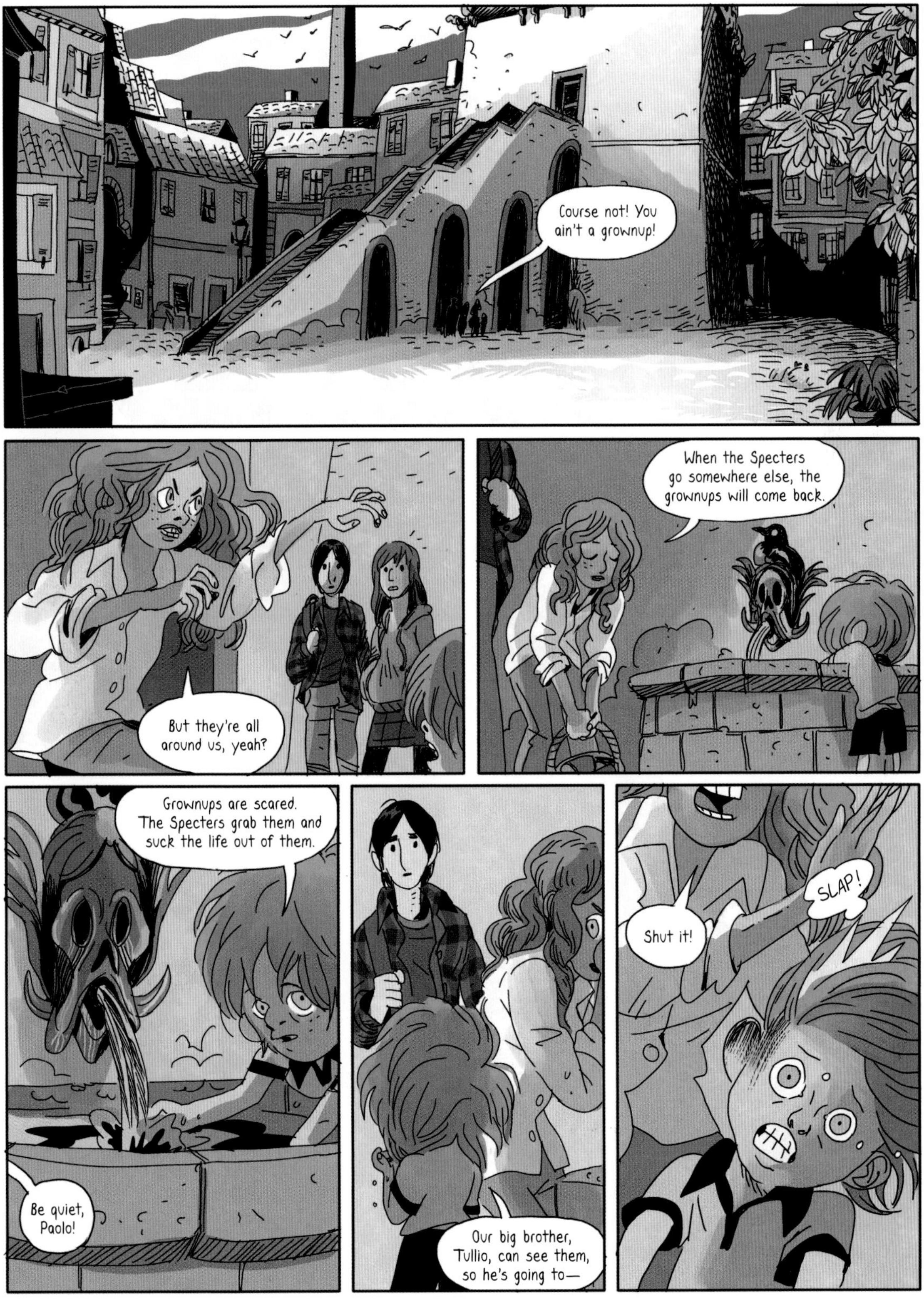
Course not! You ain't a grownup!
But they're all around us, yeah?
When the Specters go somewhere else, the grownups will come back.
Grownups are scared. The Specters grab them and suck the life out of them.
Be quiet, Paolo!
Our big brother, Tullio, can see them, so he's going to—
Shut it!
SLAP!

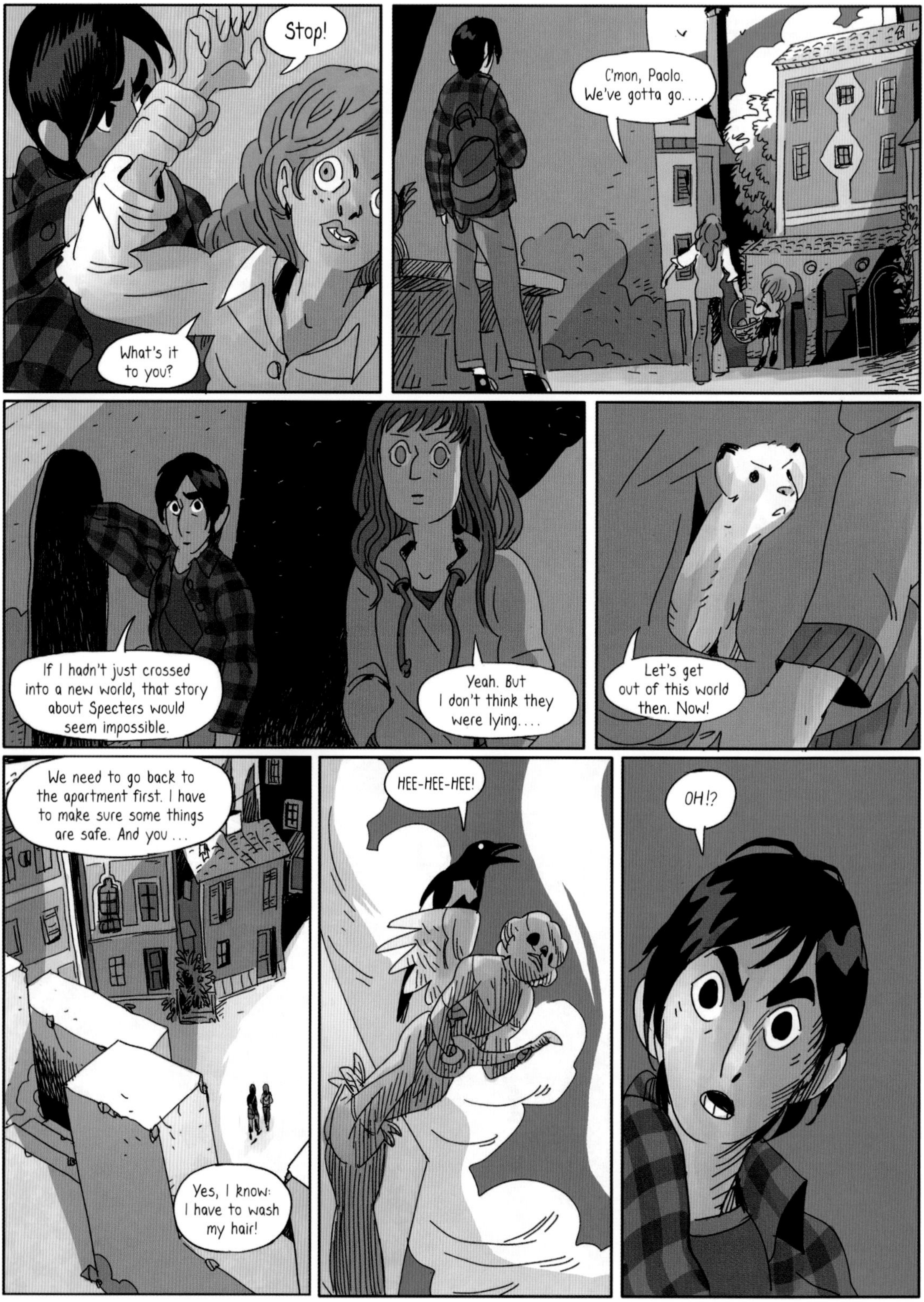
Stop!
What's it to you?
C'mon, Paolo. We've gotta go. . . .
If I hadn't just crossed into a new world, that story about Specters would seem impossible.
Yeah. But I don't think they were lying. . . .
Let's get out of this world then. Now!
We need to go back to the apartment first. I have to make sure some things are safe. And you . . .
Yes, I know: I have to wash my hair!
HEE-HEE-HEE!
OH!?

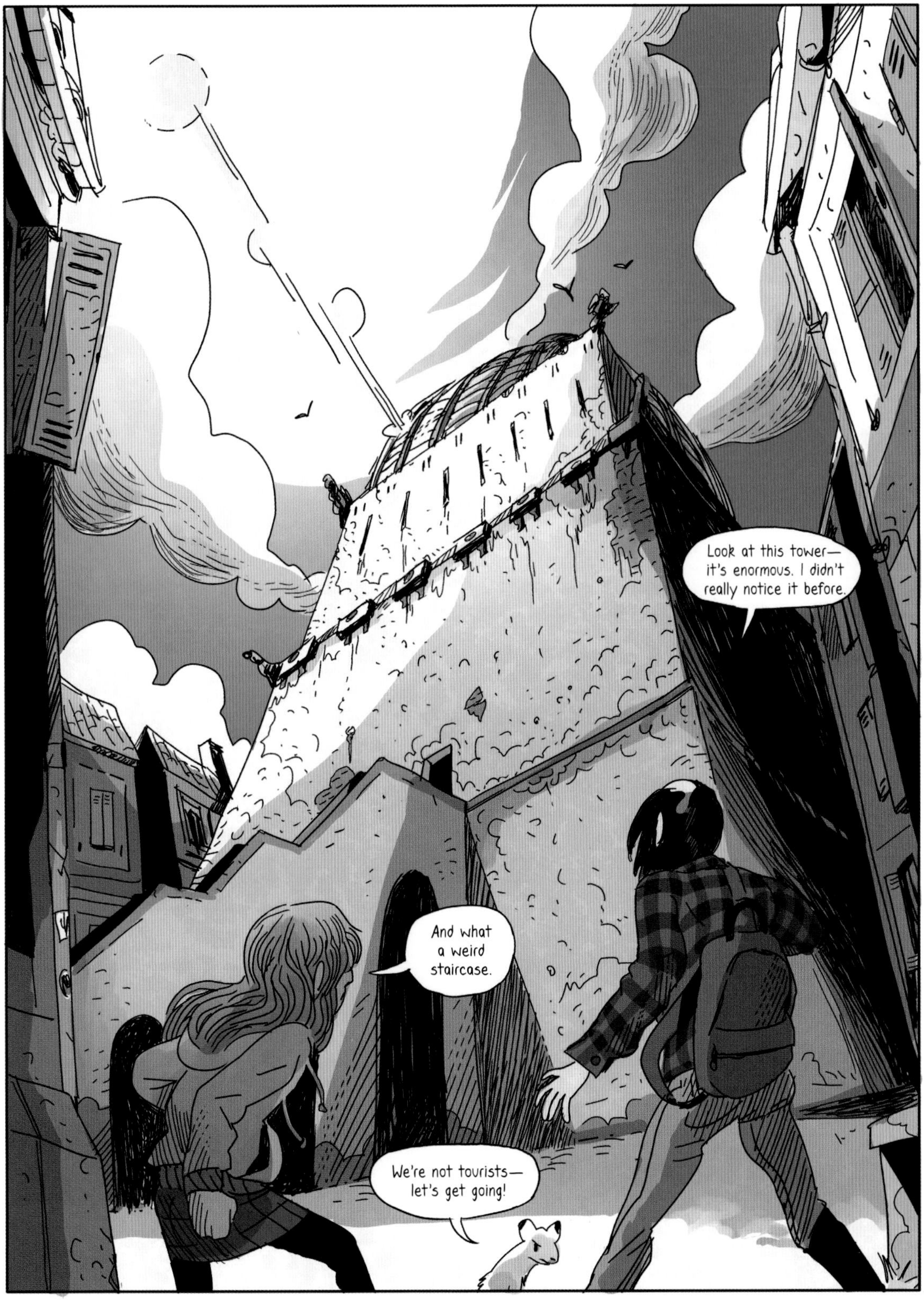
Look at this tower—it's enormous. I didn't really notice it before.
And what a weird staircase.
We're not tourists—let's get going!

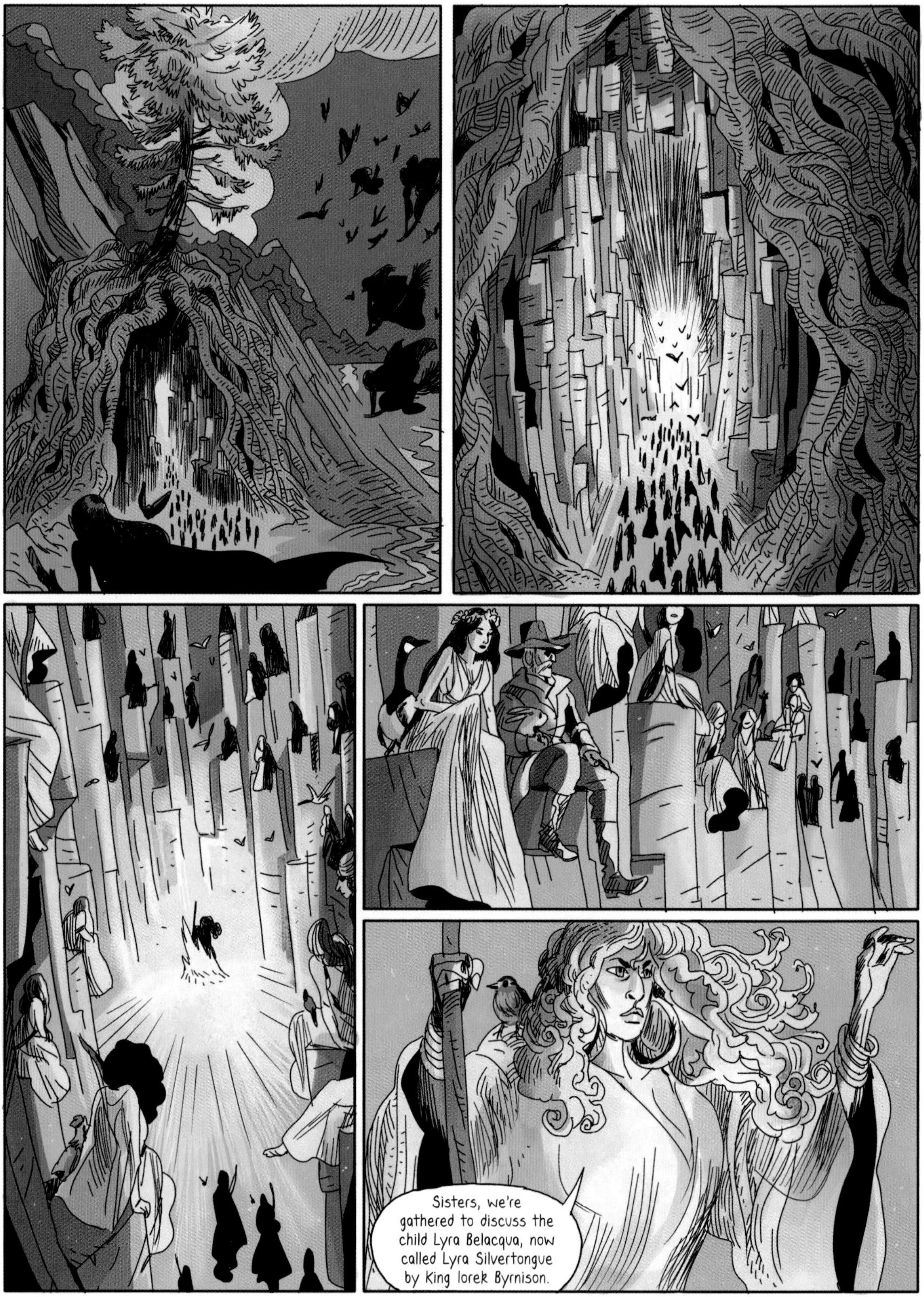
Sisters, we're gathered to discuss the child Lyra Belacqua, now called Lyra Silvertongue by King Iorek Byrnison.

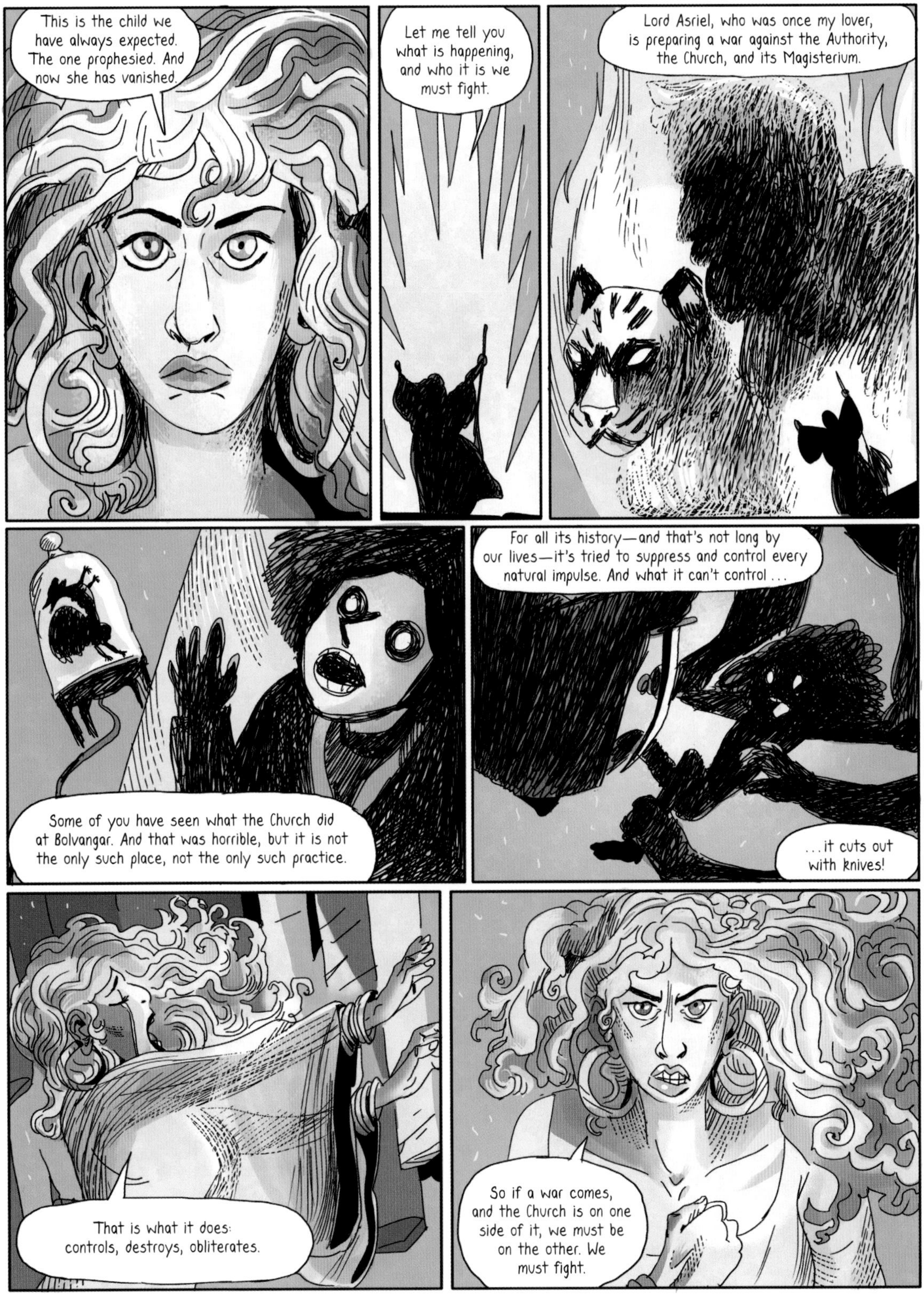
This is the child we have always expected. The one prophesied. And now she has vanished.
Let me tell you what is happening, and who it is we must fight.
Lord Asriel, who was once my lover, is preparing a war against the Authority, the Church, and its Magisterium.
Some of you have seen what the Church did at Bolvangar. And that was horrible, but it is not the only such place, not the only such practice.
For all its history—and that's not long by our lives—it's tried to suppress and control every natural impulse. And what it can't control . . .
. . . it cuts out with knives!
That is what it does: controls, destroys, obliterates.
So if a war comes, and the Church is on one side of it, we must be on the other. We must fight.

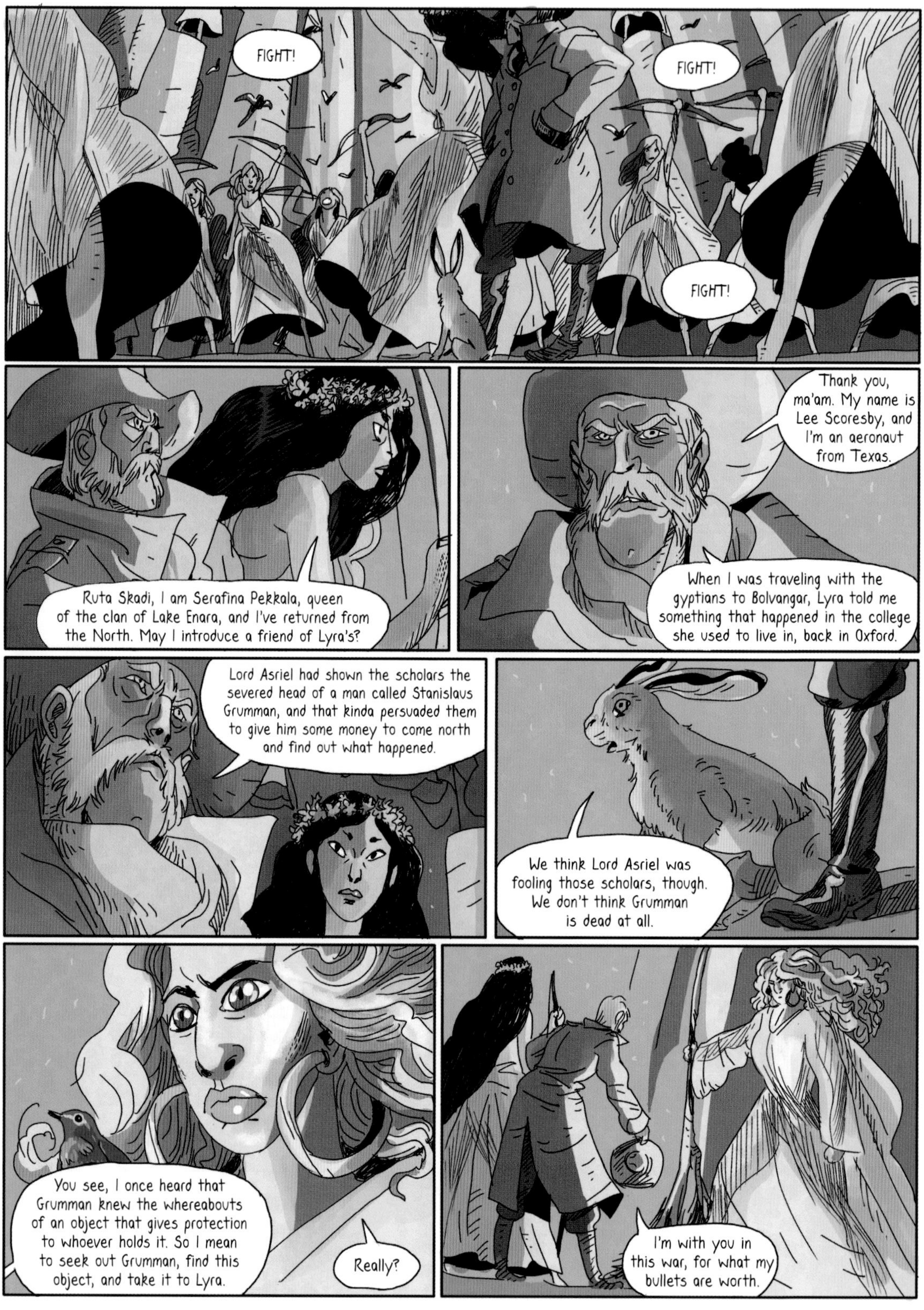
FIGHT!
FIGHT!
FIGHT!
Ruta Skadi, I am Serafina Pekkala, queen of the clan of Lake Enara, and I've returned from the North. May I introduce a friend of Lyra's?
Thank you, ma'am. My name is Lee Scoresby, and I'm an aeronaut from Texas.
When I was traveling with the gyptians to Bolvangar, Lyra told me something that happened in the college she used to live in, back in Oxford.
Lord Asriel had shown the scholars the severed head of a man called Stanislaus Grumman, and that kinda persuaded them to give him some money to come north and find out what happened.
We think Lord Asriel was fooling those scholars, though. We don't think Grumman is dead at all.
You see, I once heard that Grumman knew the whereabouts of an object that gives protection to whoever holds it. So I mean to seek out Grumman, find this object, and take it to Lyra.
Really?
I'm with you in this war, for what my bullets are worth.

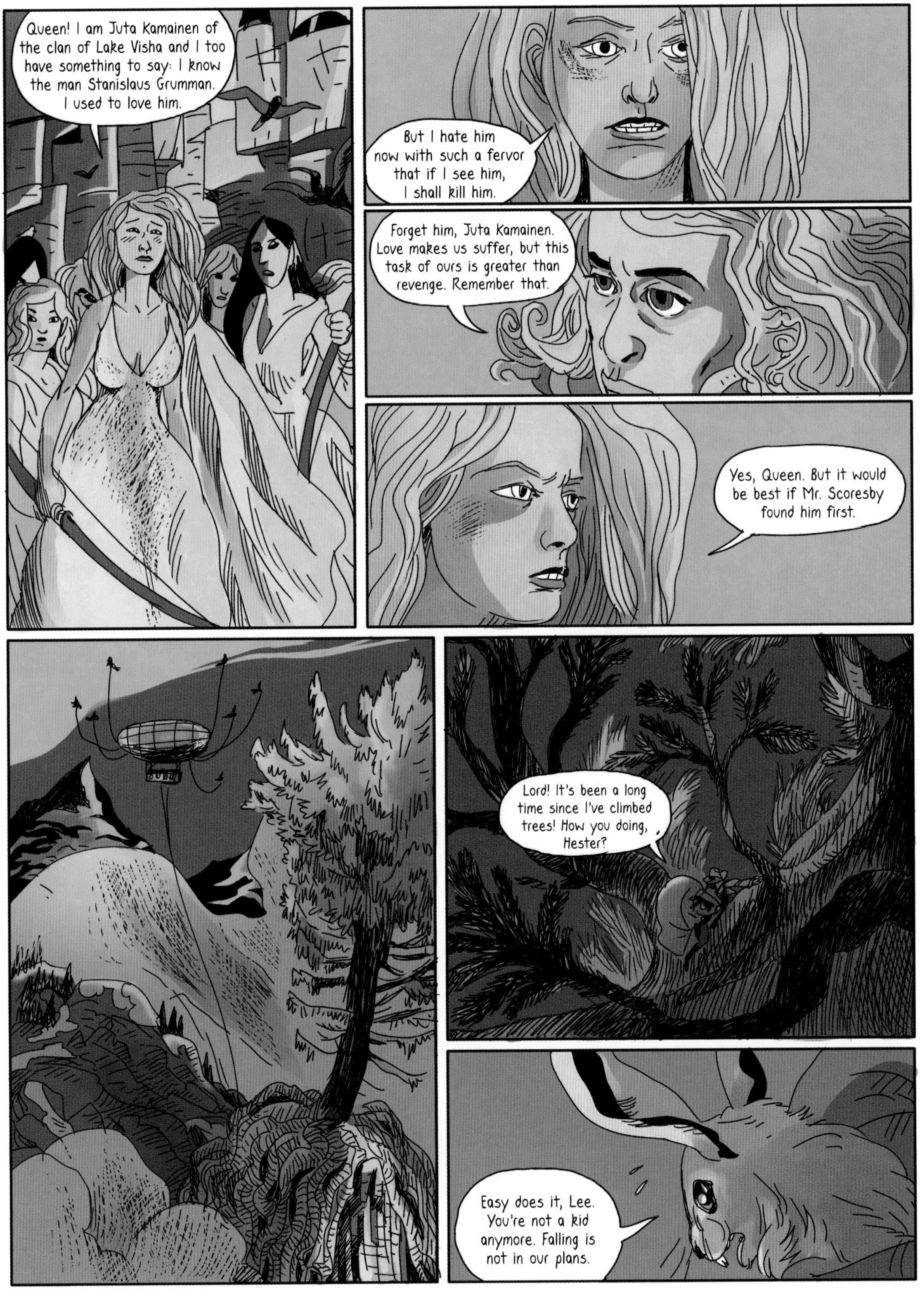
Queen! I am Juta Kamainen of the clan of Lake Visha and I too have something to say: I know the man Stanislaus Grumman. I used to love him.
But I hate him now with such a fervor that if I see him, I shall kill him.
Forget him, Juta Kamainen. Love makes us suffer, but this task of ours is greater than revenge. Remember that.
Yes, Queen. But it would be best if Mr. Scoresby found him first.
Lord! It's been a long time since I've climbed trees! How you doing, Hester?
Easy does it, Lee. You're not a kid anymore. Falling is not in our plans.

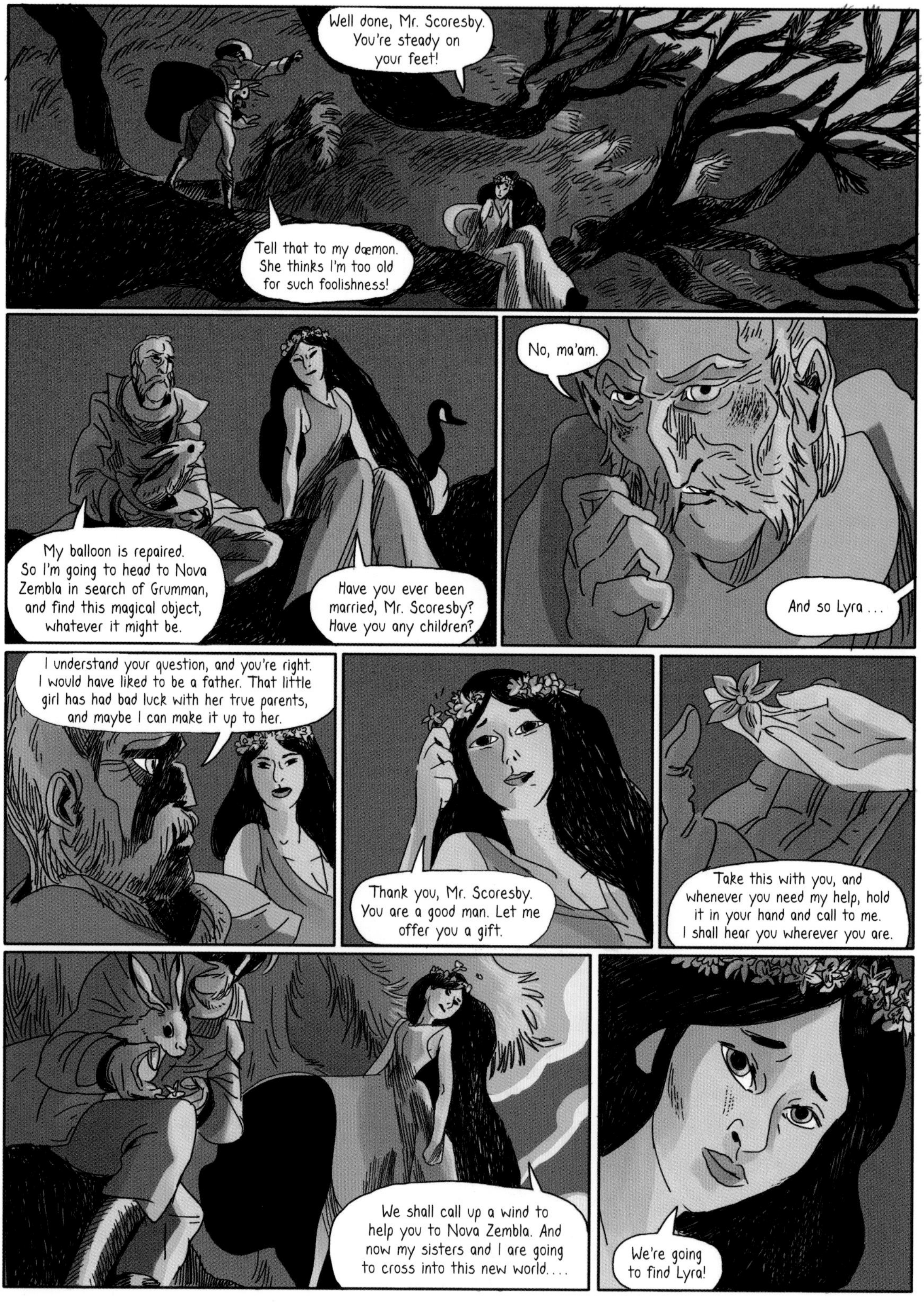

Well done, Mr. Scoresby. You're steady on your feet!
Tell that to my dæmon. She thinks I'm too old for such foolishness!
My balloon is repaired. So I'm going to head to Nova Zembla in search of Grumman, and find this magical object, whatever it might be.
Have you ever been married, Mr. Scoresby? Have you any children?
No, ma'am.
And so Lyra . . .
I understand your question, and you're right. I would have liked to be a father. That little girl has had bad luck with her true parents, and maybe I can make it up to her.
Thank you, Mr. Scoresby. You are a good man. Let me offer you a gift.
Take this with you, and whenever you need my help, hold it in your hand and call to me. I shall hear you wherever you are.
We shall call up a wind to help you to Nova Zembla. And now my sisters and I are going to cross into this new world. . . .
We're going to find Lyra!

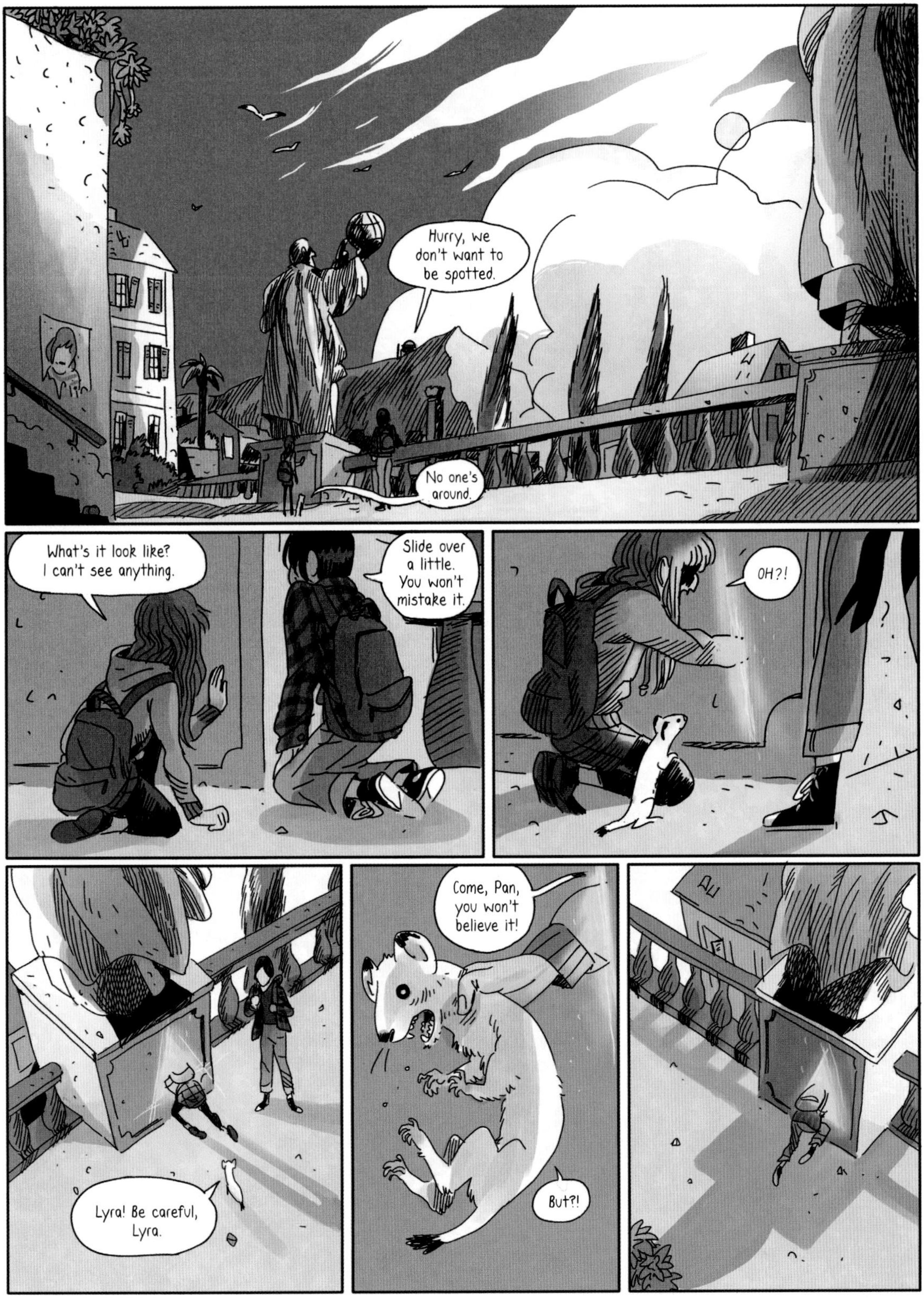
Hurry, we don't want to be spotted.
No one's around.
What's it look like? I can't see anything.
Slide over a little. You won't mistake it.
OH?!
Lyra! Be careful, Lyra.
Come, Pan, you won't believe it!
But?!

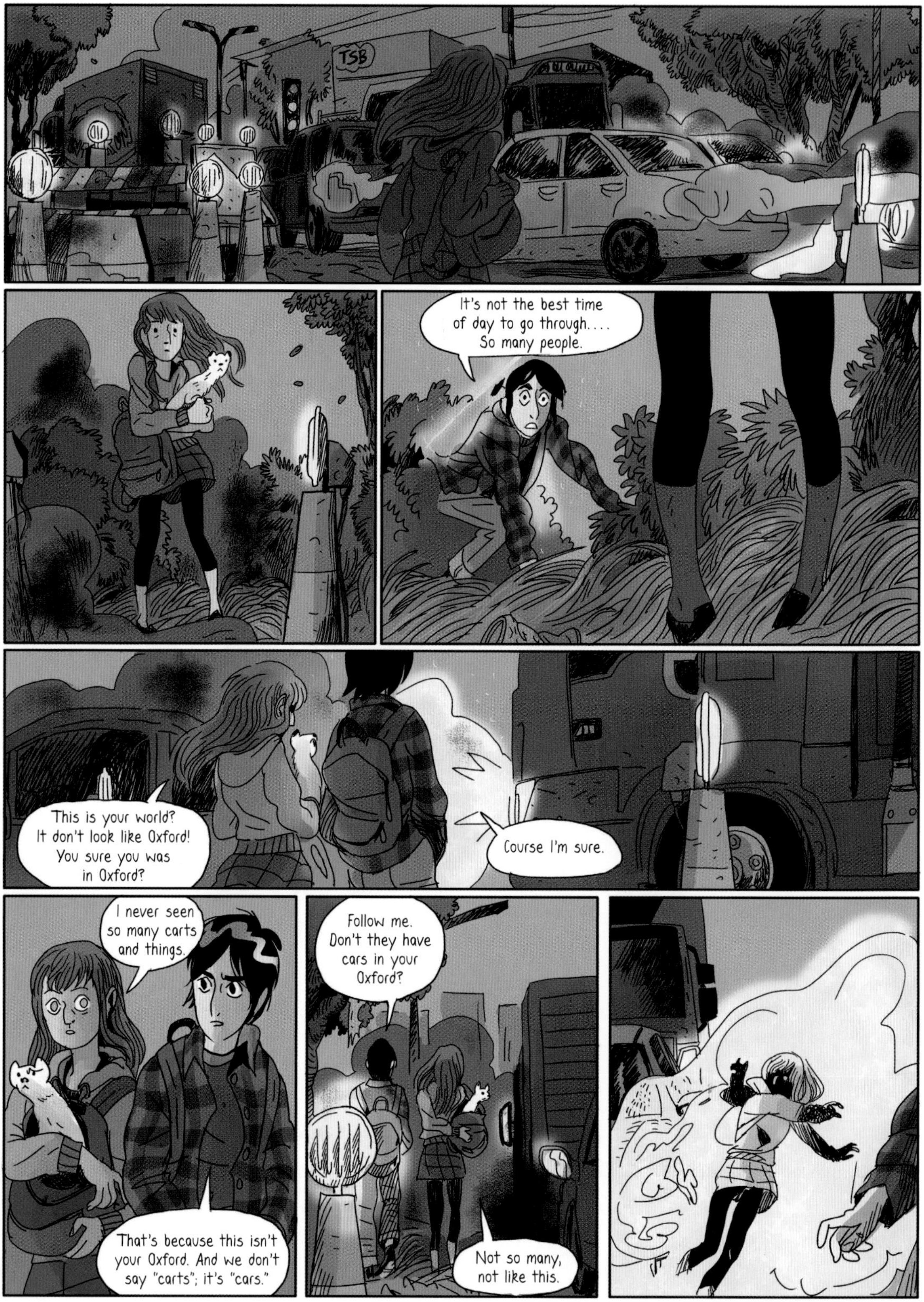
TSB
It's not the best time of day to go through. . . . So many people.
This is your world? It don't look like Oxford! You sure you was in Oxford?
Course I'm sure.
I never seen so many carts and things.
That's because this isn't your Oxford. And we don't say "carts"; it's "cars."
Follow me. Don't they have cars in your Oxford?
Not so many, not like this.

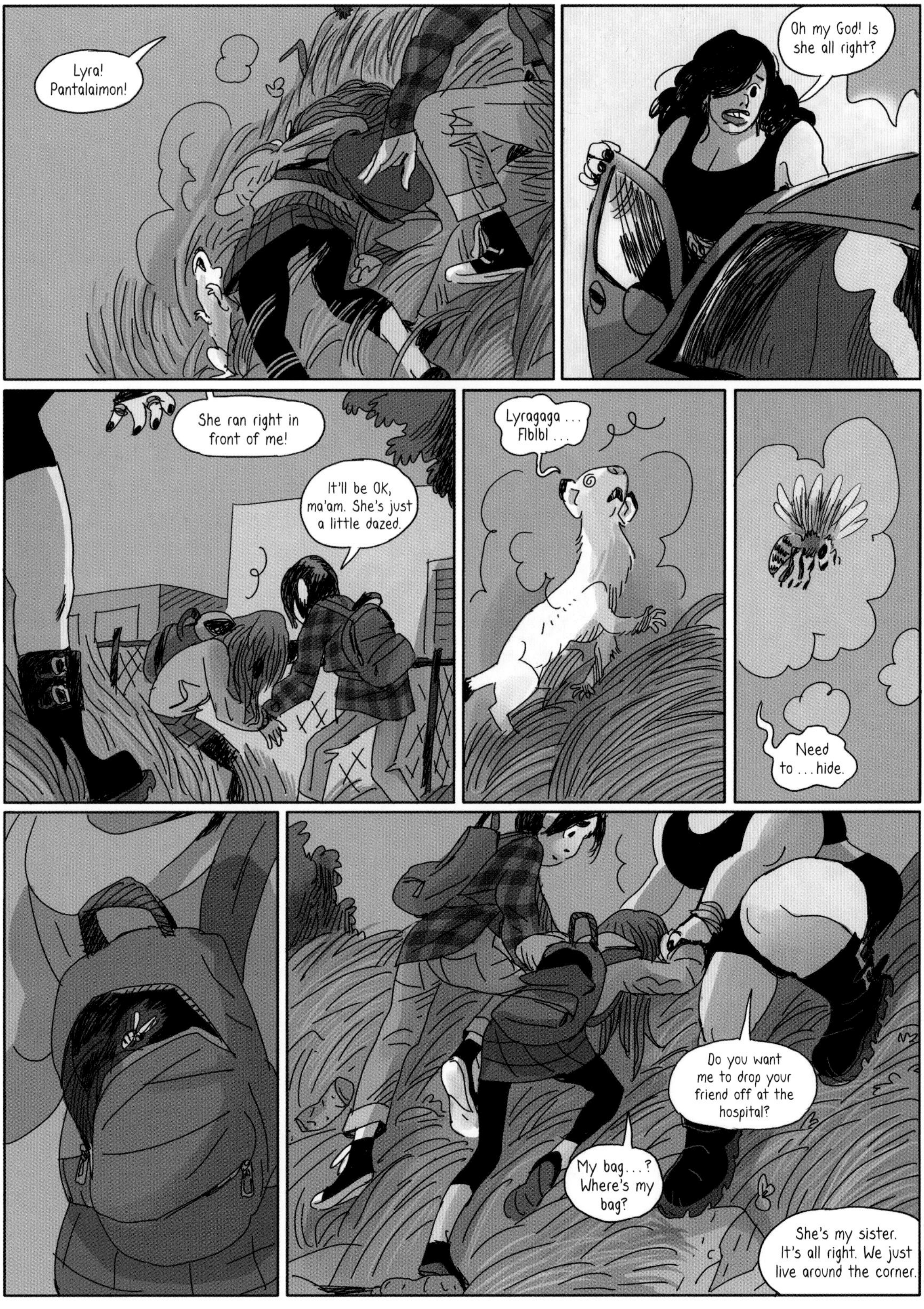
Lyra! Pantalaimon!
Oh my God! Is she all right?
She ran right in front of me!
It'll be OK, ma'am. She's just a little dazed.
Lyragaga . . . Flblbl . . .
Need to . . . hide.
Do you want me to drop your friend off at the hospital?
My bag . . .? Where's my bag?
She's my sister. It's all right. We just live around the corner.

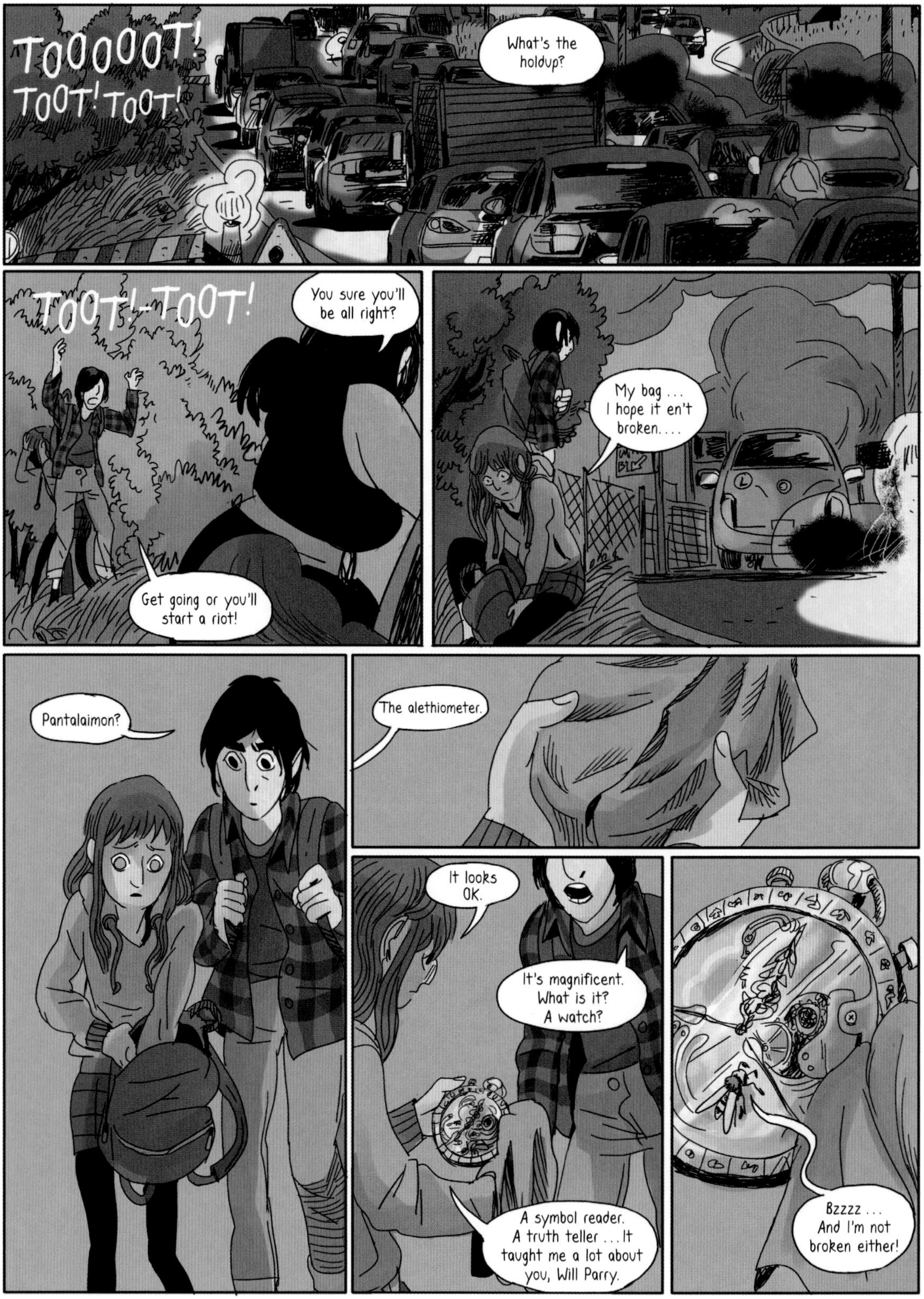
TOOOOOT!
TOOT! TOOT!
What's the holdup?
TOOT!-TOOT!
You sure you'll be all right?
Get going or you'll start a riot!
My bag . . . I hope it en't broken. . . .
Pantalaimon?
The alethiometer.
It looks OK.
It's magnificent. What is it? A watch?
A symbol reader. A truth teller . . . It taught me a lot about you, Will Parry.
Bzzzz . . . And I'm not broken either!

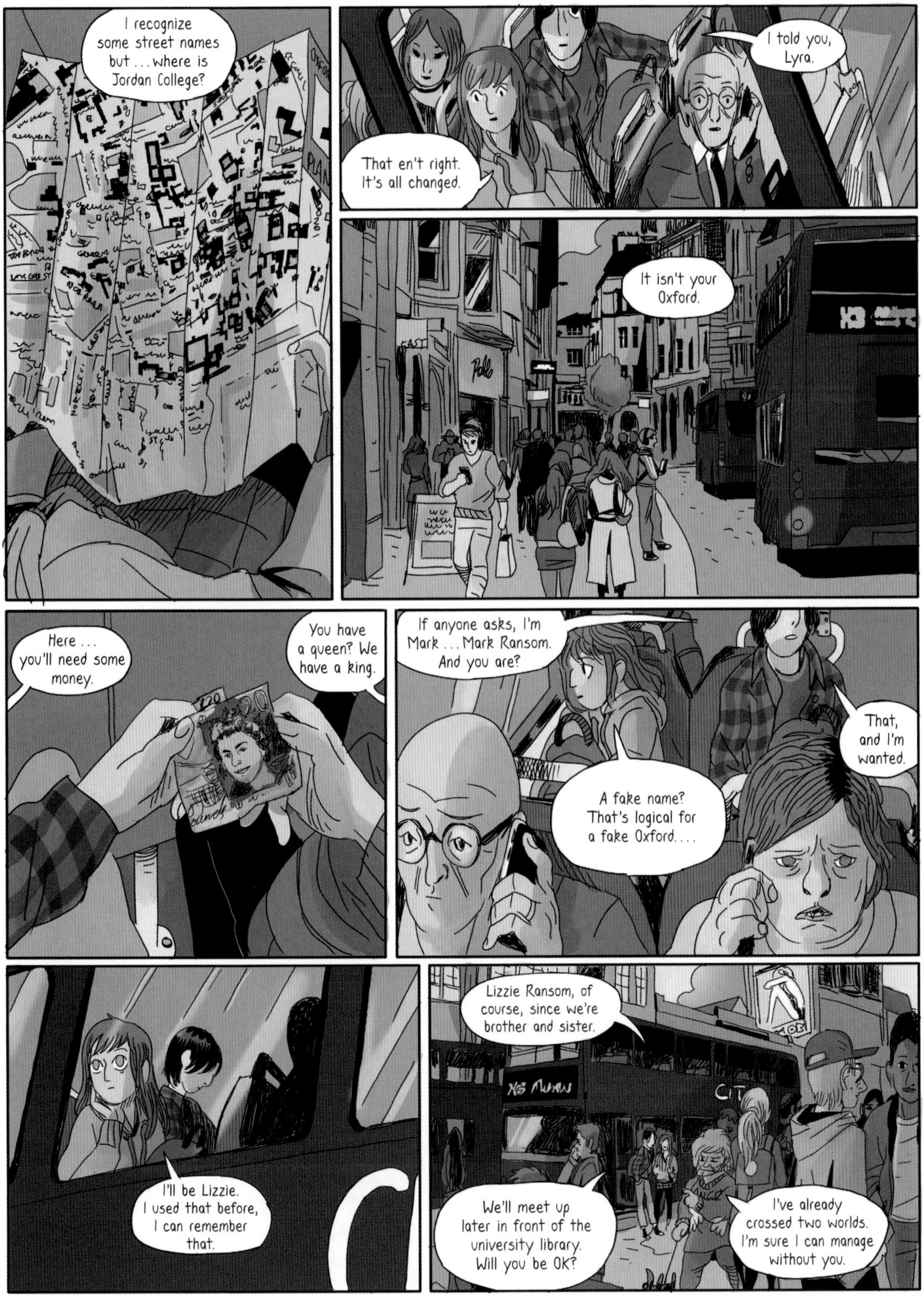
I recognize some street names but . . . where is Jordan College?
I told you, Lyra.
That en't right. It's all changed.
It isn't your Oxford.
Here . . . you'll need some money.
You have a queen? We have a king.
If anyone asks, I'm Mark . . . Mark Ransom. And you are?
That, and I'm wanted.
A fake name? That's logical for a fake Oxford. . . .
I'll be Lizzie. I used that before, I can remember that.
Lizzie Ransom, of course, since we're brother and sister.
We'll meet up later in front of the university library. Will you be OK?
I've already crossed two worlds. I'm sure I can manage without you.

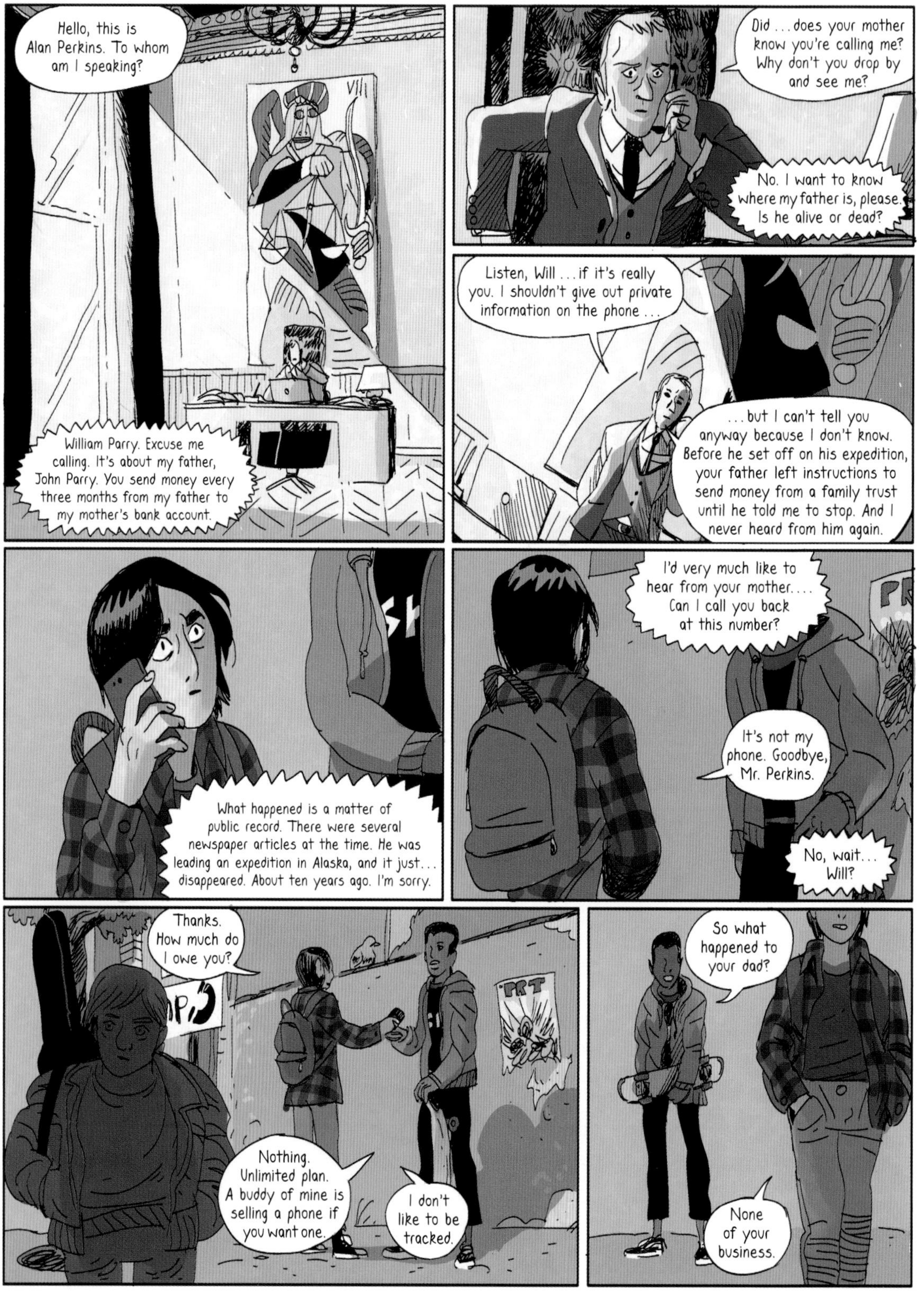
Hello, this is Alan Perkins. To whom am I speaking?
William Parry. Excuse me calling. It's about my father, John Parry. You send money every three months from my father to my mother's bank account.
Did . . . does your mother know you're calling me? Why don't you drop by and see me?
No. I want to know where my father is, please. Is he alive or dead?
Listen, Will . . . if it's really you. I shouldn't give out private information on the phone . . .
. . . but I can't tell you anyway because I don't know. Before he set off on his expedition, your father left instructions to send money from a family trust until he told me to stop. And I never heard from him again.
What happened is a matter of public record. There were several newspaper articles at the time. He was leading an expedition in Alaska, and it just . . . disappeared. About ten years ago. I'm sorry.
I'd very much like to hear from your mother. . . . Can I call you back at this number?
It's not my phone. Goodbye, Mr. Perkins.
No, wait. . . Will?
Thanks. How much do I owe you?
Nothing. Unlimited plan. A buddy of mine is selling a phone if you want one.
I don't like to be tracked.
So what happened to your dad?
None of your business.

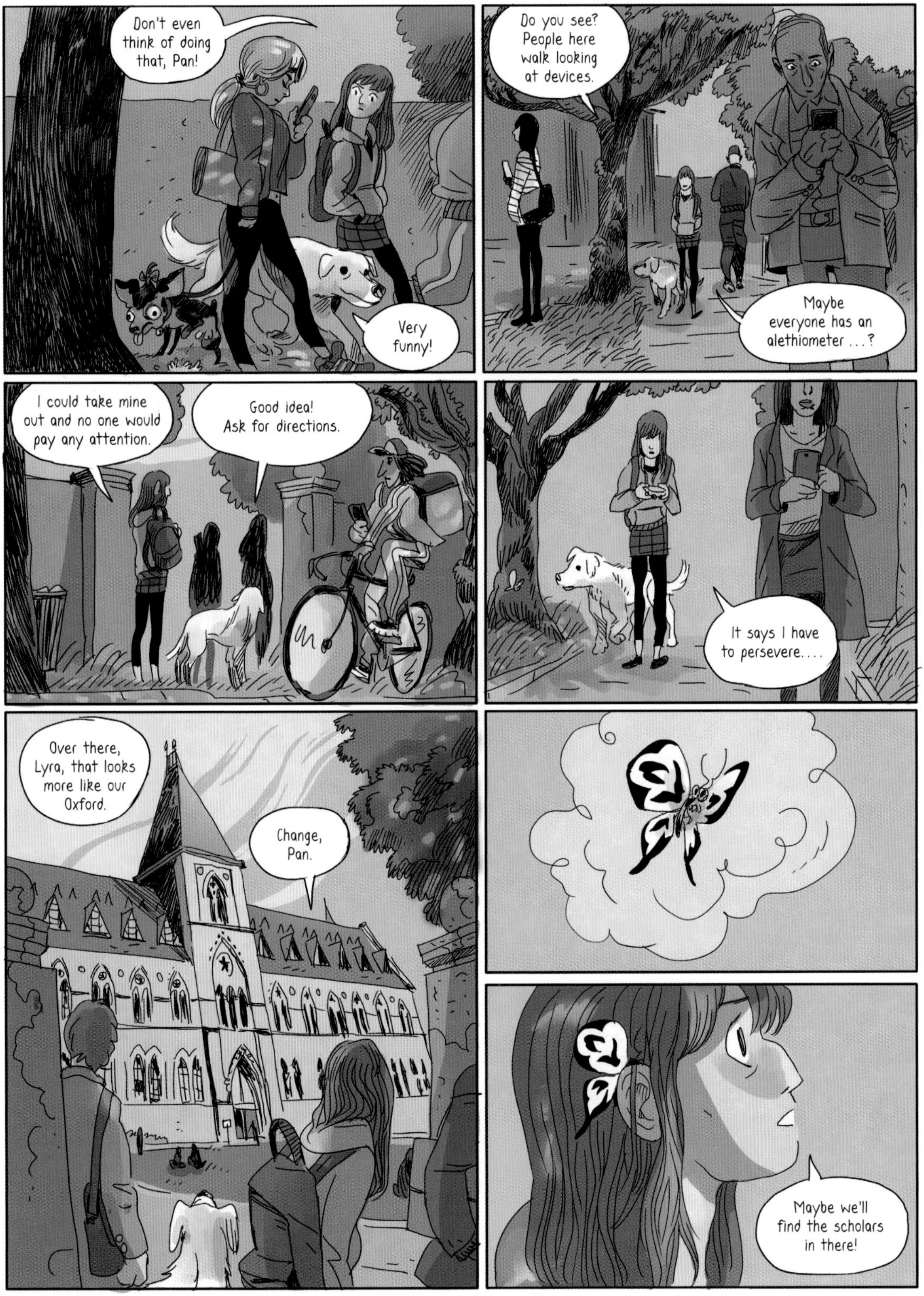
Don't even think of doing that, Pan!
Very funny!
Do you see? People here walk looking at devices.
Maybe everyone has an alethiometer . . . ?
I could take mine out and no one would pay any attention.
Good idea! Ask for directions.
It says I have to persevere. . . .
Over there, Lyra, that looks more like our Oxford.
Change, Pan.
Maybe we'll find the scholars in there!

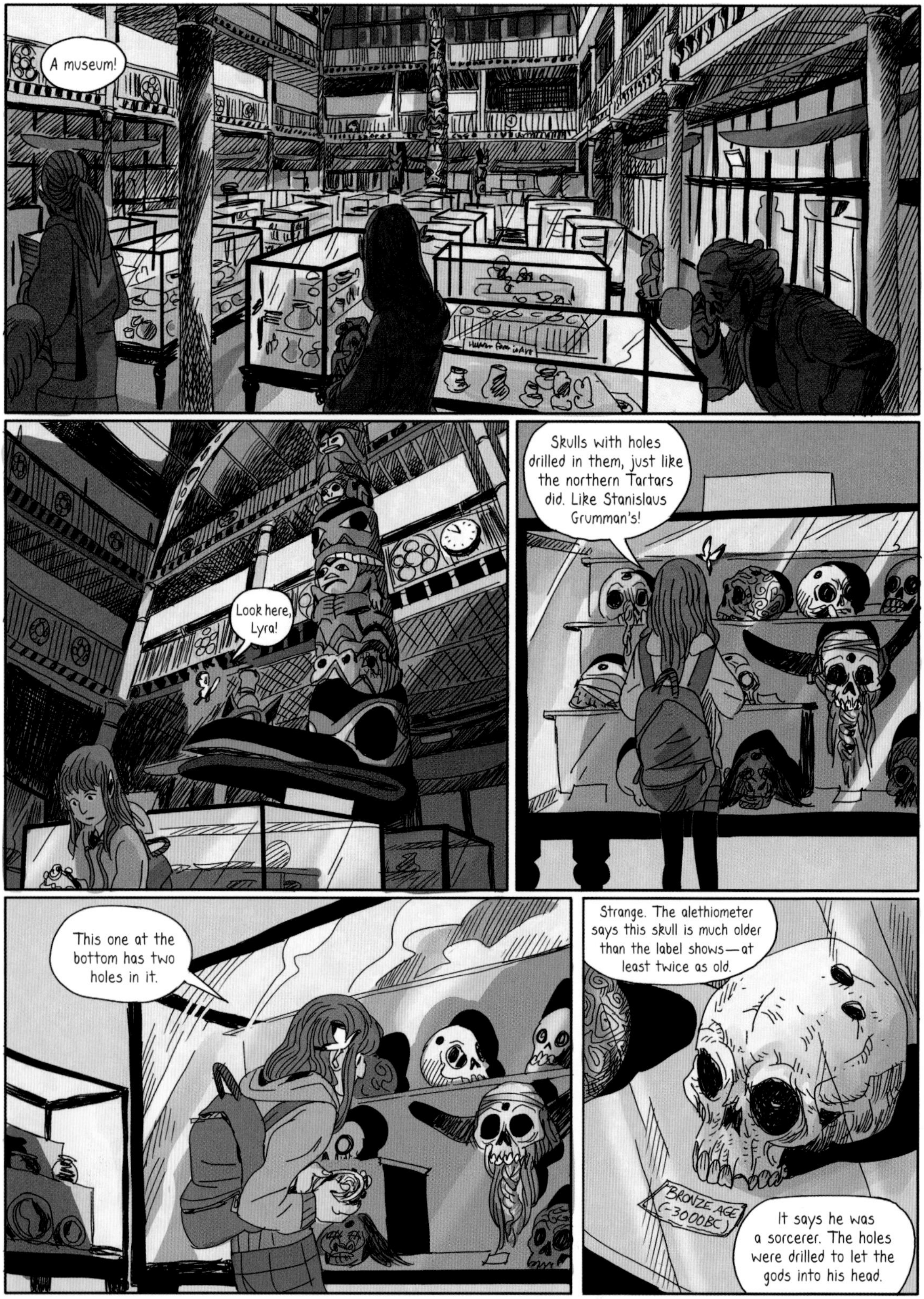
A museum!
Look here, Lyra!
Skulls with holes drilled in them, just like the northern Tartars did. Like Stanislaus Grumman's!
This one at the bottom has two holes in it.
Strange. The alethiometer says this skull is much older than the label shows—at least twice as old.
BRONZE AGE (-3000BC)
It says he was a sorcerer. The holes were drilled to let the gods into his head.

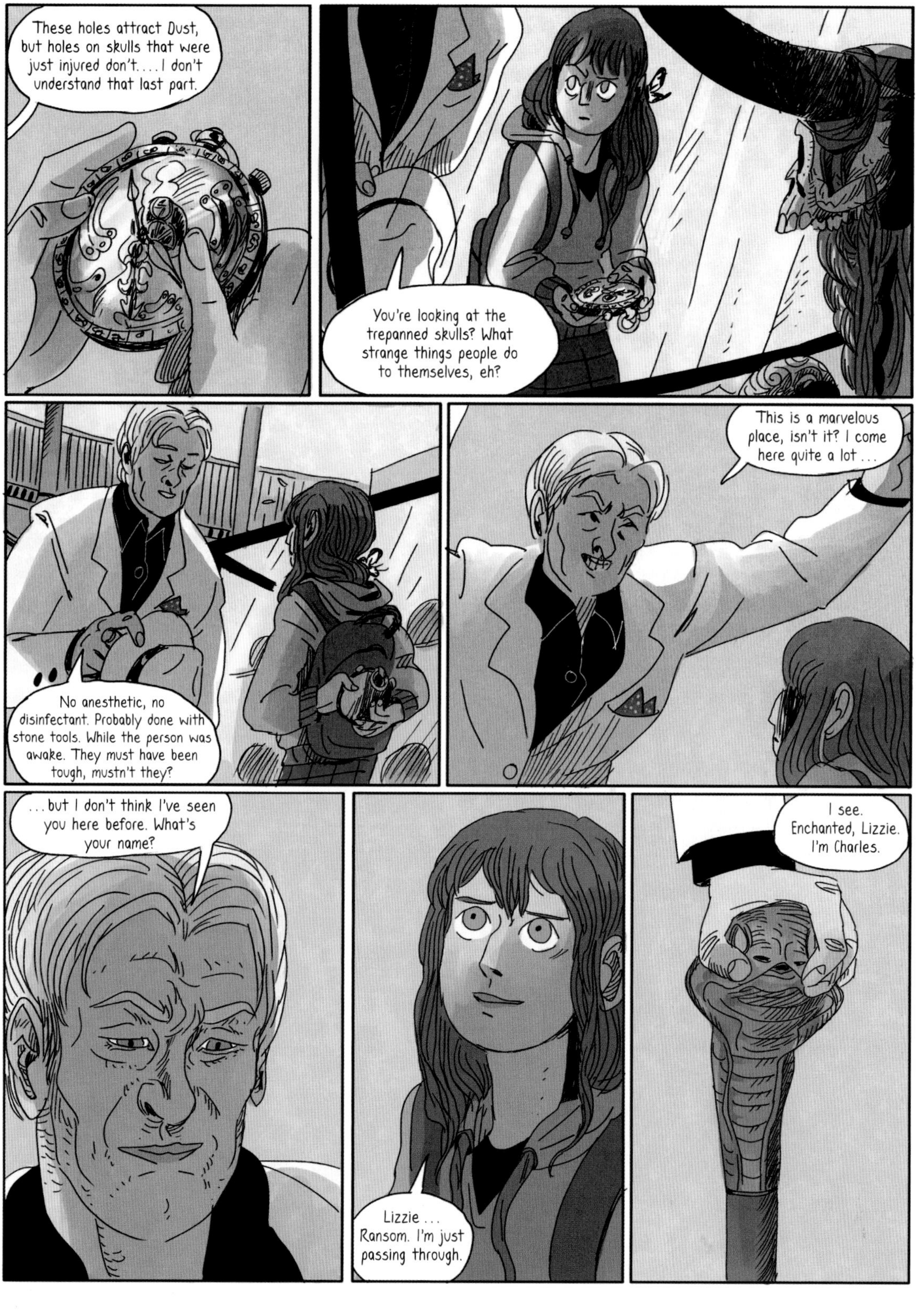
These holes attract Dust, but holes on skulls that were just injured don't. . . . I don't understand that last part.
You're looking at the trepanned skulls? What strange things people do to themselves, eh?
. . .
No anesthetic, no disinfectant. Probably done with stone tools. While the person was awake. They must have been tough, mustn't they?
This is a marvelous place, isn't it? I come here quite a lot . . .
. . . but I don't think I've seen you here before. What's your name?
Lizzie . . . Ransom. I'm just passing through.
I see. Enchanted, Lizzie. I'm Charles.

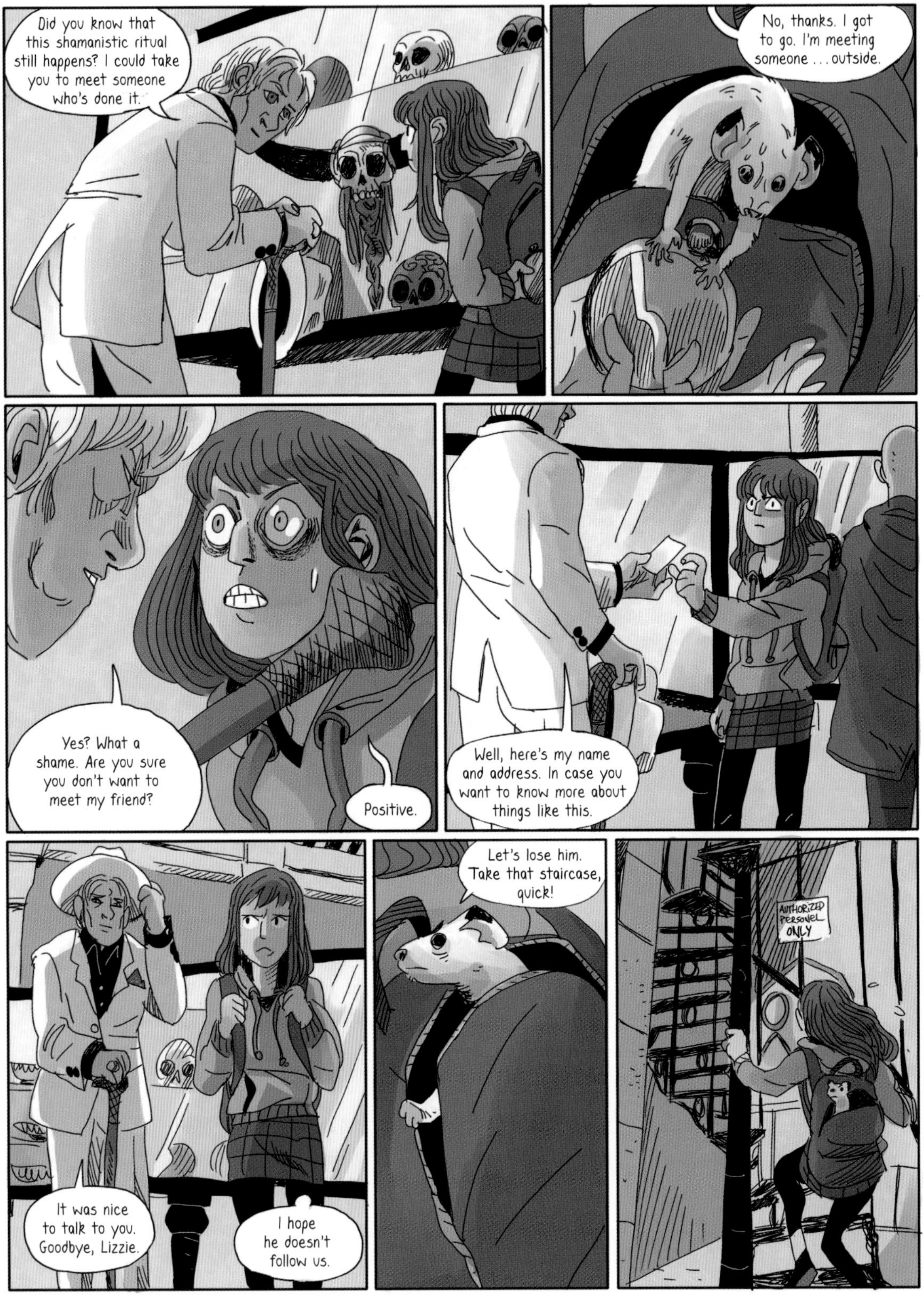
Did you know that this shamanistic ritual still happens? I could take you to meet someone who's done it.
No, thanks. I got to go. I'm meeting someone . . . outside.
Yes? What a shame. Are you sure you don't want to meet my friend?
Positive.
Well, here's my name and address. In case you want to know more about things like this.
It was nice to talk to you. Goodbye, Lizzie.
I hope he doesn't follow us.
Let's lose him. Take that staircase, quick!
AUTHORIZED PERSONEL ONLY

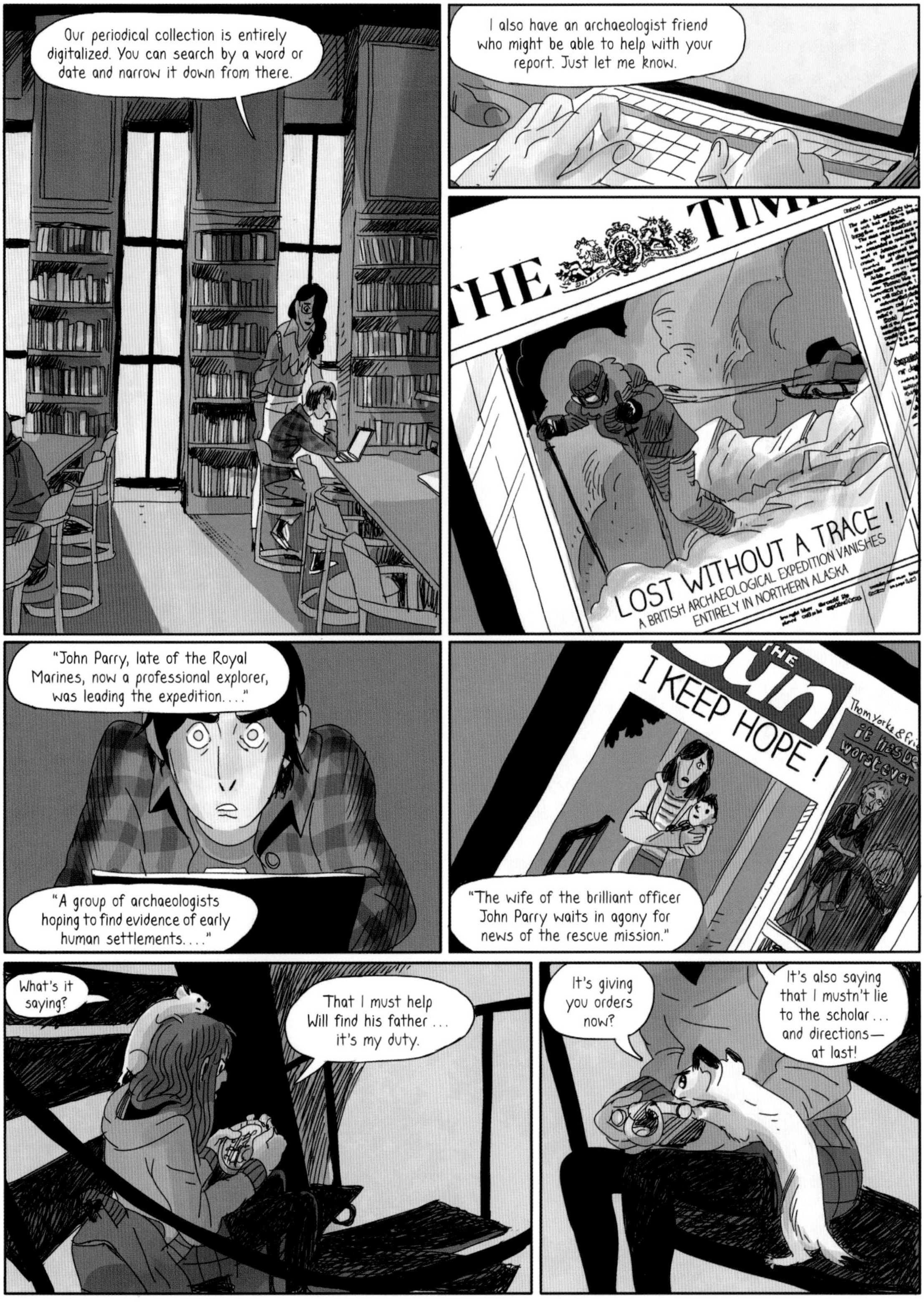
Our periodical collection is entirely digitalized. You can search by a word or date and narrow it down from there.
I also have an archaeologist friend who might be able to help with your report. Just let me know.
THE TIMES
LOST WITHOUT A TRACE !
A BRITISH ARCHAEOLOGICAL EXPEDITION VANISHES ENTIRELY IN NORTHERN ALASKA
"John Parry, late of the Royal Marines, now a professional explorer, was leading the expedition. . . ."
"A group of archaeologists hoping to find evidence of early human settlements. . . ."
THE Sun
I KEEP HOPE !
"The wife of the brilliant officer John Parry waits in agony for news of the rescue mission."
What's it saying?
That I must help Will find his father . . . it's my duty.
It's giving you orders now?
It's also saying that I mustn't lie to the scholar . . . and directions— at last!

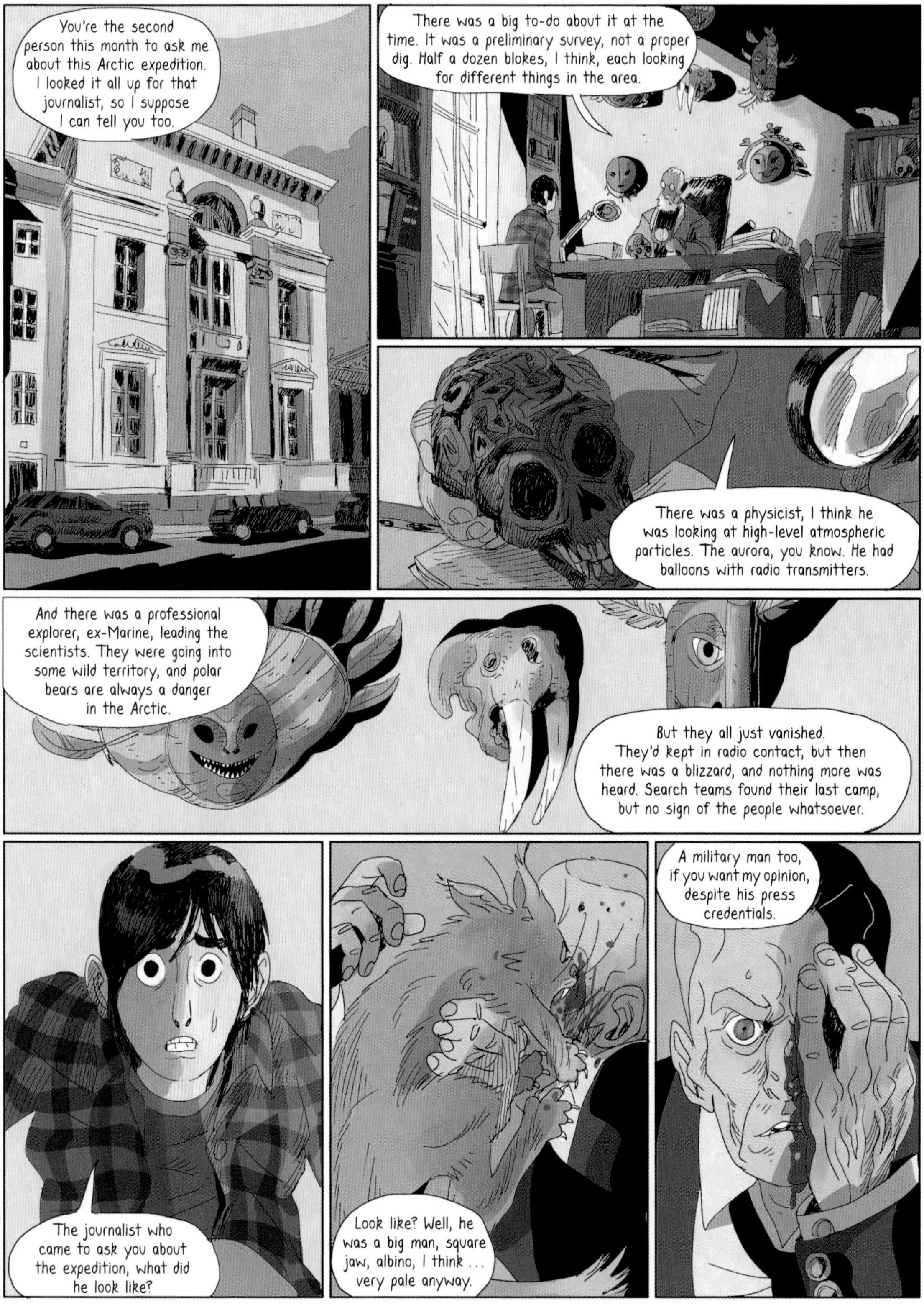
You're the second person this month to ask me about this Arctic expedition. I looked it all up for that journalist, so I suppose I can tell you too.
There was a big to-do about it at the time. It was a preliminary survey, not a proper dig. Half a dozen blokes, I think, each looking for different things in the area.
There was a physicist, I think he was looking at high-level atmospheric particles. The aurora, you know. He had balloons with radio transmitters.
And there was a professional explorer, ex-Marine, leading the scientists. They were going into some wild territory, and polar bears are always a danger in the Arctic.
But they all just vanished. They'd kept in radio contact, but then there was a blizzard, and nothing more was heard. Search teams found their last camp, but no sign of the people whatsoever.
The journalist who came to ask you about the expedition, what did he look like?
Look like? Well, he was a big man, square jaw, albino, I think . . . very pale anyway.
A military man too, if you want my opinion, despite his press credentials.

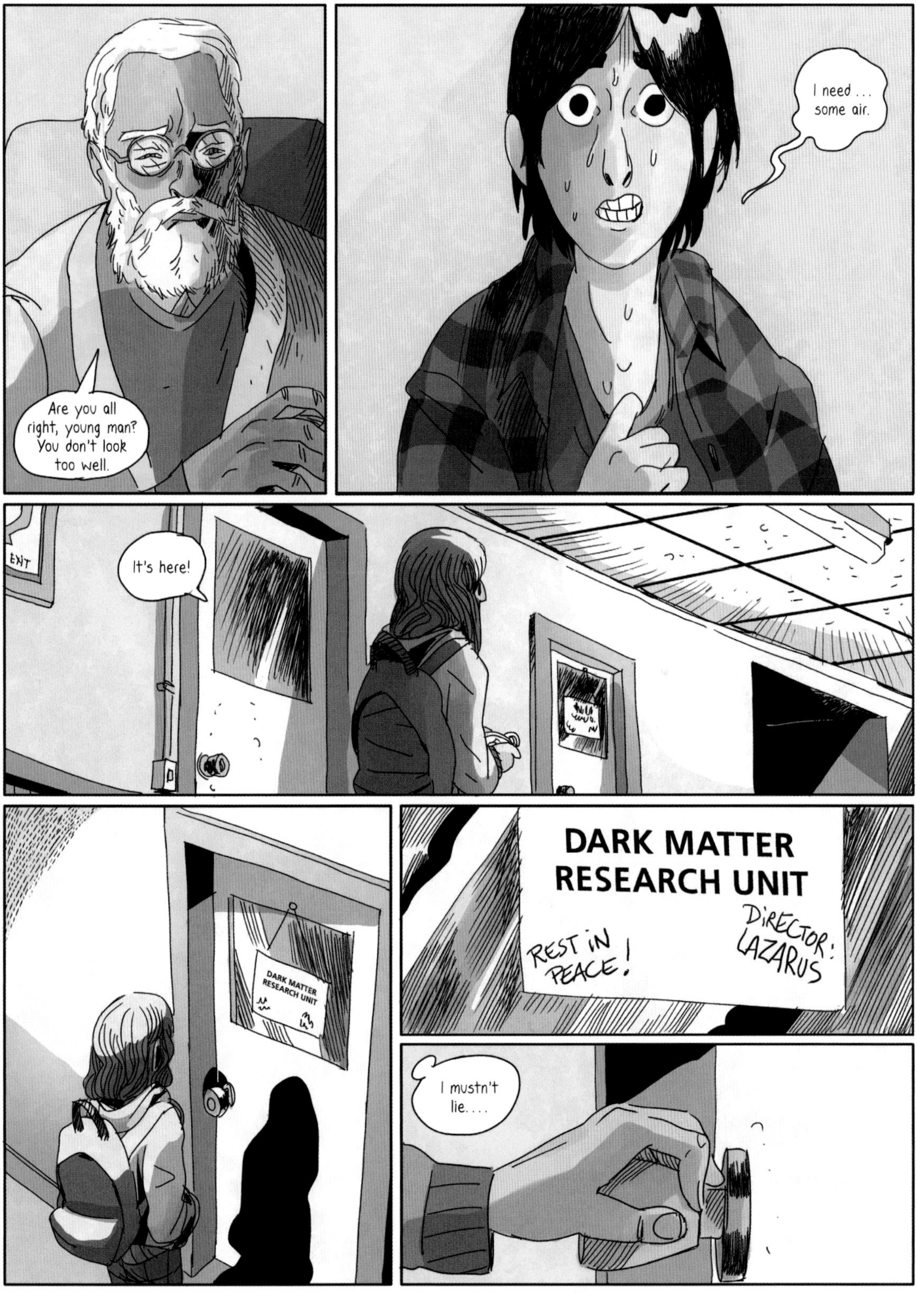
Are you all right, young man? You don't look too well.
I need . . . some air.
EXIT
It's here!
DARK MATTER RESEARCH UNIT
DARK MATTER
RESEARCH UNIT
REST IN PEACE!
DIRECTOR: LAZARUS
I mustn't lie. . . .

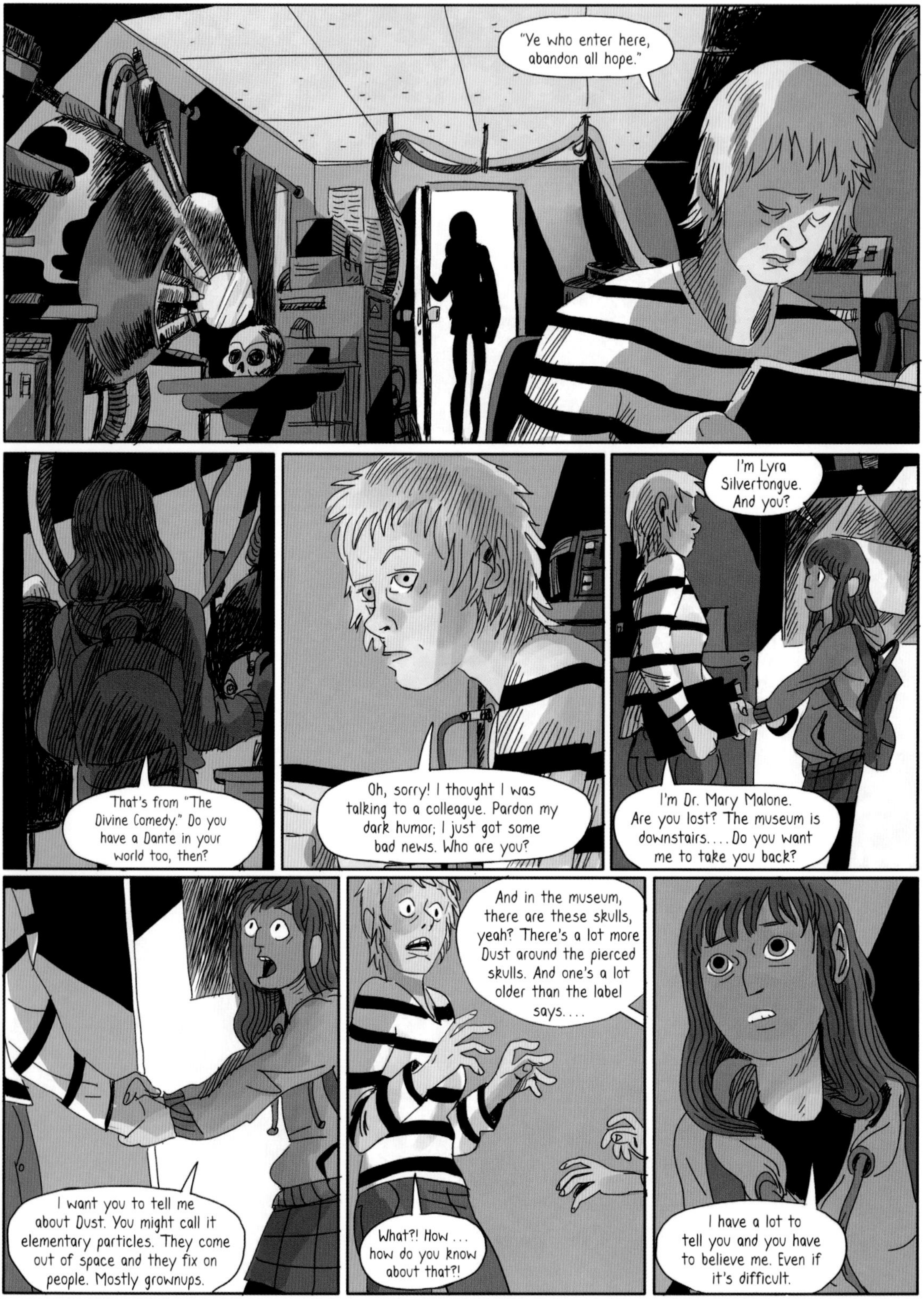
"Ye who enter here, abandon all hope."
That's from "The Divine Comedy." Do you have a Dante in your world too, then?
Oh, sorry! I thought I was talking to a colleague. Pardon my dark humor; I just got some bad news. Who are you?
I'm Lyra Silvertongue. And you?
I'm Dr. Mary Malone. Are you lost? The museum is downstairs. . . . Do you want me to take you back?
I want you to tell me about Dust. You might call it elementary particles. They come out of space and they fix on people. Mostly grownups.
And in the museum, there are these skulls, yeah? There's a lot more Dust around the pierced skulls. And one's a lot older than the label says. . . .
What?! How . . . how do you know about that?!
I have a lot to tell you and you have to believe me. Even if it's difficult.

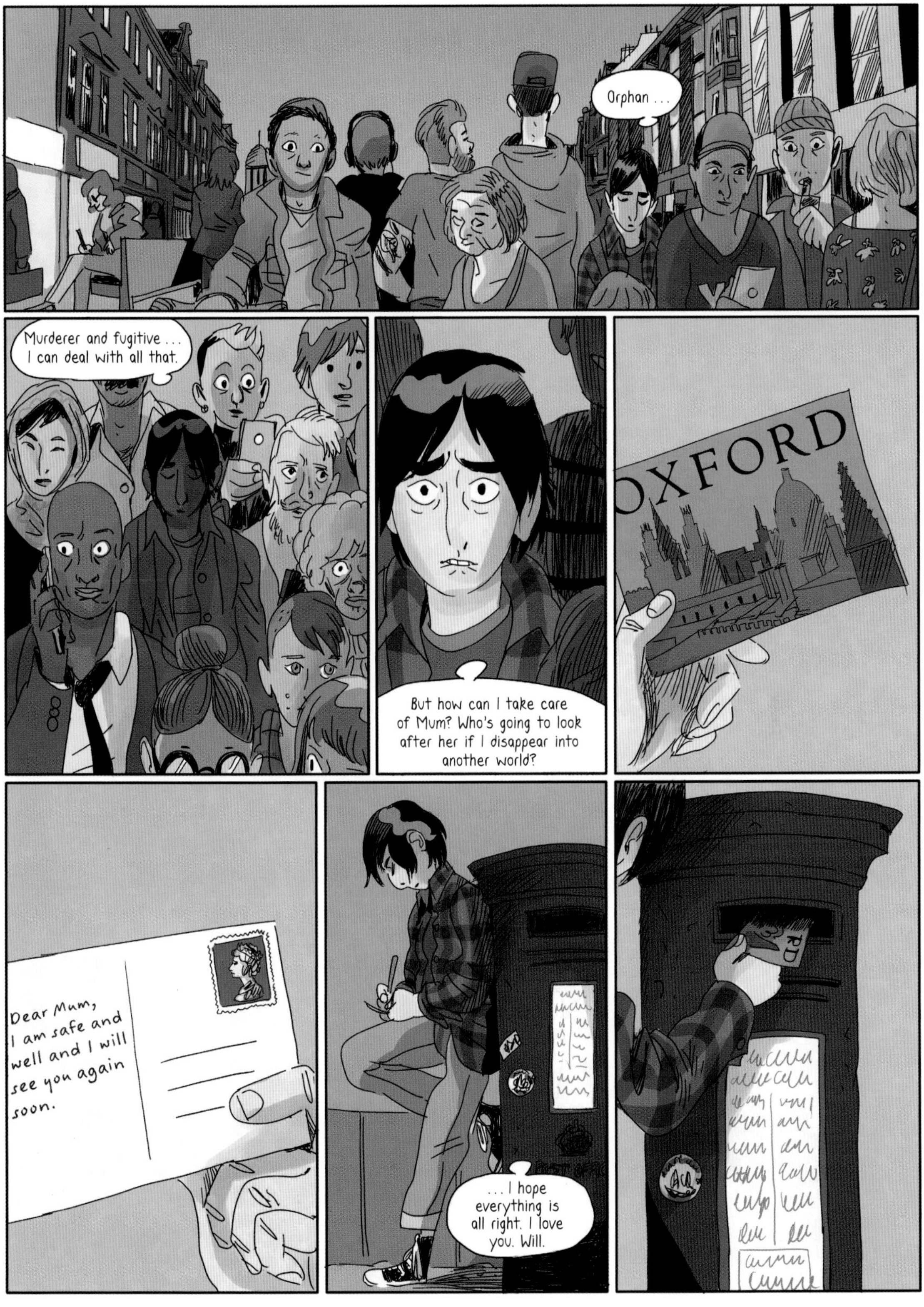
Orphan . . .
Murderer and fugitive . . . I can deal with all that.
But how can I take care of Mum? Who's going to look after her if I disappear into another world?
OXFORD
Dear Mum, I am safe and well and I will see you again soon.
. . . I hope everything is all right. I love you. Will.

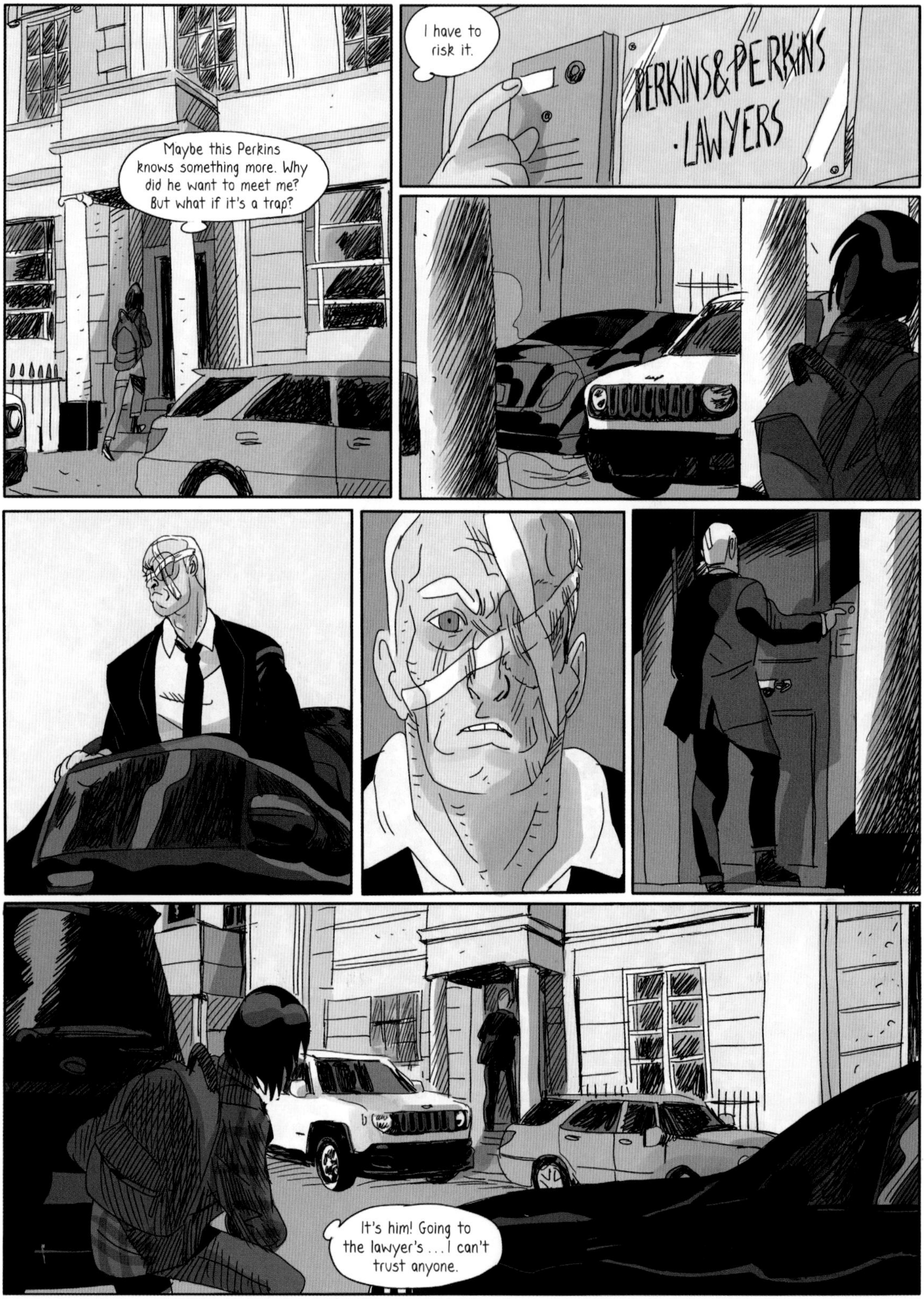
Maybe this Perkins knows something more. Why did he want to meet me? But what if it's a trap?
I have to risk it.
PERKINS&PERKINS
· LAWYERS
It's him! Going to the lawyer's . . . I can't trust anyone.

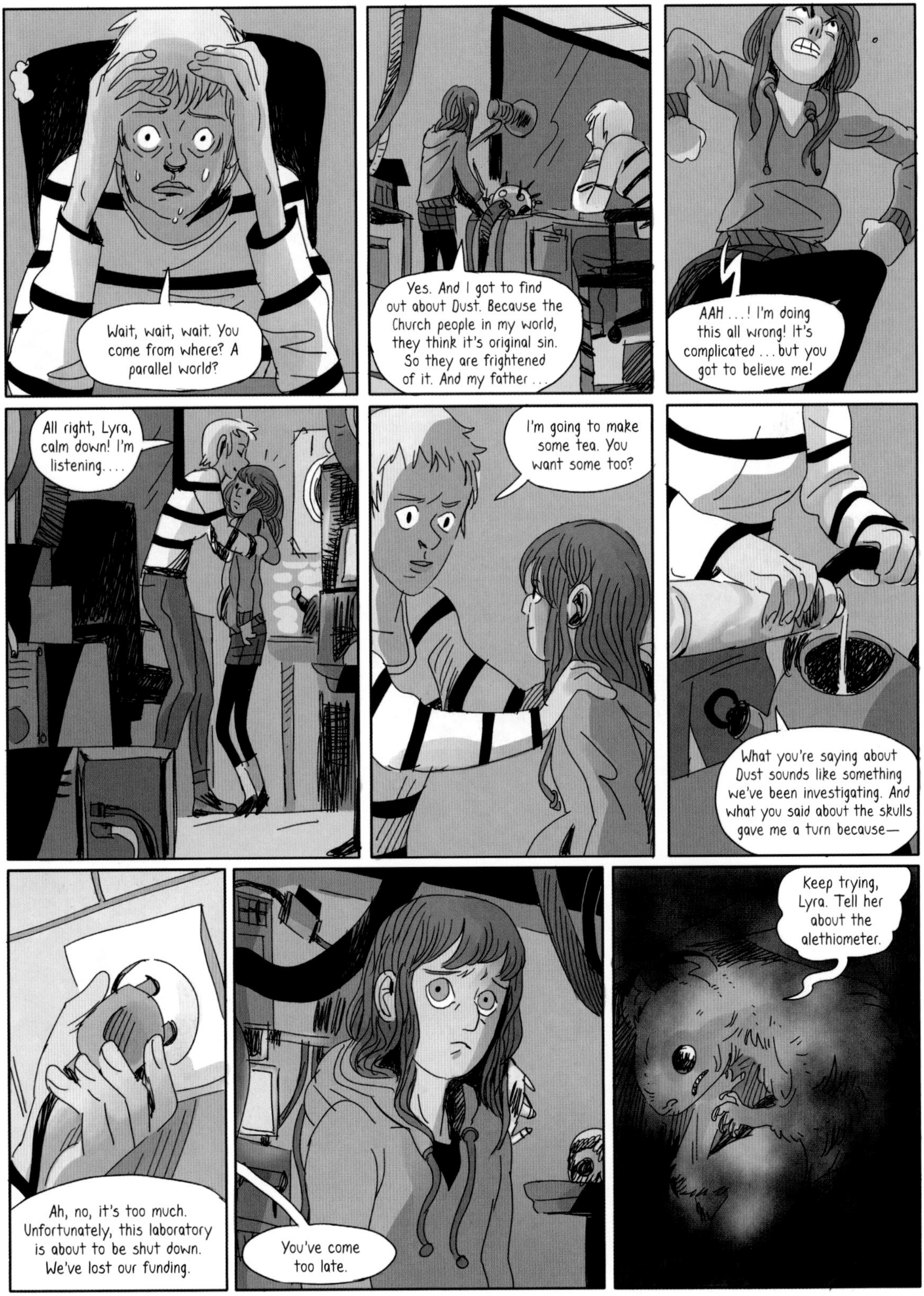
Wait, wait, wait. You come from where? A parallel world?
Yes. And I got to find out about Dust. Because the Church people in my world, they think it's original sin. So they are frightened of it. And my father . . .
AAH . . . ! I'm doing this all wrong! It's complicated . . . but you got to believe me!
All right, Lyra, calm down! I'm listening. . . .
I'm going to make some tea. You want some too?
What you're saying about Dust sounds like something we've been investigating. And what you said about the skulls gave me a turn because—
Ah, no, it's too much. Unfortunately, this laboratory is about to be shut down. We've lost our funding.
You've come too late.
Keep trying, Lyra. Tell her about the alethiometer.

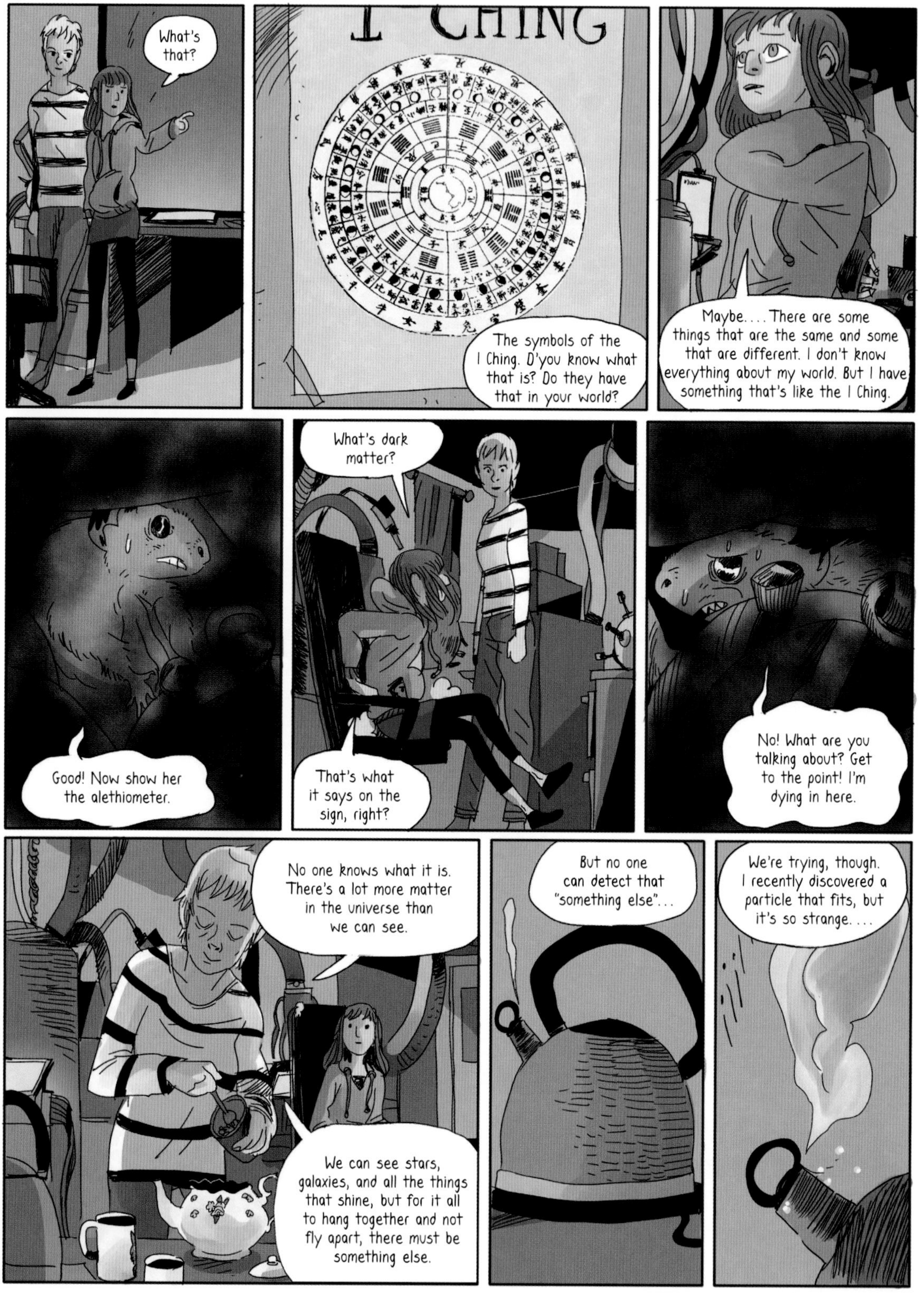
What's that?
I CHING
The symbols of the I Ching. D'you know what that is? Do they have that in your world?
Maybe. . . . There are some things that are the same and some that are different. I don't know everything about my world. But I have something that's like the I Ching.
Good! Now show her the alethiometer.
What's dark matter?
That's what it says on the sign, right?
No! What are you talking about? Get to the point! I'm dying in here.
No one knows what it is. There's a lot more matter in the universe than we can see.
We can see stars, galaxies, and all the things that shine, but for it all to hang together and not fly apart, there must be something else.
But no one can detect that "something else". . .
We're trying, though. I recently discovered a particle that fits, but it's so strange. . . .

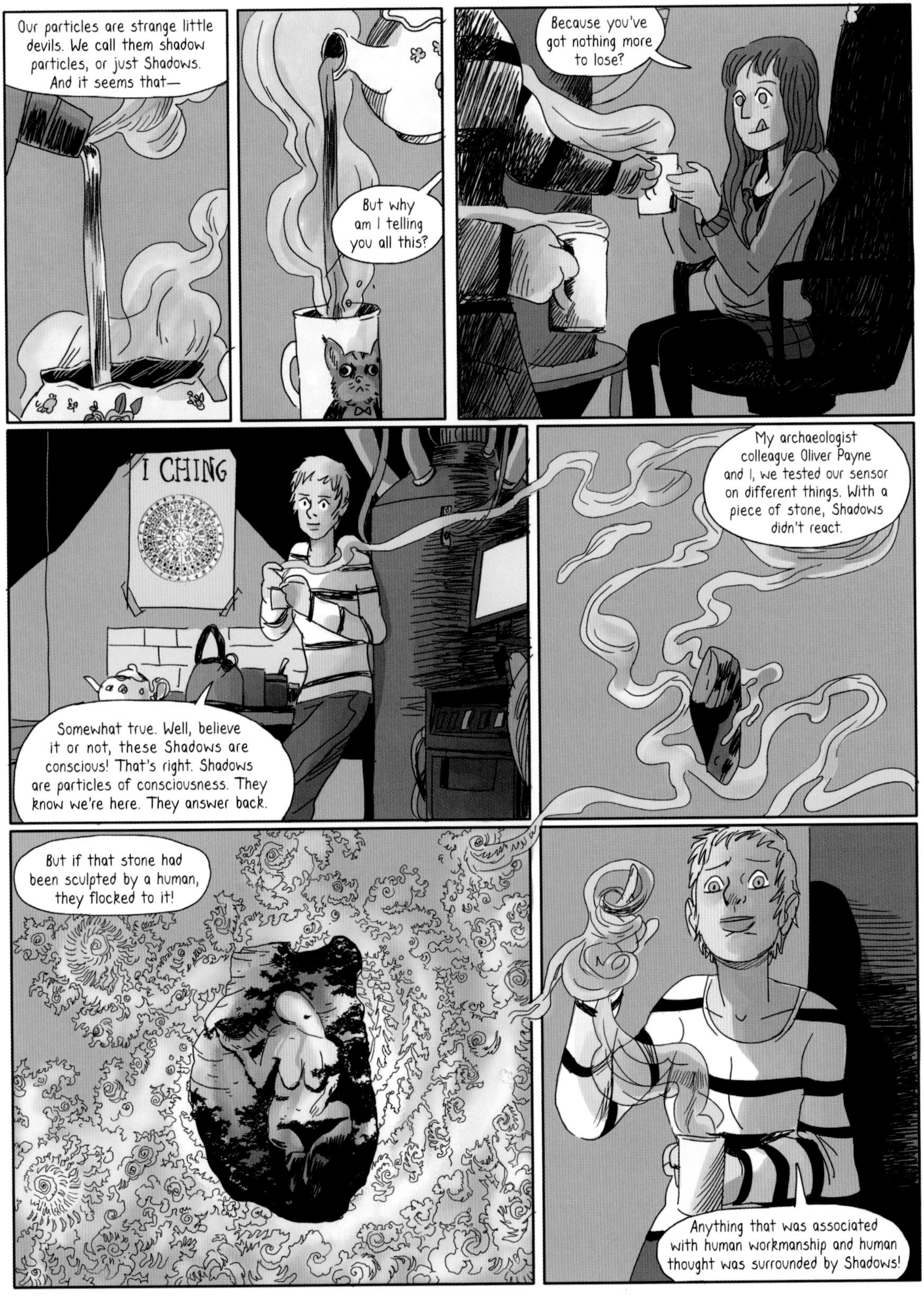
Our particles are strange little devils. We call them shadow particles, or just Shadows. And it seems that—
But why am I telling you all this?
Because you've got nothing more to lose?
I CHING
Somewhat true. Well, believe it or not, these Shadows are conscious! That's right. Shadows are particles of consciousness. They know we're here. They answer back.
My archaeologist colleague Oliver Payne and I, we tested our sensor on different things. With a piece of stone, Shadows didn't react.
But if that stone had been sculpted by a human, they flocked to it!
Anything that was associated with human workmanship and human thought was surrounded by Shadows!

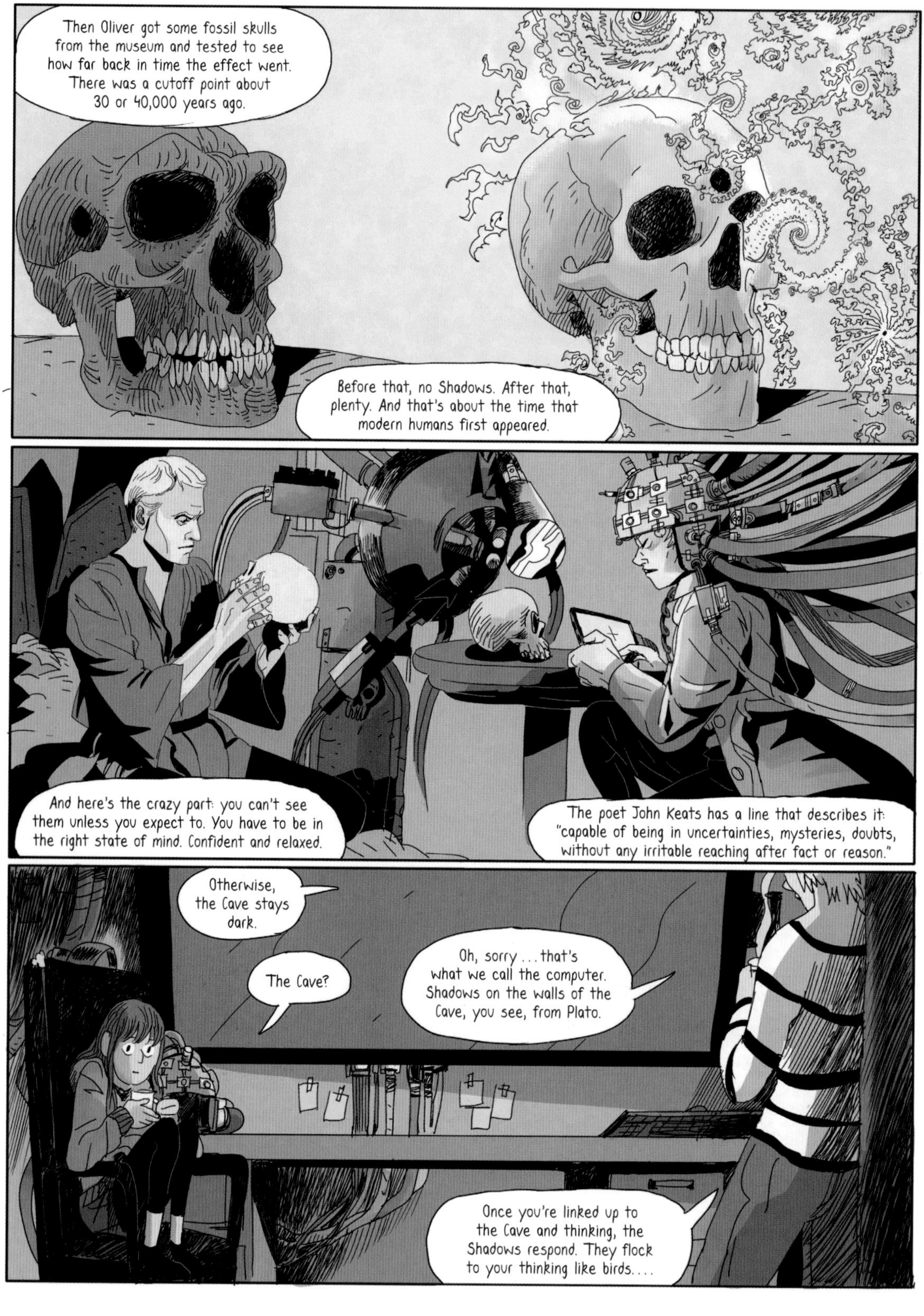

Then Oliver got some fossil skulls from the museum and tested to see how far back in time the effect went. There was a cutoff point about 30 or 40,000 years ago.
Before that, no Shadows. After that, plenty. And that's about the time that modern humans first appeared.
And here's the crazy part: you can't see them unless you expect to. You have to be in the right state of mind. Confident and relaxed.
The poet John Keats has a line that describes it: "capable of being in uncertainties, mysteries, doubts, without any irritable reaching after fact or reason."
Otherwise, the Cave stays dark.
The Cave?
Oh, sorry . . . that's what we call the computer. Shadows on the walls of the Cave, you see, from Plato.
Once you're linked up to the Cave and thinking, the Shadows respond. They flock to your thinking like birds. . . .

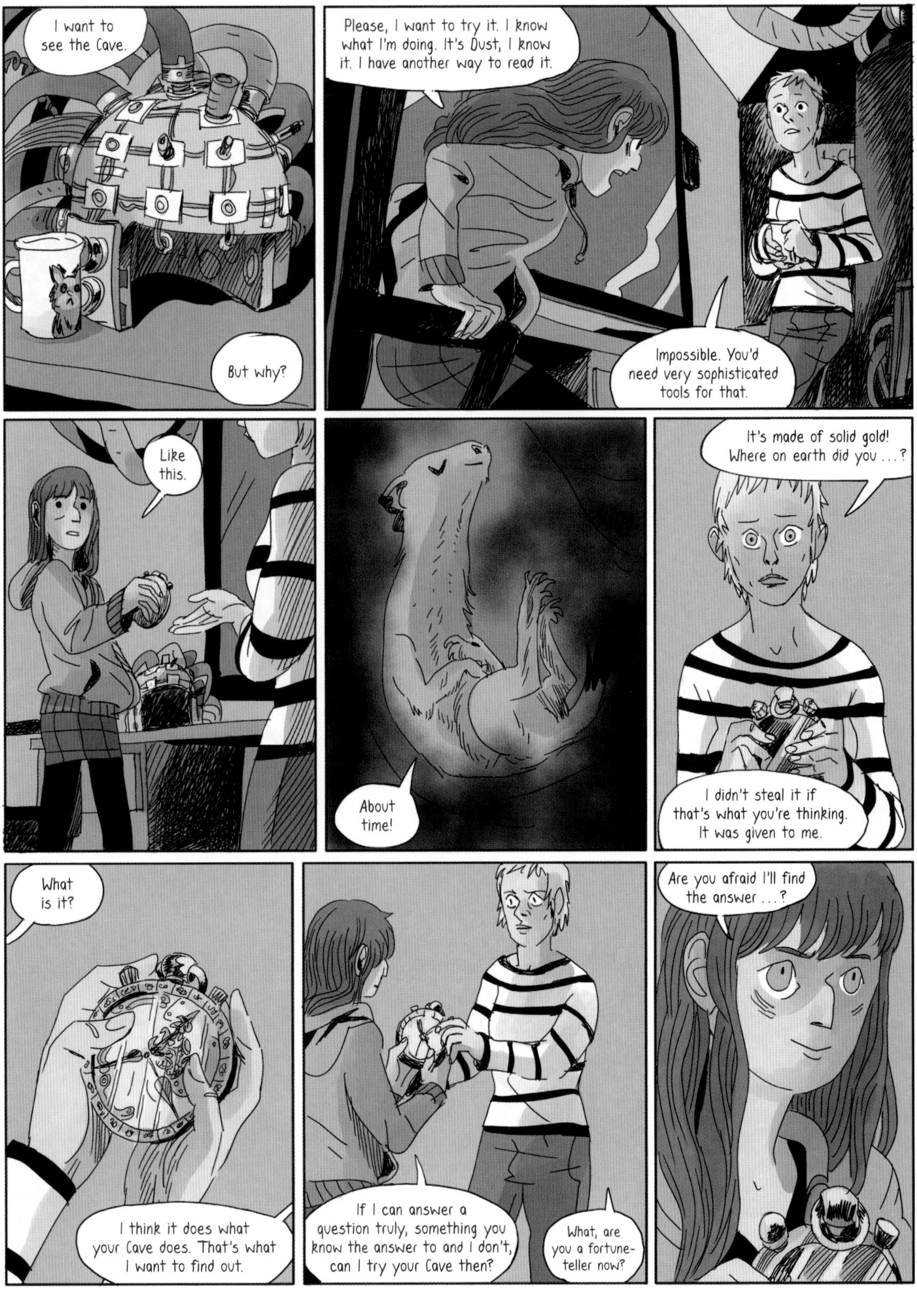
I want to see the Cave.
But why?
Please, I want to try it. I know what I'm doing. It's Dust, I know it. I have another way to read it.
Impossible. You'd need very sophisticated tools for that.
Like this.
About time!
It's made of solid gold! Where on earth did you . . . ?
I didn't steal it if that's what you're thinking. It was given to me.
What is it?
I think it does what your Cave does. That's what I want to find out.
If I can answer a question truly, something you know the answer to and I don't, can I try your Cave then?
What, are you a fortune-teller now?
Are you afraid I'll find the answer . . . ?

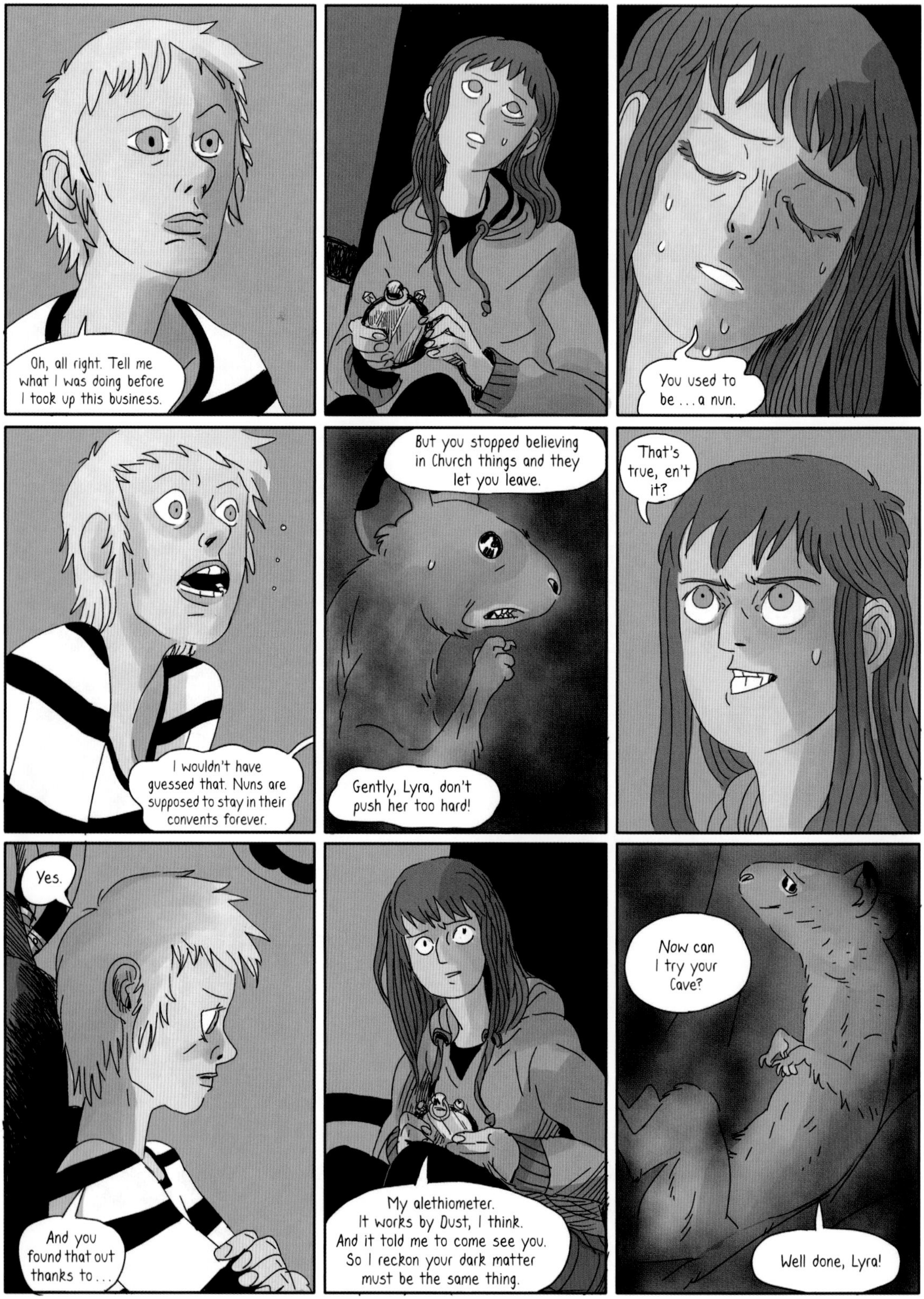
Oh, all right. Tell me what I was doing before I took up this business.
You used to be . . . a nun.
I wouldn't have guessed that. Nuns are supposed to stay in their convents forever.
But you stopped believing in Church things and they let you leave.
Gently, Lyra, don't push her too hard!
That's true, en't it?
Yes.
And you found that out thanks to . . .
My alethiometer. It works by Dust, I think. And it told me to come see you. So I reckon your dark matter must be the same thing.
Now can I try your Cave?
Well done, Lyra!

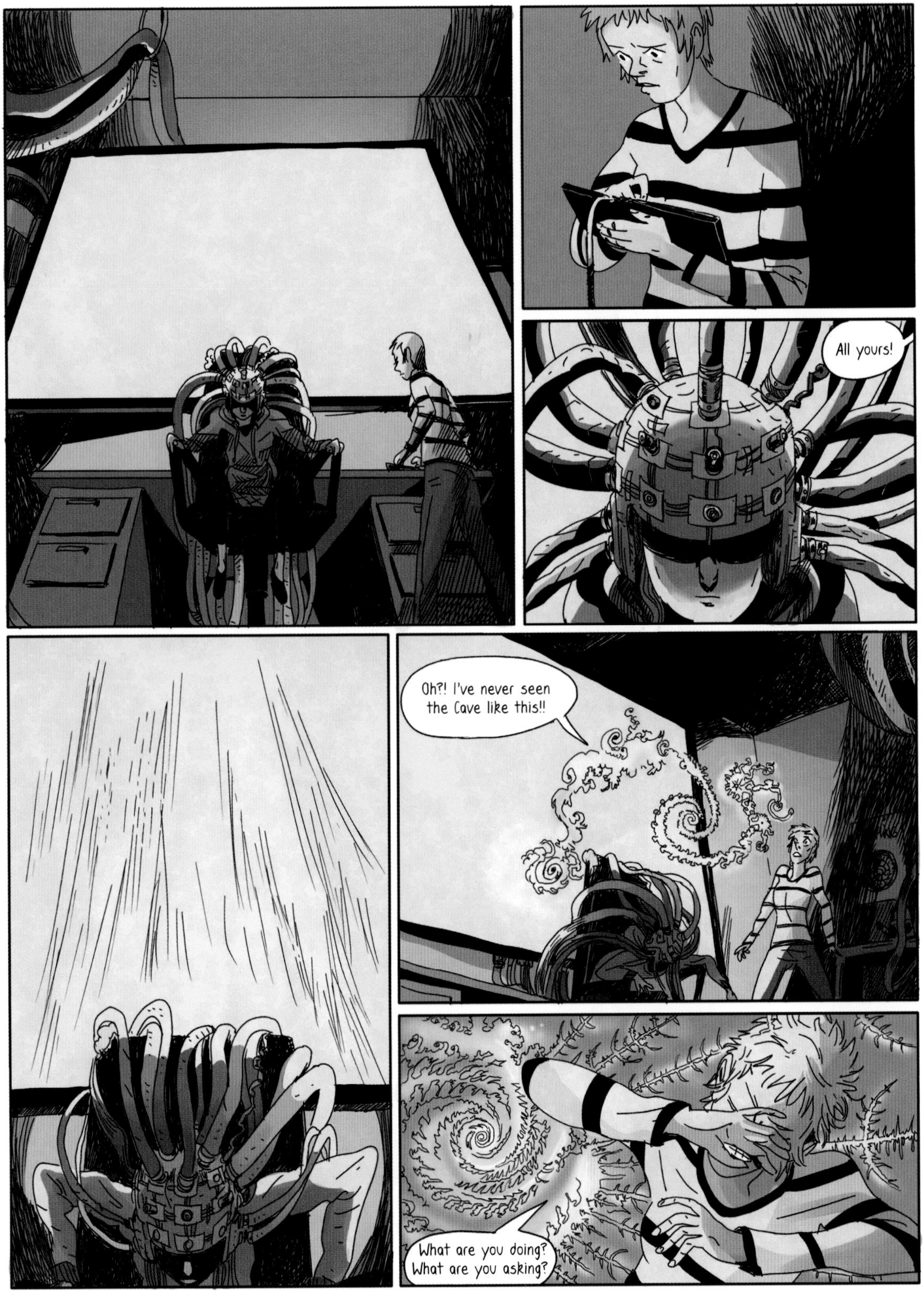
All yours!
Oh?! I've never seen the Cave like this!!
What are you doing? What are you asking?

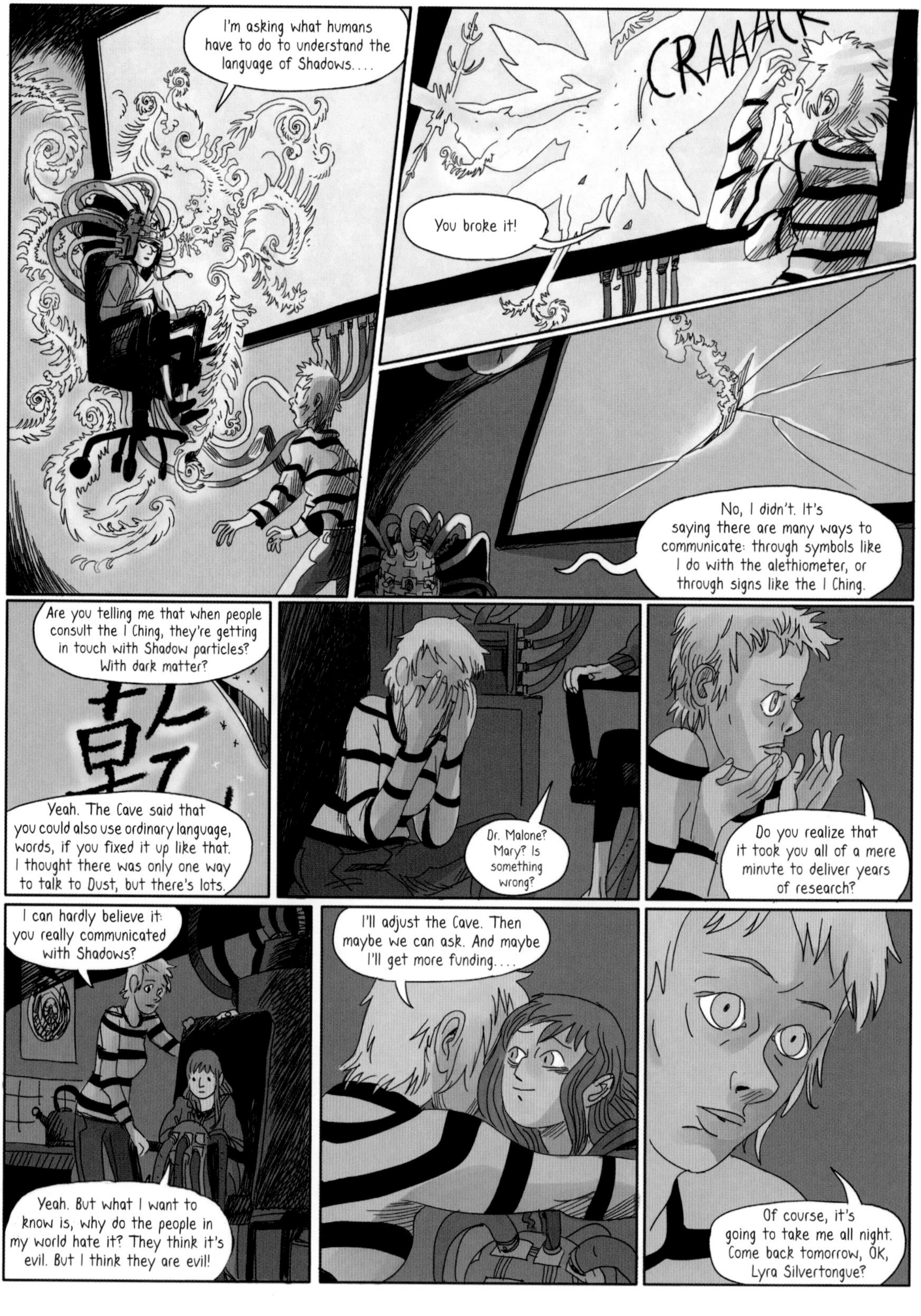
I'm asking what humans have to do to understand the language of Shadows. . . .
CRAAACK
You broke it!
No, I didn't. It's saying there are many ways to communicate: through symbols like I do with the alethiometer, or through signs like the I Ching.
Are you telling me that when people consult the I Ching, they're getting in touch with Shadow particles? With dark matter?
Yeah. The Cave said that you could also use ordinary language, words, if you fixed it up like that. I thought there was only one way to talk to Dust, but there's lots.
Dr. Malone? Mary? Is something wrong?
Do you realize that it took you all of a mere minute to deliver years of research?
I can hardly believe it: you really communicated with Shadows?
Yeah. But what I want to know is, why do the people in my world hate it? They think it's evil. But I think they are evil!
I'll adjust the Cave. Then maybe we can ask. And maybe I'll get more funding. . . .
Of course, it's going to take me all night. Come back tomorrow, OK, Lyra Silvertongue?

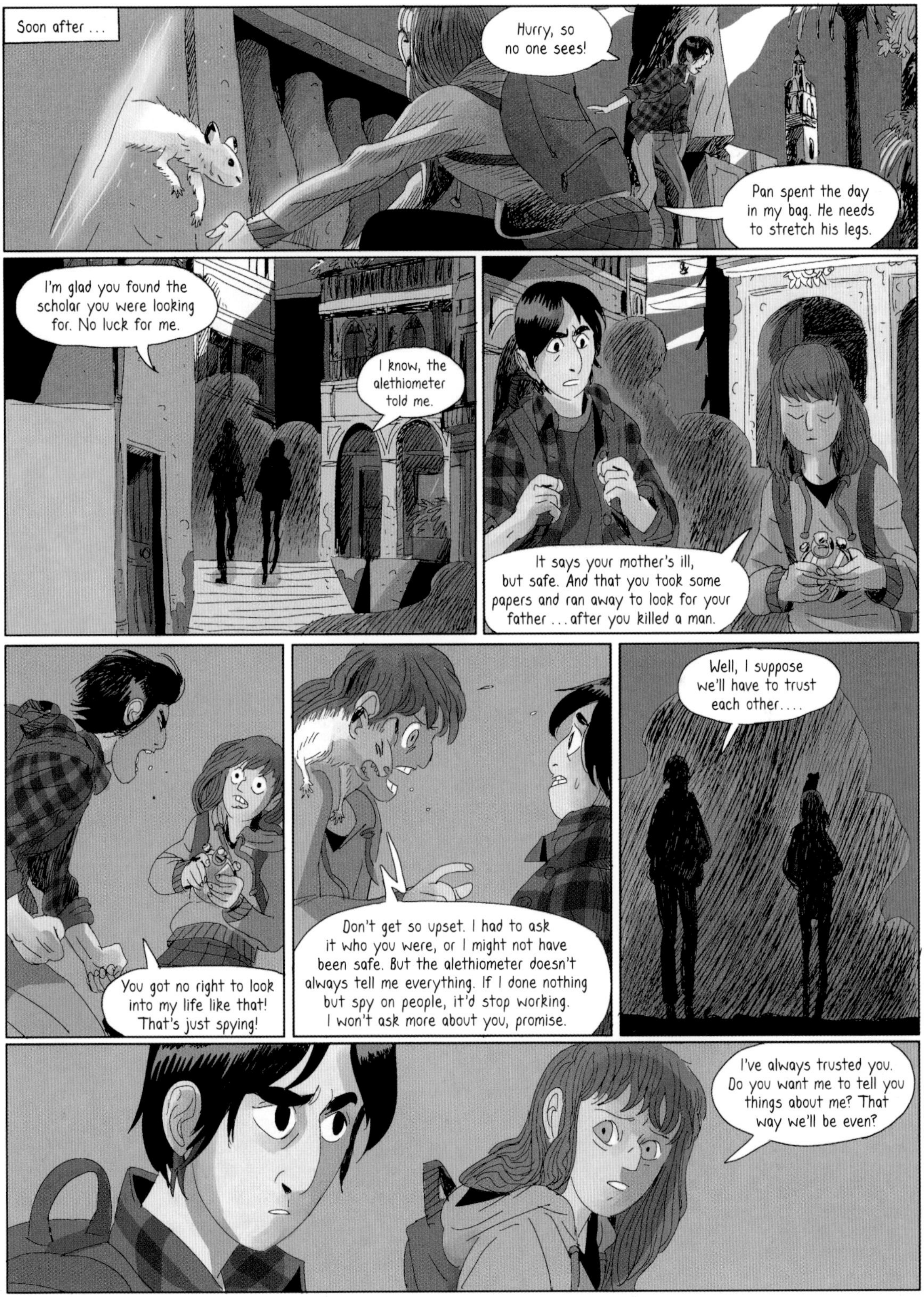
Soon after . . .
Hurry, so no one sees!
Pan spent the day in my bag. He needs to stretch his legs.
I'm glad you found the scholar you were looking for. No luck for me.
I know, the alethiometer told me.
It says your mother's ill, but safe. And that you took some papers and ran away to look for your father . . . after you killed a man.
You got no right to look into my life like that! That's just spying!
Don't get so upset. I had to ask it who you were, or I might not have been safe. But the alethiometer doesn't always tell me everything. If I done nothing but spy on people, it'd stop working. I won't ask more about you, promise.
Well, I suppose we'll have to trust each other. . . .
I've always trusted you. Do you want me to tell you things about me? That way we'll be even?

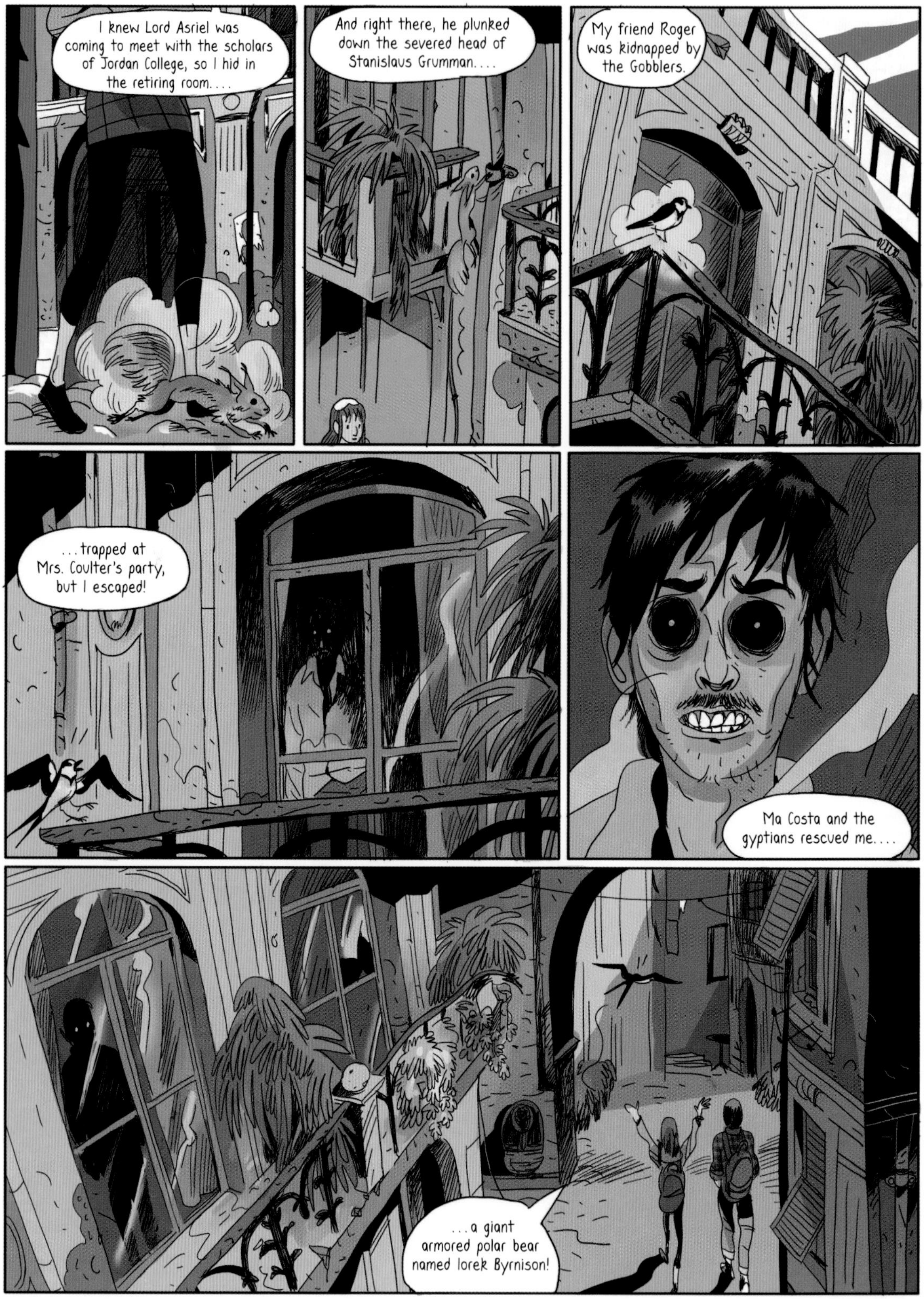
I knew Lord Asriel was coming to meet with the scholars of Jordan College, so I hid in the retiring room....
And right there, he plunked down the severed head of Stanislaus Grumman....
My friend Roger was kidnapped by the Gobblers.
...trapped at Mrs. Coulter's party, but I escaped!
Ma Costa and the gyptians rescued me....
...a giant armored polar bear named Iorek Byrnison!

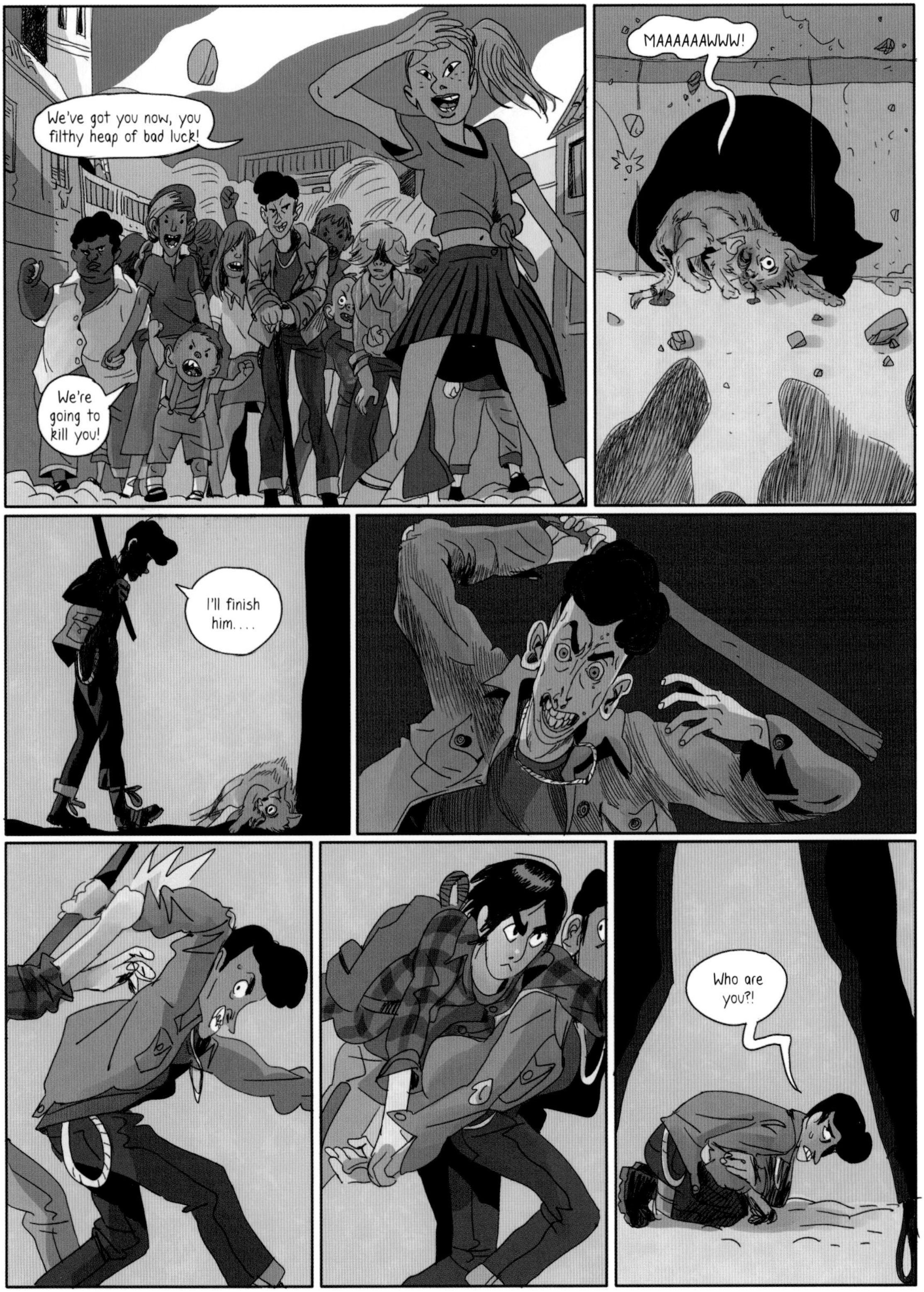
We've got you now, you filthy heap of bad luck!
We're going to kill you!
MAAAAAAWWW!
I'll finish him. . . .
Who are you?!

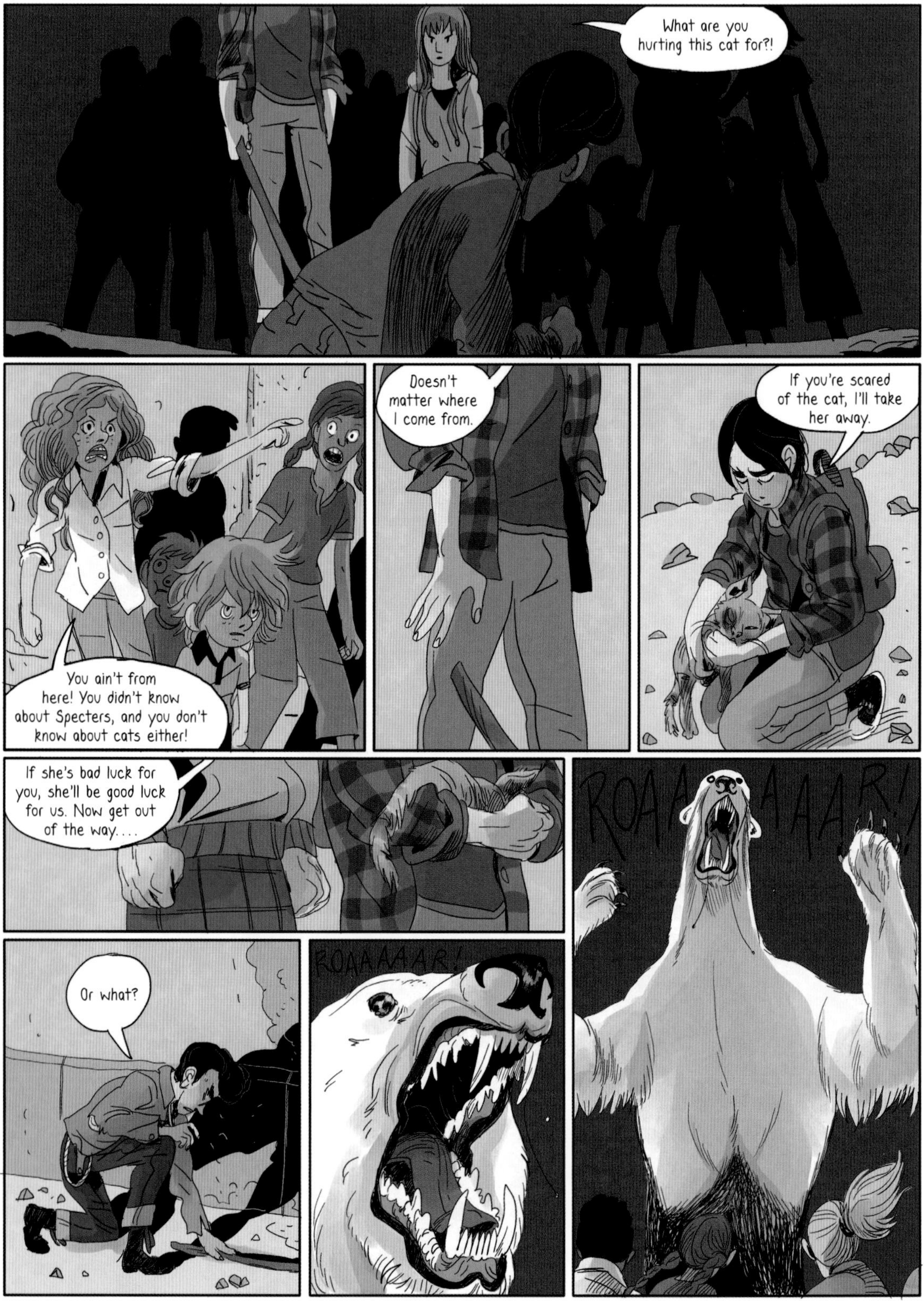
What are you hurting this cat for?!
You ain't from here! You didn't know about Specters, and you don't know about cats either!
Doesn't matter where I come from.
If you're scared of the cat, I'll take her away.
If she's bad luck for you, she'll be good luck for us. Now get out of the way....
ROAAAAAAR!!
Or what?
ROAAAAAAR!

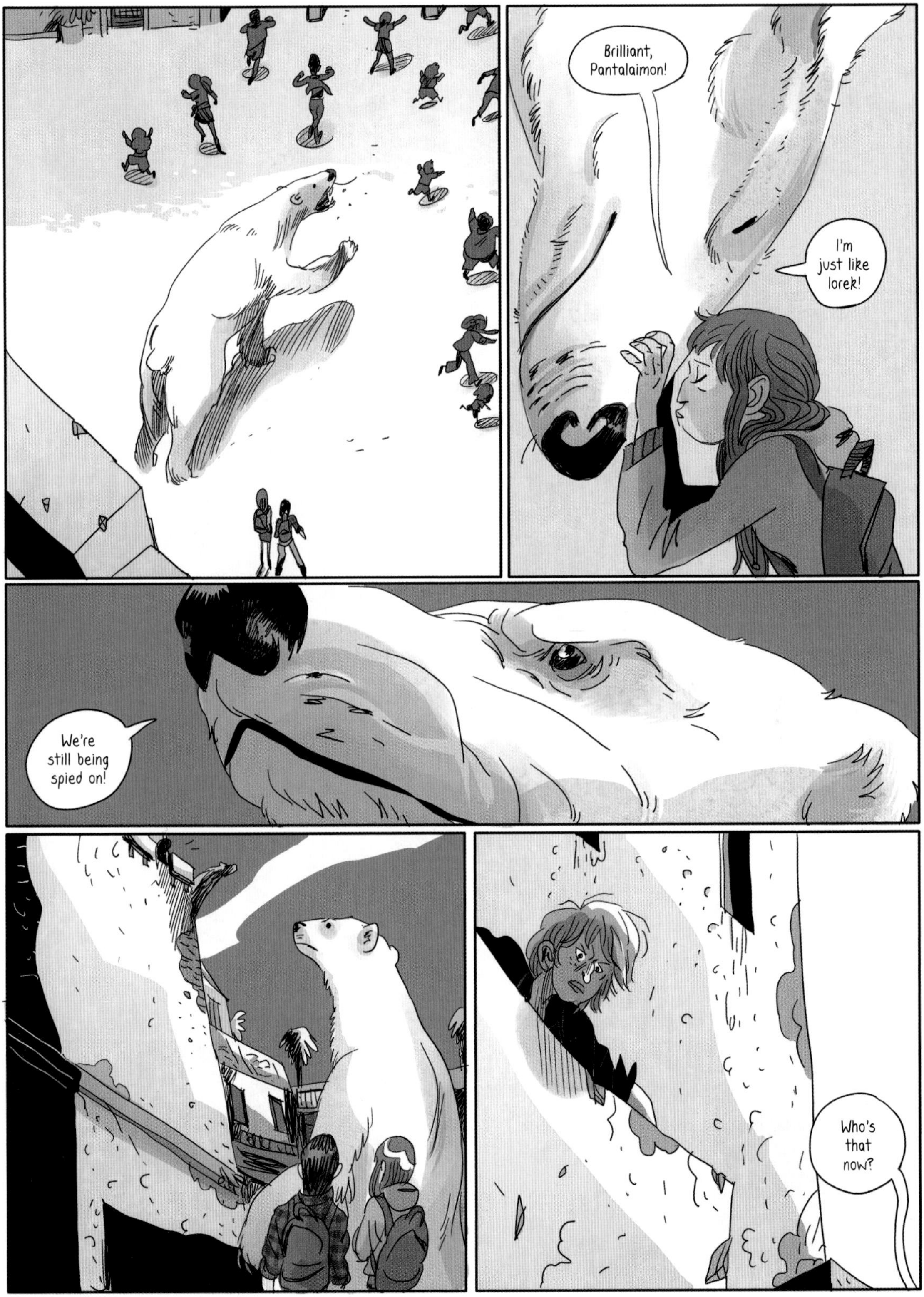
Brilliant, Pantalaimon!
I'm just like Iorek!
We're still being spied on!
Who's that now?

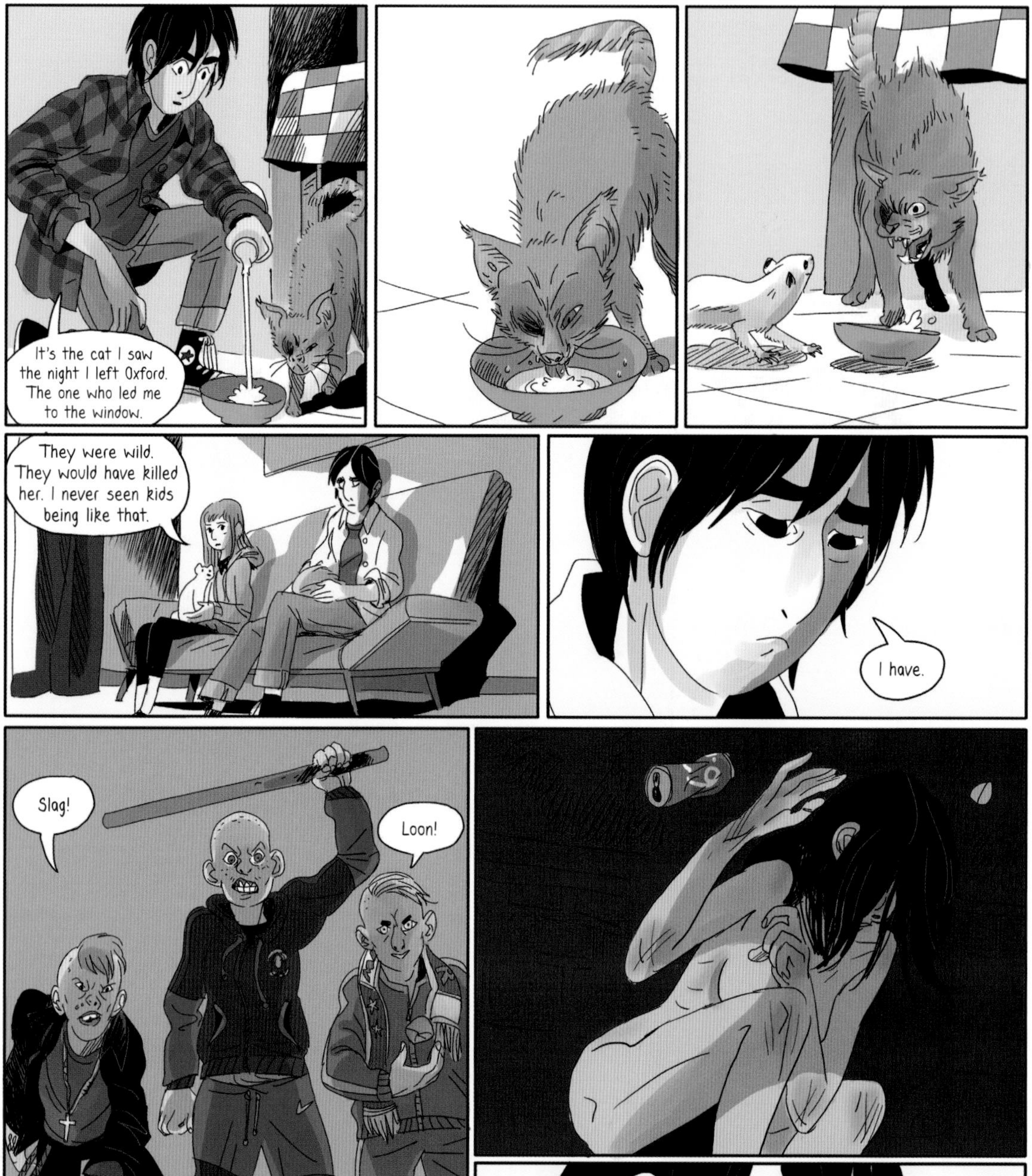
It's the cat I saw the night I left Oxford. The one who led me to the window.
They were wild. They would have killed her. I never seen kids being like that.
I have.
Slag!
Loon!
Loony slag!

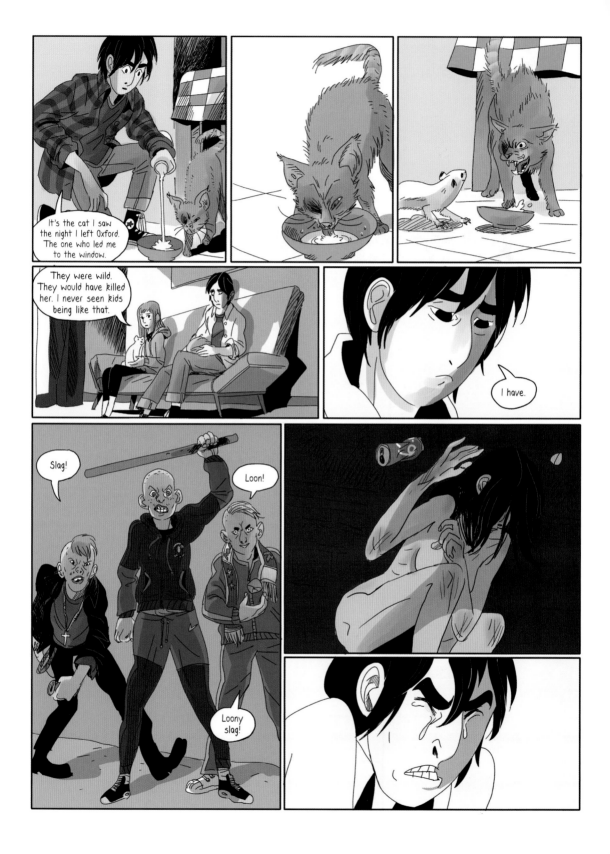

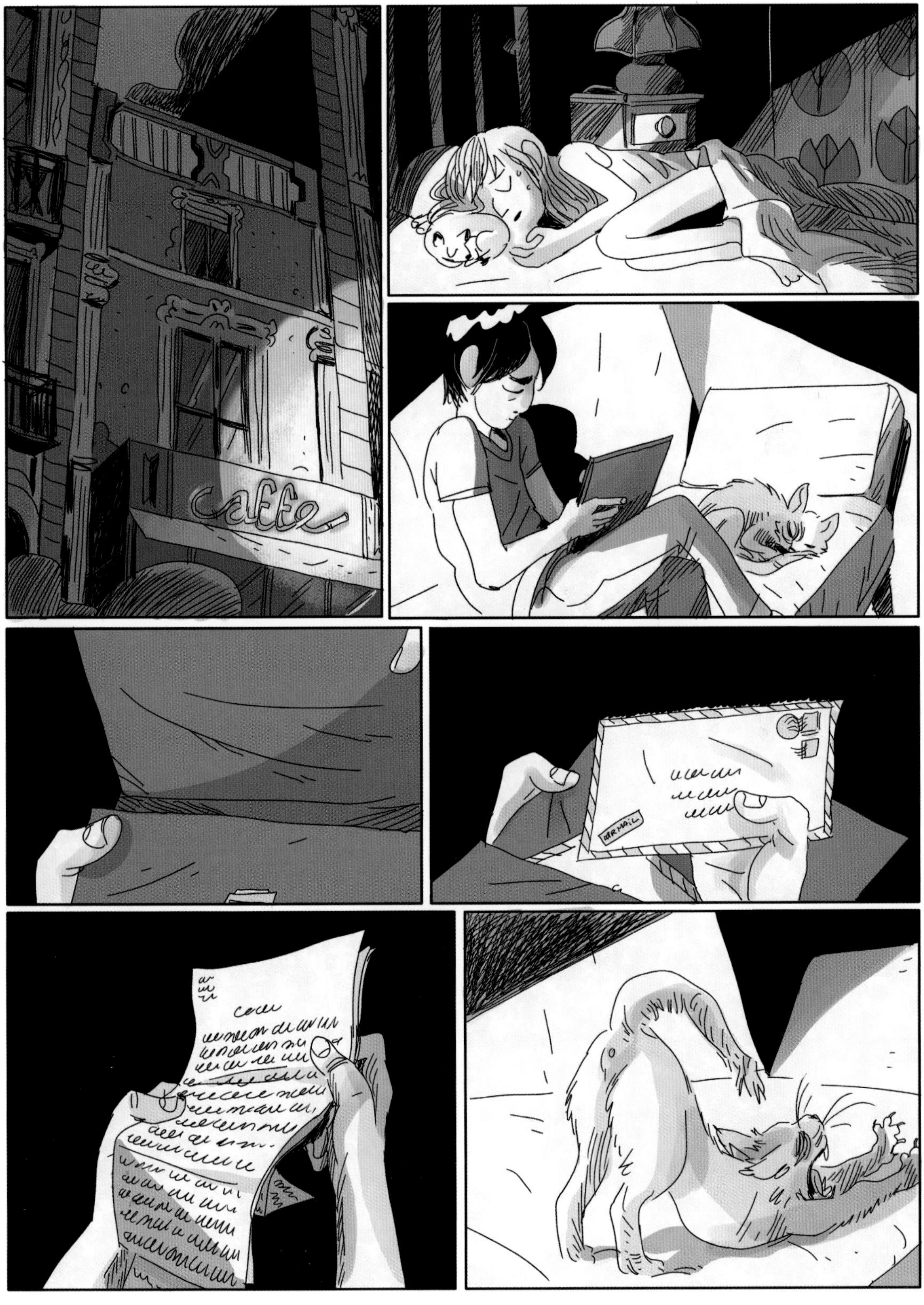
caffe

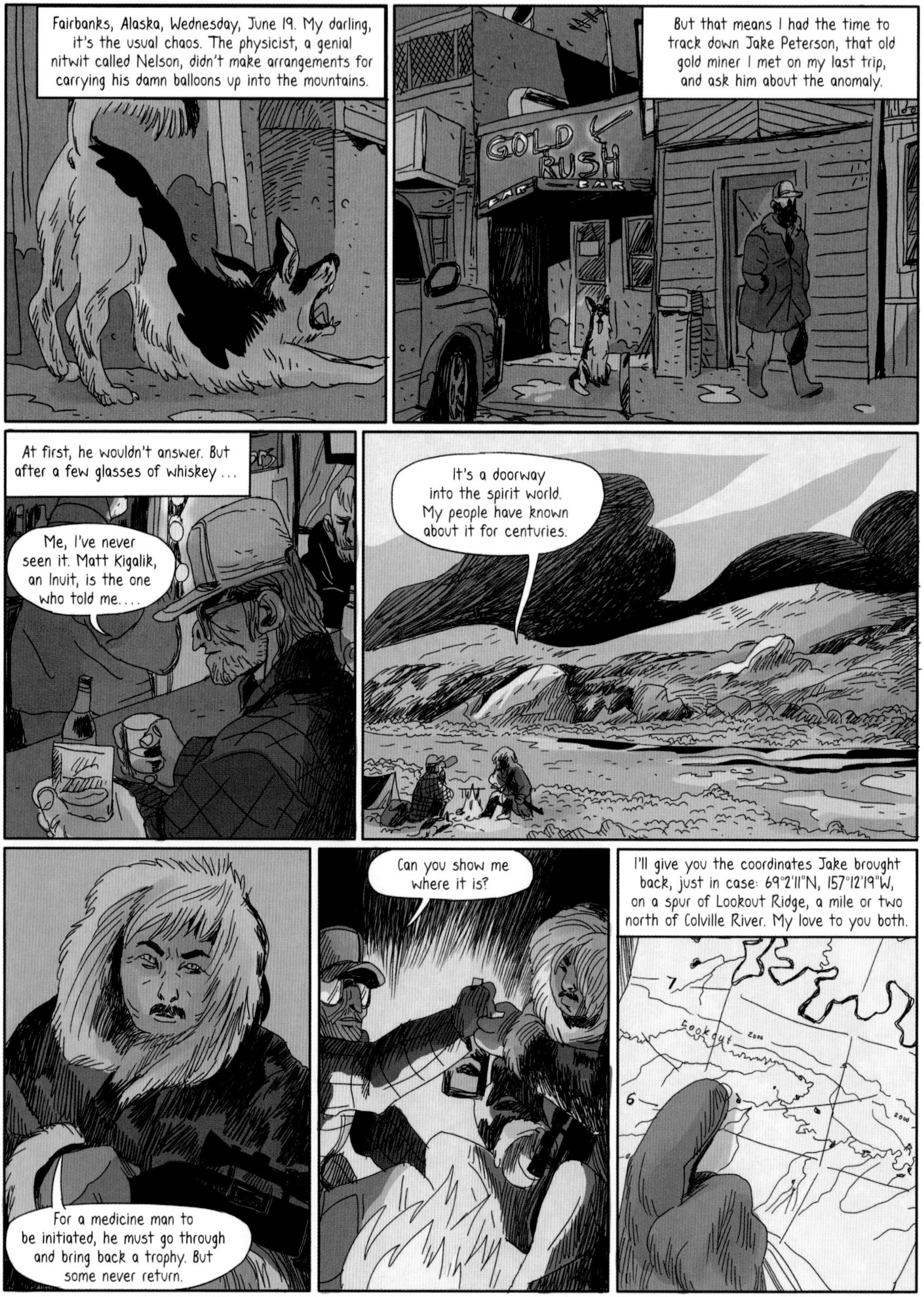
Fairbanks, Alaska, Wednesday, June 19. My darling, it's the usual chaos. The physicist, a genial nitwit called Nelson, didn't make arrangements for carrying his damn balloons up into the mountains.
But that means I had the time to track down Jake Peterson, that old gold miner I met on my last trip, and ask him about the anomaly.
GOLD RUSH
BAR
BAR
At first, he wouldn't answer. But after a few glasses of whiskey . . .
Me, I've never seen it. Matt Kigalik, an Inuit, is the one who told me. . . .
It's a doorway into the spirit world. My people have known about it for centuries.
For a medicine man to be initiated, he must go through and bring back a trophy. But some never return.
Can you show me where it is?
I'll give you the coordinates Jake brought back, just in case: 69°2'11"N, 157°12'19"W, on a spur of Lookout Ridge, a mile or two north of Colville River. My love to you both.
7
Lookout
2000
6
2000

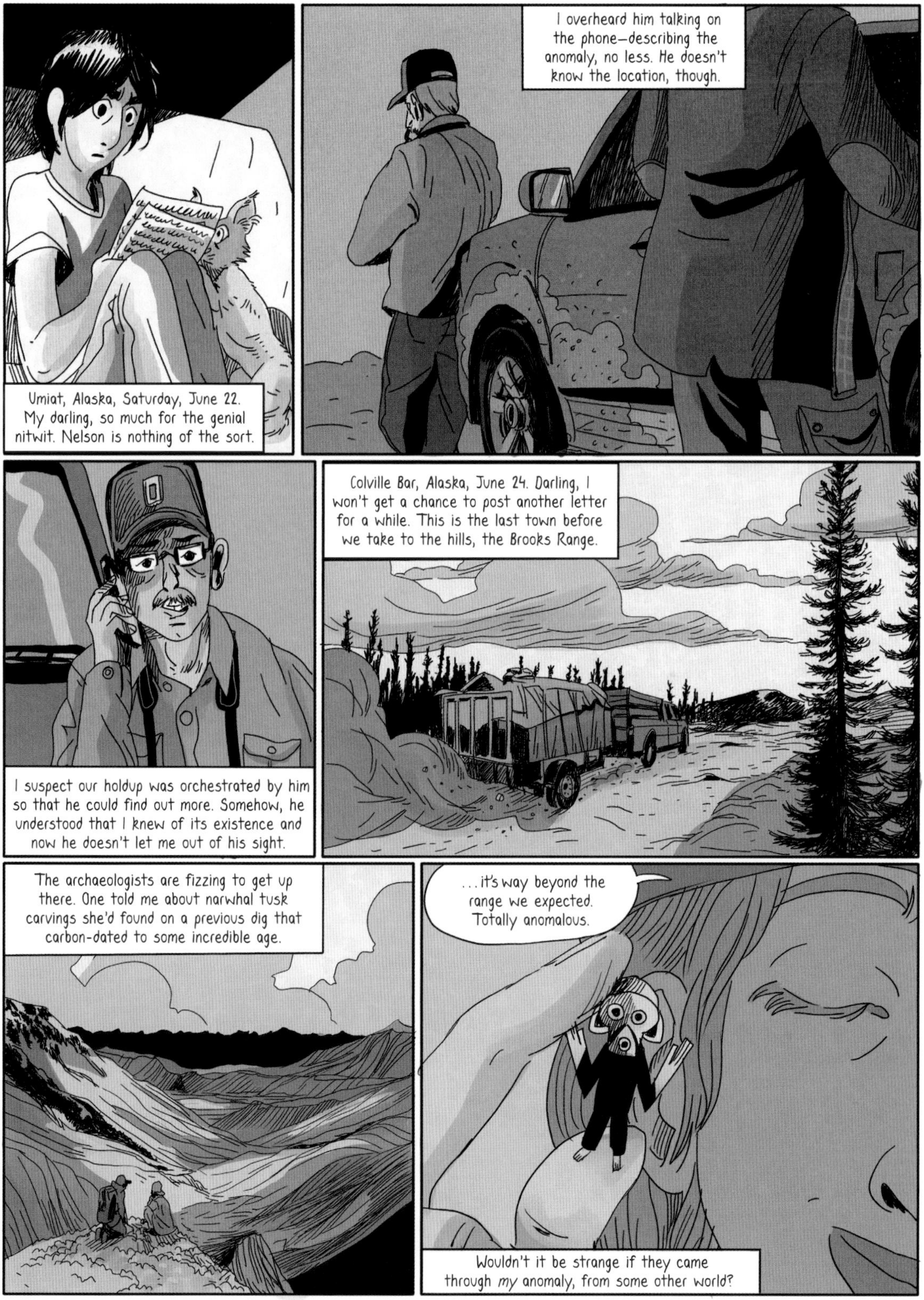
Umiat, Alaska, Saturday, June 22. My darling, so much for the genial nitwit. Nelson is nothing of the sort.
I overheard him talking on the phone—describing the anomaly, no less. He doesn't know the location, though.
I suspect our holdup was orchestrated by him so that he could find out more. Somehow, he understood that I knew of its existence and now he doesn't let me out of his sight.
Colville Bar, Alaska, June 24. Darling, I won't get a chance to post another letter for a while. This is the last town before we take to the hills, the Brooks Range.
The archaeologists are fizzing to get up there. One told me about narwhal tusk carvings she'd found on a previous dig that carbon-dated to some incredible age.
. . . it's way beyond the range we expected. Totally anomalous.
Wouldn't it be strange if they came through *my* anomaly, from some other world?

Perhaps they originate in the spirit world the Inuits believe in.

I must be careful. Nelson's funding is from the Ministry of Defense— I know their codes. I'll stick to my plan: take the archaeologists to their spot and go off by myself for a few days to look for the anomaly.

A bit of real luck. I met Matt Kigalik. He told me the Russians are looking for the anomaly too. He watched a man poking around in the mountains who turned out to be a Russian spy.

I got the impression he bumped him off.

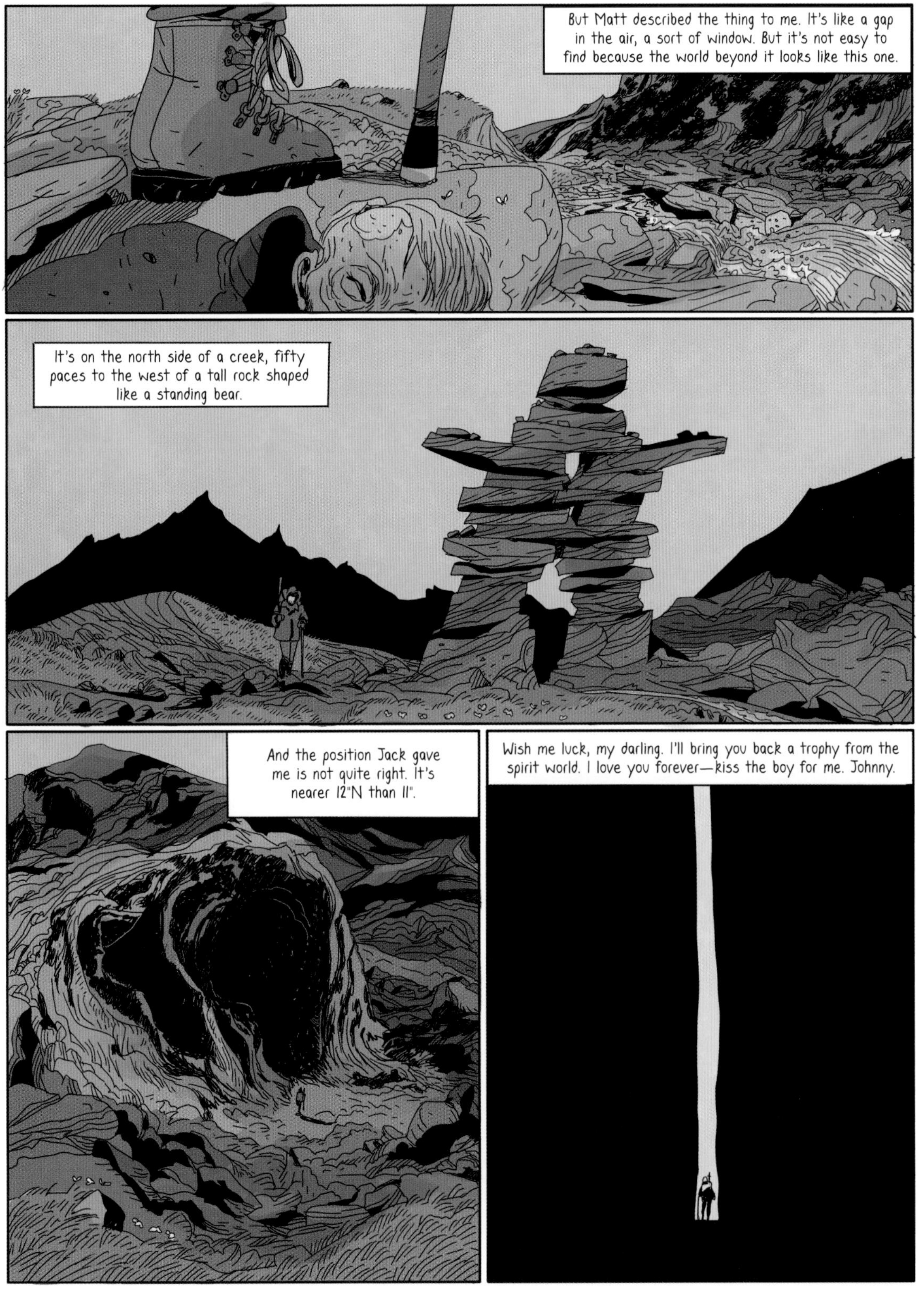
But Matt described the thing to me. It's like a gap in the air, a sort of window. But it's not easy to find because the world beyond it looks like this one.
It's on the north side of a creek, fifty paces to the west of a tall rock shaped like a standing bear.
And the position Jack gave me is not quite right. It's nearer 12"N than 11".
Wish me luck, my darling. I'll bring you back a trophy from the spirit world. I love you forever—kiss the boy for me. Johnny.

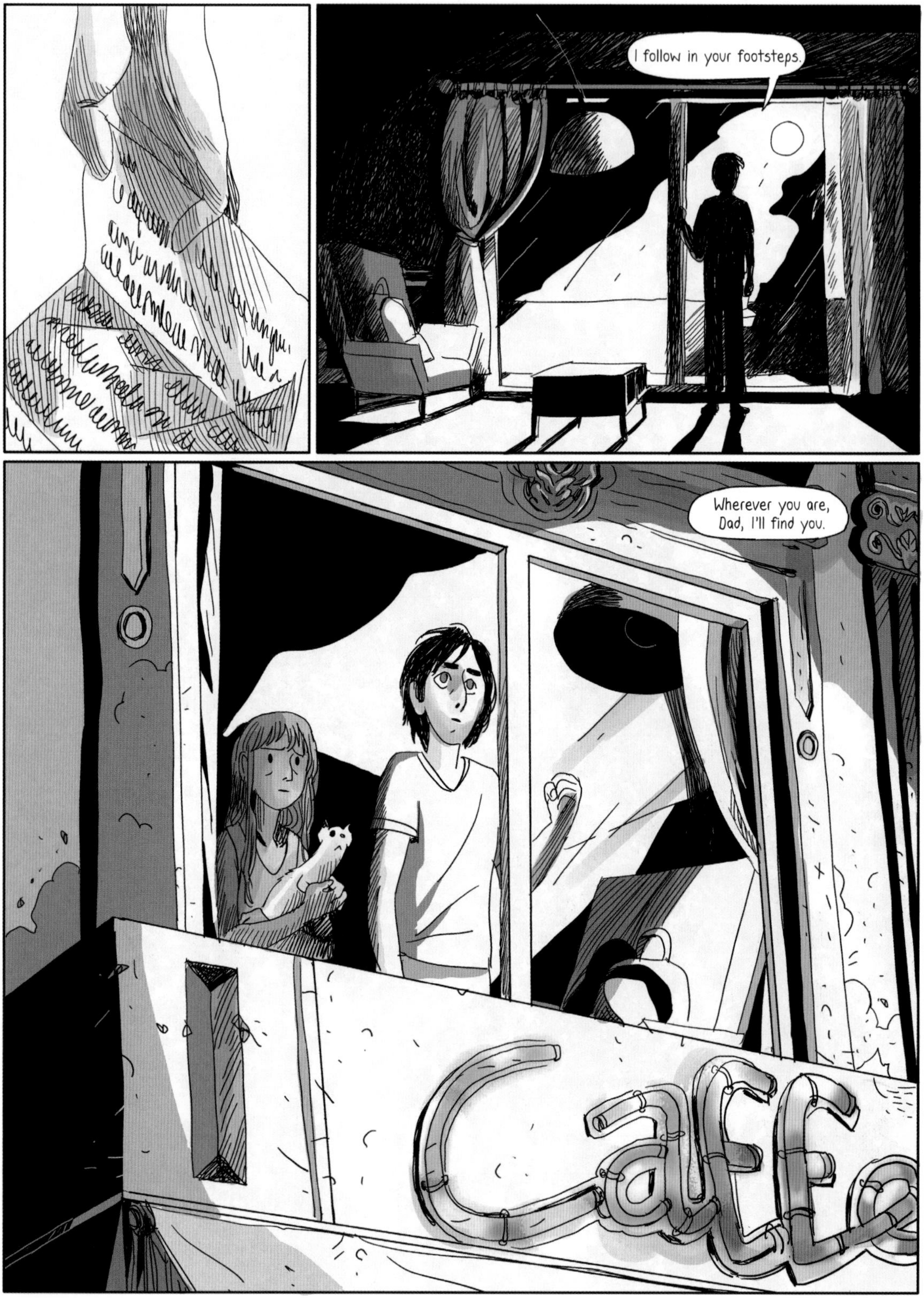
I follow in your footsteps.
Wherever you are, Dad, I'll find you.
Caffe

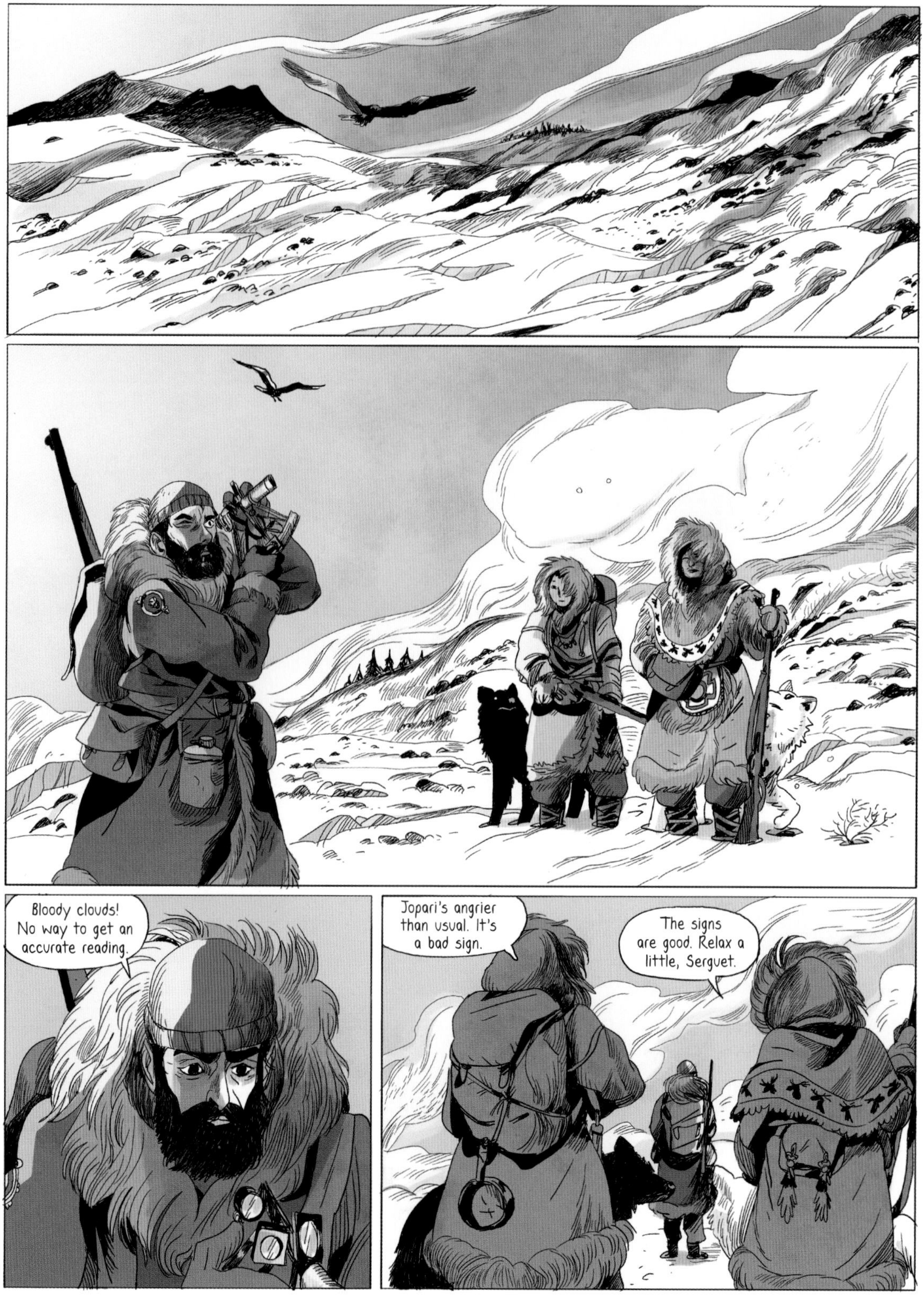
Bloody clouds! No way to get an accurate reading.
Jopari's angrier than usual. It's a bad sign.
The signs are good. Relax a little, Serguet.

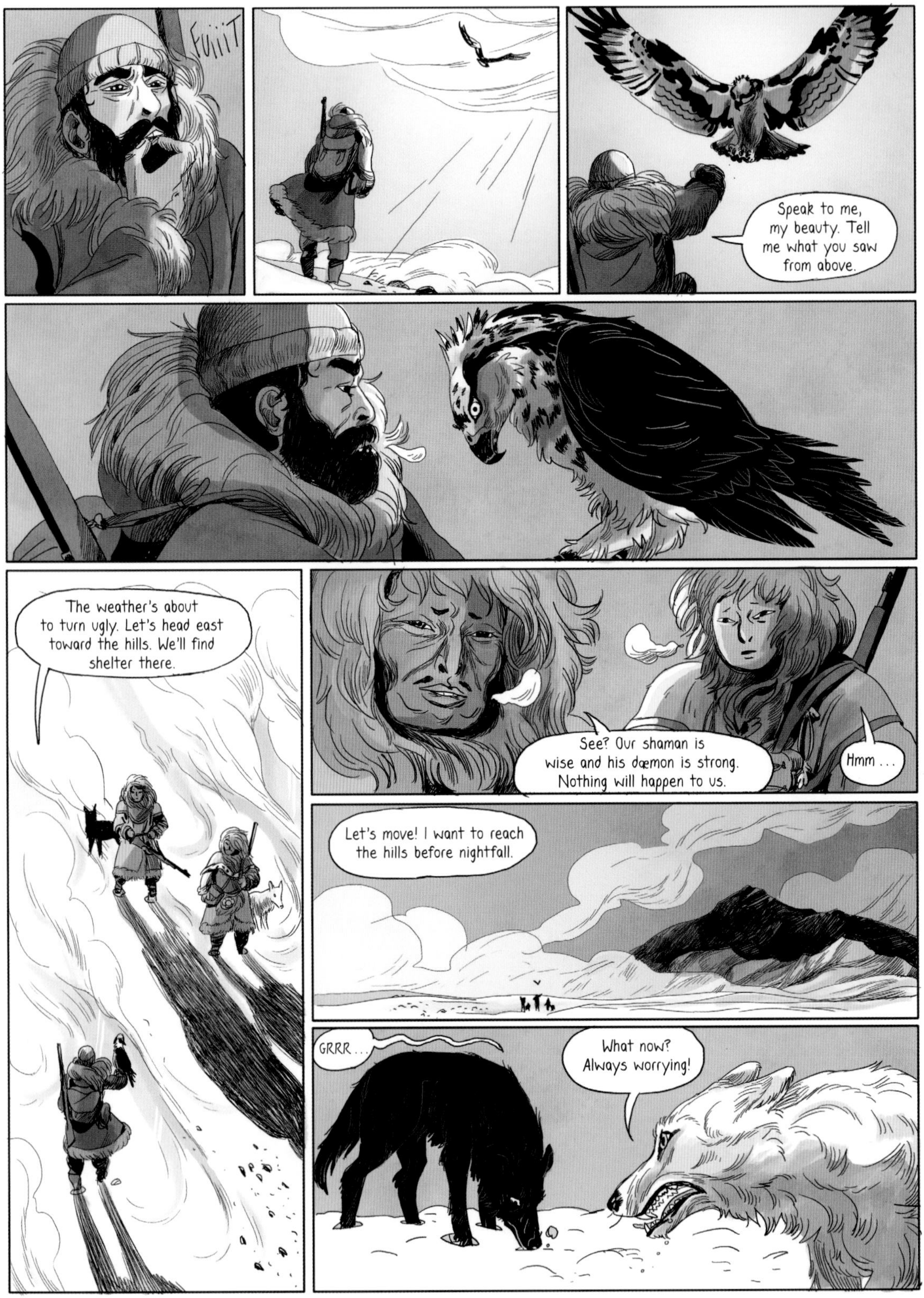
FUIIIT
Speak to me, my beauty. Tell me what you saw from above.
The weather's about to turn ugly. Let's head east toward the hills. We'll find shelter there.
See? Our shaman is wise and his dæmon is strong. Nothing will happen to us.
Hmm . . .
Let's move! I want to reach the hills before nightfall.
GRRR . . .
What now? Always worrying!

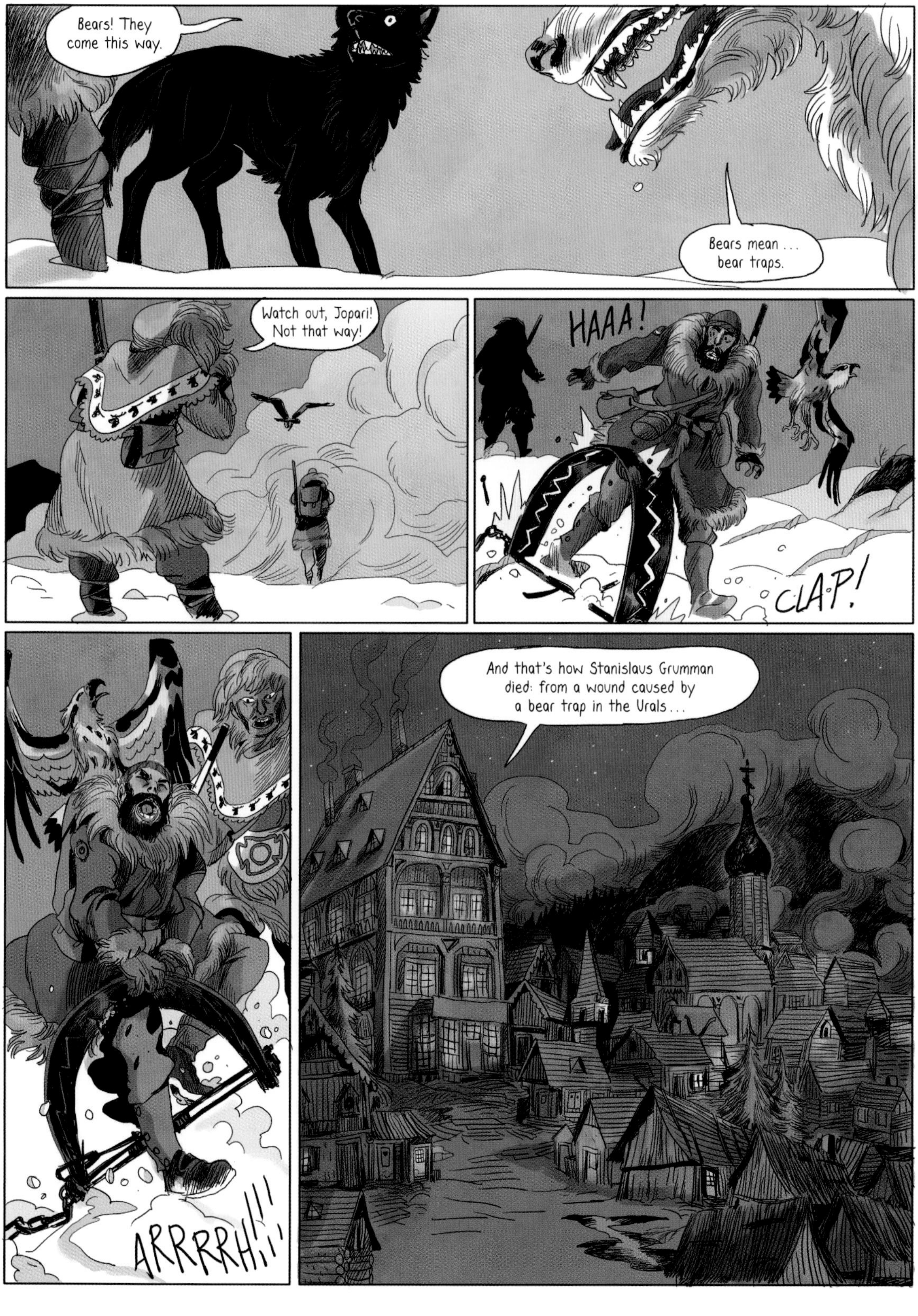
Bears! They come this way.
Bears mean . . . bear traps.
Watch out, Jopari! Not that way!
HAAA!
CLAP!
ARRRRH!!!
And that's how Stanislaus Grumman died: from a wound caused by a bear trap in the Urals . . .

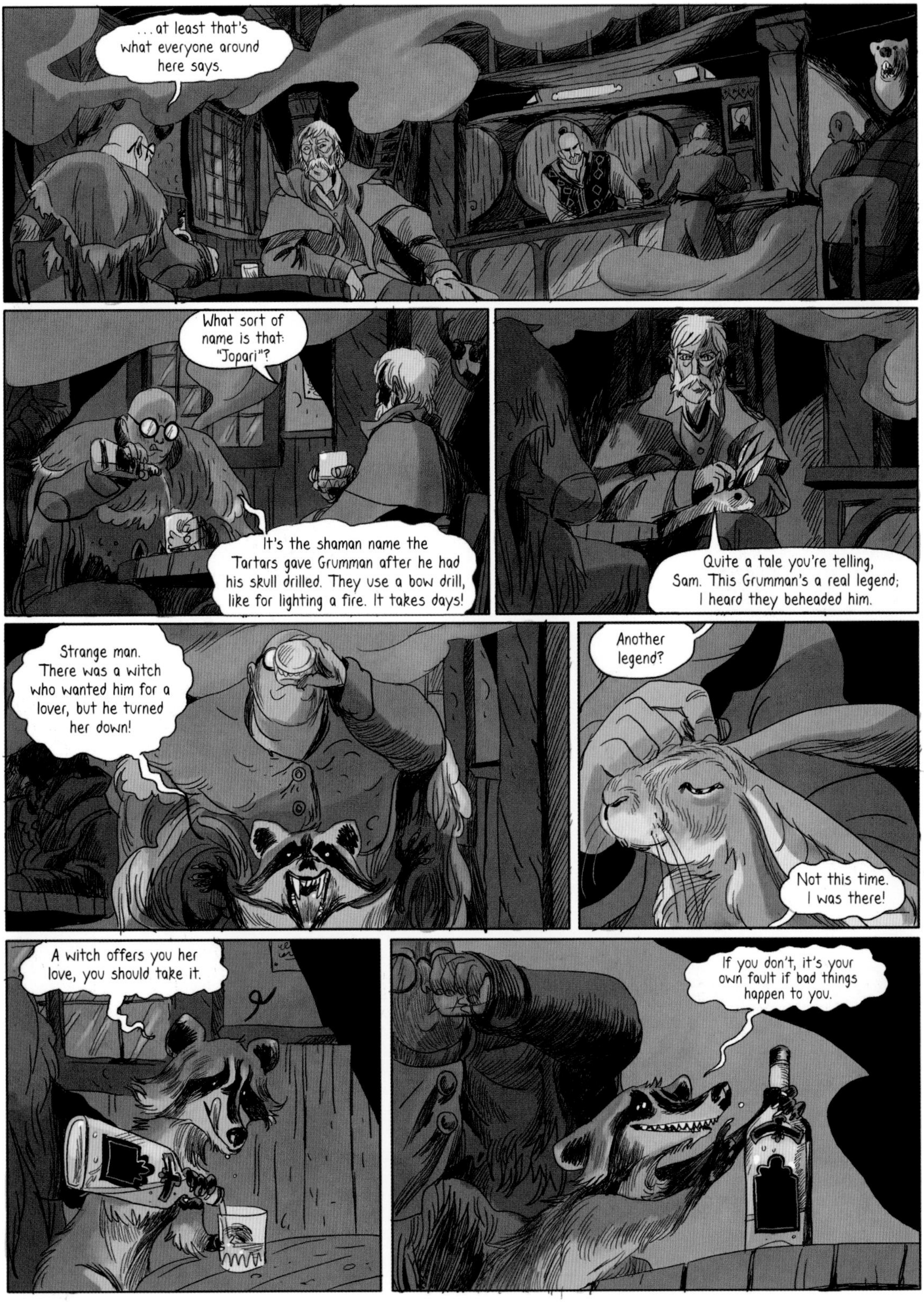

...at least that's what everyone around here says.
What sort of name is that: "Jopari"?
It's the shaman name the Tartars gave Grumman after he had his skull drilled. They use a bow drill, like for lighting a fire. It takes days!
Quite a tale you're telling, Sam. This Grumman's a real legend; I heard they beheaded him.
Strange man. There was a witch who wanted him for a lover, but he turned her down!
Another legend?
Not this time. I was there!
A witch offers you her love, you should take it.
If you don't, it's your own fault if bad things happen to you.

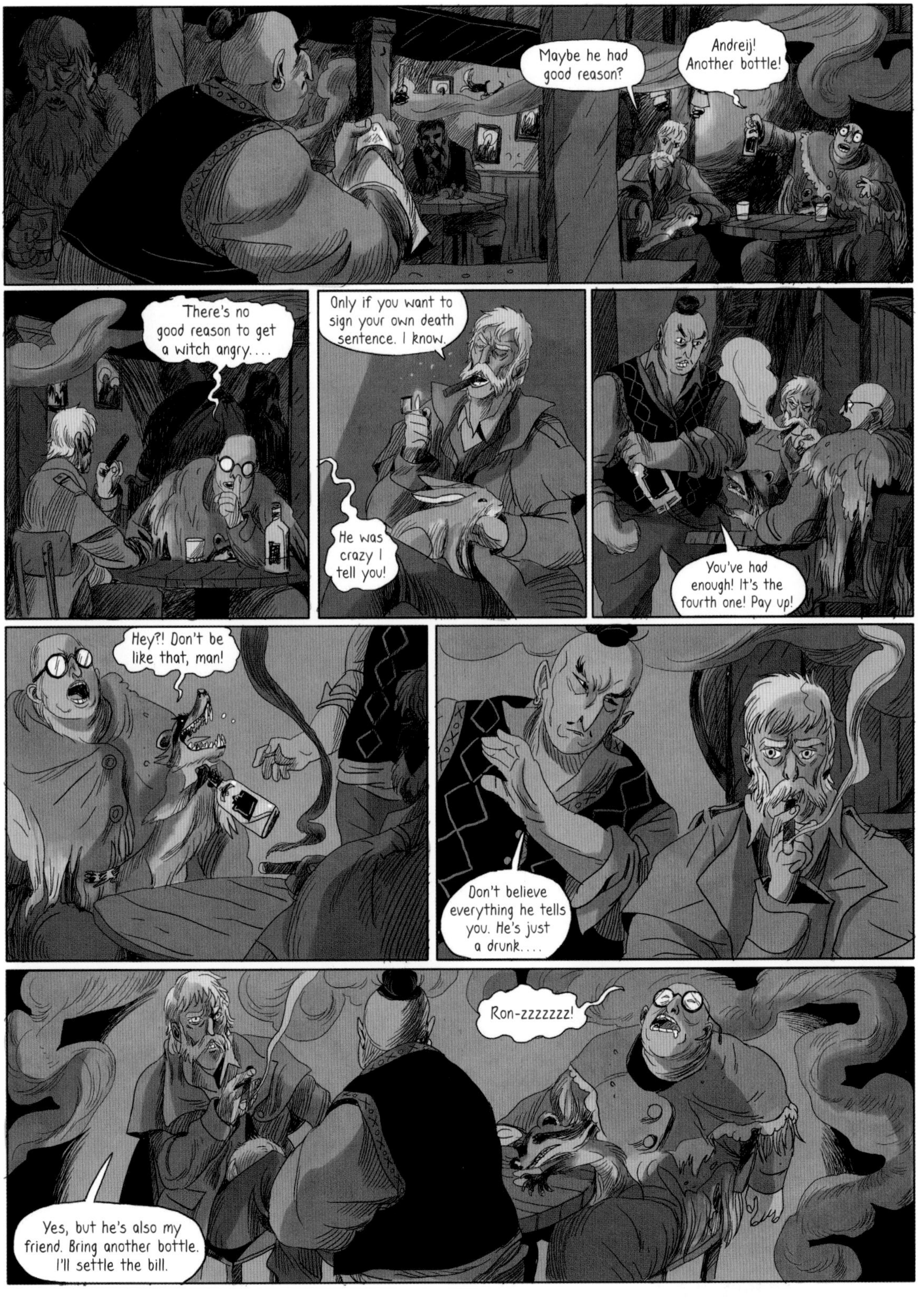
Maybe he had good reason?
Andreij! Another bottle!
There's no good reason to get a witch angry....
Only if you want to sign your own death sentence. I know.
He was crazy I tell you!
You've had enough! It's the fourth one! Pay up!
Hey?! Don't be like that, man!
Don't believe everything he tells you. He's just a drunk....
Ron-zzzzzzz!
Yes, but he's also my friend. Bring another bottle. I'll settle the bill.

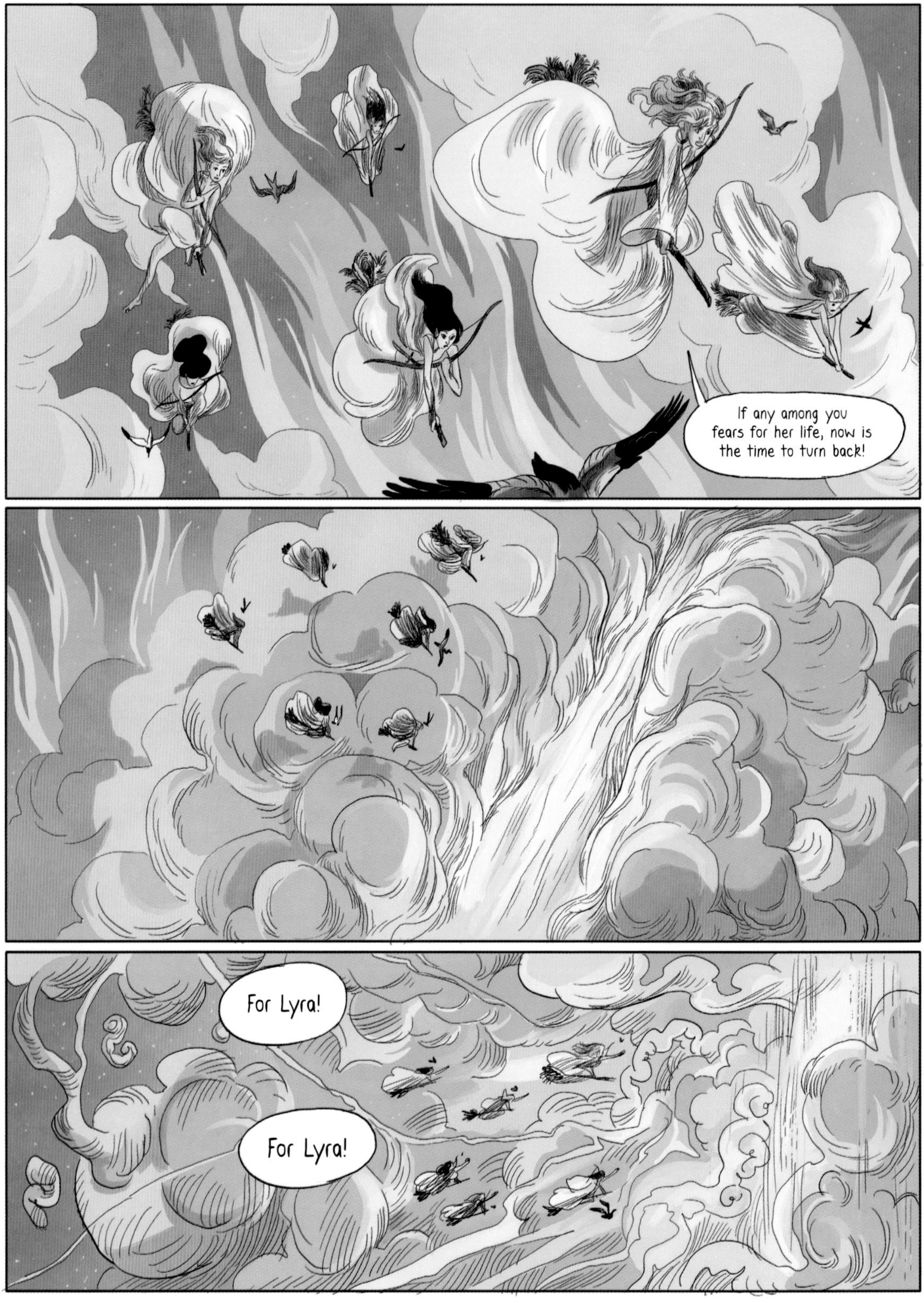
If any among you fears for her life, now is the time to turn back!
For Lyra!
For Lyra!

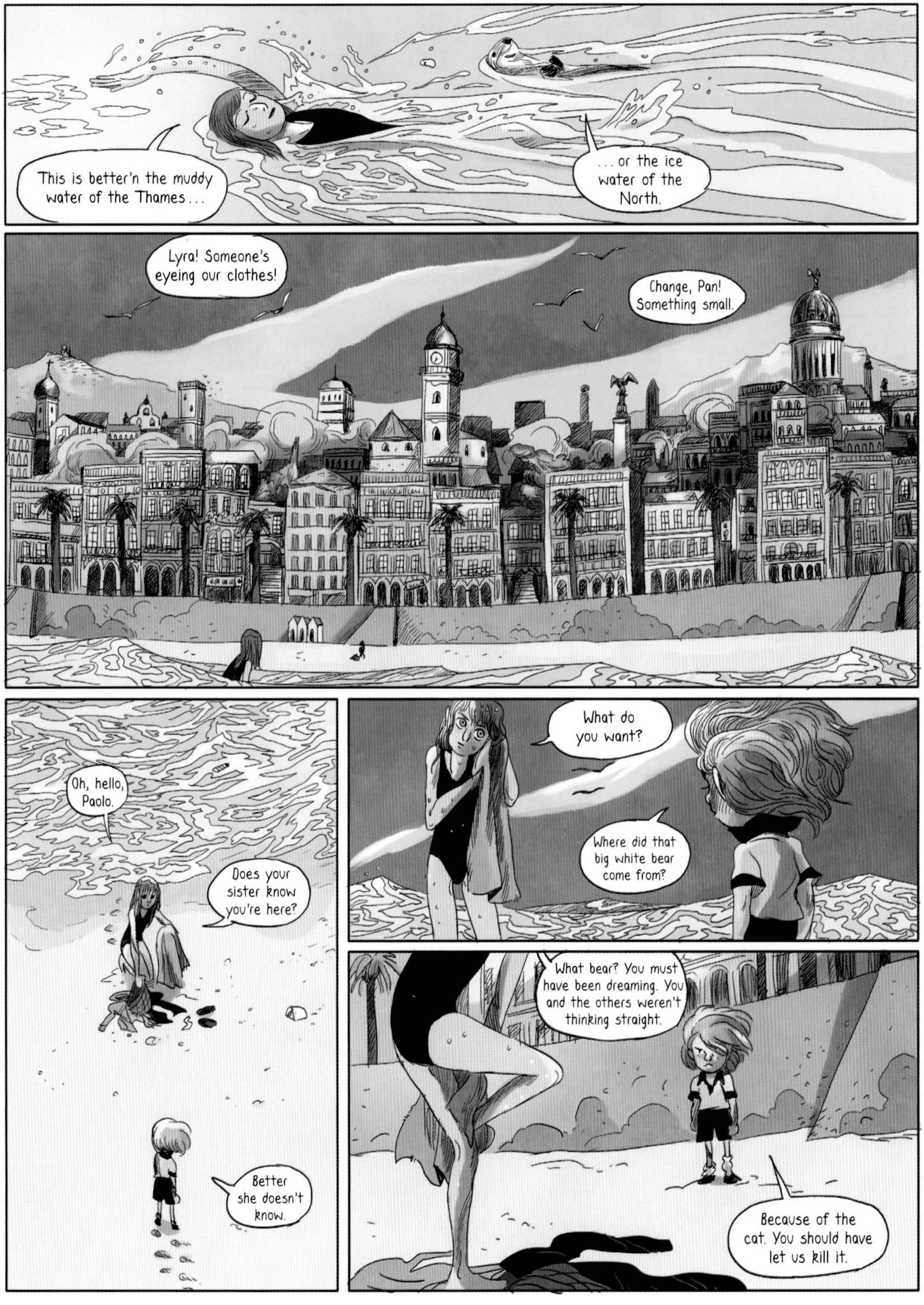
This is better'n the muddy water of the Thames...
...or the ice water of the North.
Lyra! Someone's eyeing our clothes!
Change, Pan! Something small.
Oh, hello, Paolo.
Does your sister know you're here?
Better she doesn't know.
What do you want?
Where did that big white bear come from?
What bear? You must have been dreaming. You and the others weren't thinking straight.
Because of the cat. You should have let us kill it.

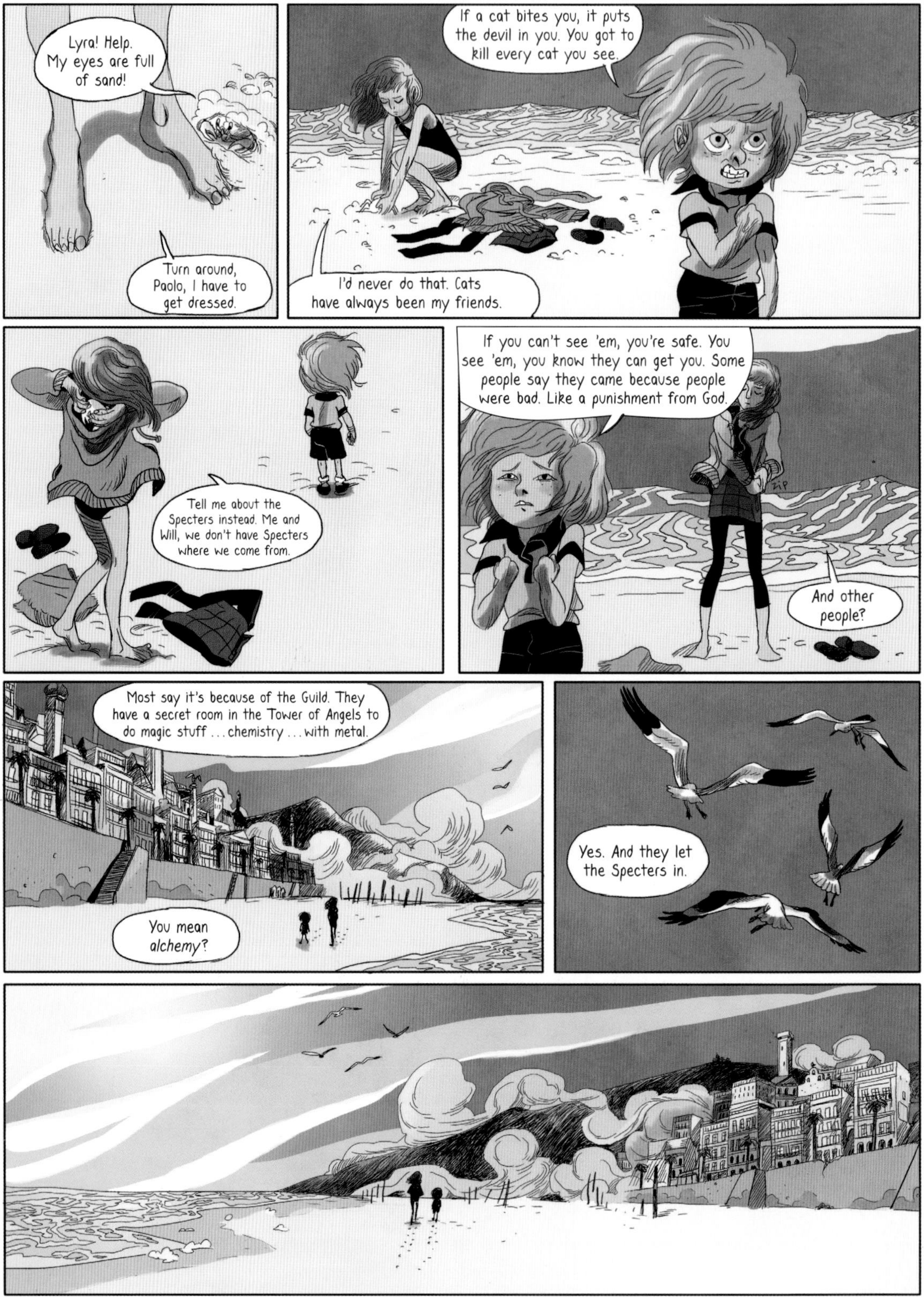

Lyra! Help. My eyes are full of sand!
Turn around, Paolo, I have to get dressed.
If a cat bites you, it puts the devil in you. You got to kill every cat you see.
I'd never do that. Cats have always been my friends.
Tell me about the Specters instead. Me and Will, we don't have Specters where we come from.
If you can't see 'em, you're safe. You see 'em, you know they can get you. Some people say they came because people were bad. Like a punishment from God.
ZIP
And other people?
Most say it's because of the Guild. They have a secret room in the Tower of Angels to do magic stuff . . . chemistry . . . with metal.
You mean *alchemy*?
Yes. And they let the Specters in.

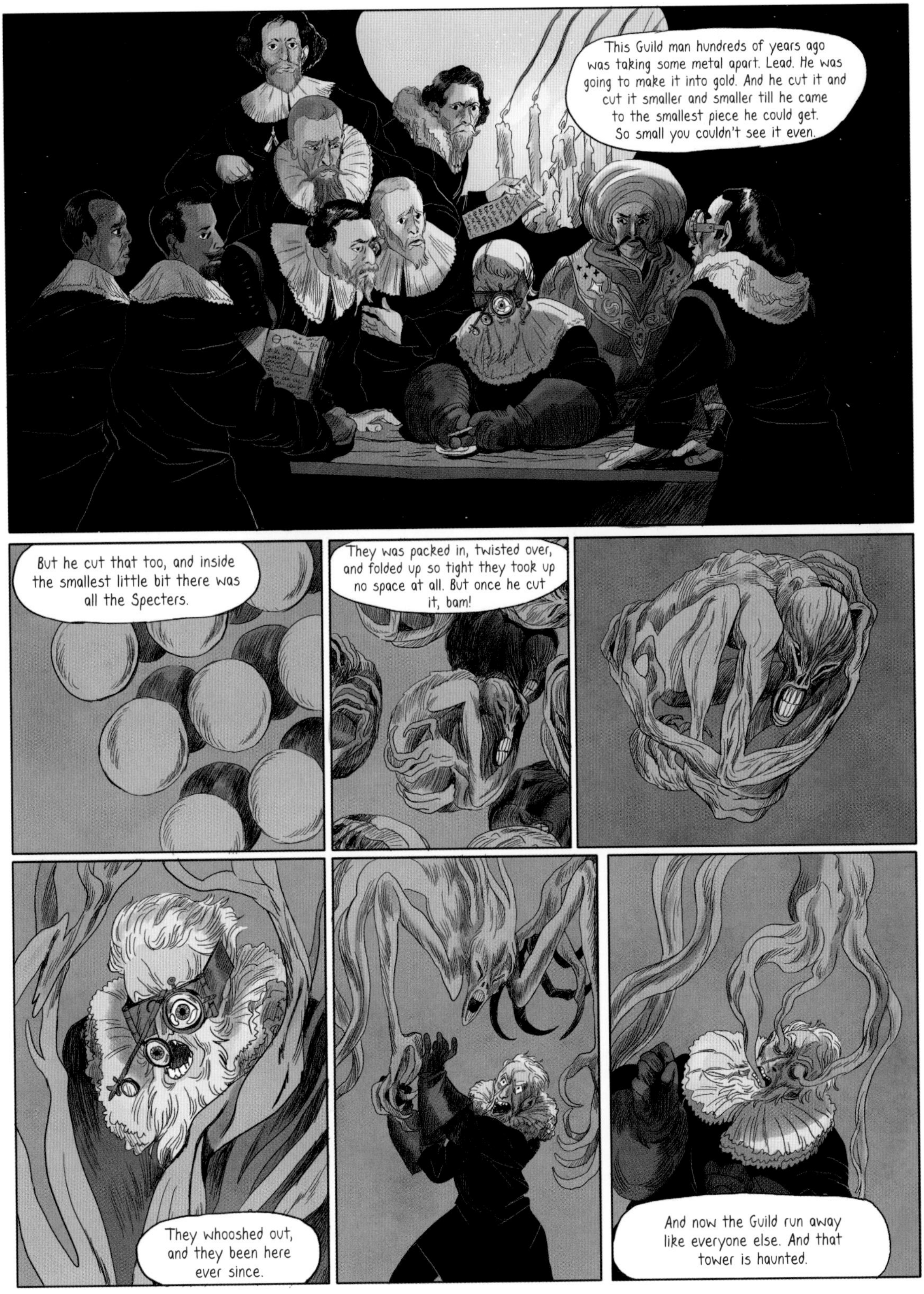
This Guild man hundreds of years ago was taking some metal apart. Lead. He was going to make it into gold. And he cut it and cut it smaller and smaller till he came to the smallest piece he could get. So small you couldn't see it even.
But he cut that too, and inside the smallest little bit there was all the Specters.
They was packed in, twisted over, and folded up so tight they took up no space at all. But once he cut it, bam!
They whooshed out, and they been here ever since.
And now the Guild run away like everyone else. And that tower is haunted.

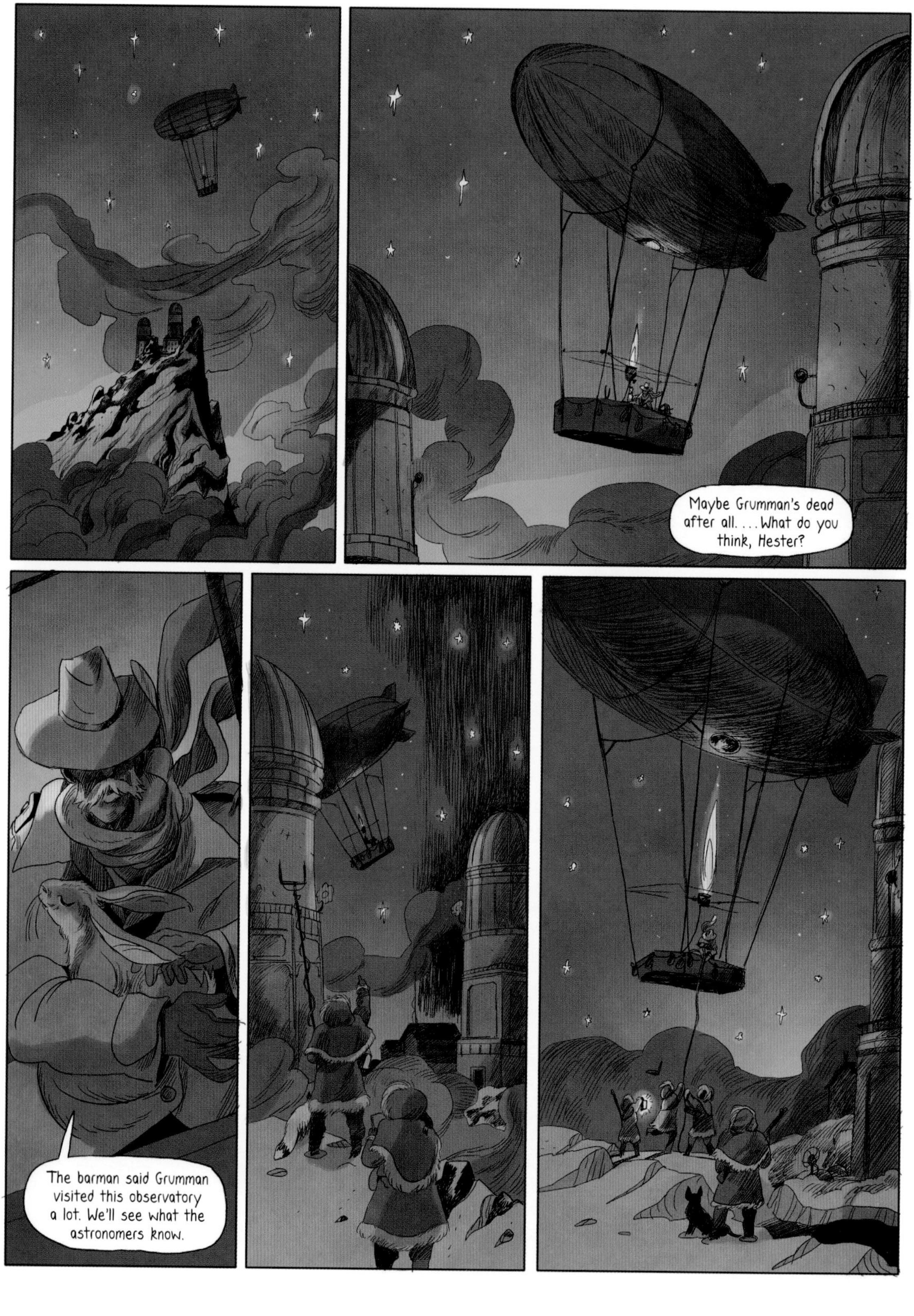
Maybe Grumman's dead after all. . . . What do you think, Hester?
The barman said Grumman visited this observatory a lot. We'll see what the astronomers know.

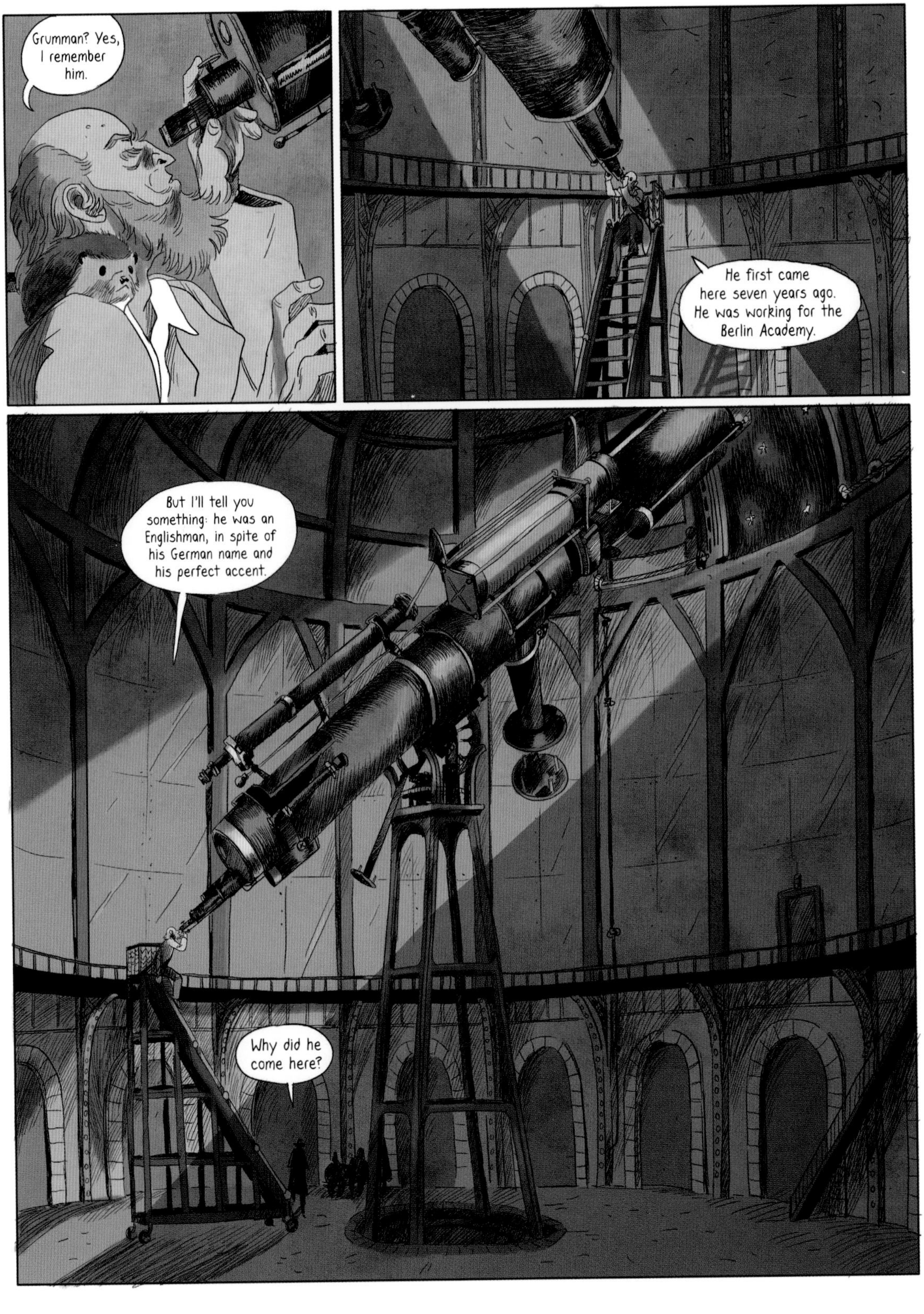
Grumman? Yes, I remember him.
He first came here seven years ago. He was working for the Berlin Academy.
But I'll tell you something: he was an Englishman, in spite of his German name and his perfect accent.
Why did he come here?

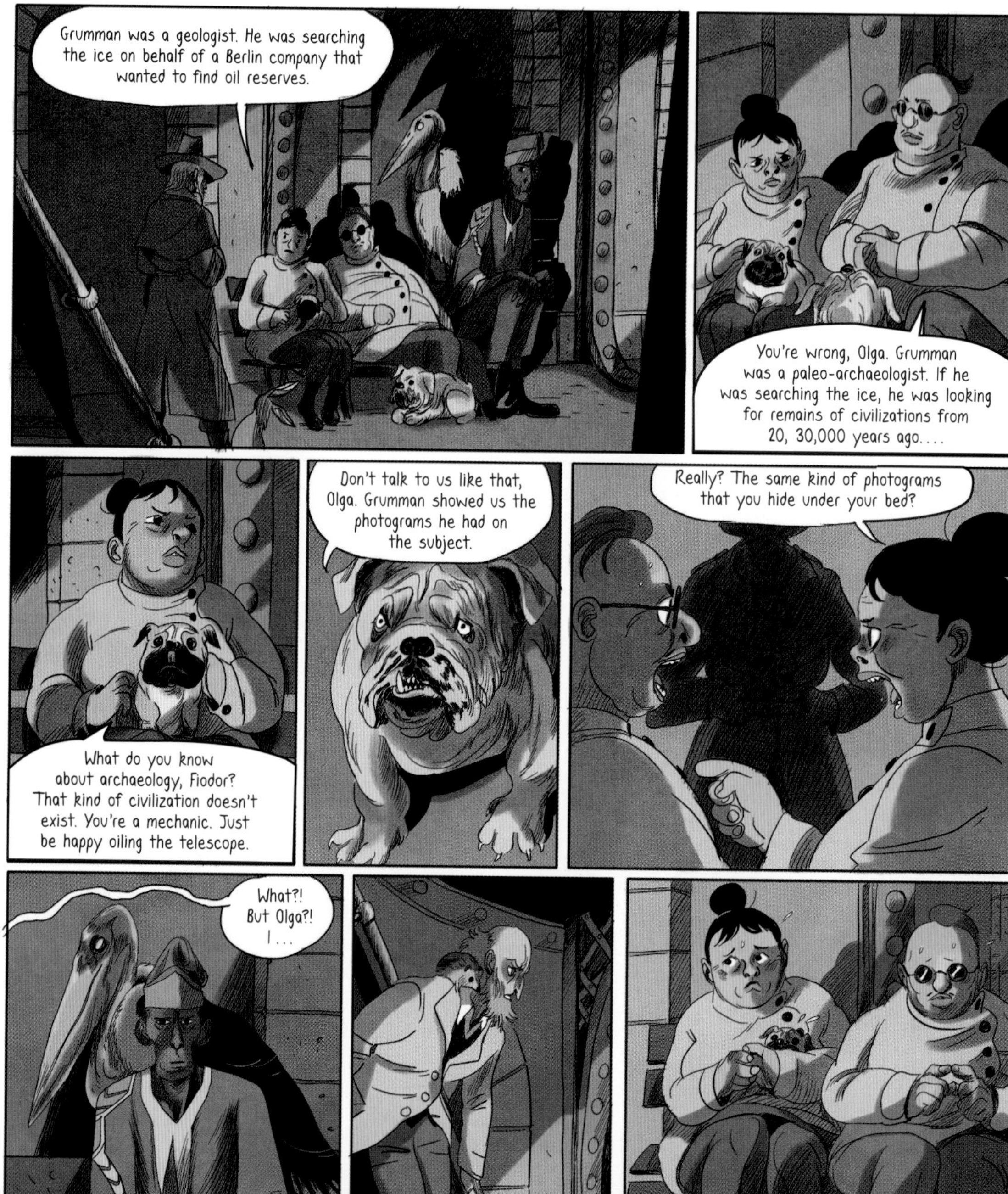
Grumman was a geologist. He was searching the ice on behalf of a Berlin company that wanted to find oil reserves.
You're wrong, Olga. Grumman was a paleo-archaeologist. If he was searching the ice, he was looking for remains of civilizations from 20, 30,000 years ago. . . .
What do you know about archaeology, Fiodor? That kind of civilization doesn't exist. You're a mechanic. Just be happy oiling the telescope.
Don't talk to us like that, Olga. Grumman showed us the photograms he had on the subject.
Really? The same kind of photograms that you hide under your bed?
What?! But Olga?! I . . .
Enough, you two! You're making a spectacle of yourselves in front of our visitor! Off with you!
Excuse us, Mr. Director.
Right away, Mr. Director.

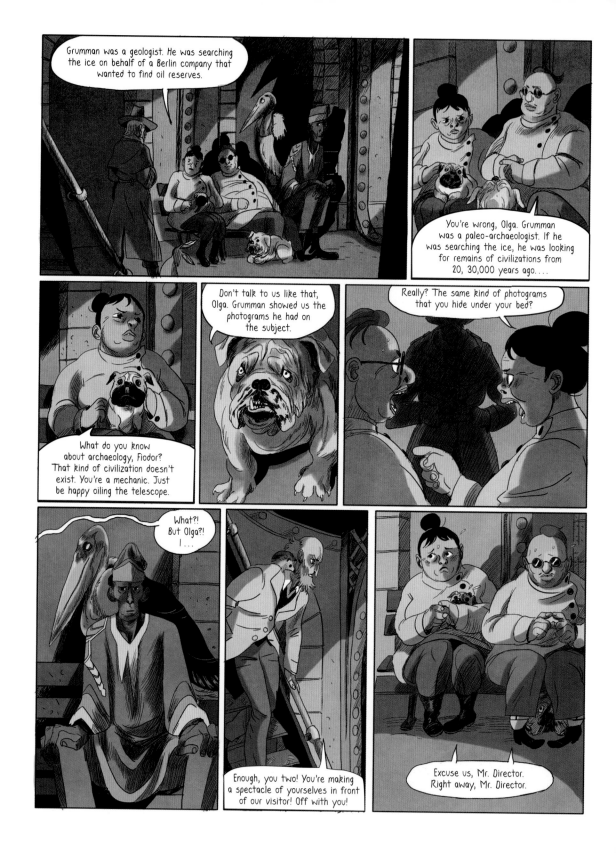

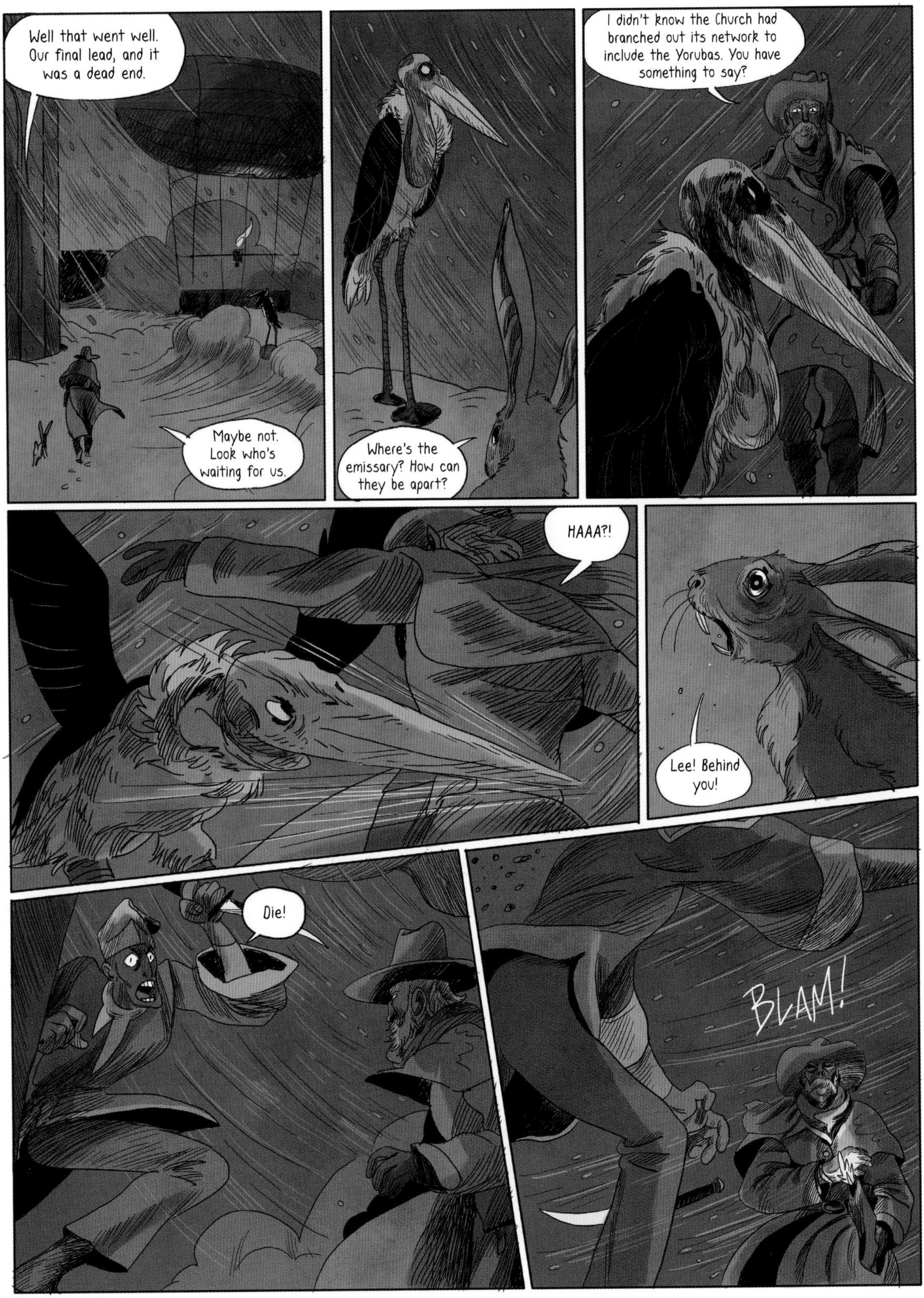
Well that went well. Our final lead, and it was a dead end.
Maybe not. Look who's waiting for us.
Where's the emissary? How can they be apart?
I didn't know the Church had branched out its network to include the Yorubas. You have something to say?
HAAA?!
Lee! Behind you!
Die!
BLAM!

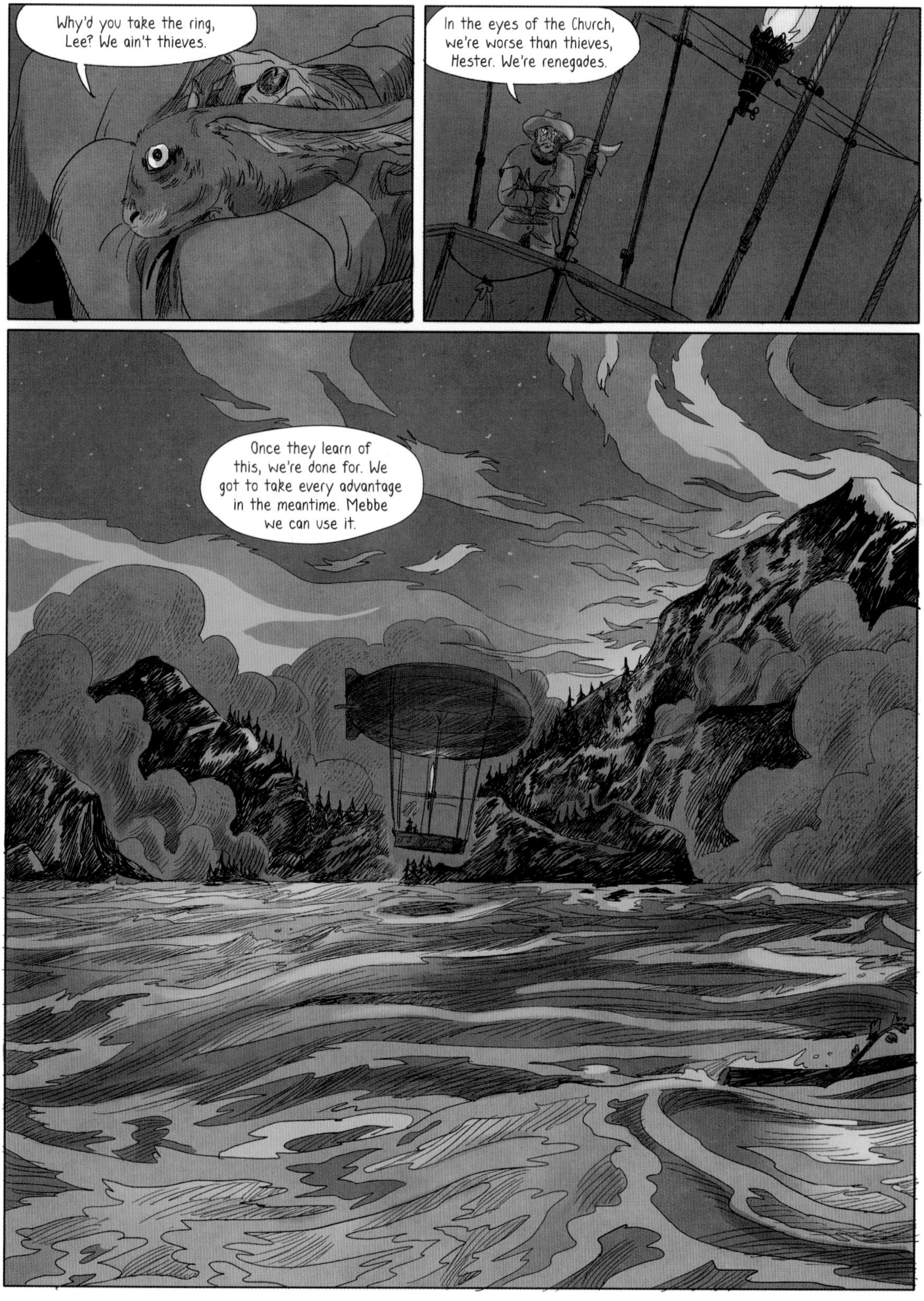
Why'd you take the ring, Lee? We ain't thieves.
In the eyes of the Church, we're worse than thieves, Hester. We're renegades.
Once they learn of this, we're done for. We got to take every advantage in the meantime. Mebbe we can use it.

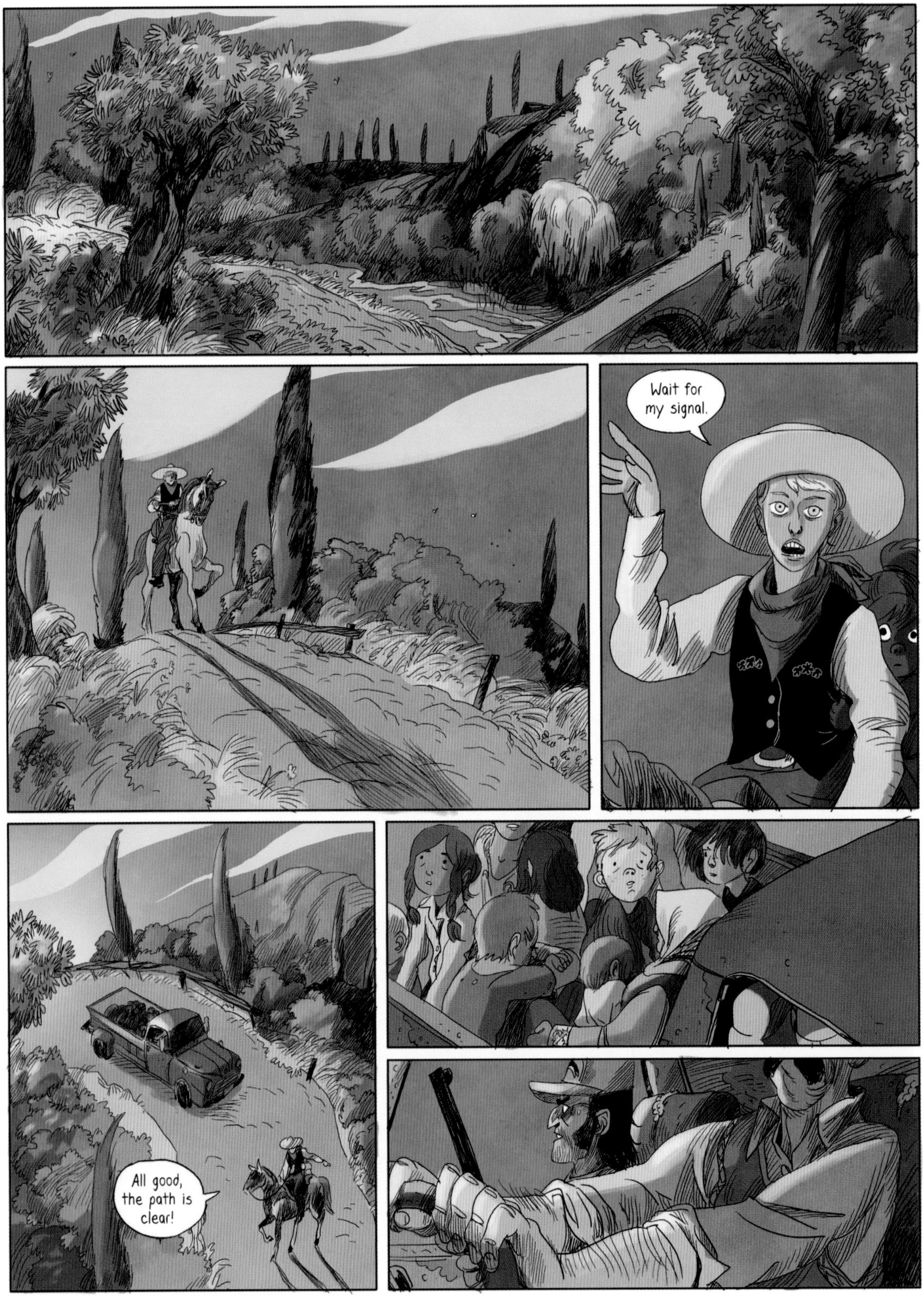
Wait for my signal.
All good, the path is clear!

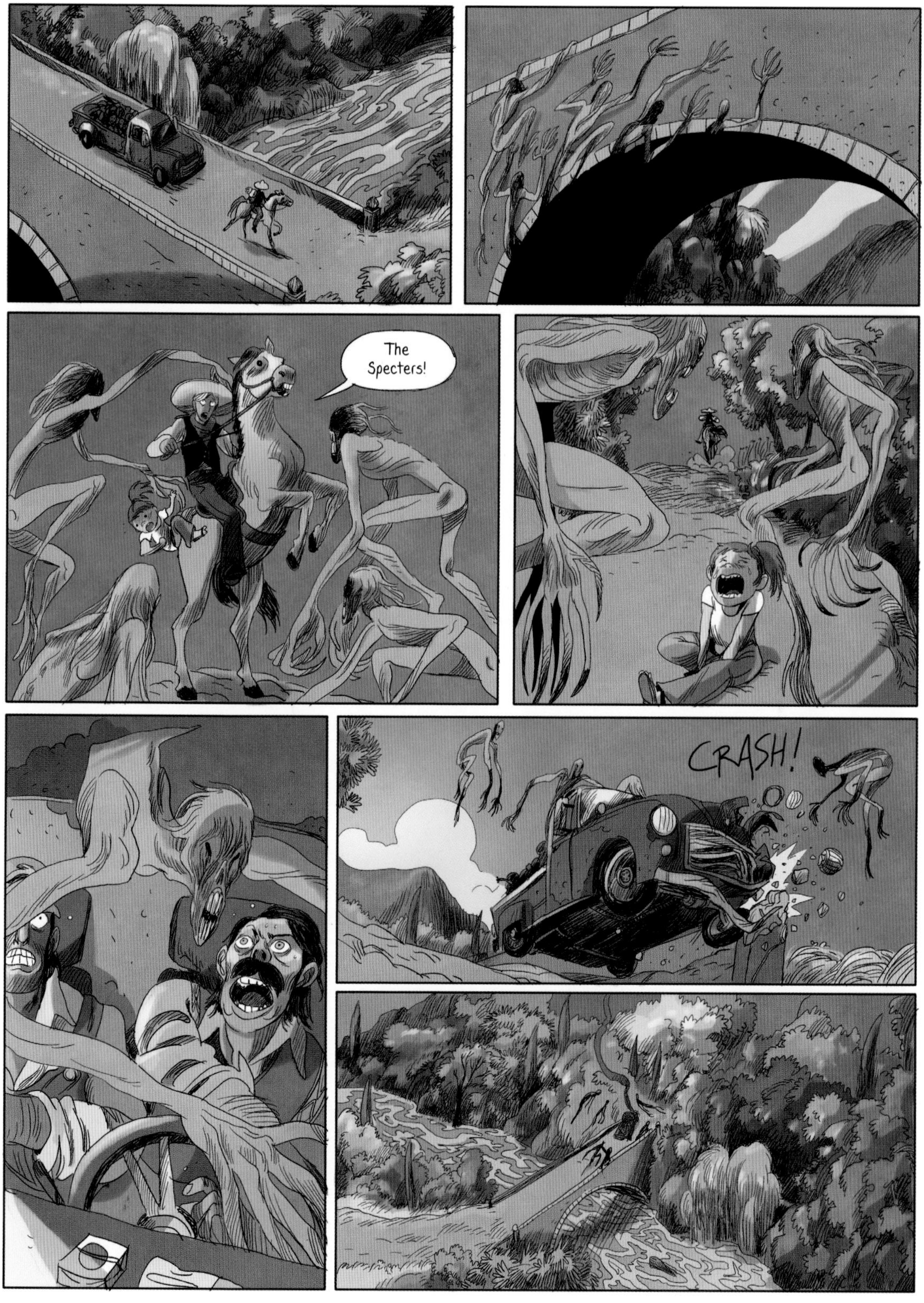
The Specters!
CRASH!

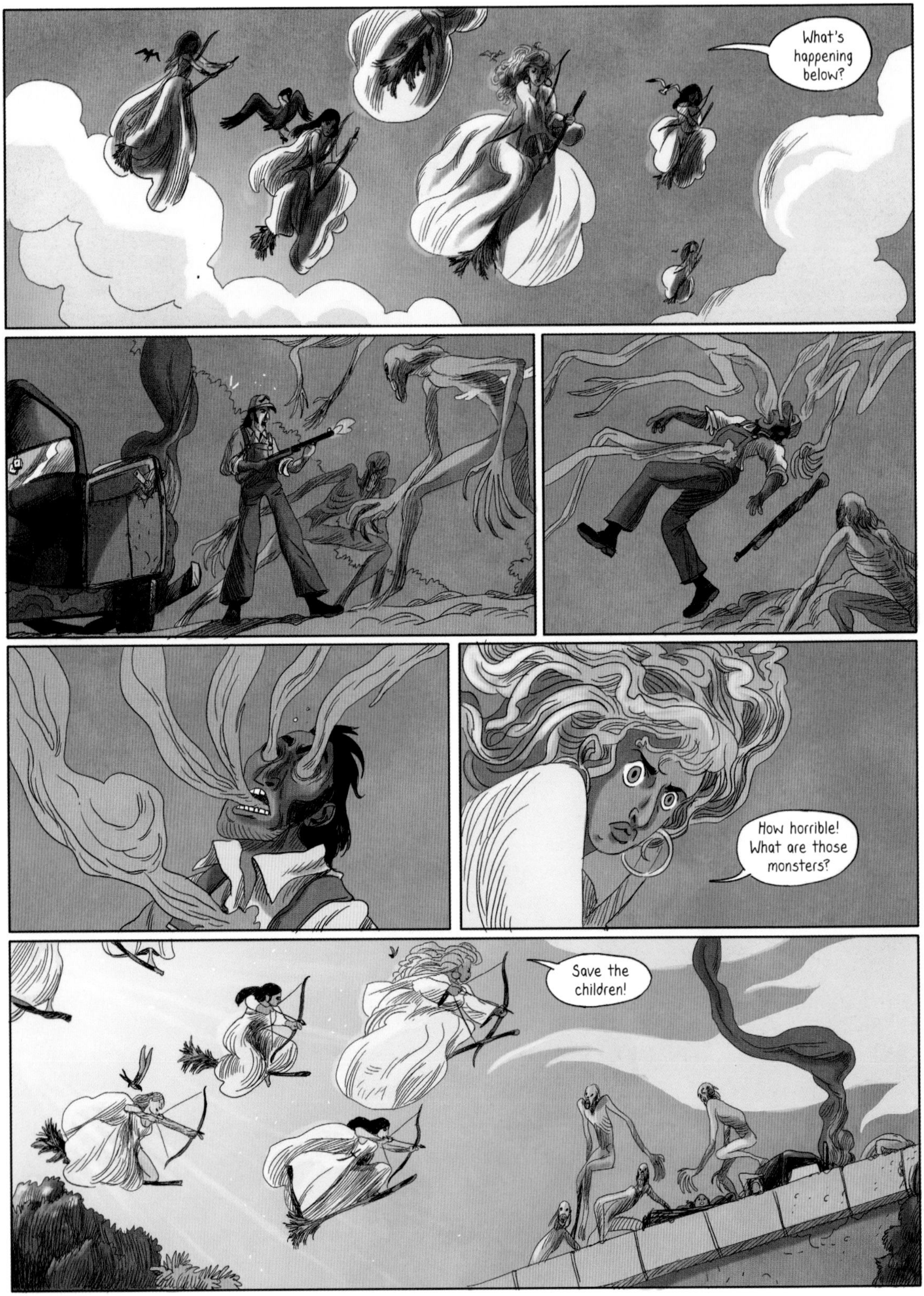
What's happening below?
How horrible! What are those monsters?
Save the children!

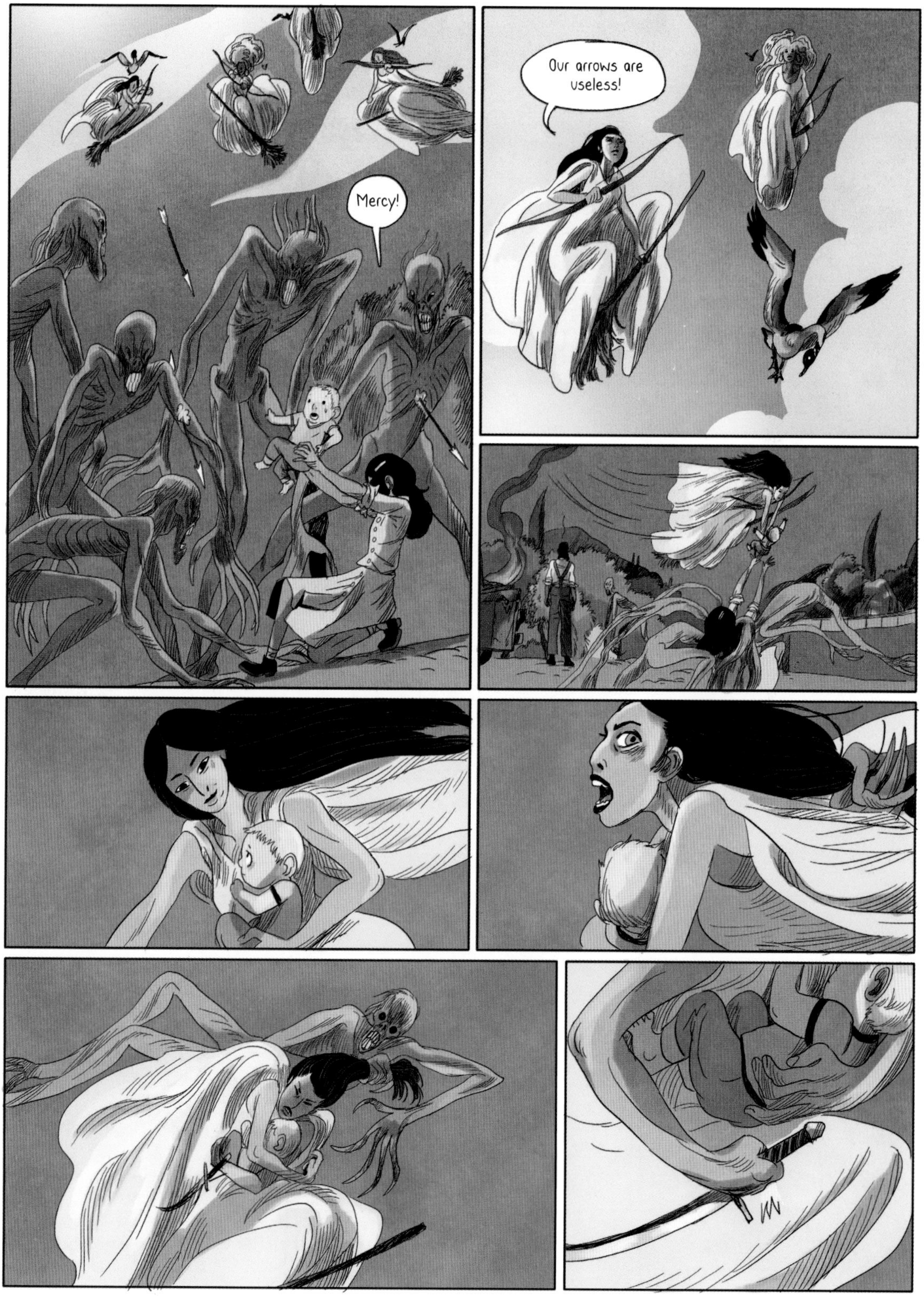
Our arrows are useless!
Mercy!

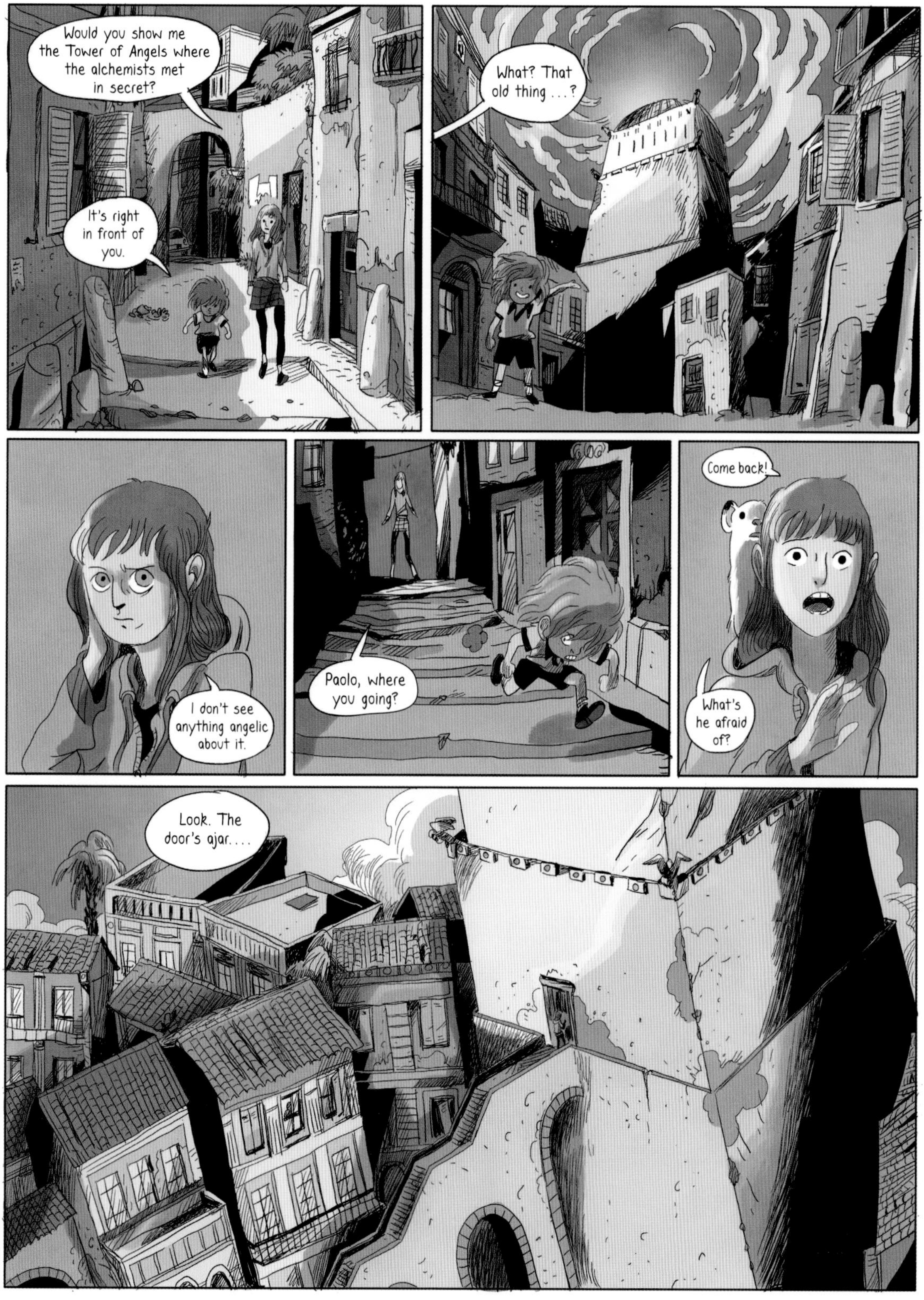
Would you show me the Tower of Angels where the alchemists met in secret?
It's right in front of you.
What? That old thing . . . ?
I don't see anything angelic about it.
Paolo, where you going?
Come back!
What's he afraid of?
Look. The door's ajar. . . .

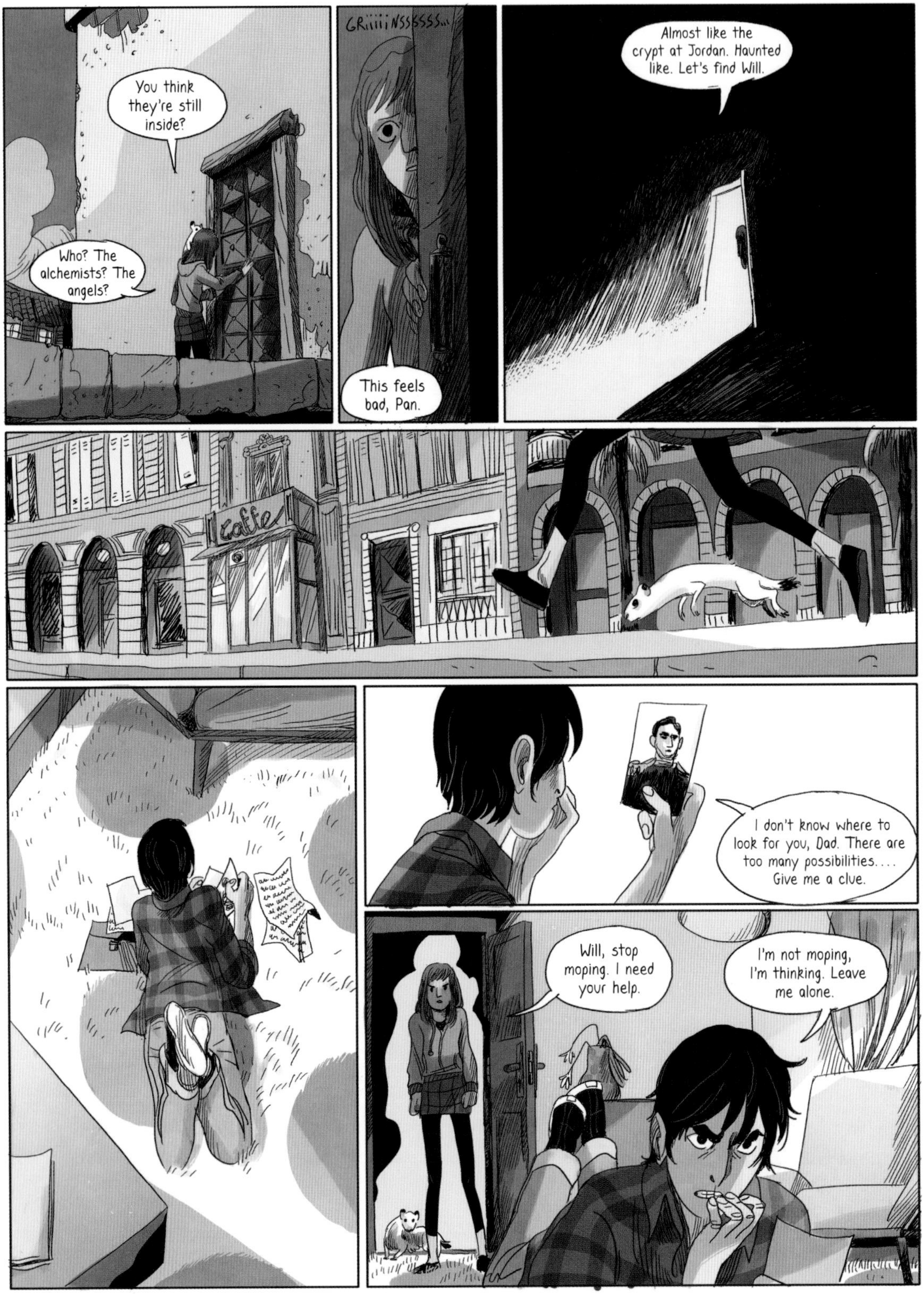
You think they're still inside?
Who? The alchemists? The angels?
GRiiiiNSSSSSS...
This feels bad, Pan.
Almost like the crypt at Jordan. Haunted like. Let's find Will.
Caffe
I don't know where to look for you, Dad. There are too many possibilities.... Give me a clue.
Will, stop moping. I need your help.
I'm not moping, I'm thinking. Leave me alone.

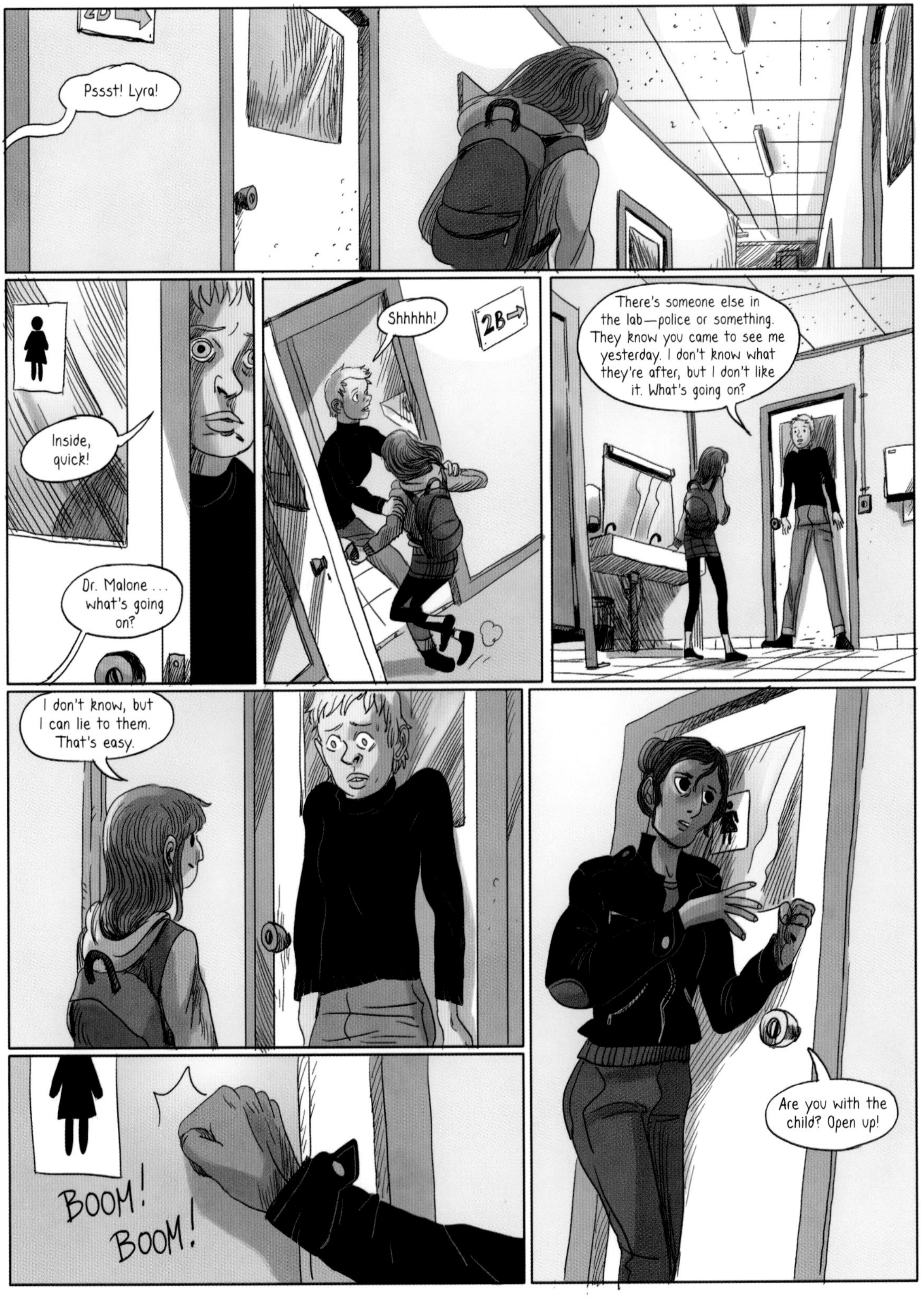
Pssst! Lyra!
Inside, quick!
Dr. Malone . . . what's going on?
Shhhhh!
2B
There's someone else in the lab—police or something. They know you came to see me yesterday. I don't know what they're after, but I don't like it. What's going on?
I don't know, but I can lie to them. That's easy.
BOOM! BOOM!
Are you with the child? Open up!

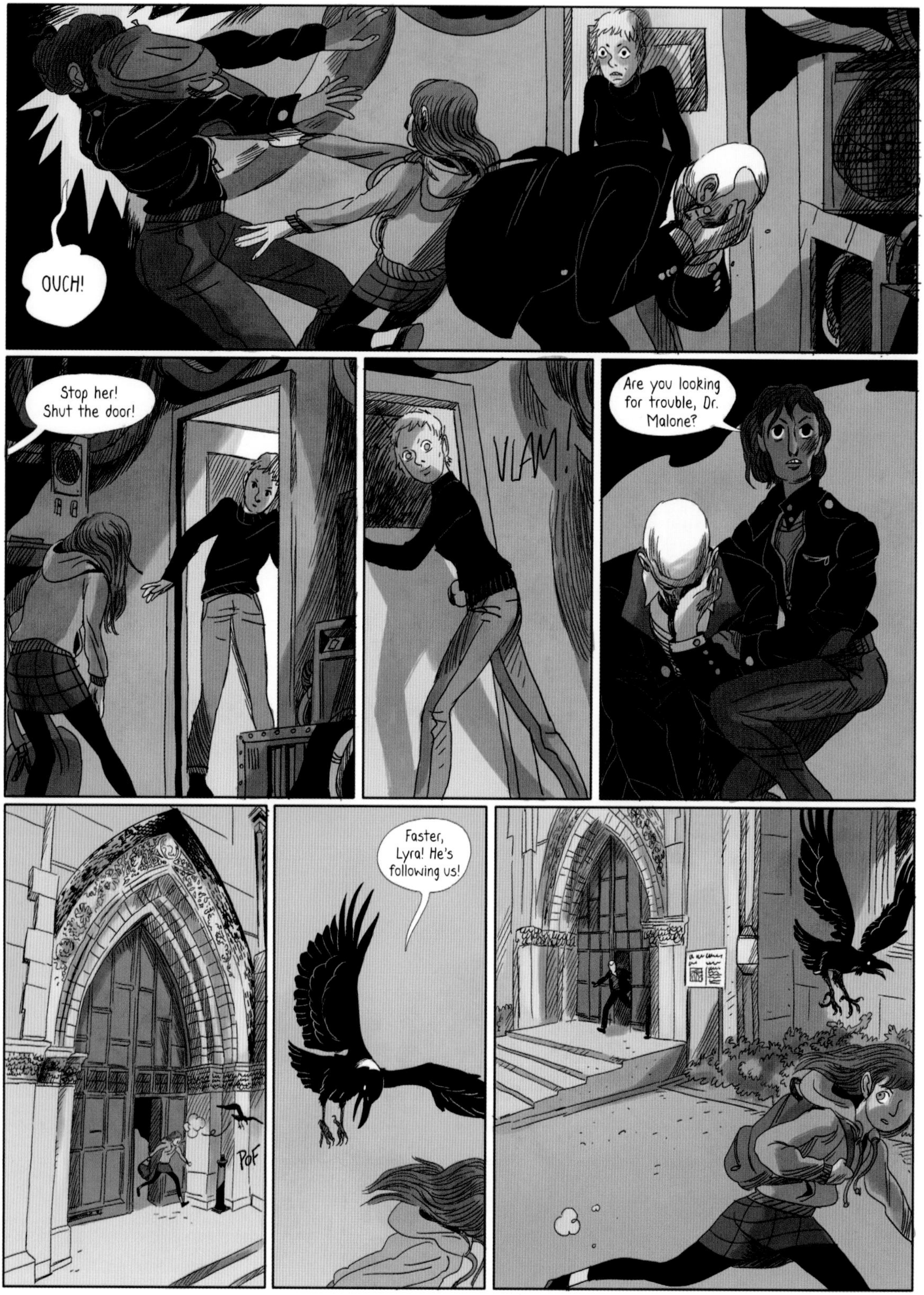
OUCH!
Stop her! Shut the door!
VLAM!
Are you looking for trouble, Dr. Malone?
POF
Faster, Lyra! He's following us!

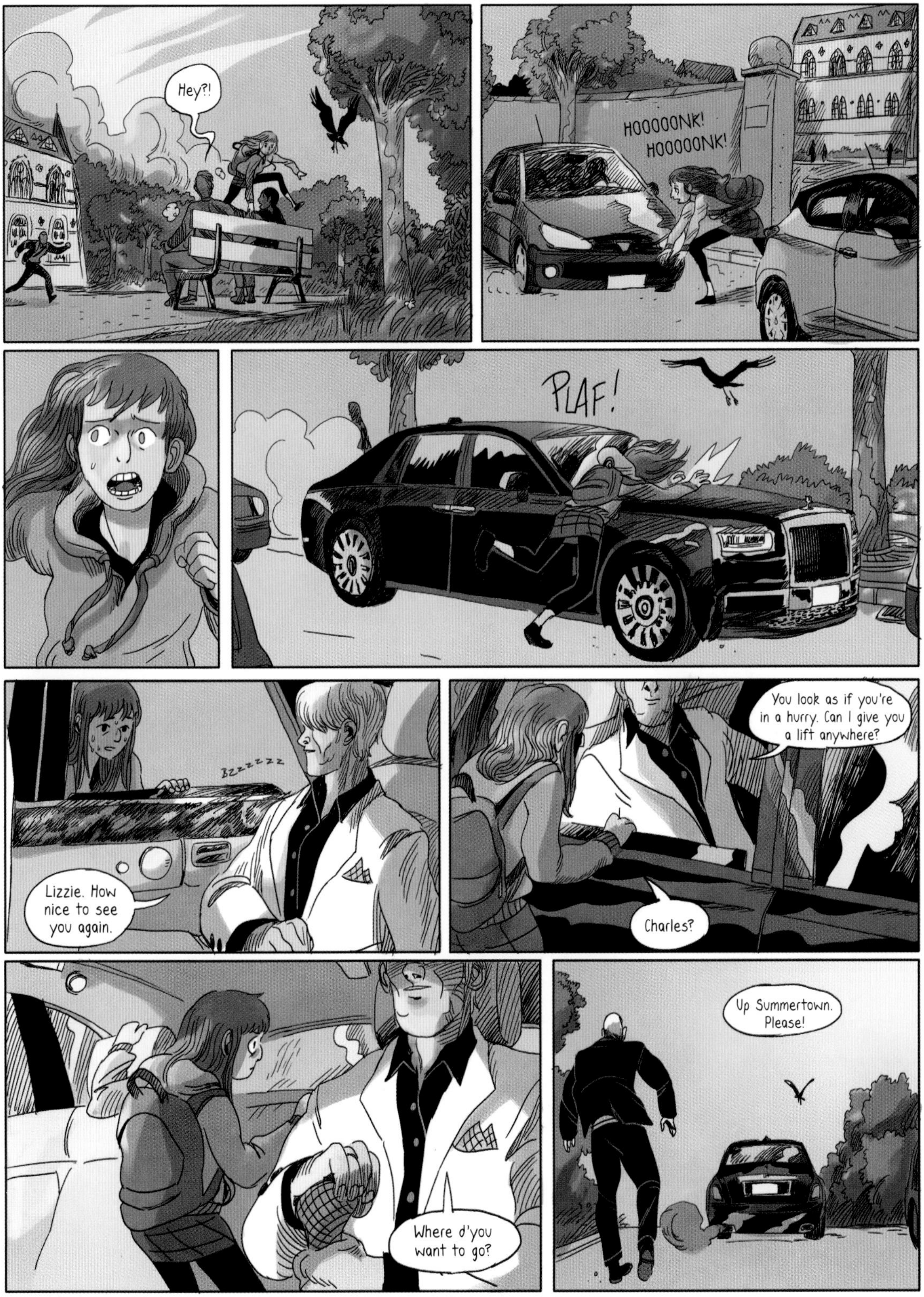
Hey?!
HOOOOONK!
HOOOOONK!
PLAF!
Bzzzzzz
Lizzie. How nice to see you again.
You look as if you're in a hurry. Can I give you a lift anywhere?
Charles?
Where d'you want to go?
Up Summertown. Please!

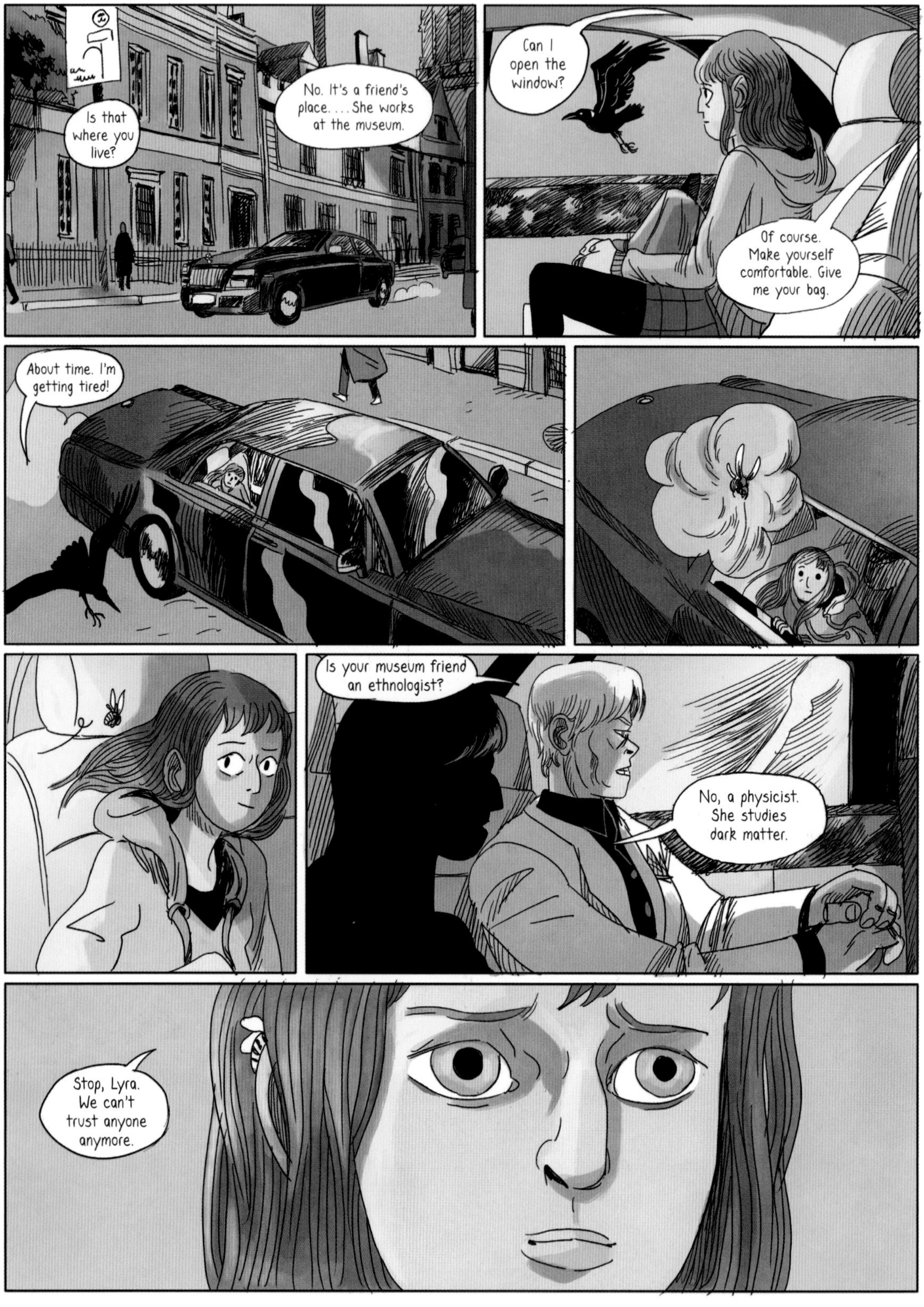
Is that where you live?
No. It's a friend's place. . . . She works at the museum.
Can I open the window?
Of course. Make yourself comfortable. Give me your bag.
About time. I'm getting tired!
Is your museum friend an ethnologist?
No, a physicist. She studies dark matter.
Stop, Lyra. We can't trust anyone anymore.

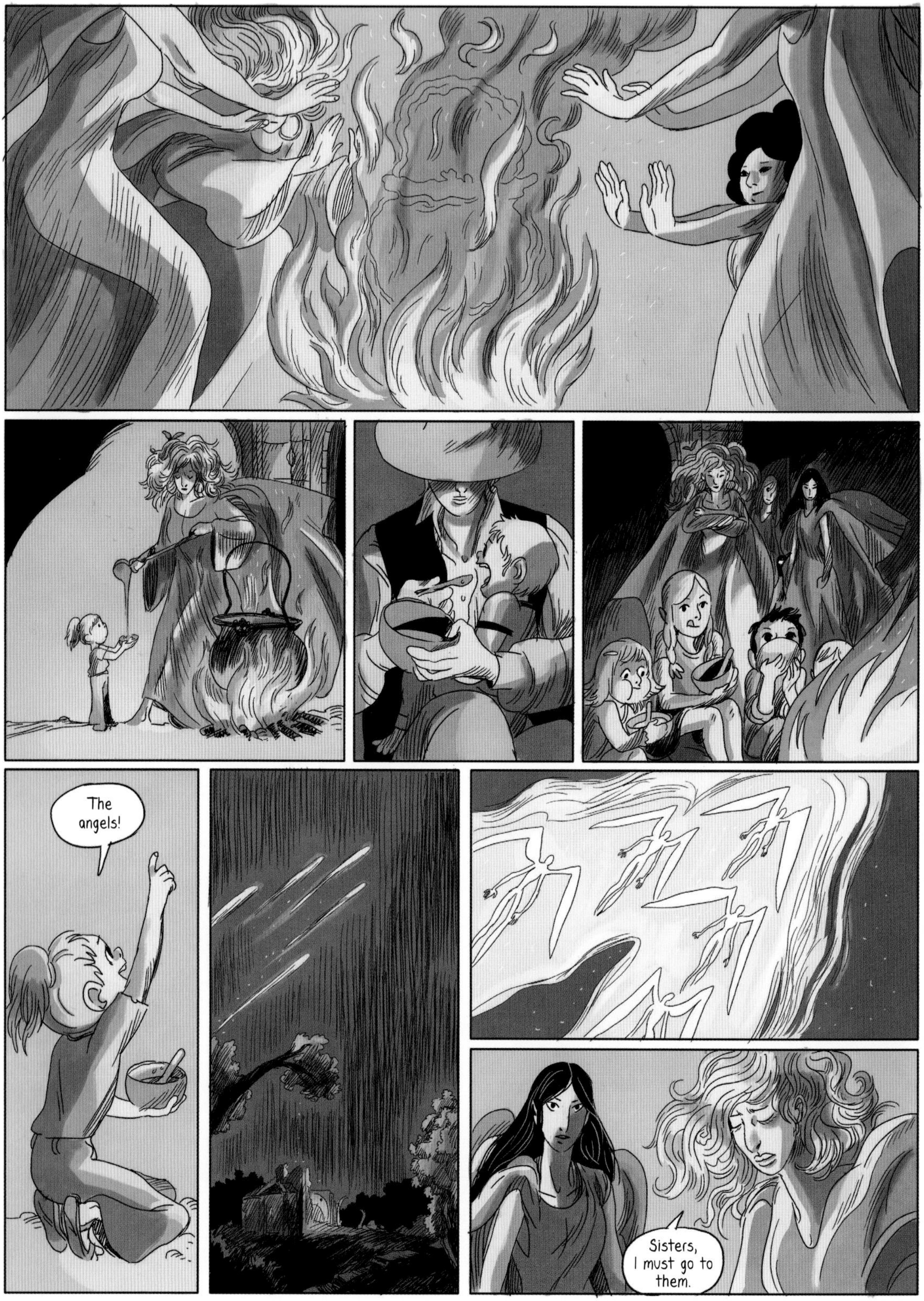

The angels!
Sisters, I must go to them.

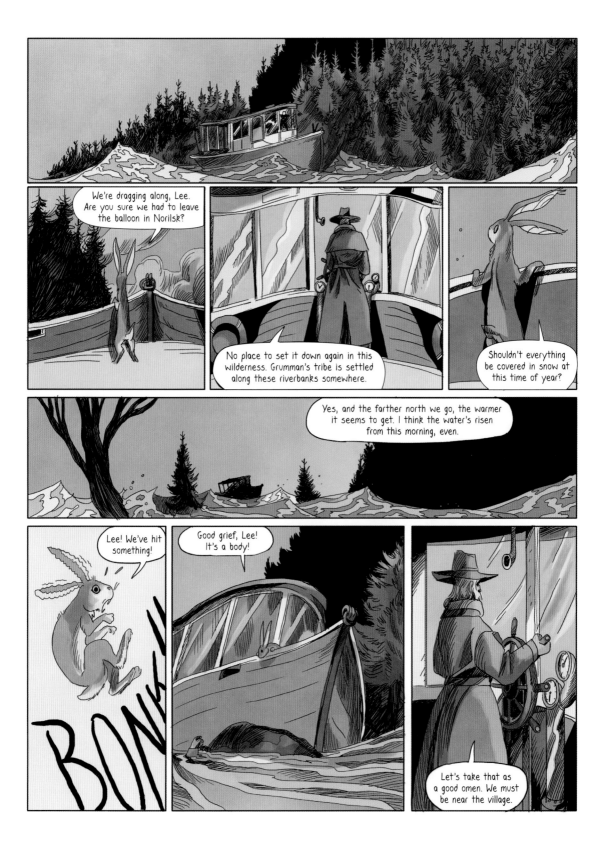

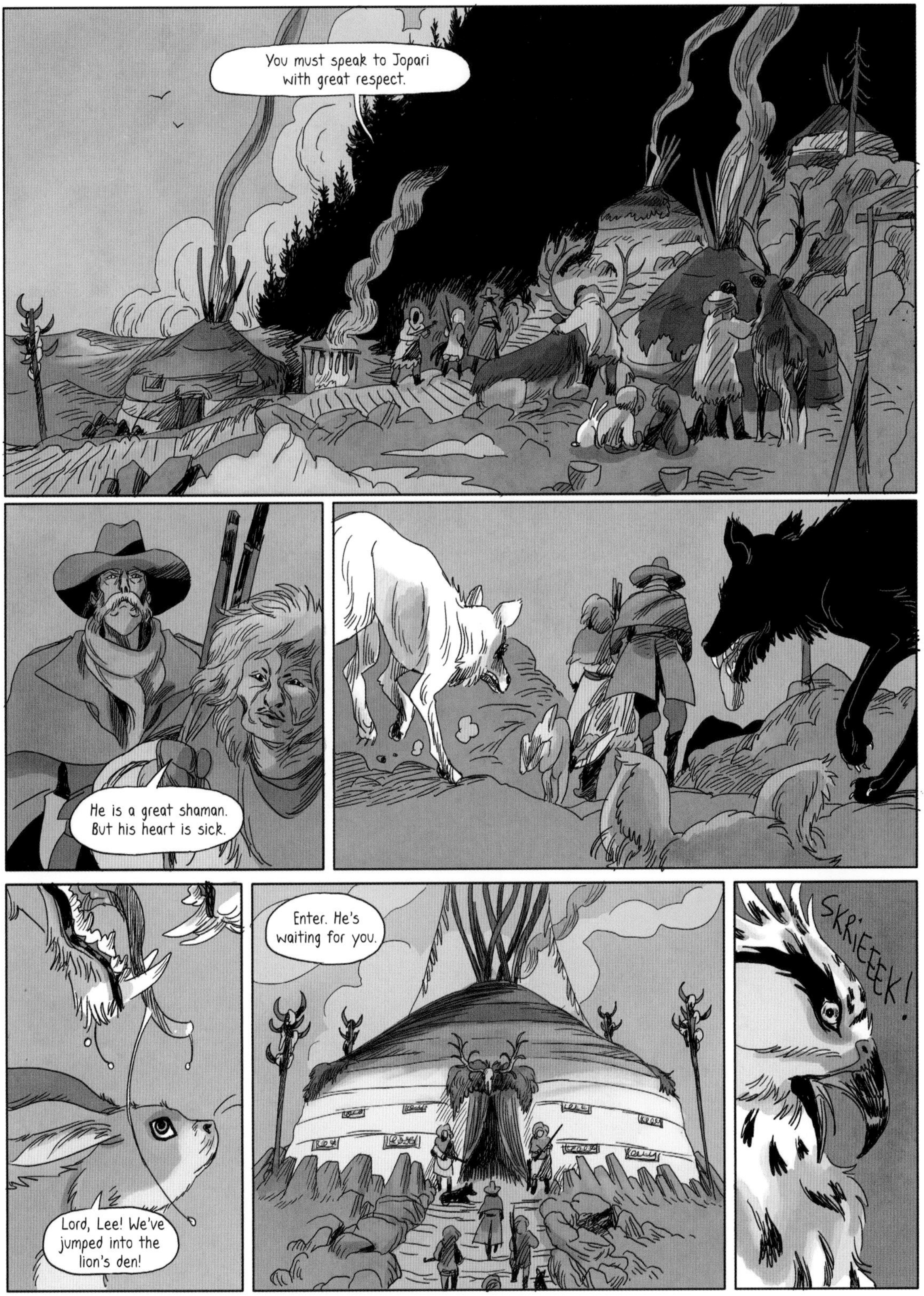
You must speak to Jopari with great respect.
He is a great shaman. But his heart is sick.
Lord, Lee! We've jumped into the lion's den!
Enter. He's waiting for you.
SKRIEEEK!

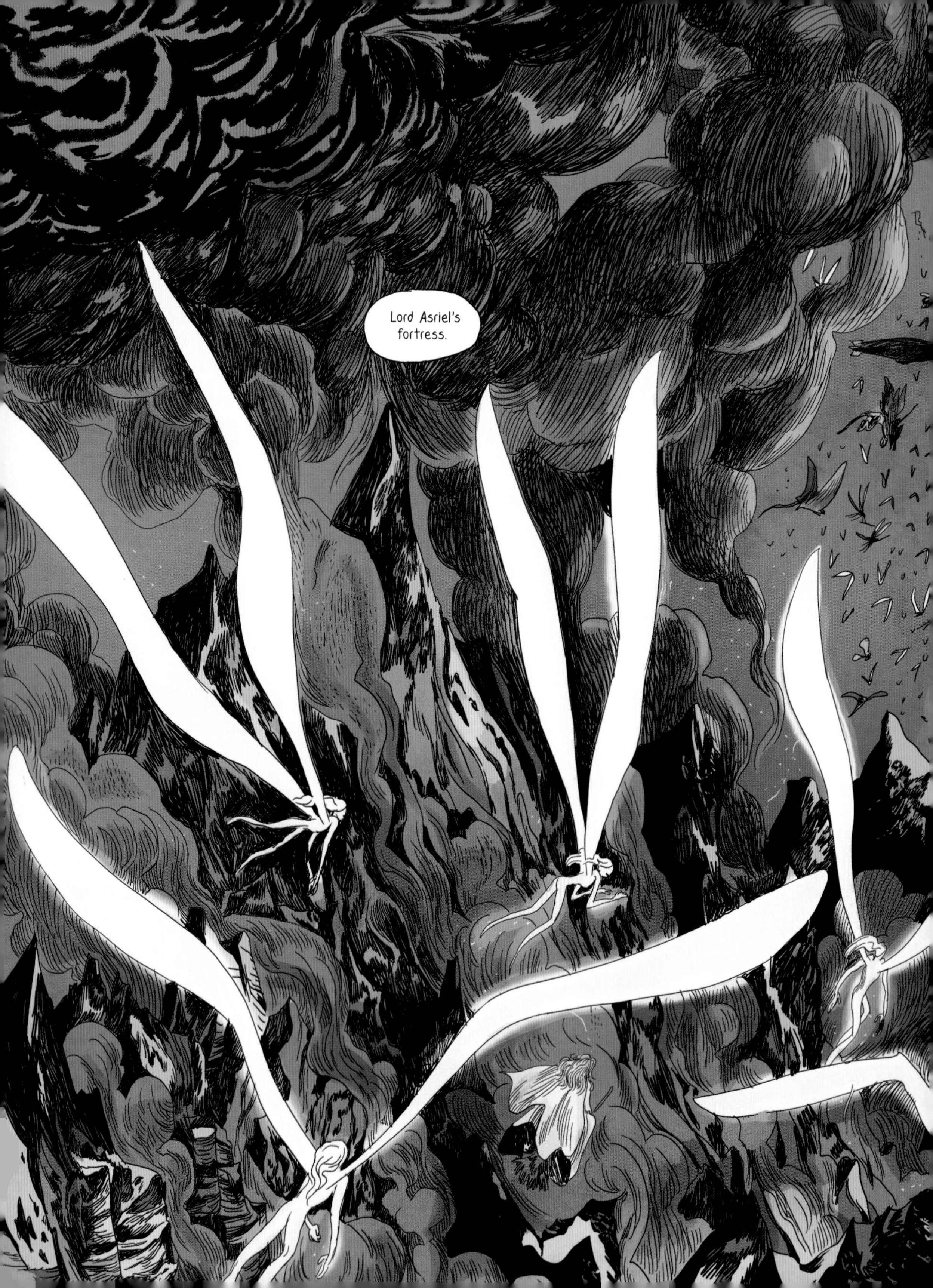
Lord Asriel's fortress.

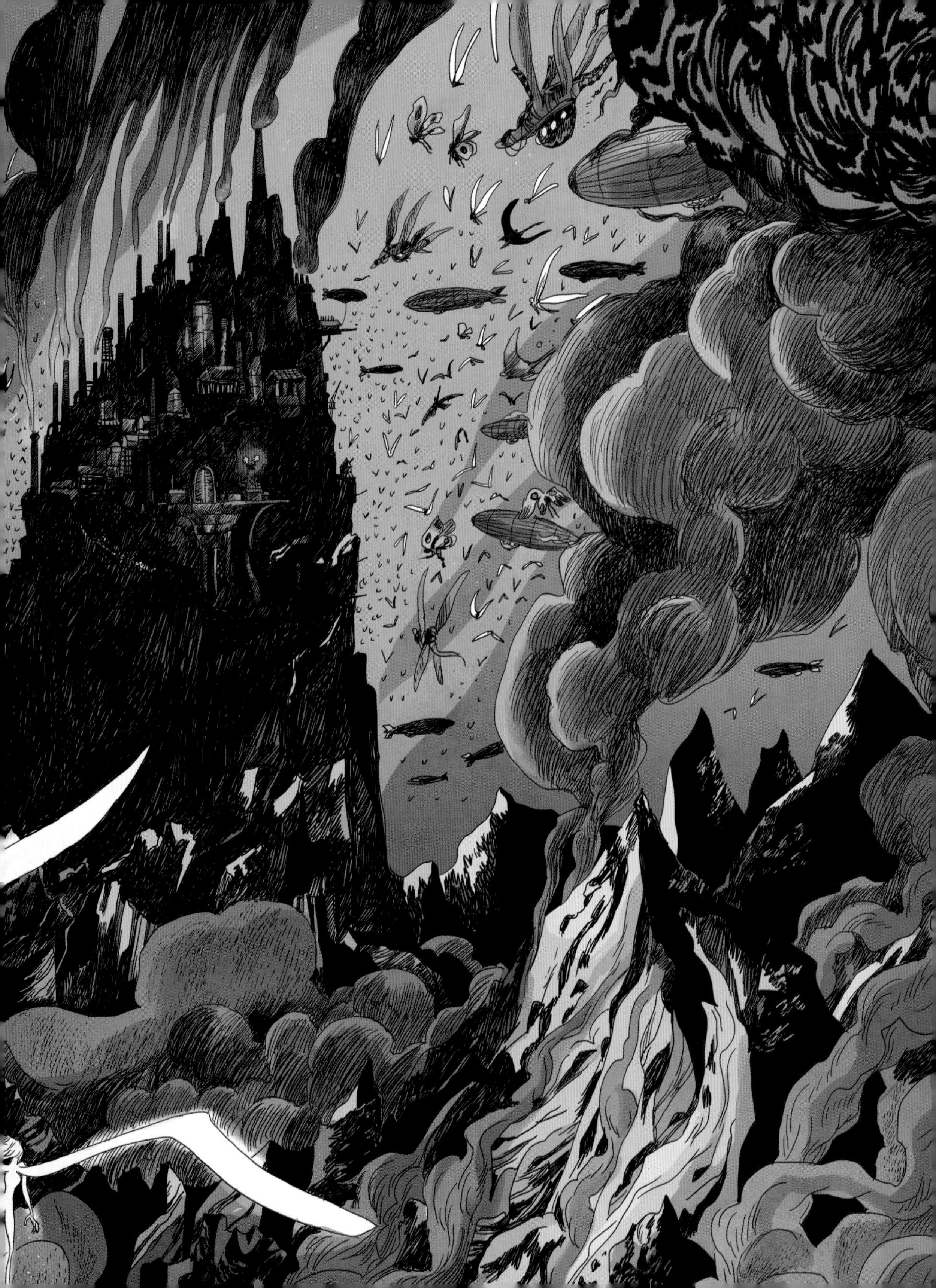

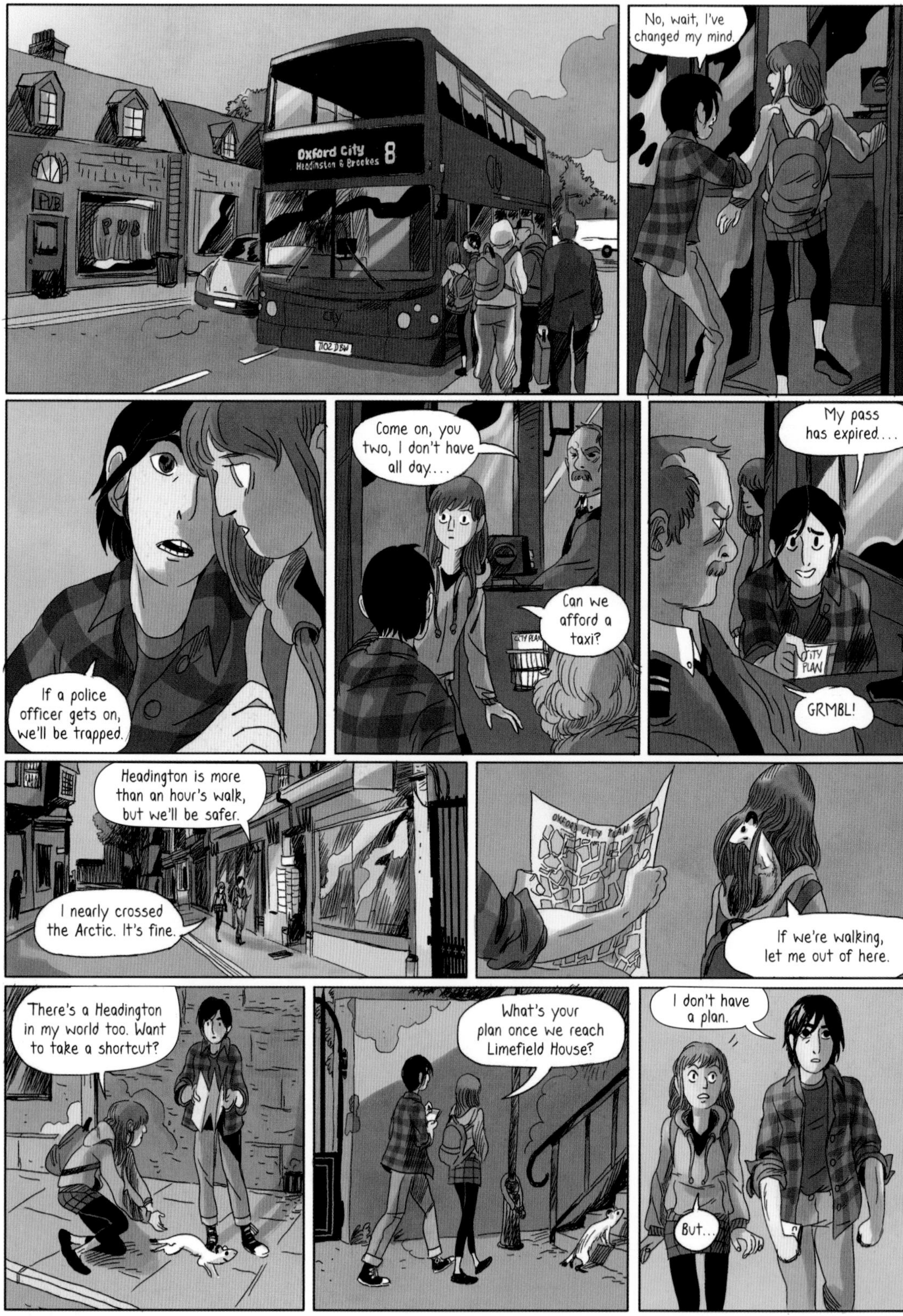
PUB
PUB
Oxford City 8
Headinston & Brookes
No, wait, I've changed my mind.
If a police officer gets on, we'll be trapped.
Come on, you two, I don't have all day...
Can we afford a taxi?
CITY PLAN
My pass has expired....
CITY PLAN
GRMBL!
Headington is more than an hour's walk, but we'll be safer.
I nearly crossed the Arctic. It's fine.
OXFORD CITY PLAN
If we're walking, let me out of here.
There's a Headington in my world too. Want to take a shortcut?
What's your plan once we reach Limefield House?
I don't have a plan.
But...

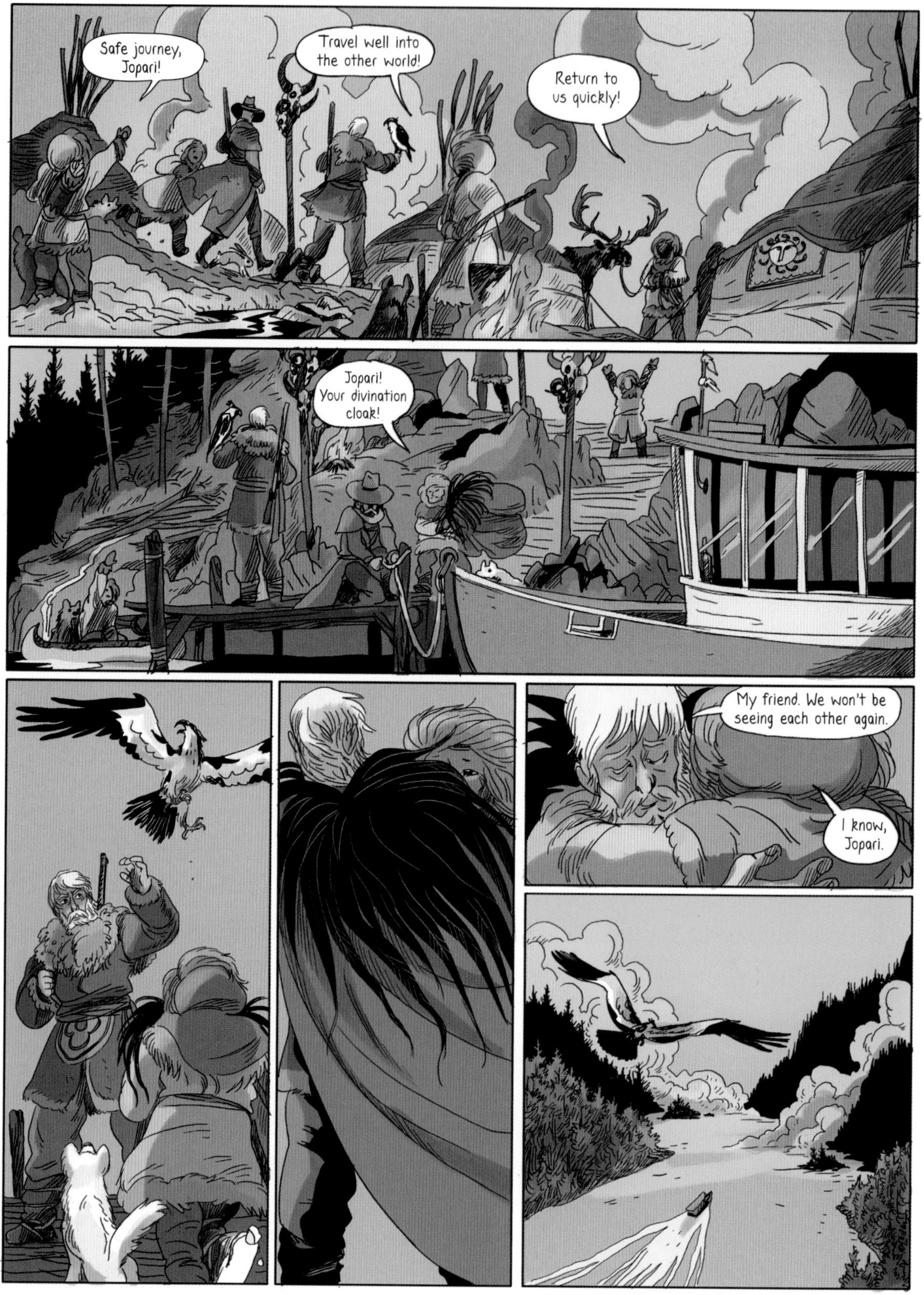
Safe journey, Jopari!
Travel well into the other world!
Return to us quickly!
Jopari! Your divination cloak!
My friend. We won't be seeing each other again.
I know, Jopari.

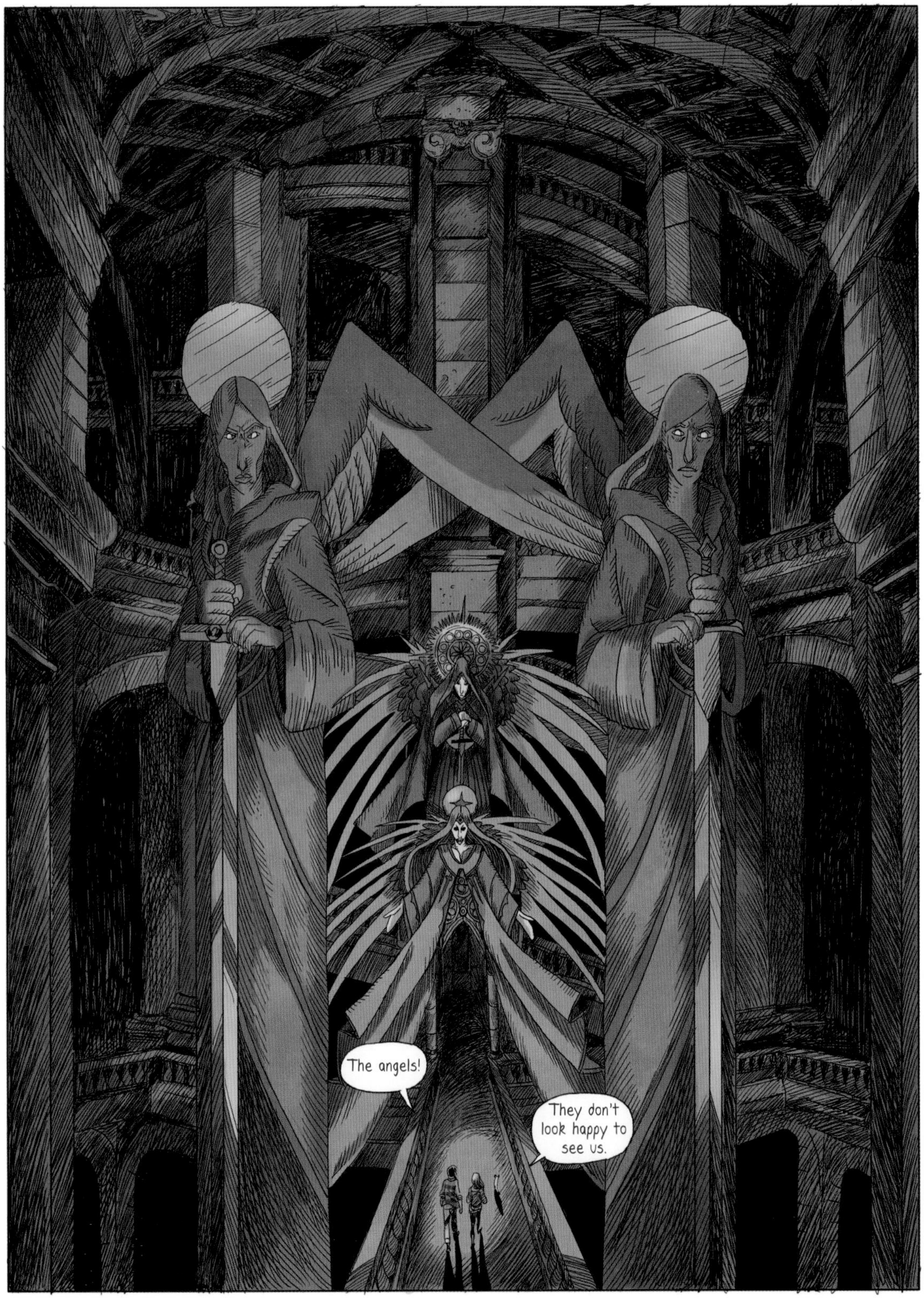
The angels!
They don't look happy to see us.

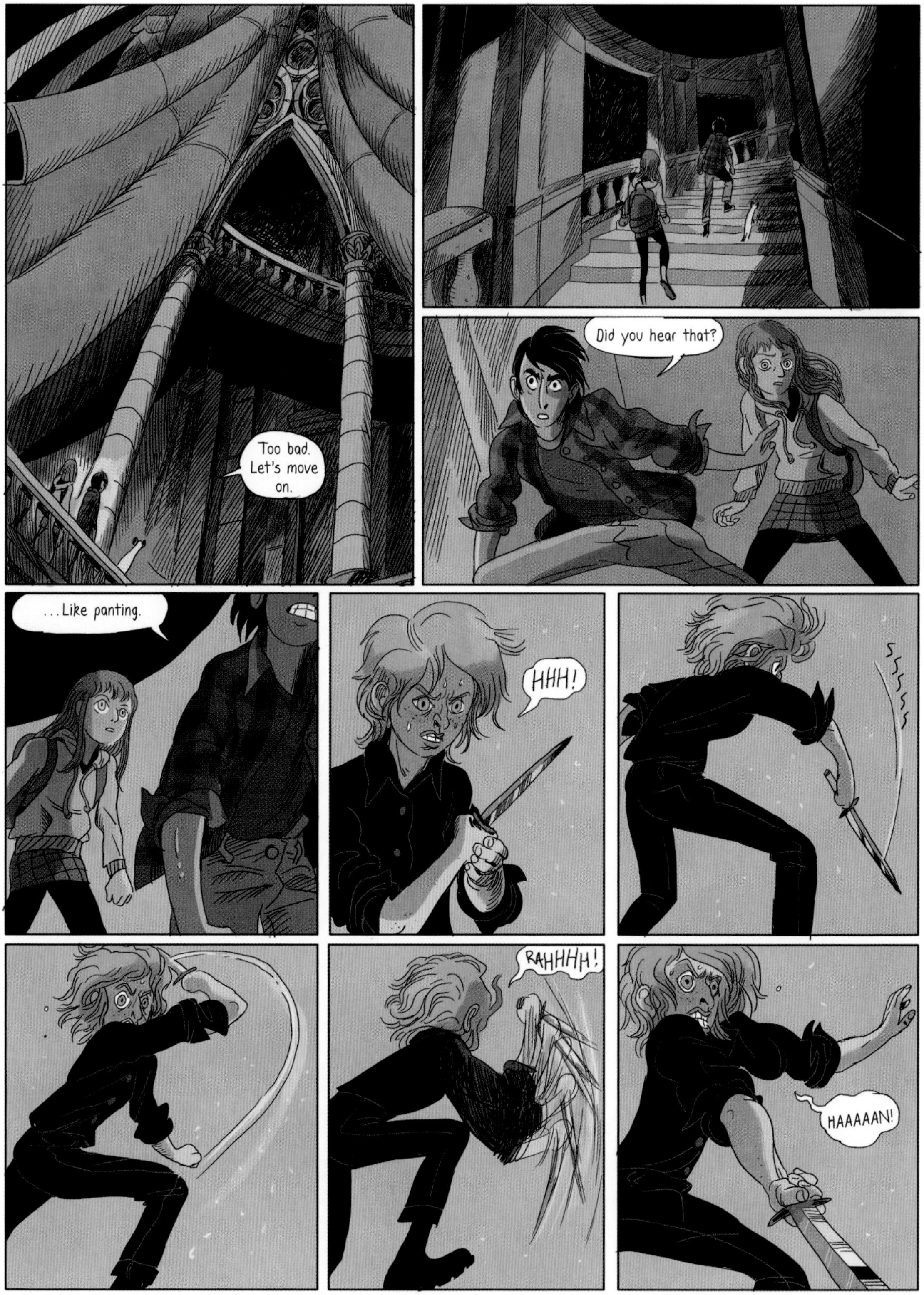
Too bad. Let's move on.
Did you hear that?
...Like panting.
HHH!
SSSSS
RAHHHH!
HAAAAAN!

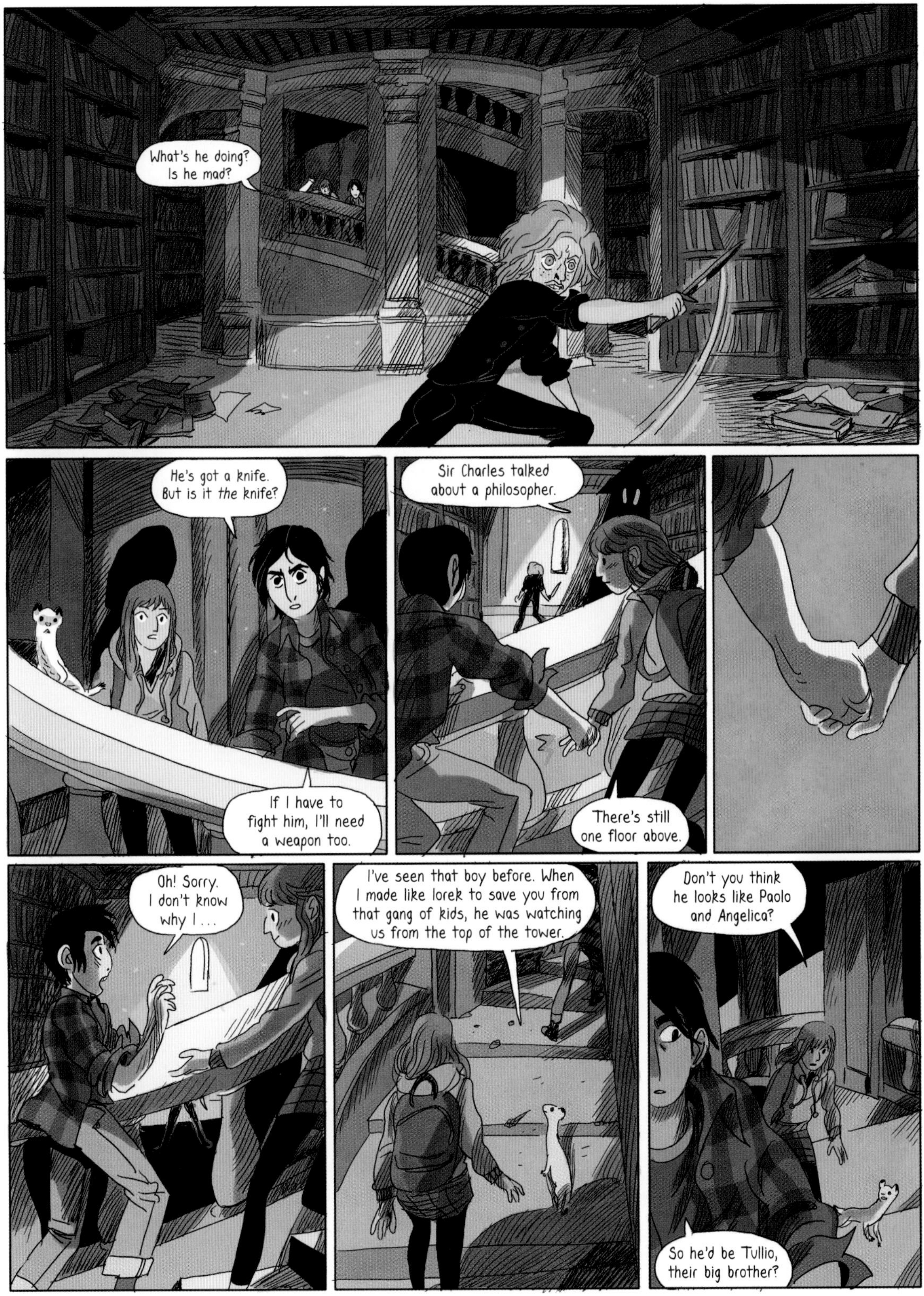
What's he doing? Is he mad?
He's got a knife. But is it *the* knife?
If I have to fight him, I'll need a weapon too.
Sir Charles talked about a philosopher.
There's still one floor above.
Oh! Sorry. I don't know why I . . .
I've seen that boy before. When I made like Iorek to save you from that gang of kids, he was watching us from the top of the tower.
Don't you think he looks like Paolo and Angelica?
So he'd be Tullio, their big brother?

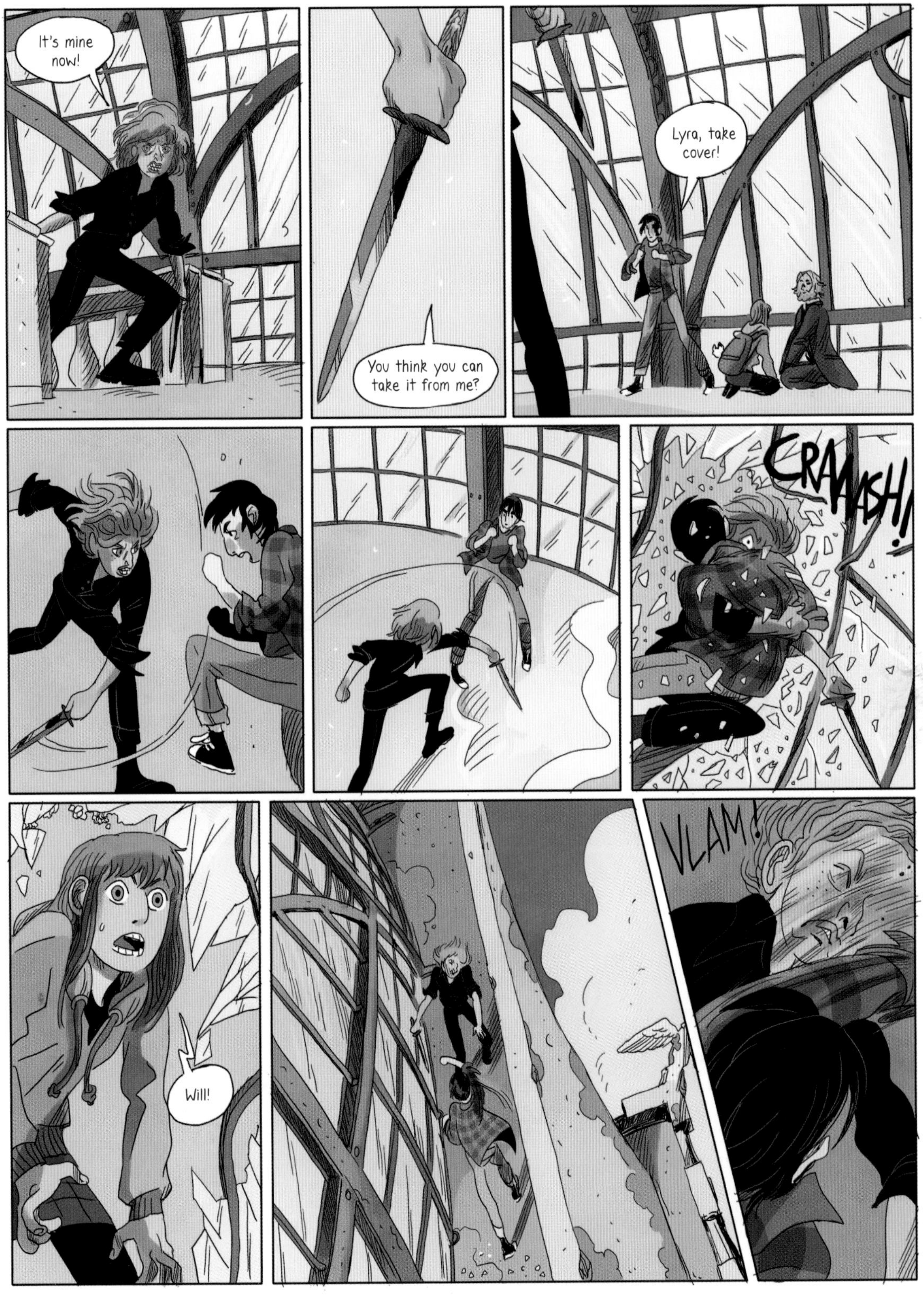
It's mine now!
You think you can take it from me?
Lyra, take cover!
CRAAASH!
Will!
VLAM!

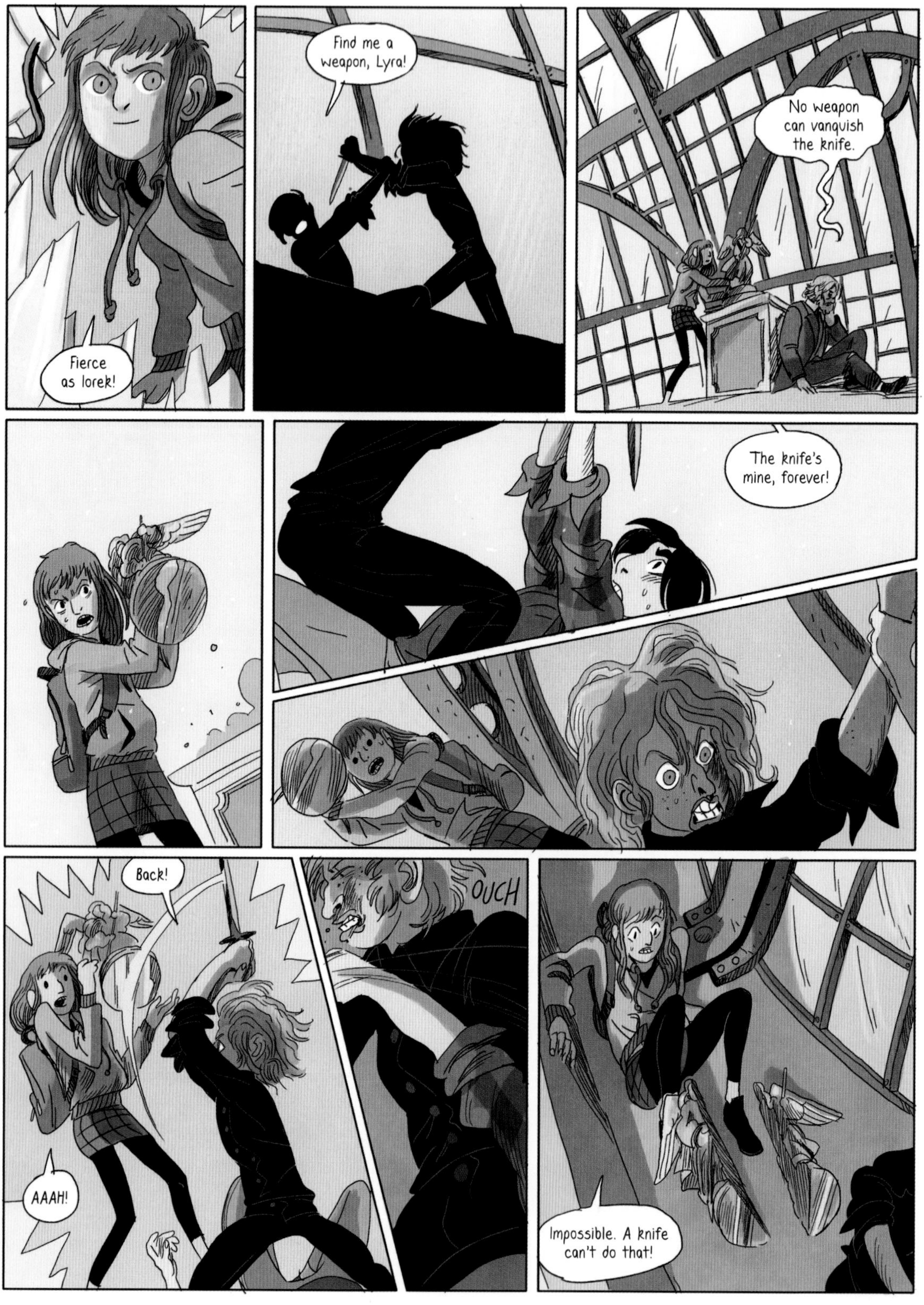
Fierce as Iorek!
Find me a weapon, Lyra!
No weapon can vanquish the knife.
The knife's mine, forever!
Back!
AAAH!
OUCH
Impossible. A knife can't do that!

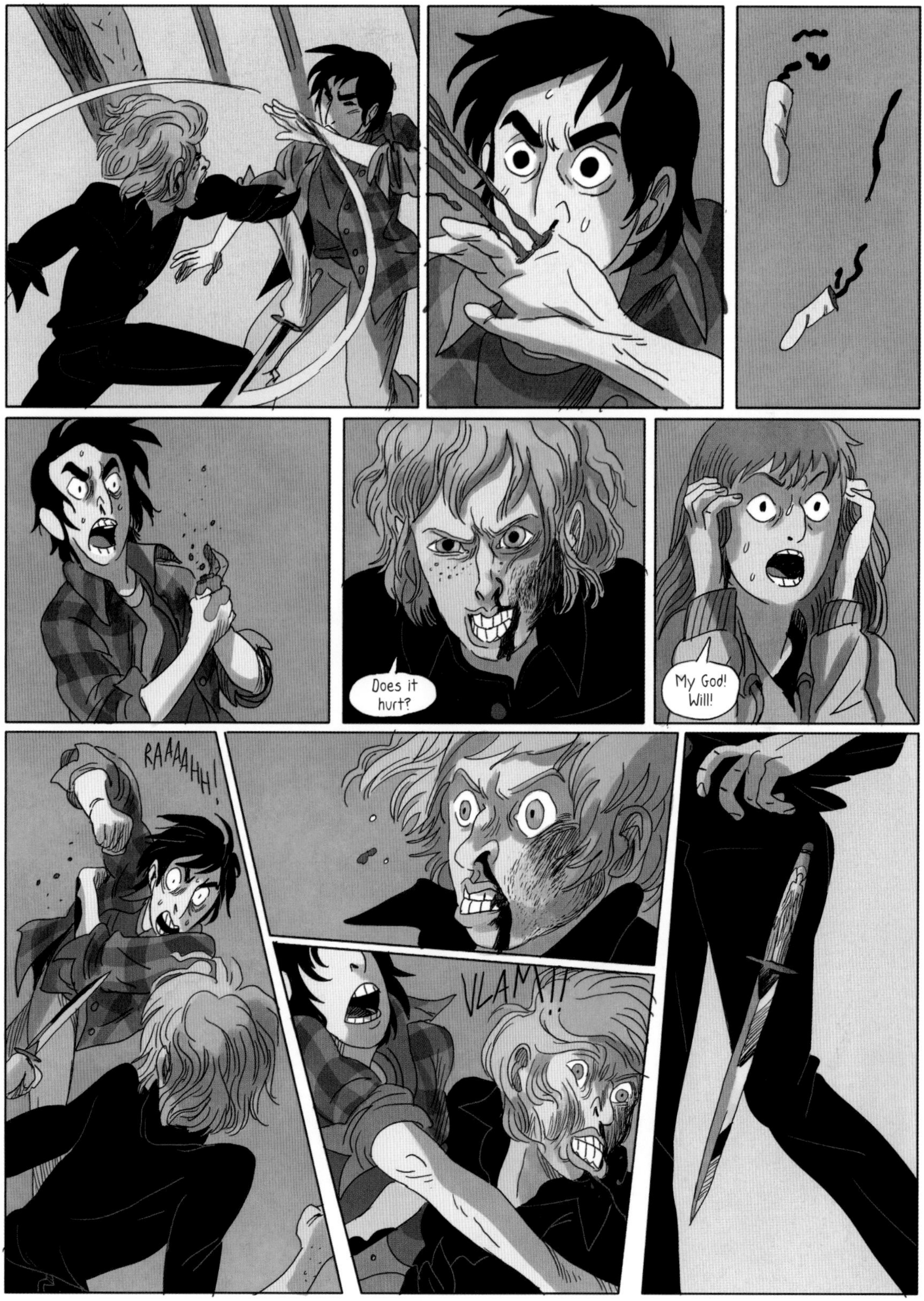
Does it hurt?
My God! Will!
RAAAAHH!
VLAM!!

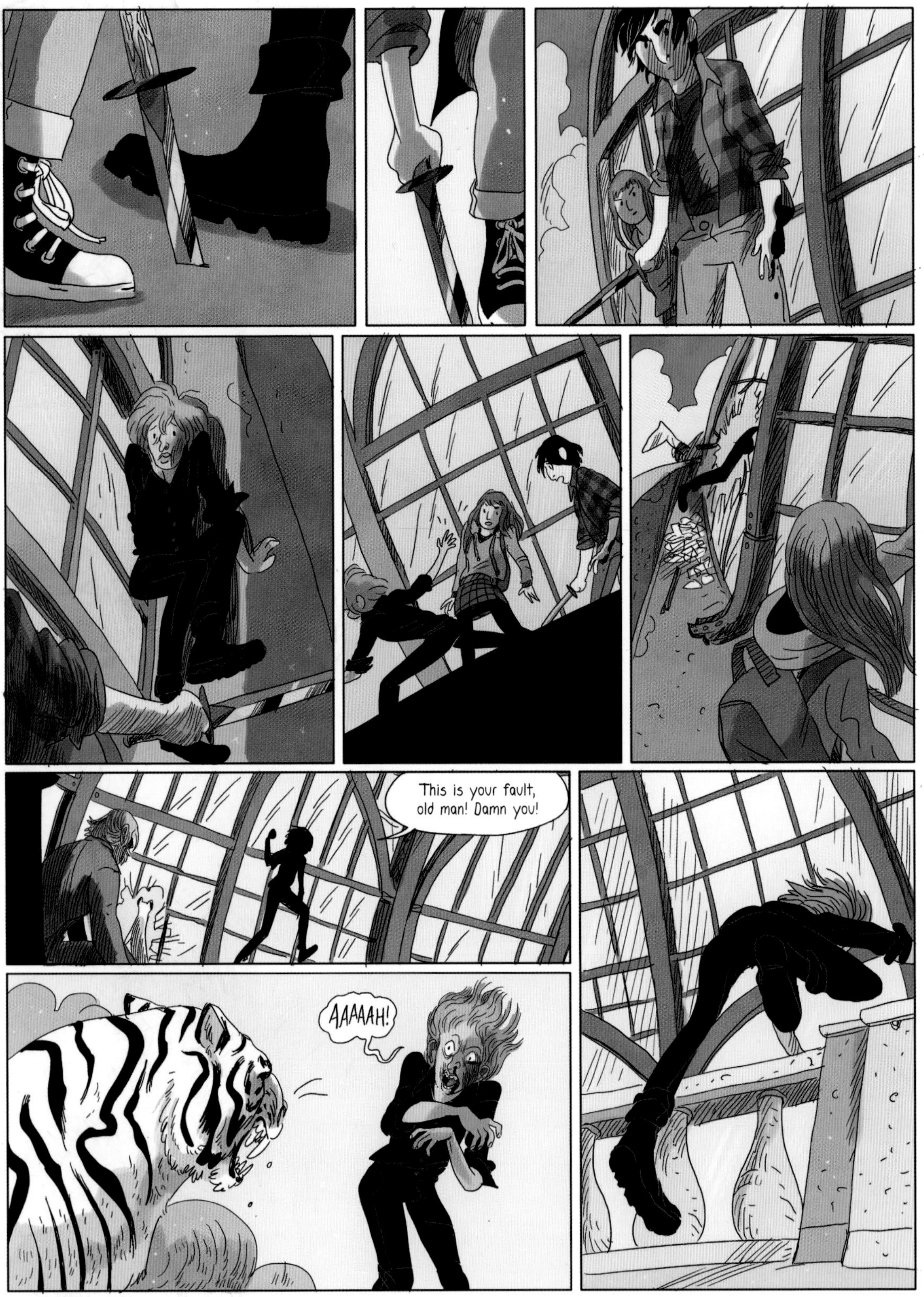
This is your fault, old man! Damn you!
AAAAAH!

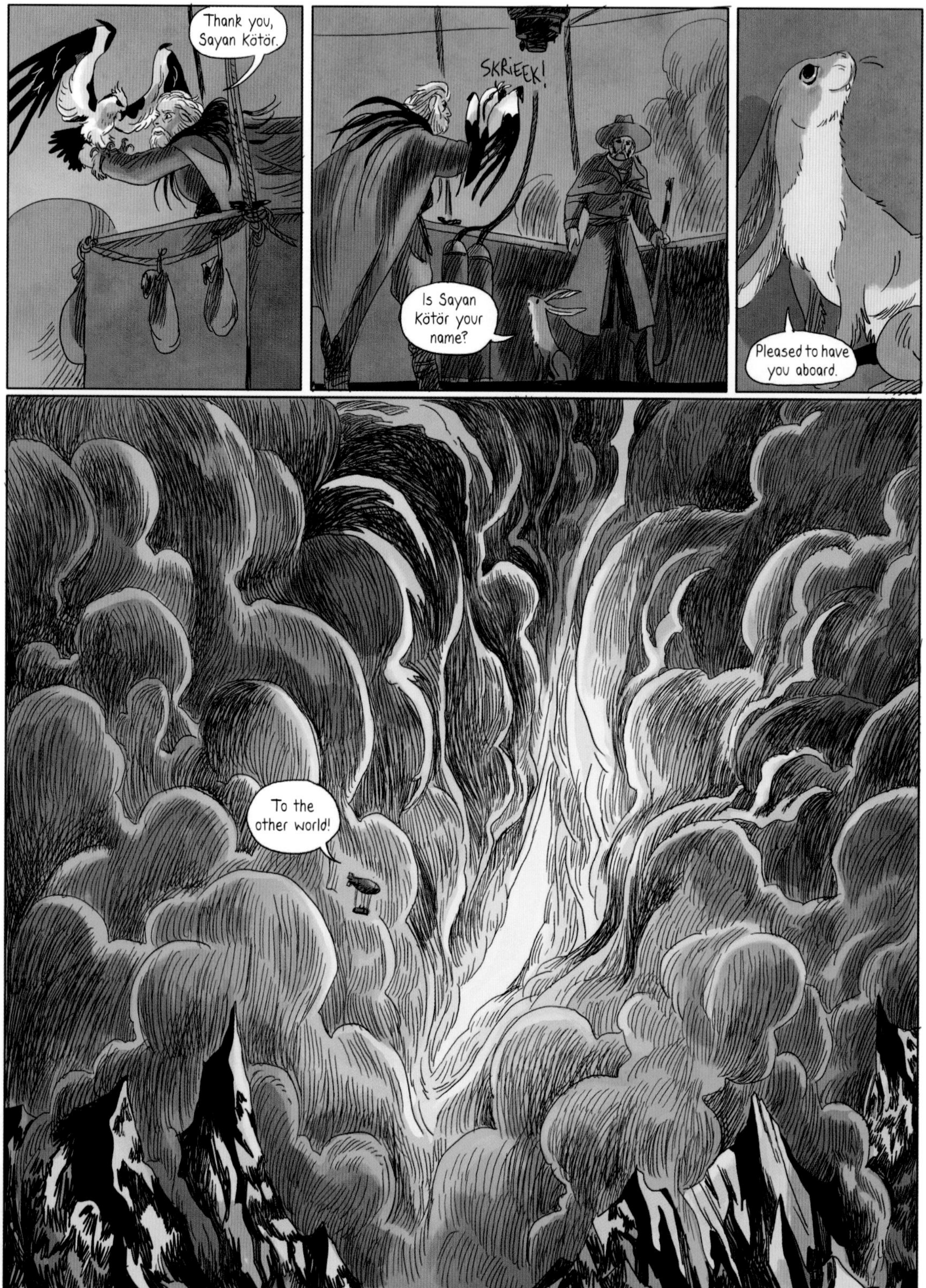
Thank you, Sayan Kötör.
SKRIEEK!
Is Sayan Kötör your name?
Pleased to have you aboard.
To the other world!

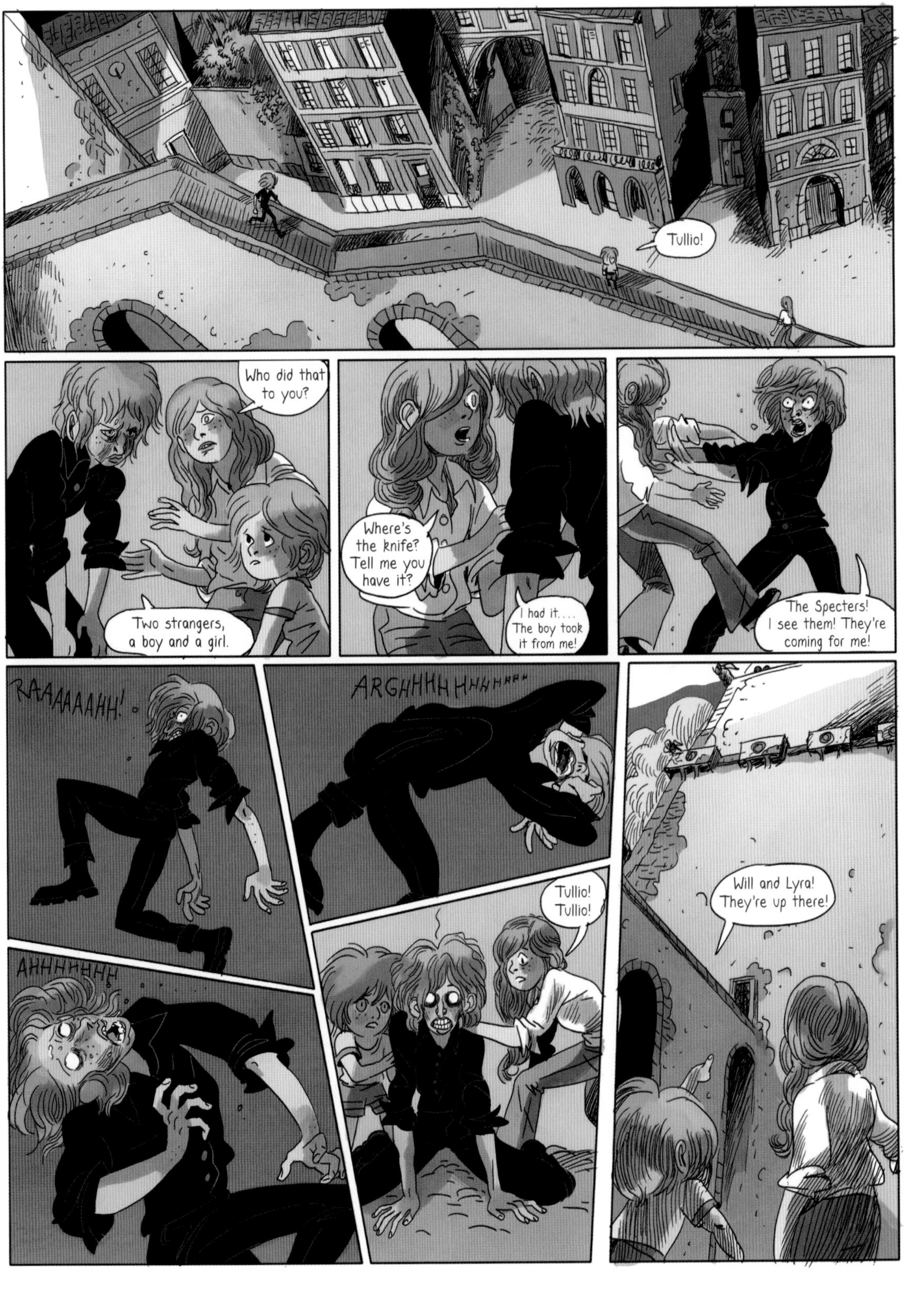
Tullio!
Who did that to you?
Two strangers, a boy and a girl.
Where's the knife? Tell me you have it?
I had it. . . . The boy took it from me!
The Specters! I see them! They're coming for me!
RAAAAAAHH!
ARGHHHHHhhhhh
AHHHHHHH
Tullio! Tullio!
Will and Lyra! They're up there!

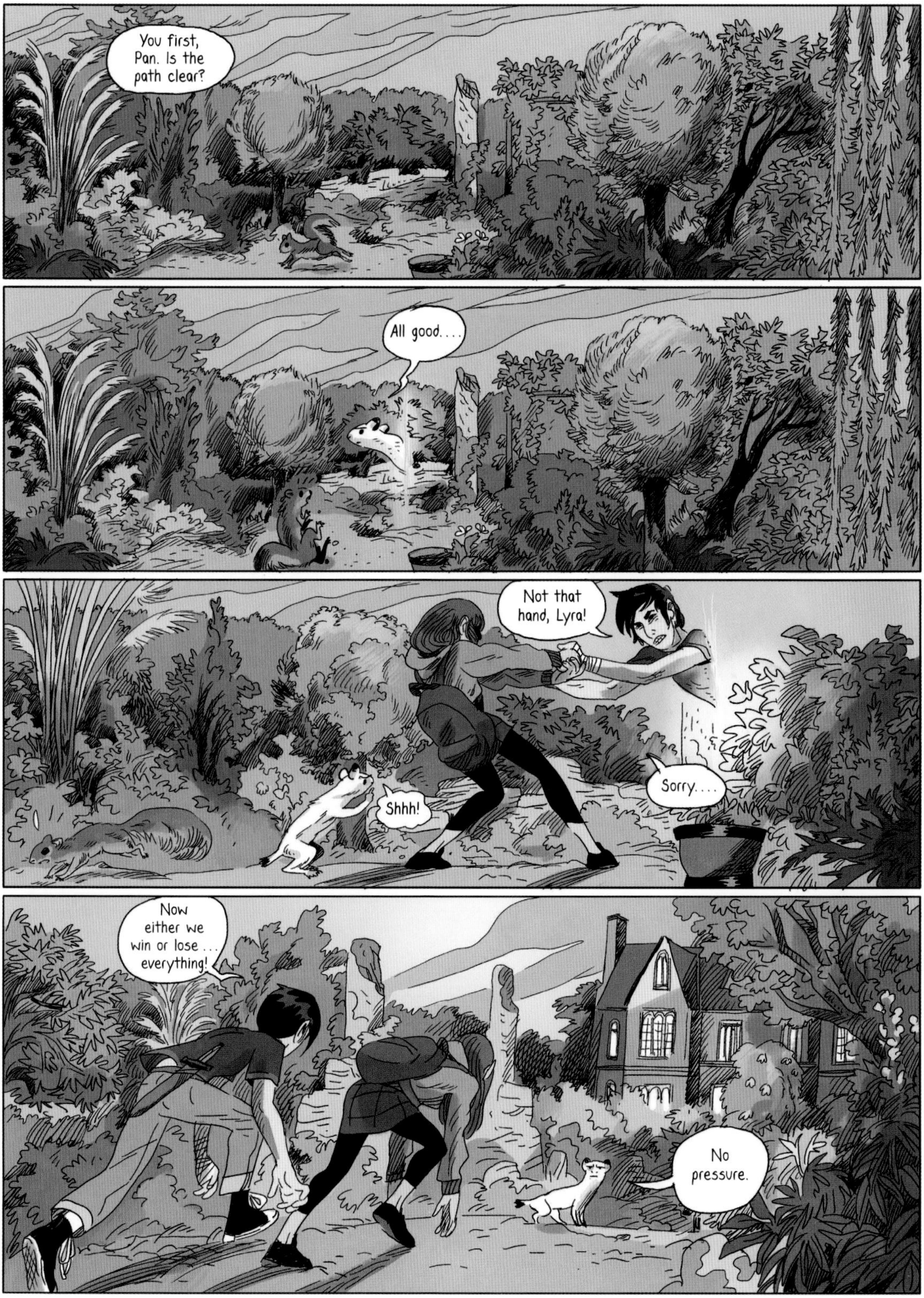
You first, Pan. Is the path clear?
All good. . . .
Not that hand, Lyra!
Shhh!
Sorry. . . .
Now either we win or lose . . . everything!
No pressure.

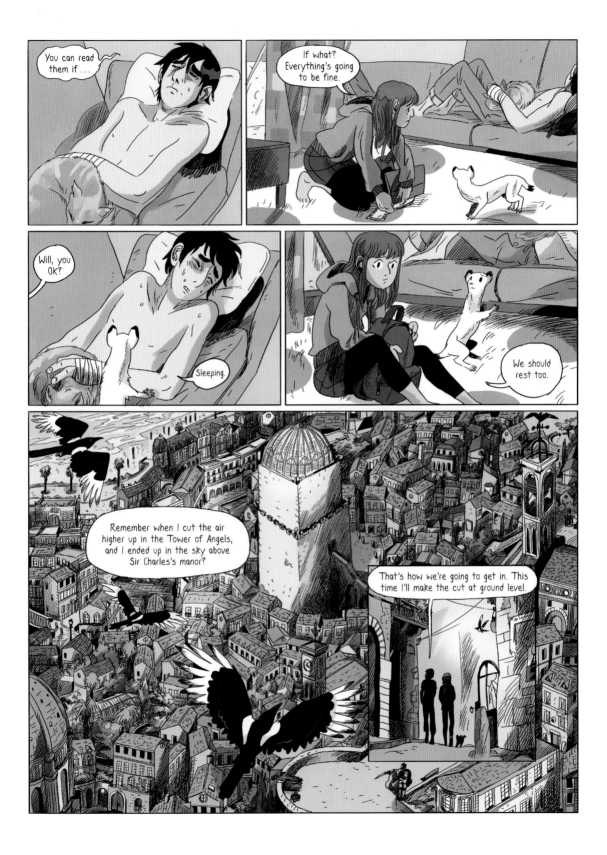

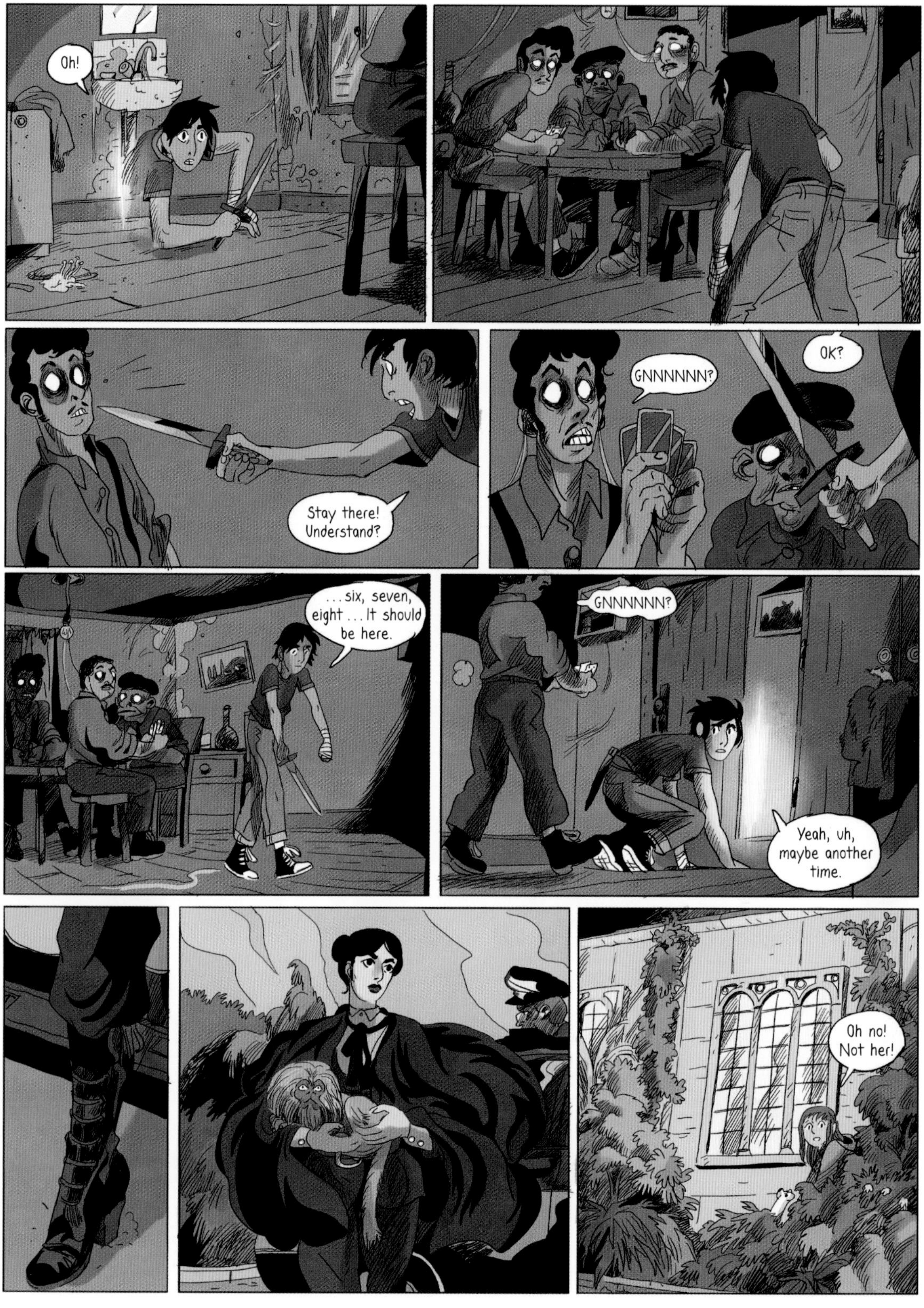
Oh!
GNNNNNN?
OK?
Stay there! Understand?
. . . six, seven, eight . . . It should be here.
GNNNNNN?
Yeah, uh, maybe another time.
Oh no! Not her!

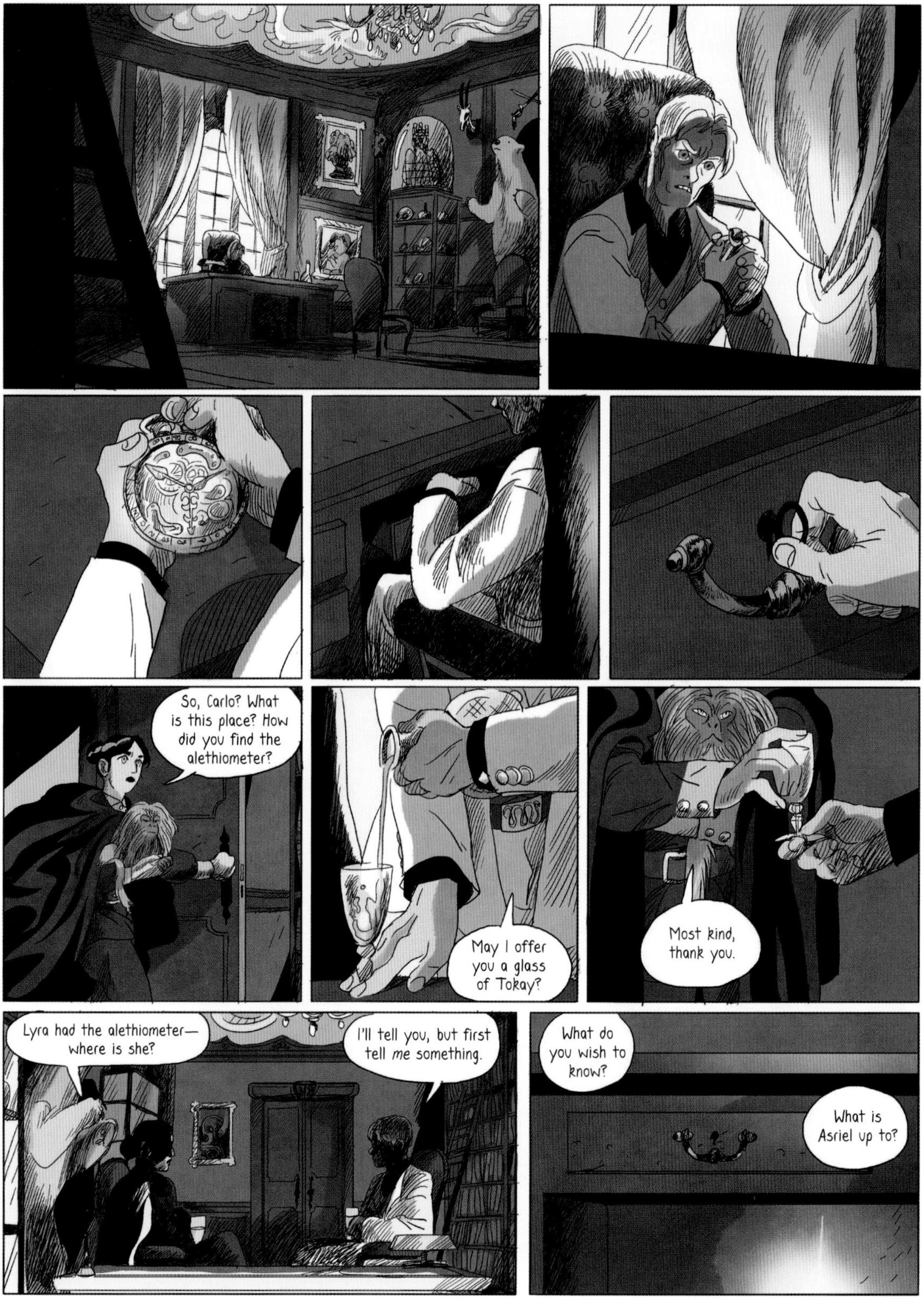
So, Carlo? What is this place? How did you find the alethiometer?
May I offer you a glass of Tokay?
Most kind, thank you.
Lyra had the alethiometer— where is she?
I'll tell you, but first tell *me* something.
What do you wish to know?
What is Asriel up to?

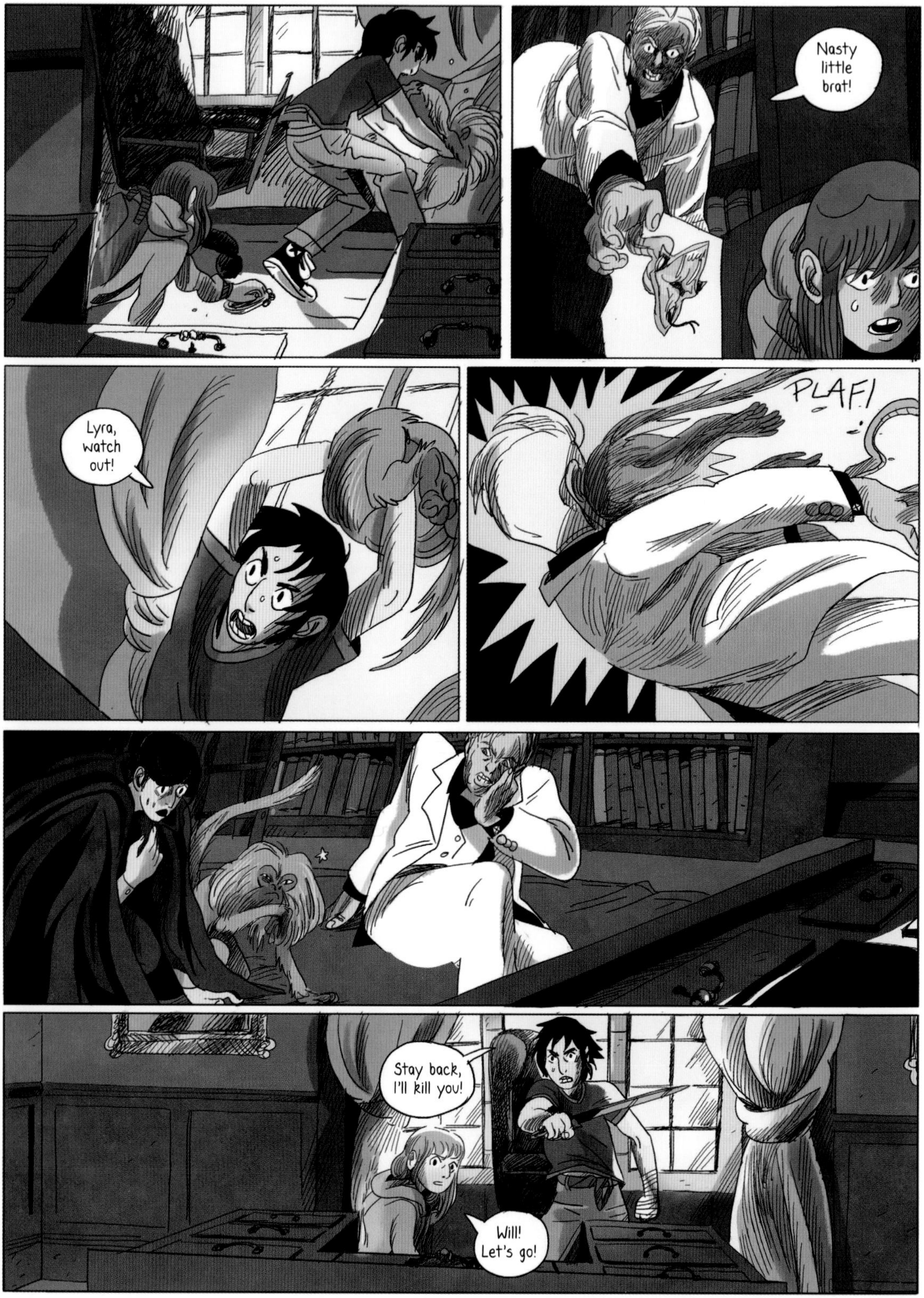
Nasty little brat!
Lyra, watch out!
PLAF!
Stay back, I'll kill you!
Will! Let's go!

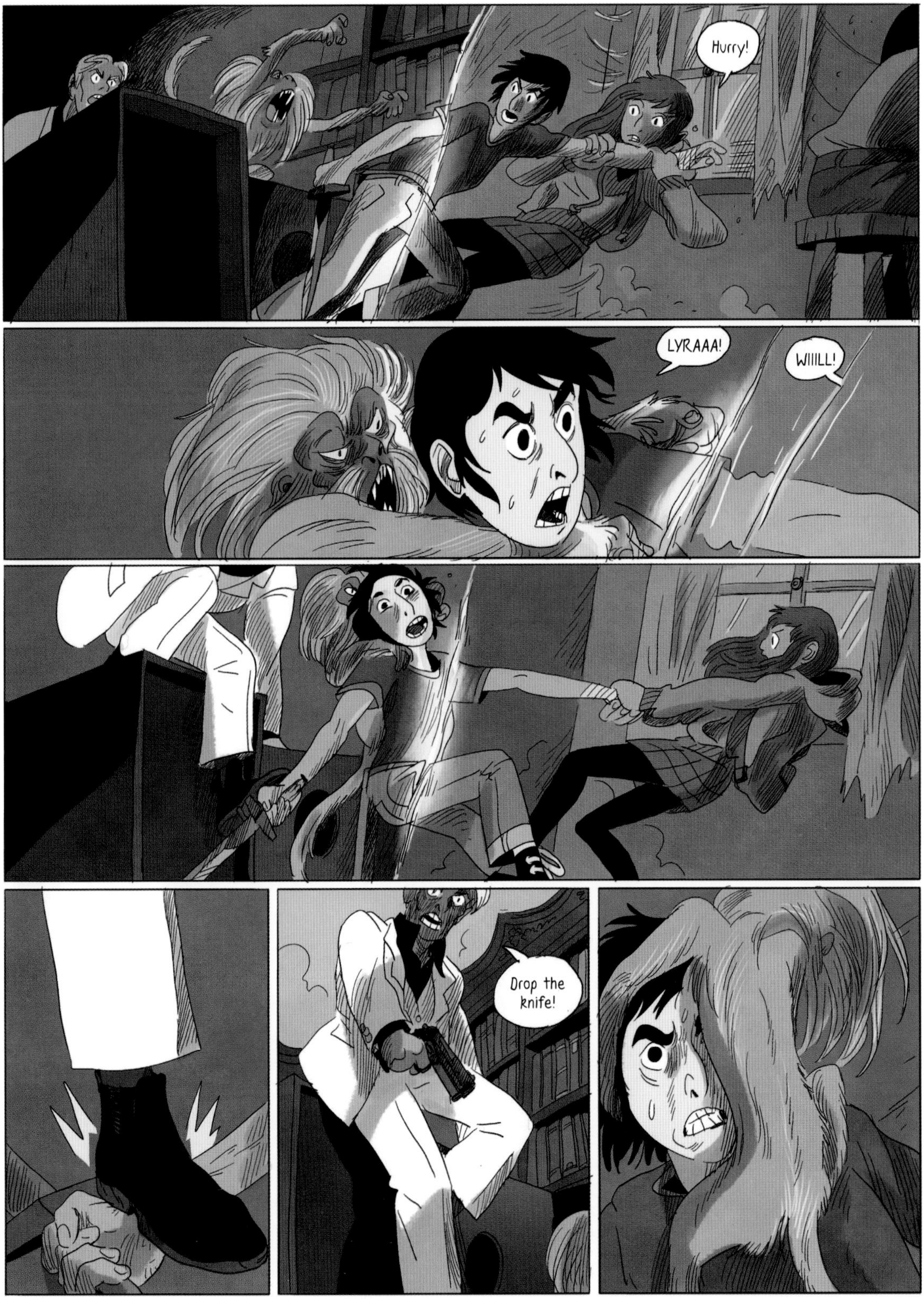
Hurry!
LYRAAA!
WIIILL!
Drop the knife!

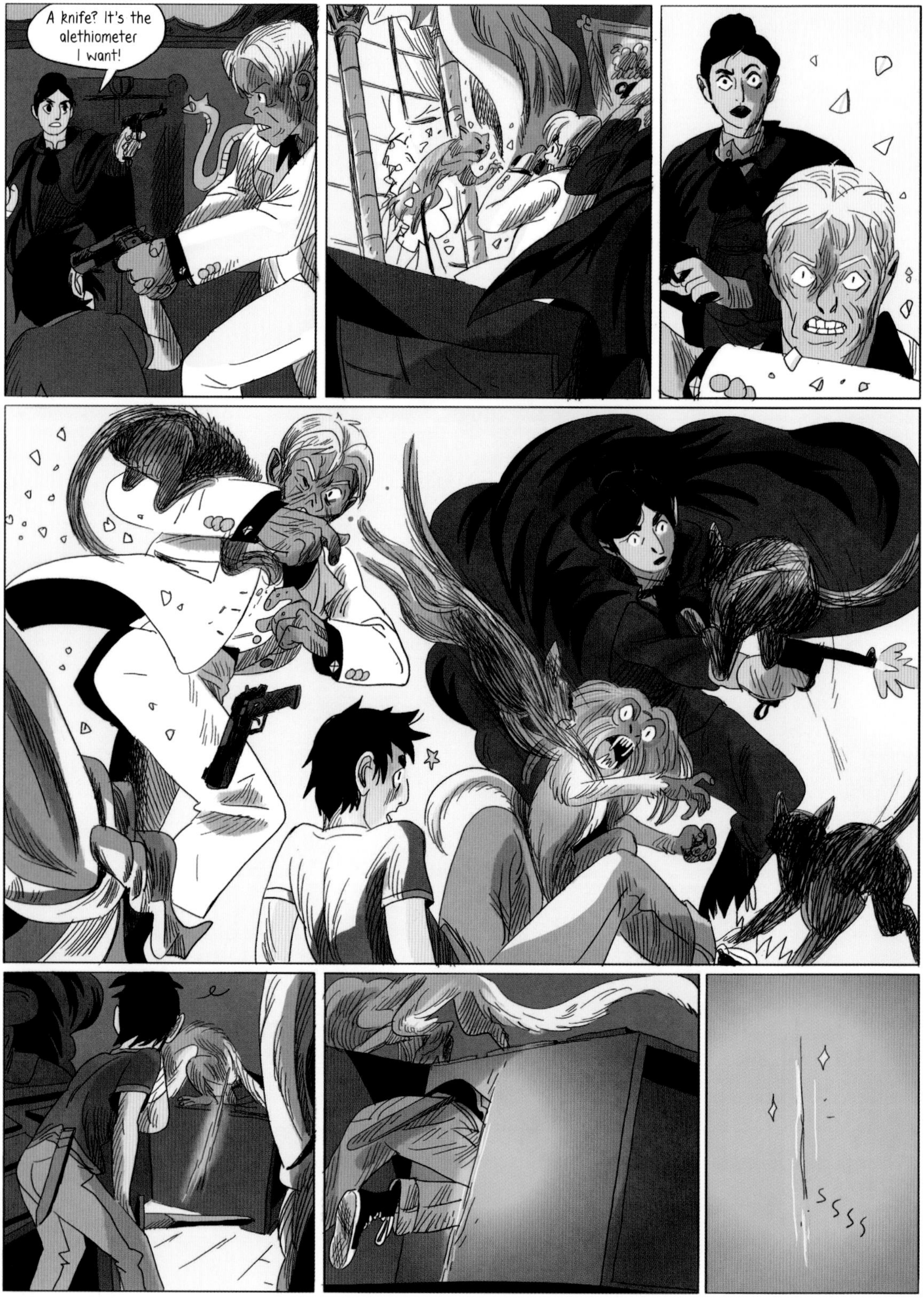
A knife? It's the alethiometer I want!
SSSS

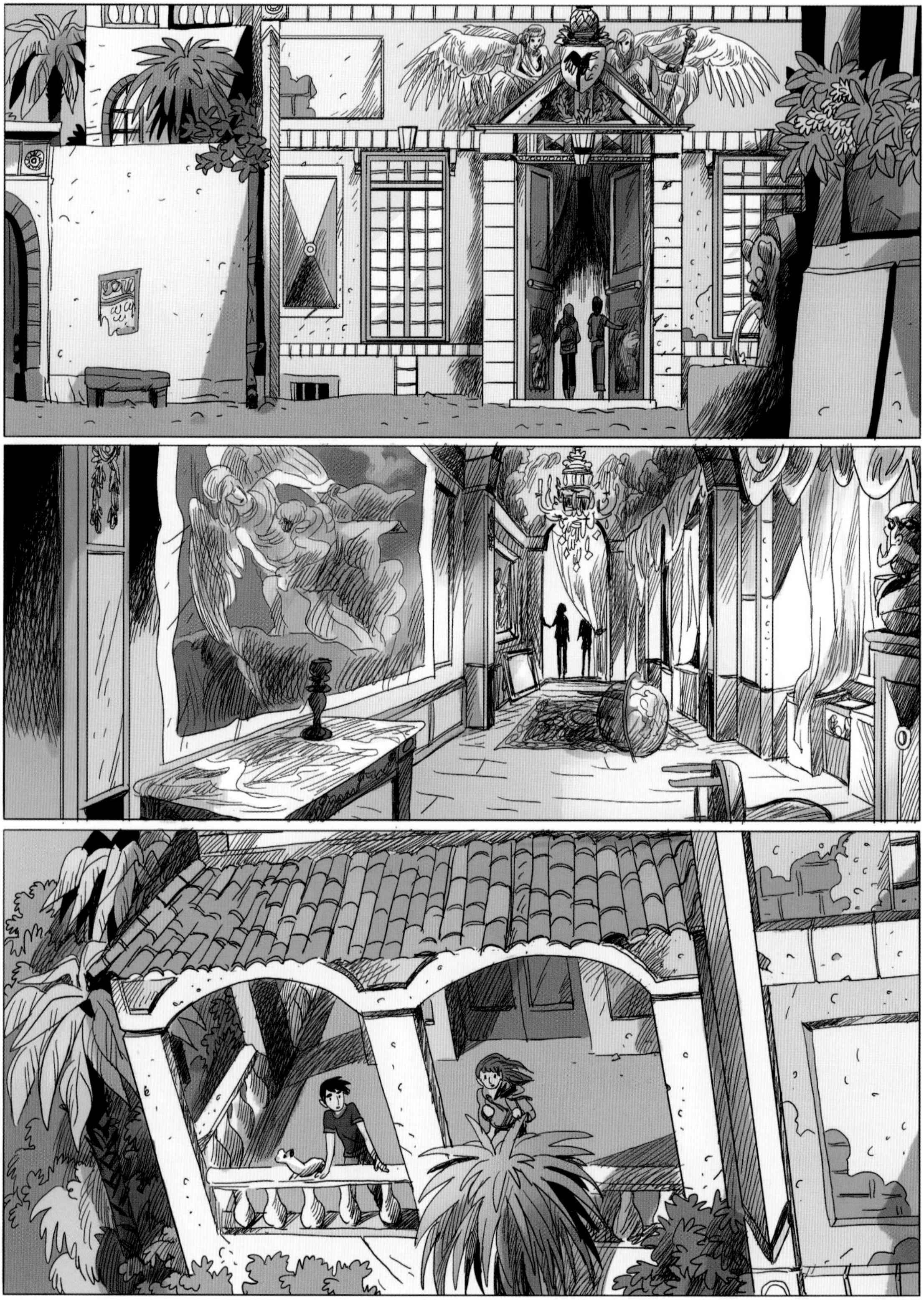

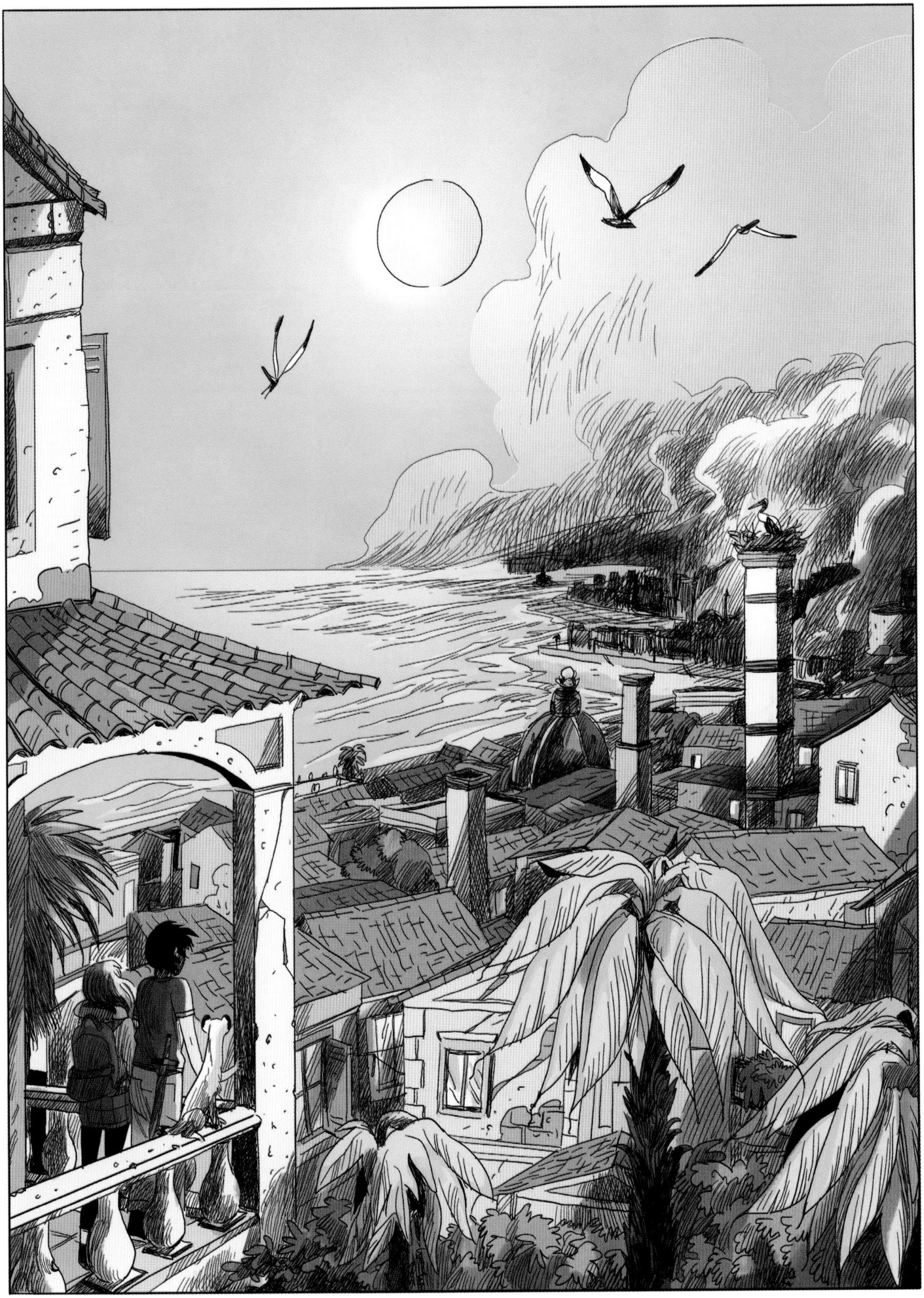

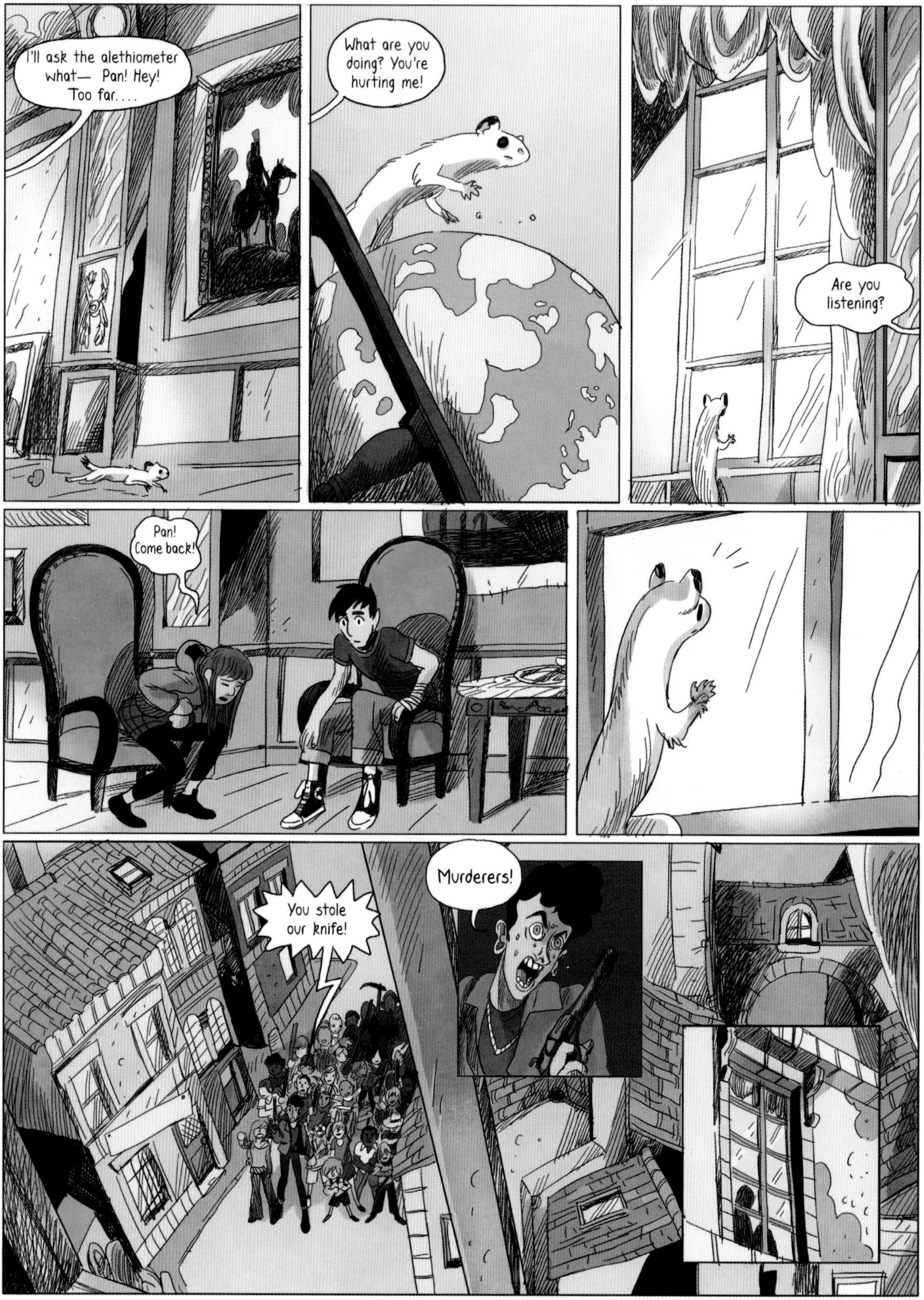
I'll ask the alethiometer what— Pan! Hey! Too far. . . .
What are you doing? You're hurting me!
Are you listening?
Pan! Come back!
You stole our knife!
Murderers!

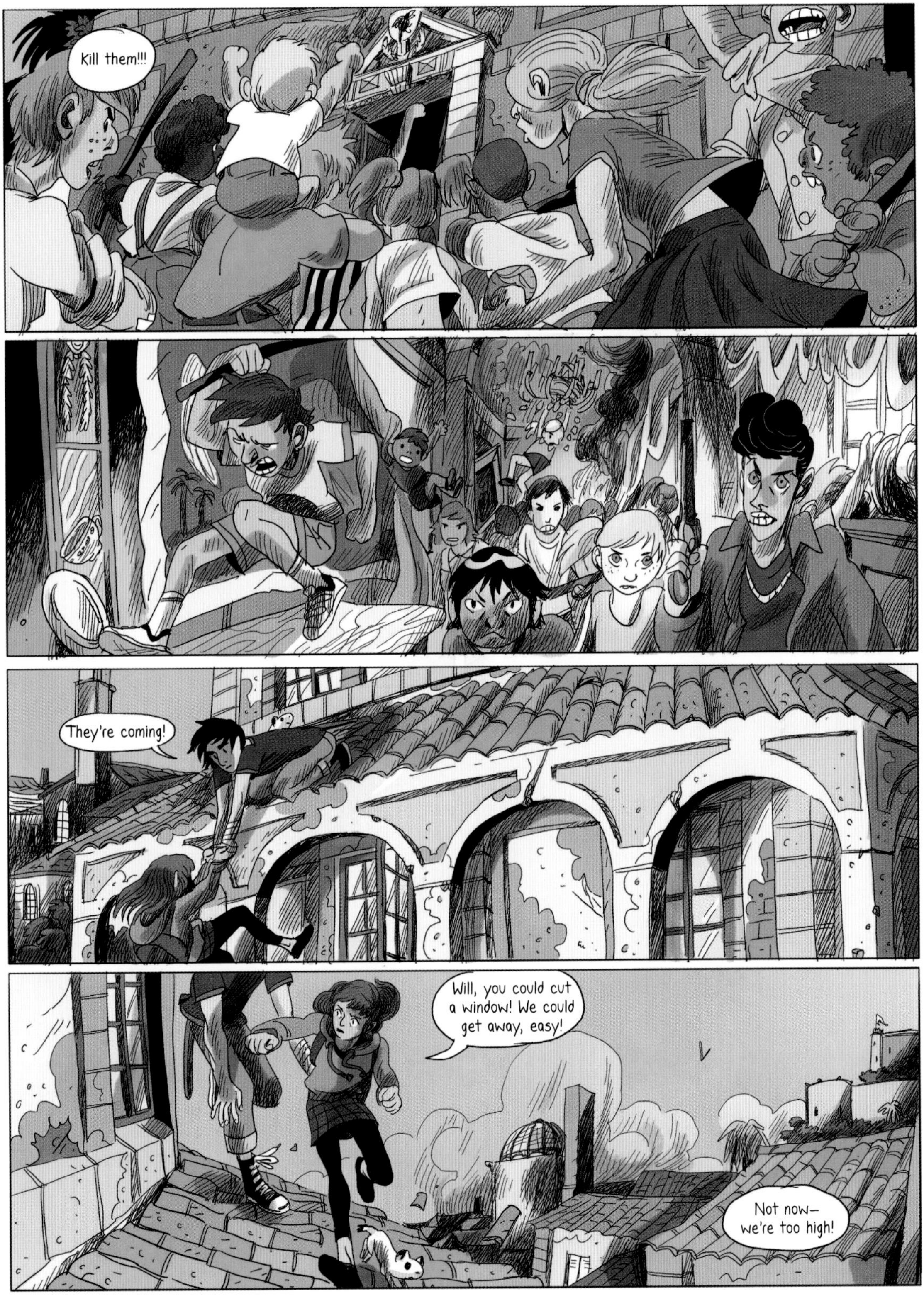
Kill them!!!
They're coming!
Will, you could cut a window! We could get away, easy!
Not now—we're too high!

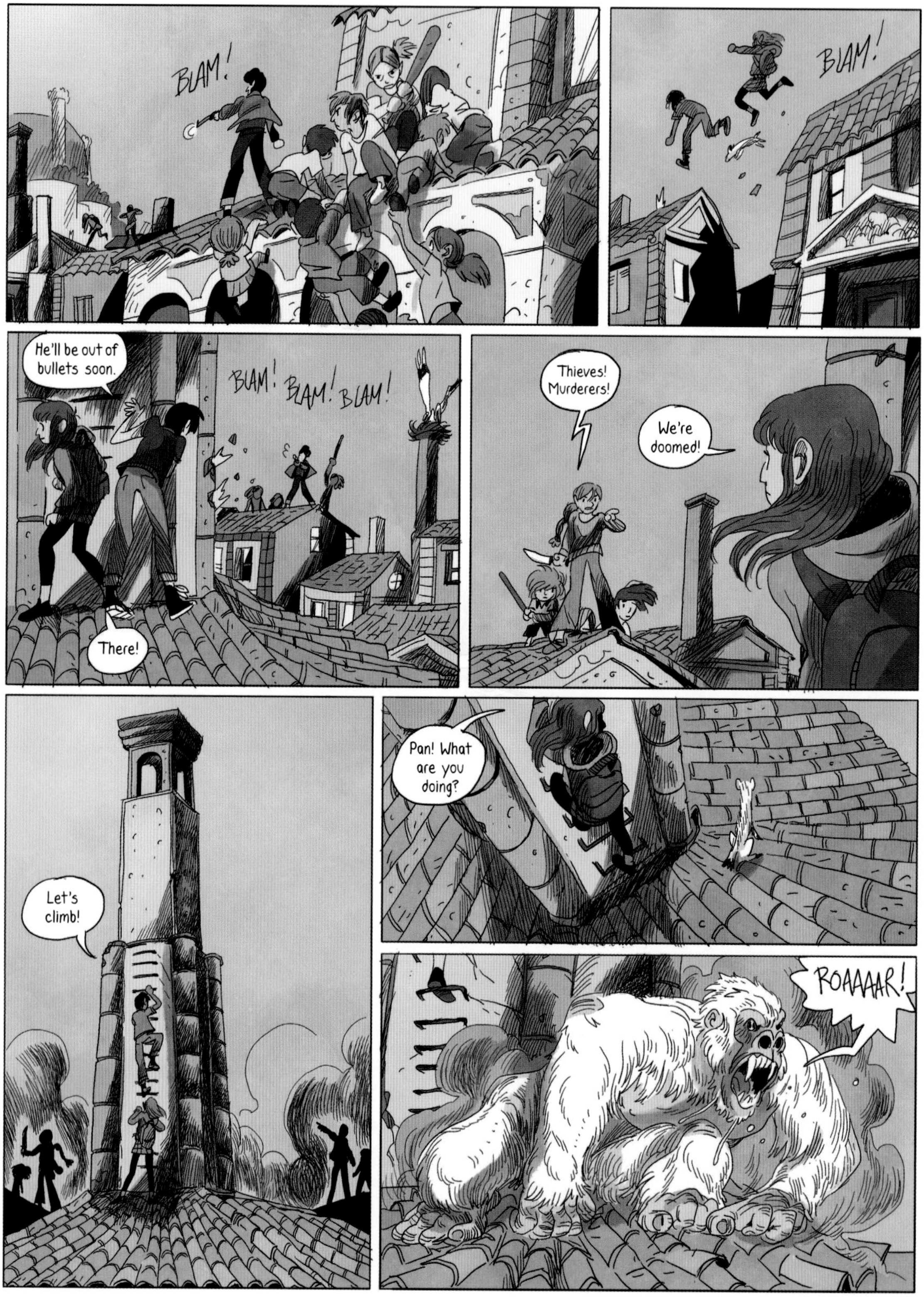
BLAM!
BLAM!
He'll be out of bullets soon.
BLAM! BLAM! BLAM!
There!
Thieves! Murderers!
We're doomed!
Let's climb!
Pan! What are you doing?
ROAAAAR!

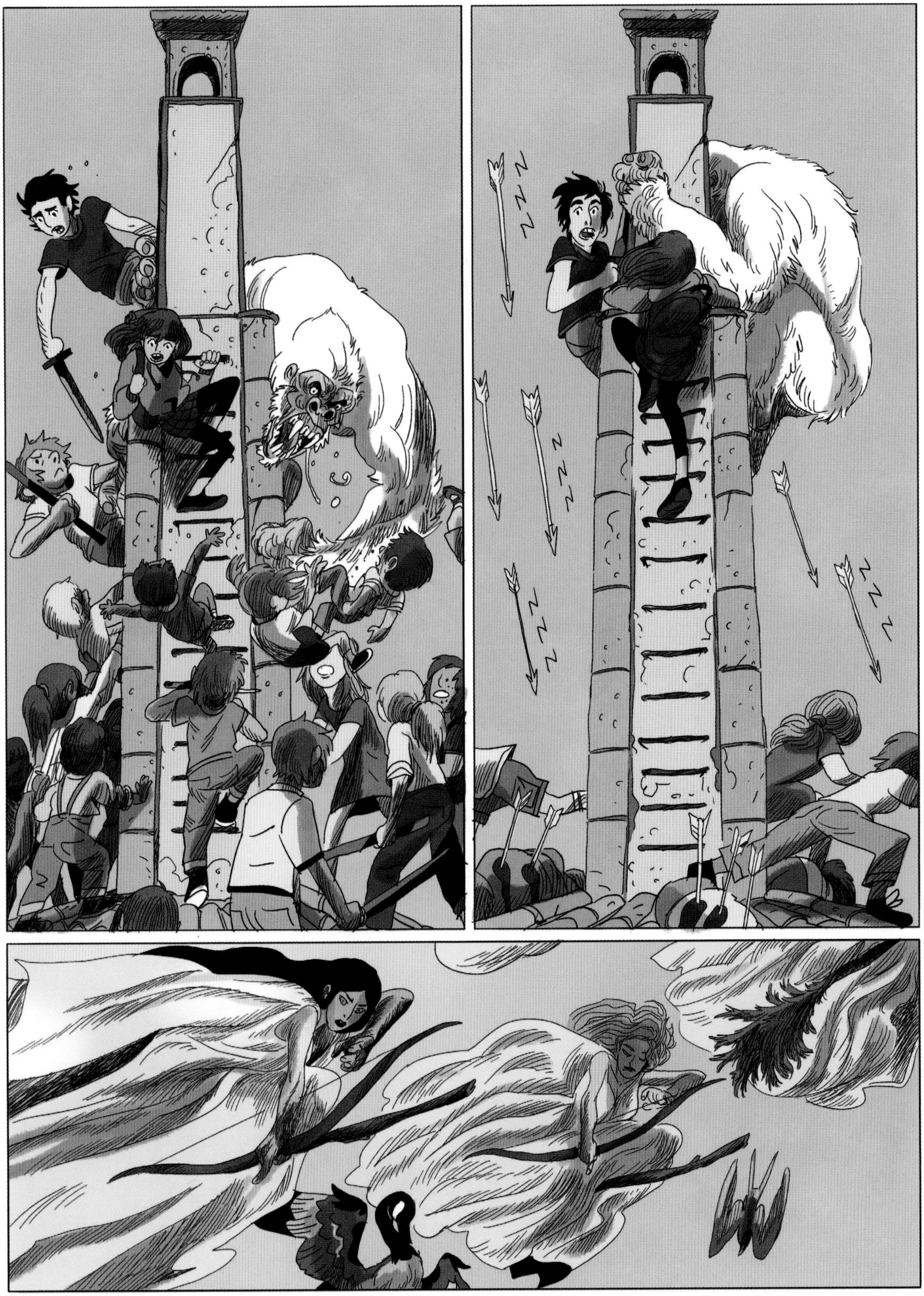

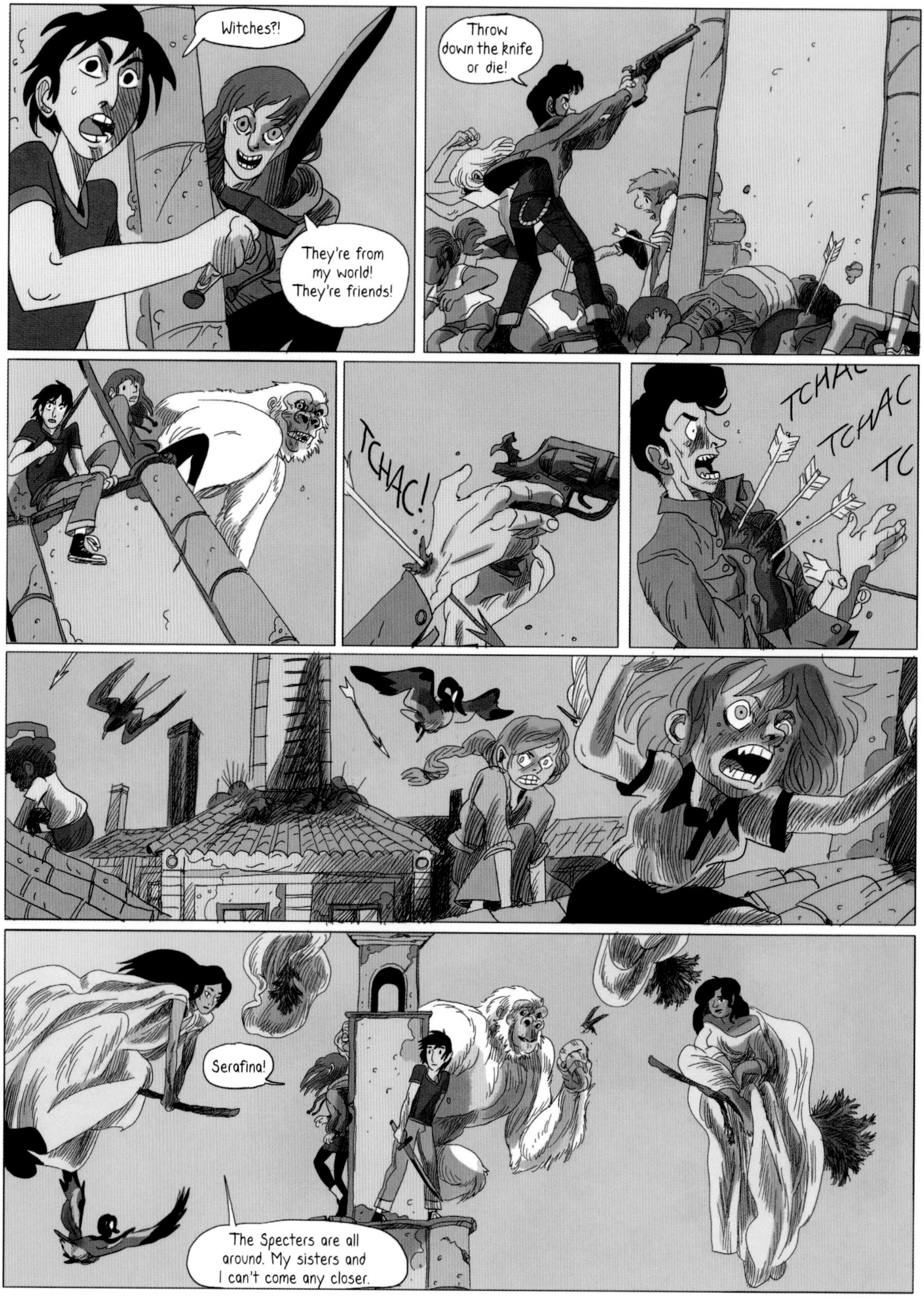
Witches?!
They're from my world! They're friends!
Throw down the knife or die!
TCHAC!
TCHAC
TCHAC
TC
Serafina!
The Specters are all around. My sisters and I can't come any closer.

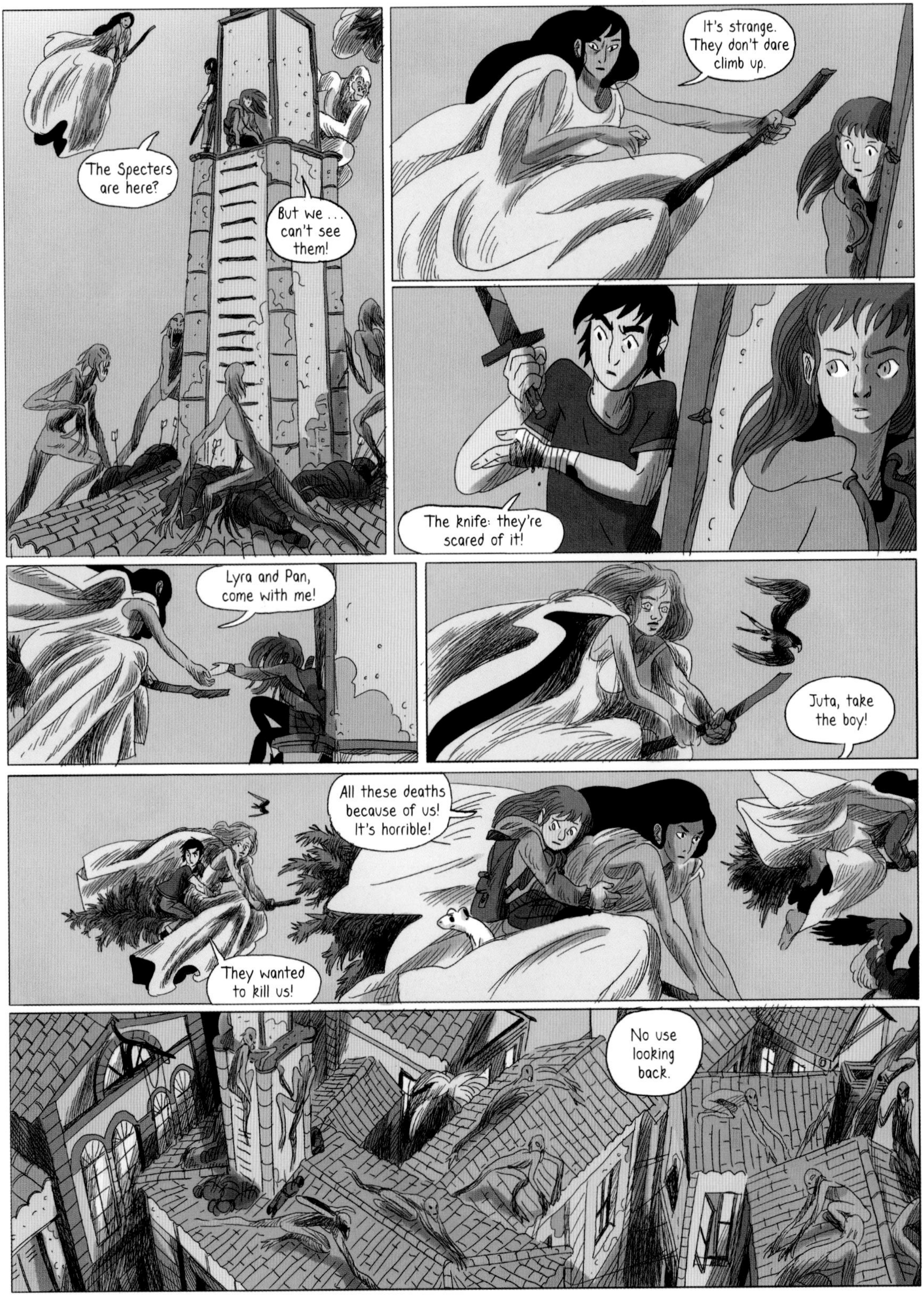
The Specters are here?
But we . . . can't see them!
It's strange. They don't dare climb up.
The knife: they're scared of it!
Lyra and Pan, come with me!
Juta, take the boy!
All these deaths because of us! It's horrible!
They wanted to kill us!
No use looking back.

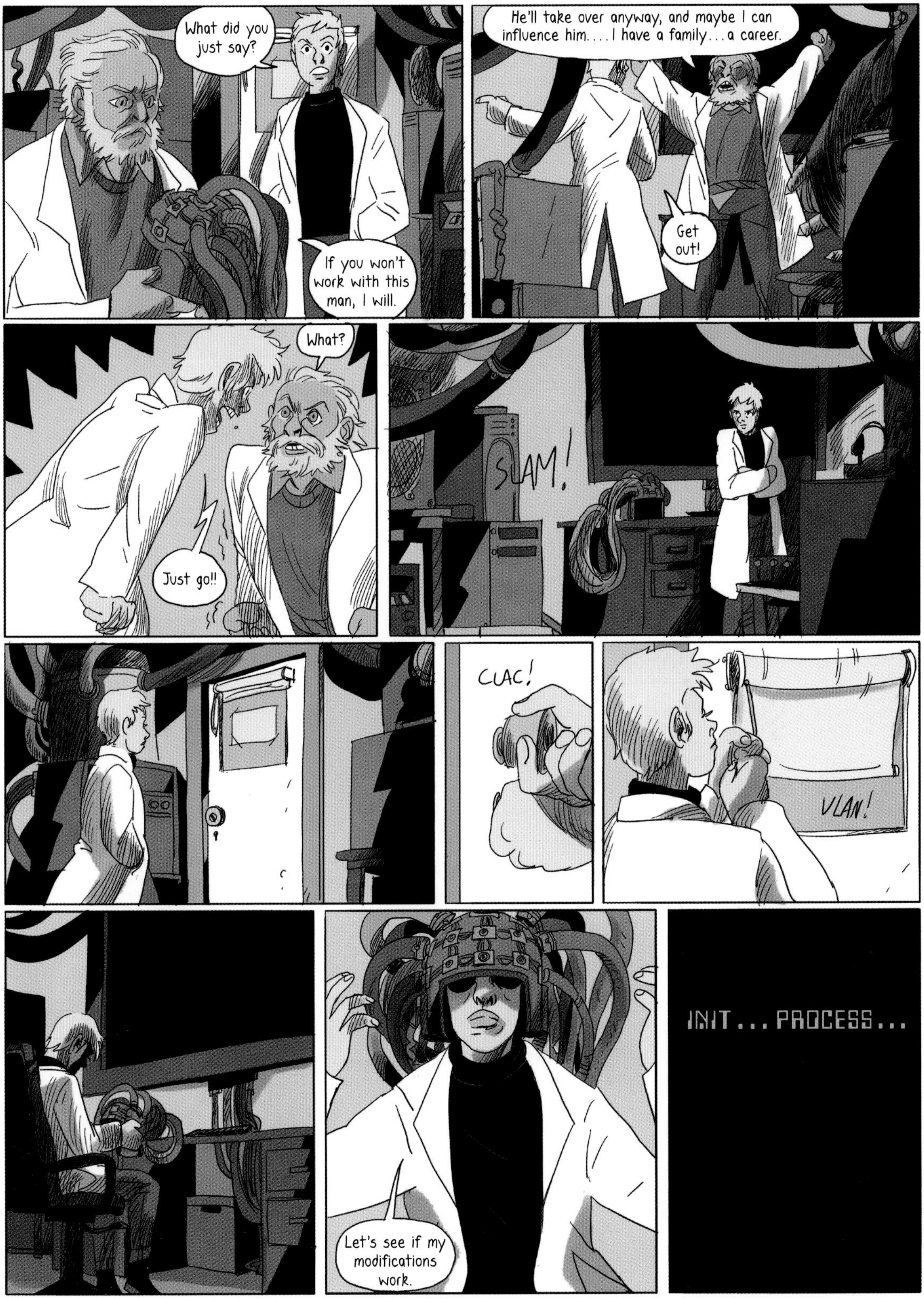
What did you just say?
If you won't work with this man, I will.
He'll take over anyway, and maybe I can influence him.... I have a family... a career.
Get out!
What?
Just go!!
SLAM!
CLAC!
VLAN!
Let's see if my modifications work.
INIT... PROCESS...

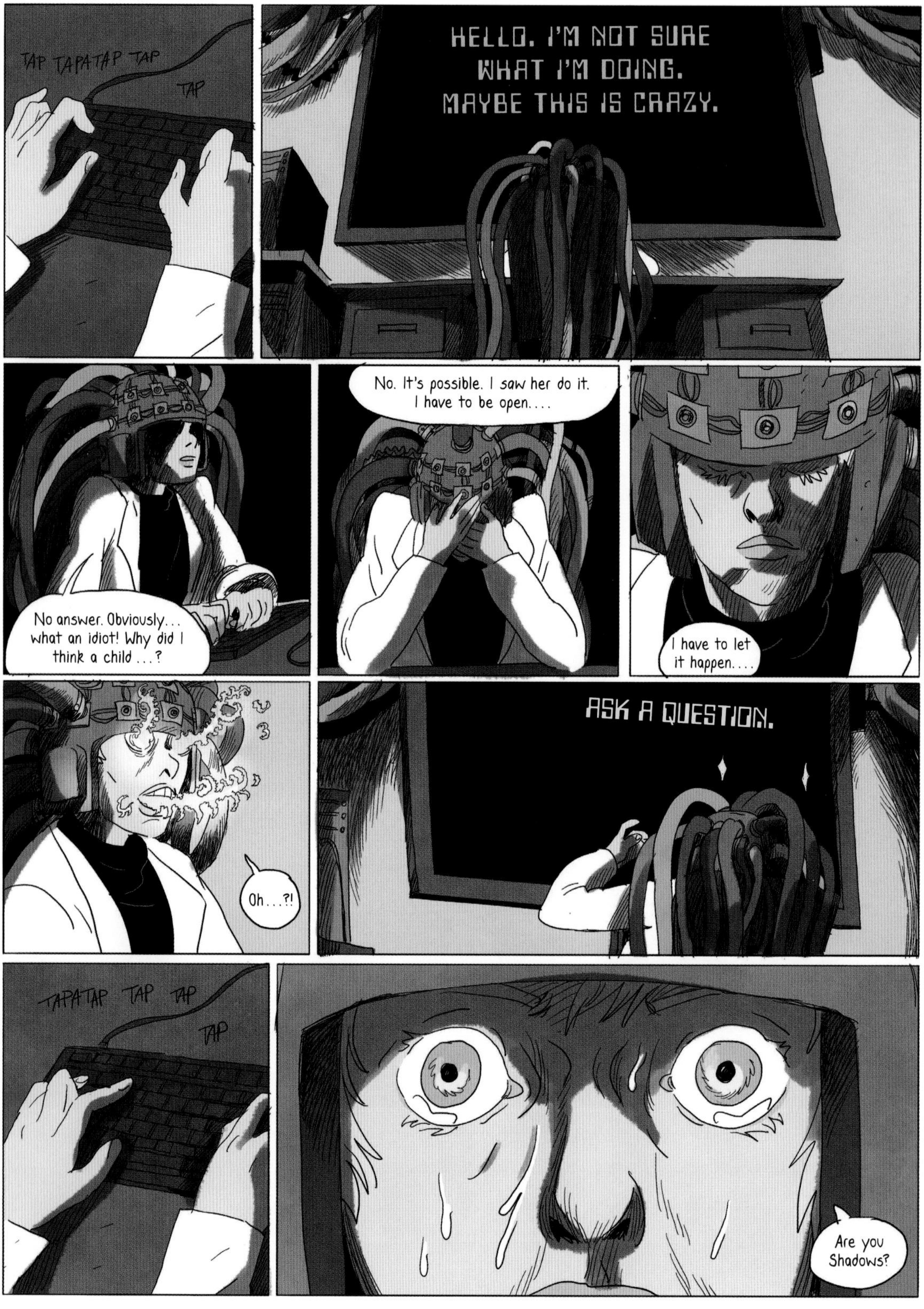
TAP TAPATAP TAP
TAP
HELLO. I'M NOT SURE WHAT I'M DOING. MAYBE THIS IS CRAZY.
No answer. Obviously... what an idiot! Why did I think a child...?
No. It's possible. I saw her do it. I have to be open....
I have to let it happen....
Oh...?!
ASK A QUESTION.
TAPATAP TAP TAP
TAP
Are you Shadows?

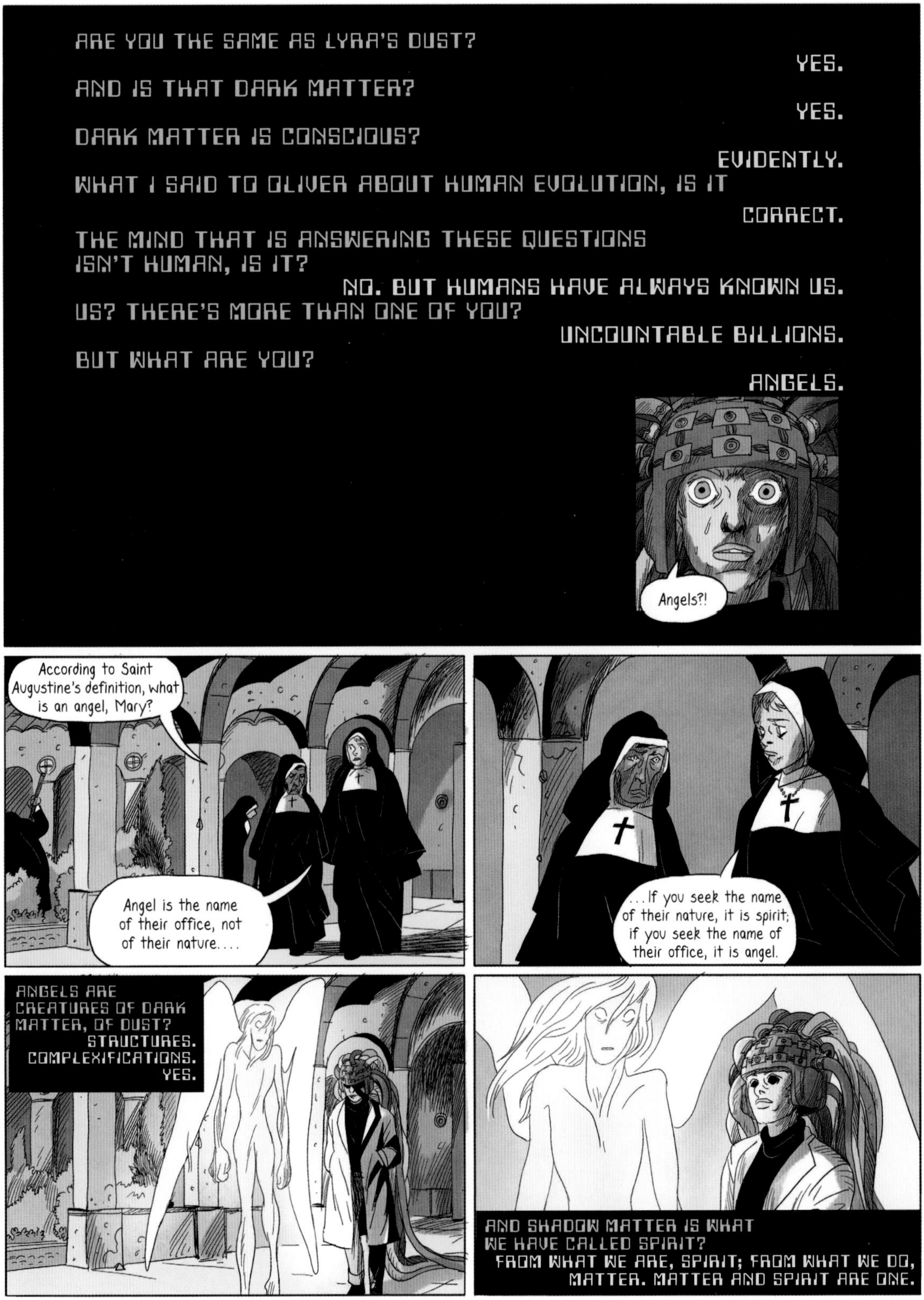
ARE YOU THE SAME AS LYRA'S DUST?
YES.
AND IS THAT DARK MATTER?
YES.
DARK MATTER IS CONSCIOUS?
EVIDENTLY.
WHAT I SAID TO OLIVER ABOUT HUMAN EVOLUTION, IS IT
CORRECT.
THE MIND THAT IS ANSWERING THESE QUESTIONS ISN'T HUMAN, IS IT?
NO. BUT HUMANS HAVE ALWAYS KNOWN US.
US? THERE'S MORE THAN ONE OF YOU?
UNCOUNTABLE BILLIONS.
BUT WHAT ARE YOU?
ANGELS.
Angels?!
According to Saint Augustine's definition, what is an angel, Mary?
Angel is the name of their office, not of their nature. . . .
. . . If you seek the name of their nature, it is spirit; if you seek the name of their office, it is angel.
ANGELS ARE CREATURES OF DARK MATTER, OF DUST?
STRUCTURES. COMPLEXIFICATIONS. YES.
AND SHADOW MATTER IS WHAT WE HAVE CALLED SPIRIT?
FROM WHAT WE ARE, SPIRIT; FROM WHAT WE DO, MATTER. MATTER AND SPIRIT ARE ONE.

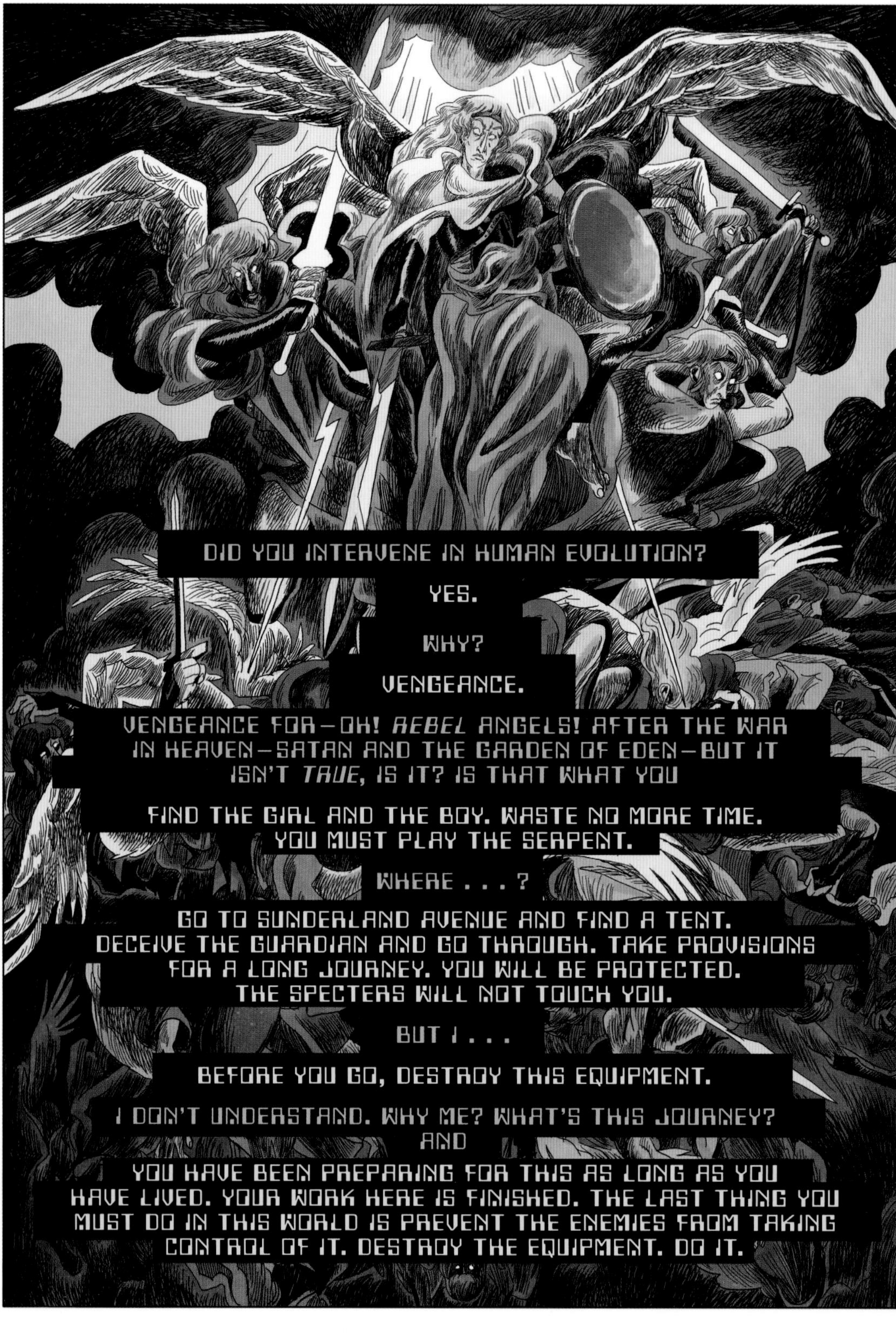
DID YOU INTERVENE IN HUMAN EVOLUTION?
YES.
WHY?
VENGEANCE.
VENGEANCE FOR—OH! *REBEL* ANGELS! AFTER THE WAR IN HEAVEN—SATAN AND THE GARDEN OF EDEN—BUT IT ISN'T *TRUE*, IS IT? IS THAT WHAT YOU
FIND THE GIRL AND THE BOY. WASTE NO MORE TIME. YOU MUST PLAY THE SERPENT.
WHERE . . . ?
GO TO SUNDERLAND AVENUE AND FIND A TENT. DECEIVE THE GUARDIAN AND GO THROUGH. TAKE PROVISIONS FOR A LONG JOURNEY. YOU WILL BE PROTECTED. THE SPECTERS WILL NOT TOUCH YOU.
BUT I . . .
BEFORE YOU GO, DESTROY THIS EQUIPMENT.
I DON'T UNDERSTAND. WHY ME? WHAT'S THIS JOURNEY? AND
YOU HAVE BEEN PREPARING FOR THIS AS LONG AS YOU HAVE LIVED. YOUR WORK HERE IS FINISHED. THE LAST THING YOU MUST DO IN THIS WORLD IS PREVENT THE ENEMIES FROM TAKING CONTROL OF IT. DESTROY THE EQUIPMENT. DO IT.

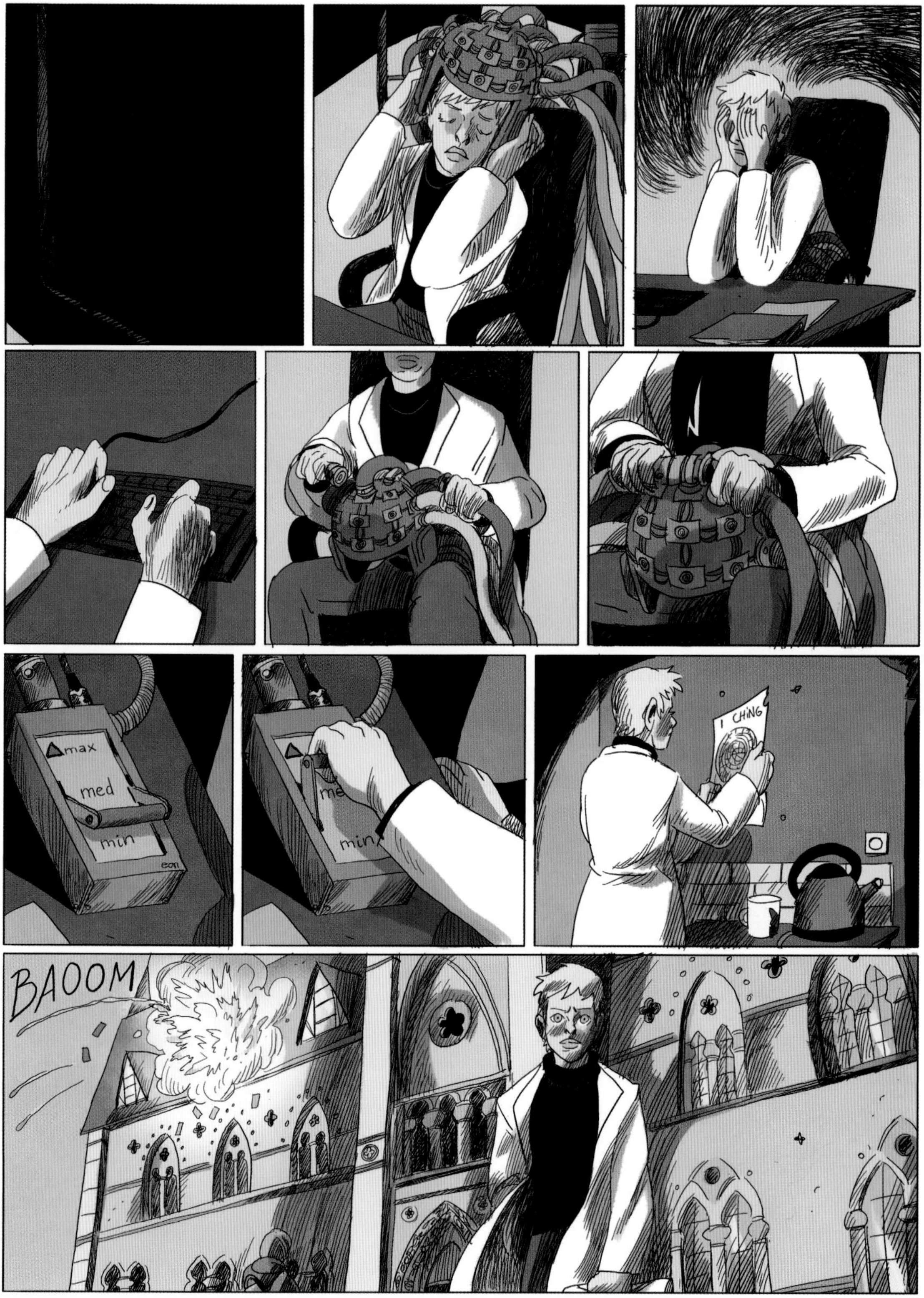
max
med
min
eon
me
min
I CHING
BAOOM

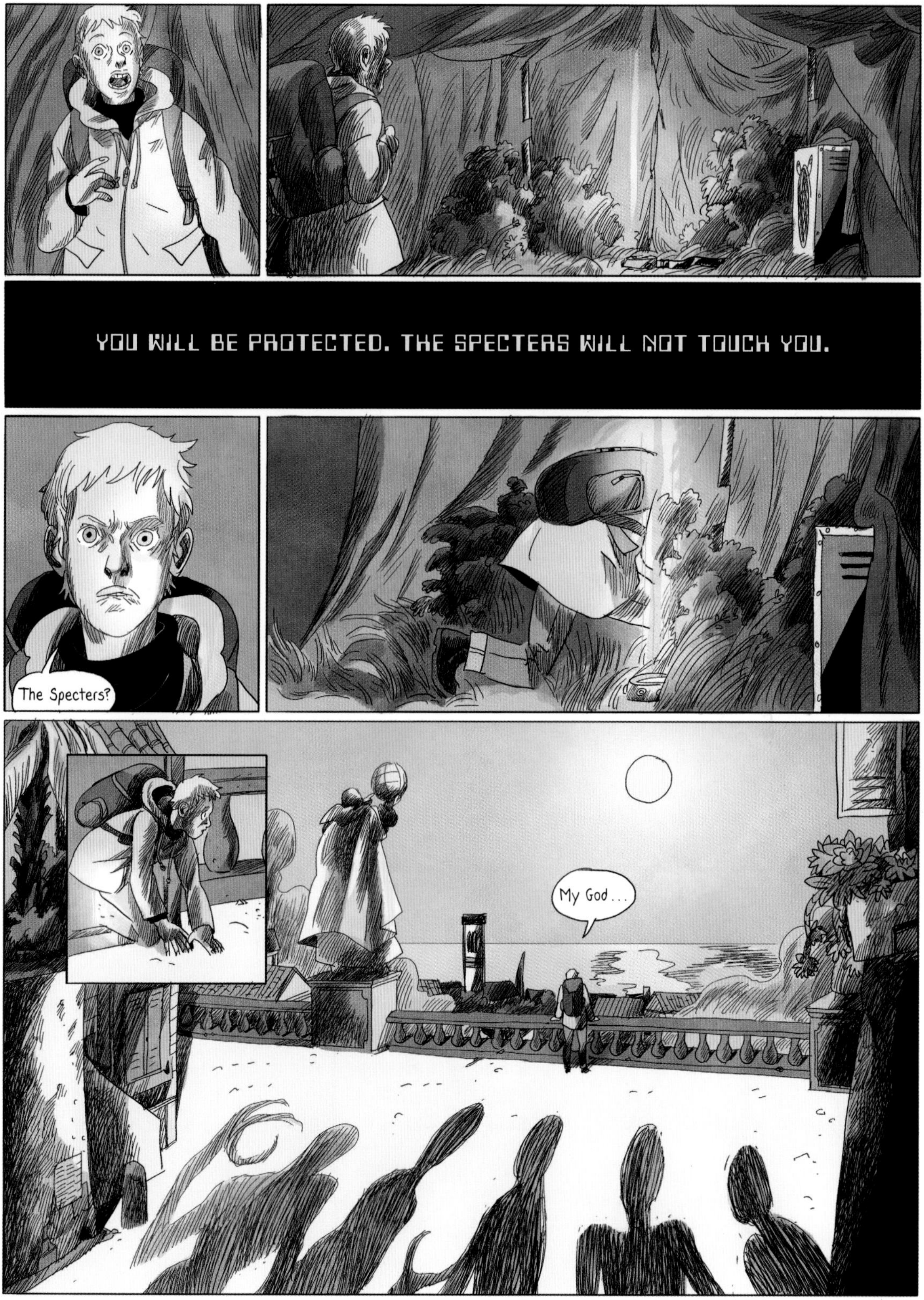
YOU WILL BE PROTECTED. THE SPECTERS WILL NOT TOUCH YOU.
The Specters?
My God...

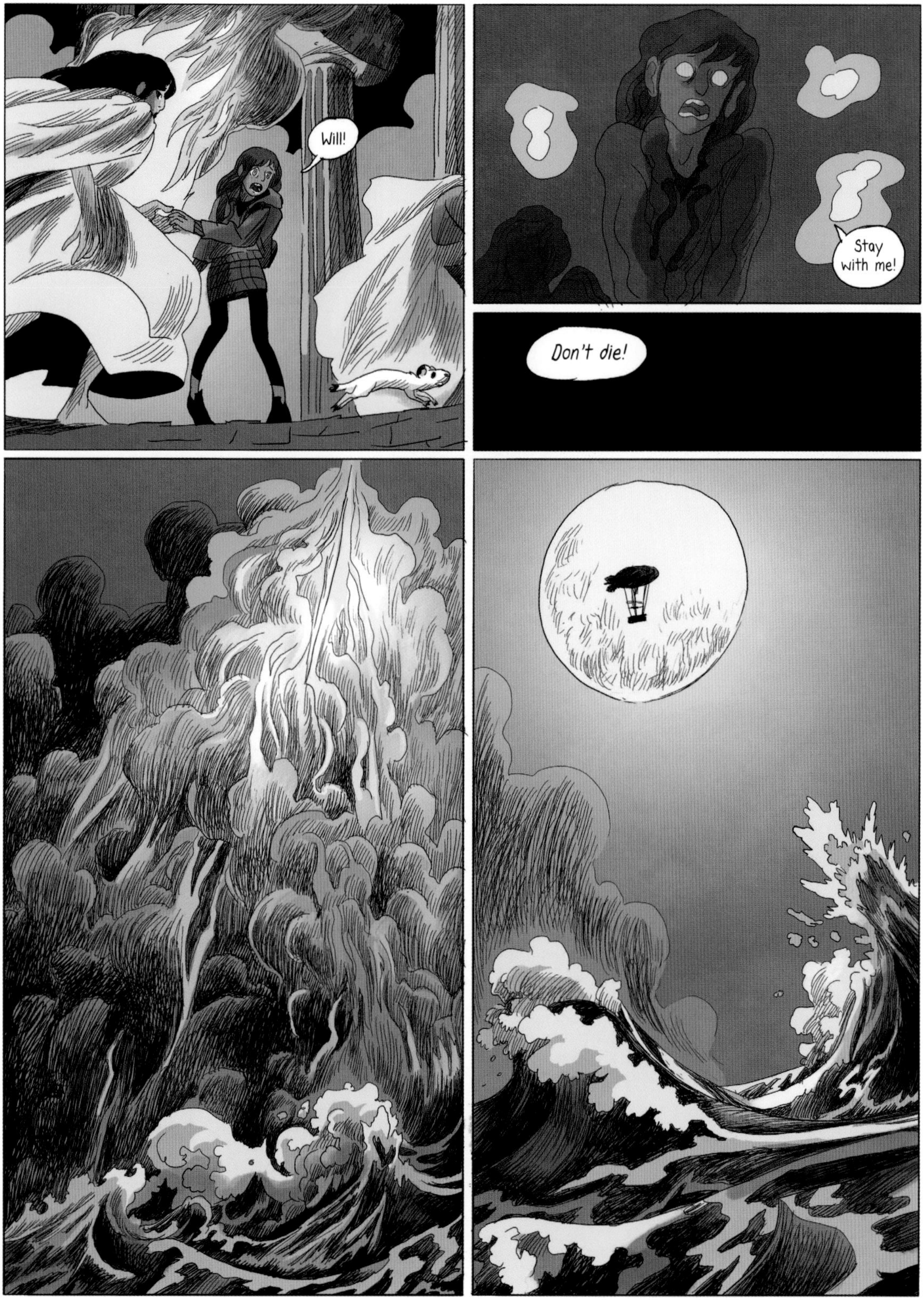
Will!
Stay with me!
Don't die!

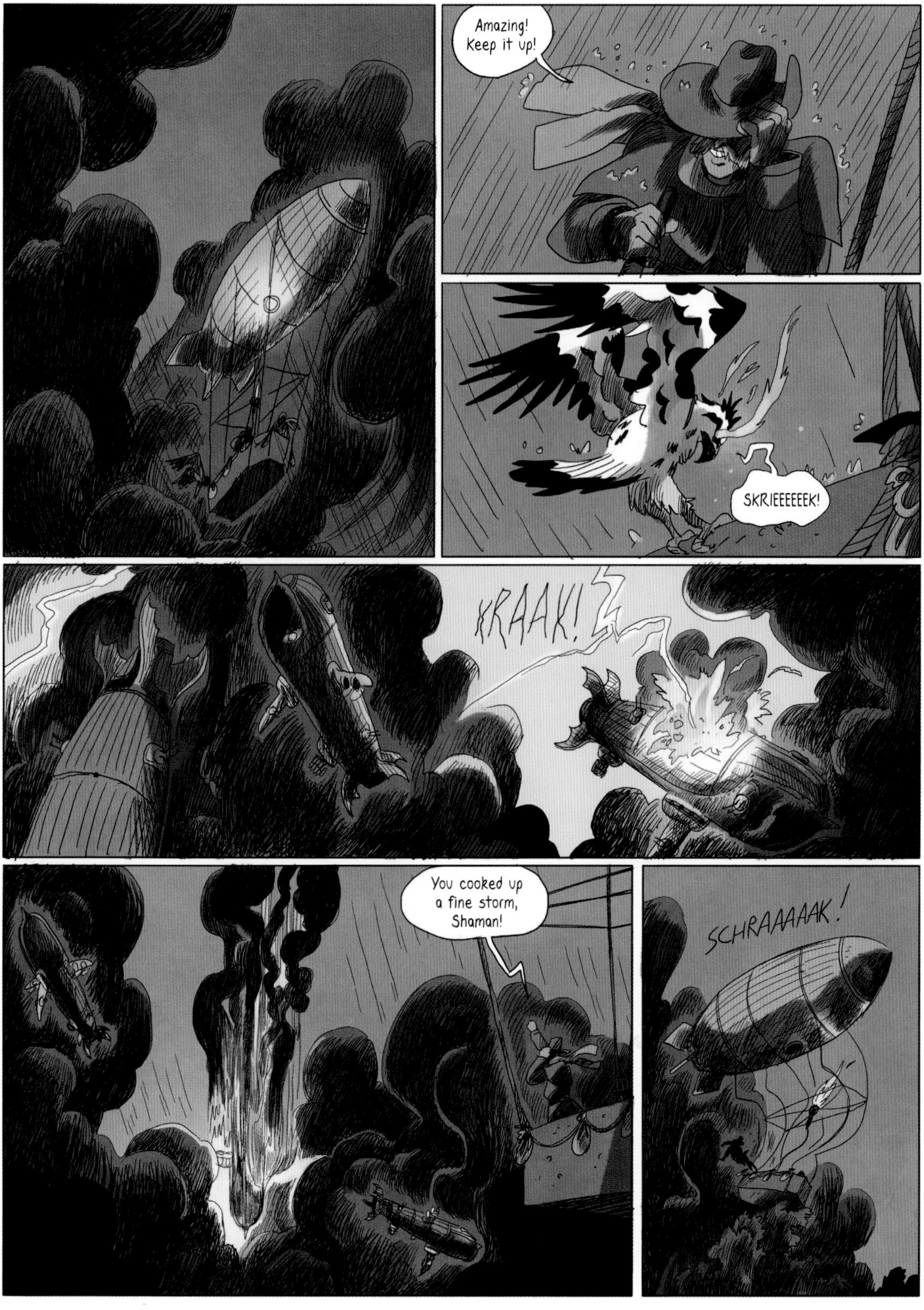
Amazing!
Keep it up!
SKRIEEEEEEK!
KRAAK!
You cooked up
a fine storm,
Shaman!
SCHRAAAAAK!

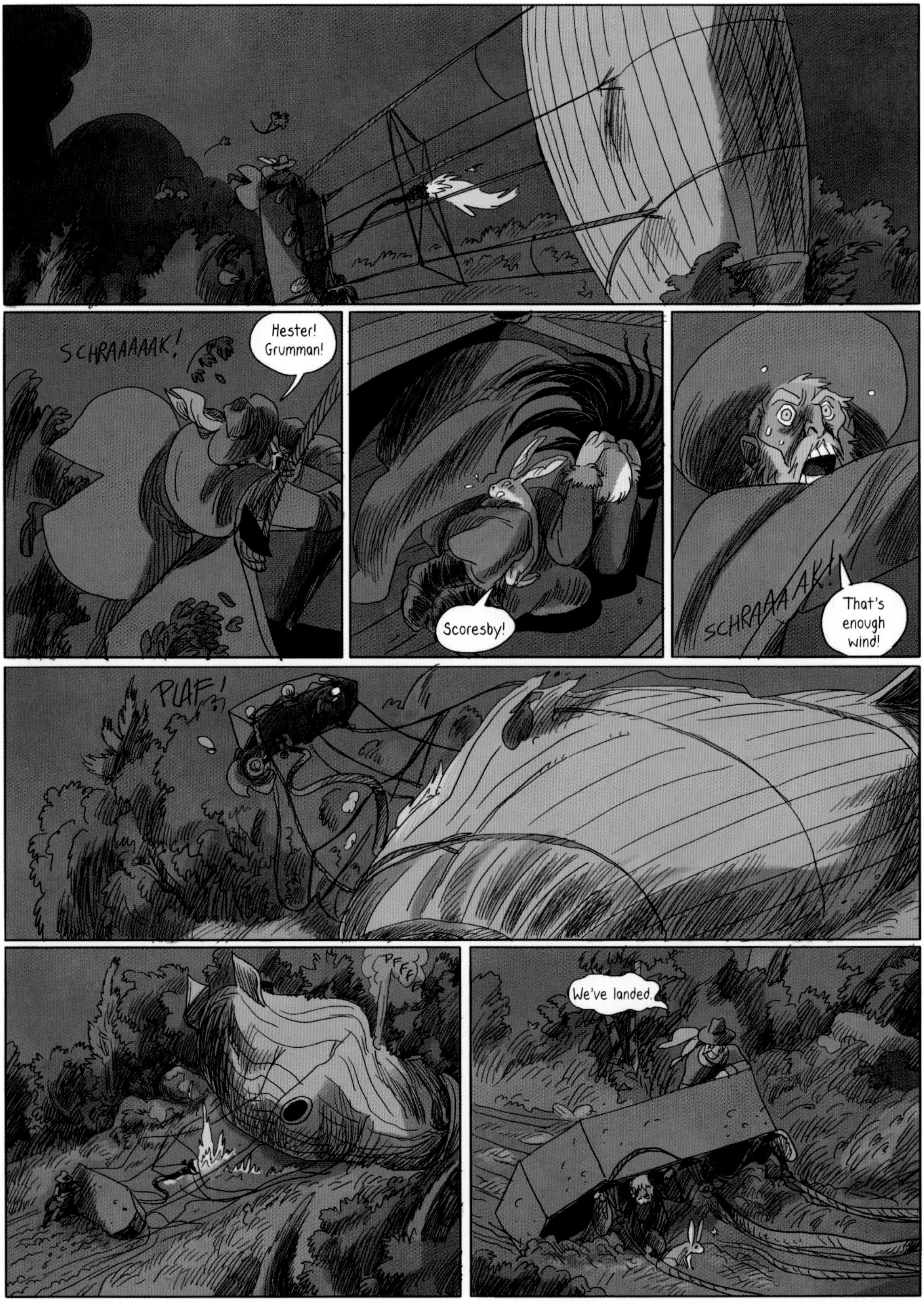
SCHRAAAAAK!
Hester! Grumman!
Scoresby!
SCHRAAAAK!
That's enough wind!
PLAF!
PFFF
We've landed.

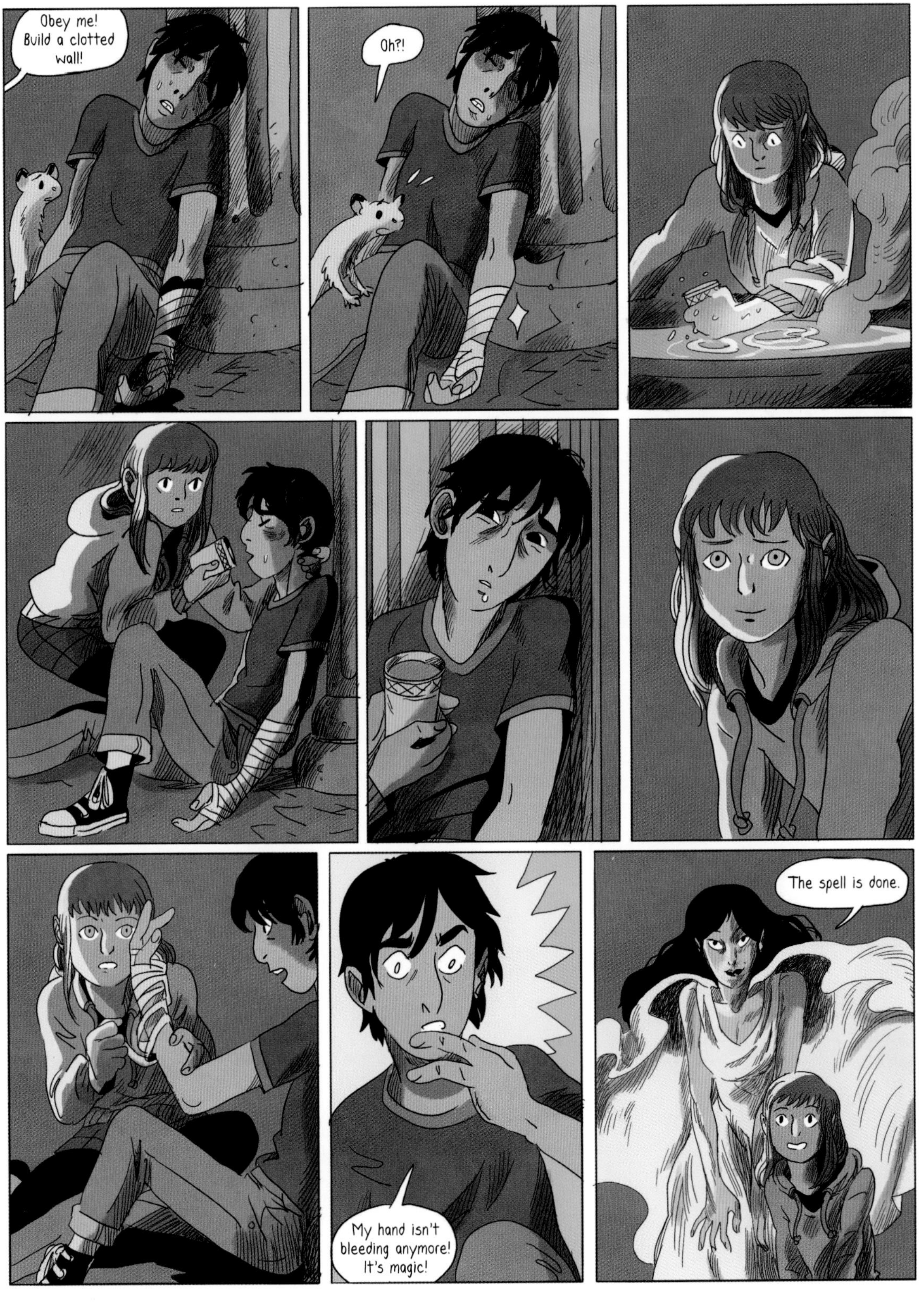
Obey me! Build a clotted wall!
Oh?!
My hand isn't bleeding anymore! It's magic!
The spell is done.

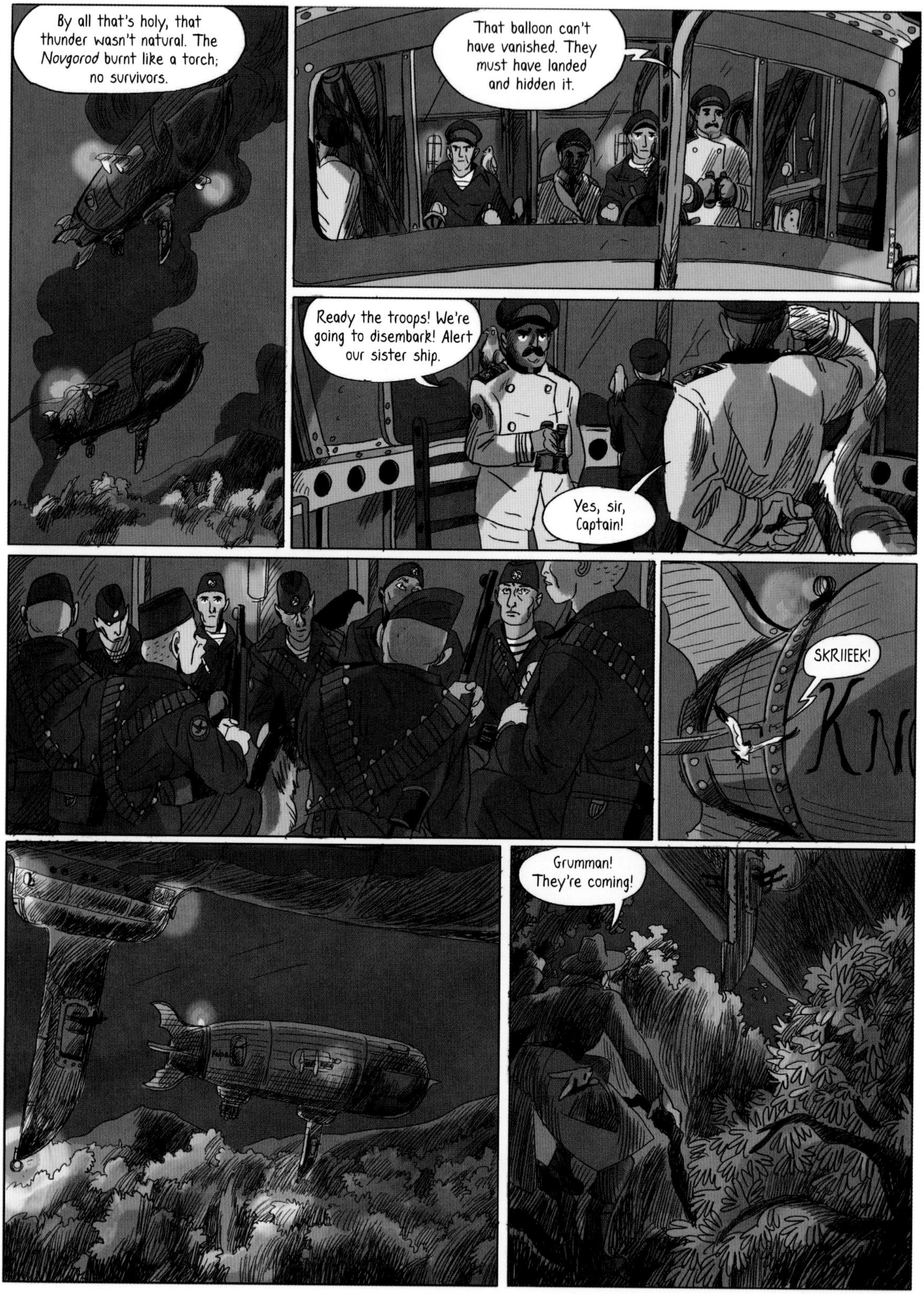
By all that's holy, that thunder wasn't natural. The *Novgorod* burnt like a torch; no survivors.
That balloon can't have vanished. They must have landed and hidden it.
Ready the troops! We're going to disembark! Alert our sister ship.
Yes, sir, Captain!
SKRIIEEK!
Grumman! They're coming!

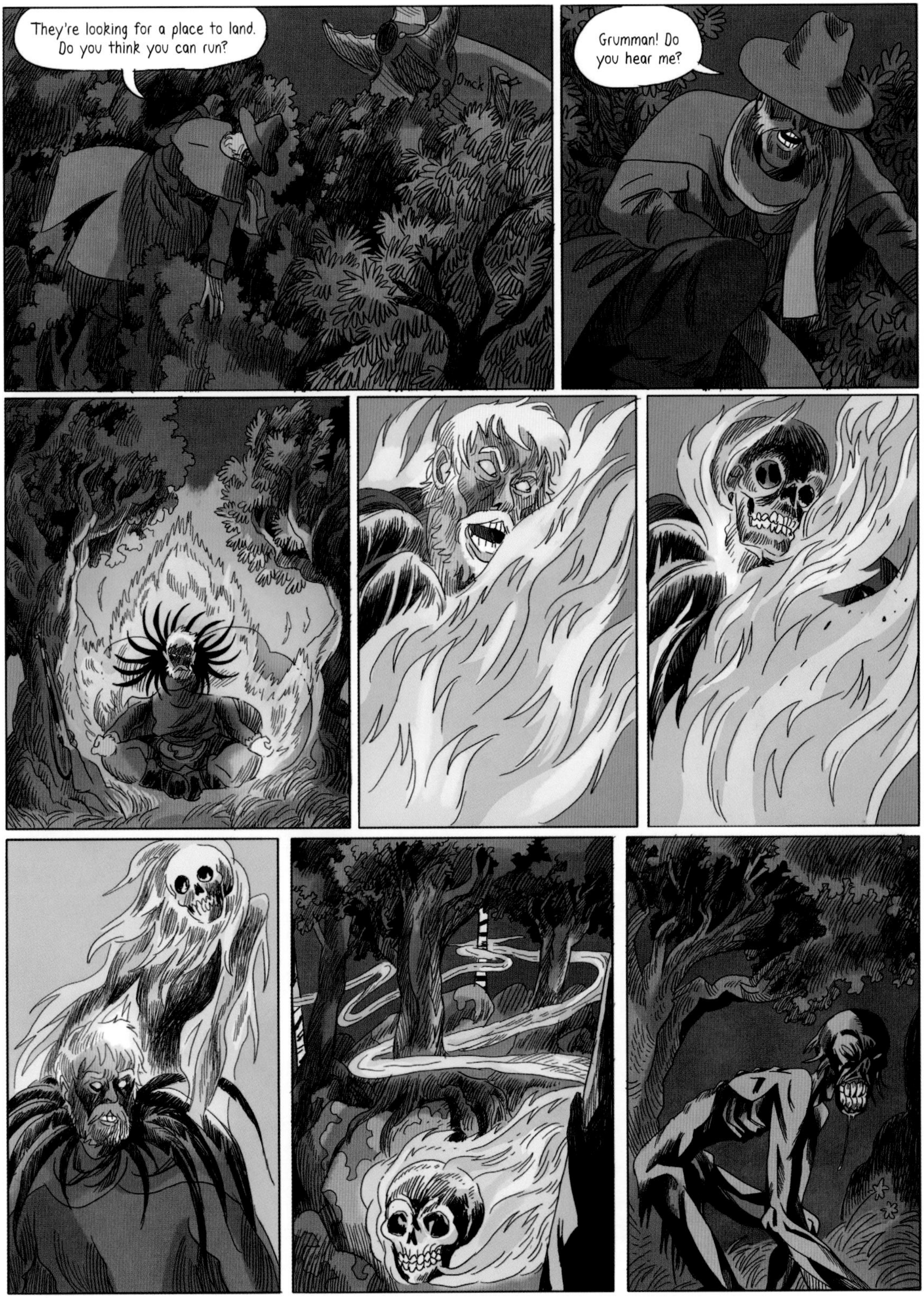
They're looking for a place to land. Do you think you can run?
Grumman! Do you hear me?

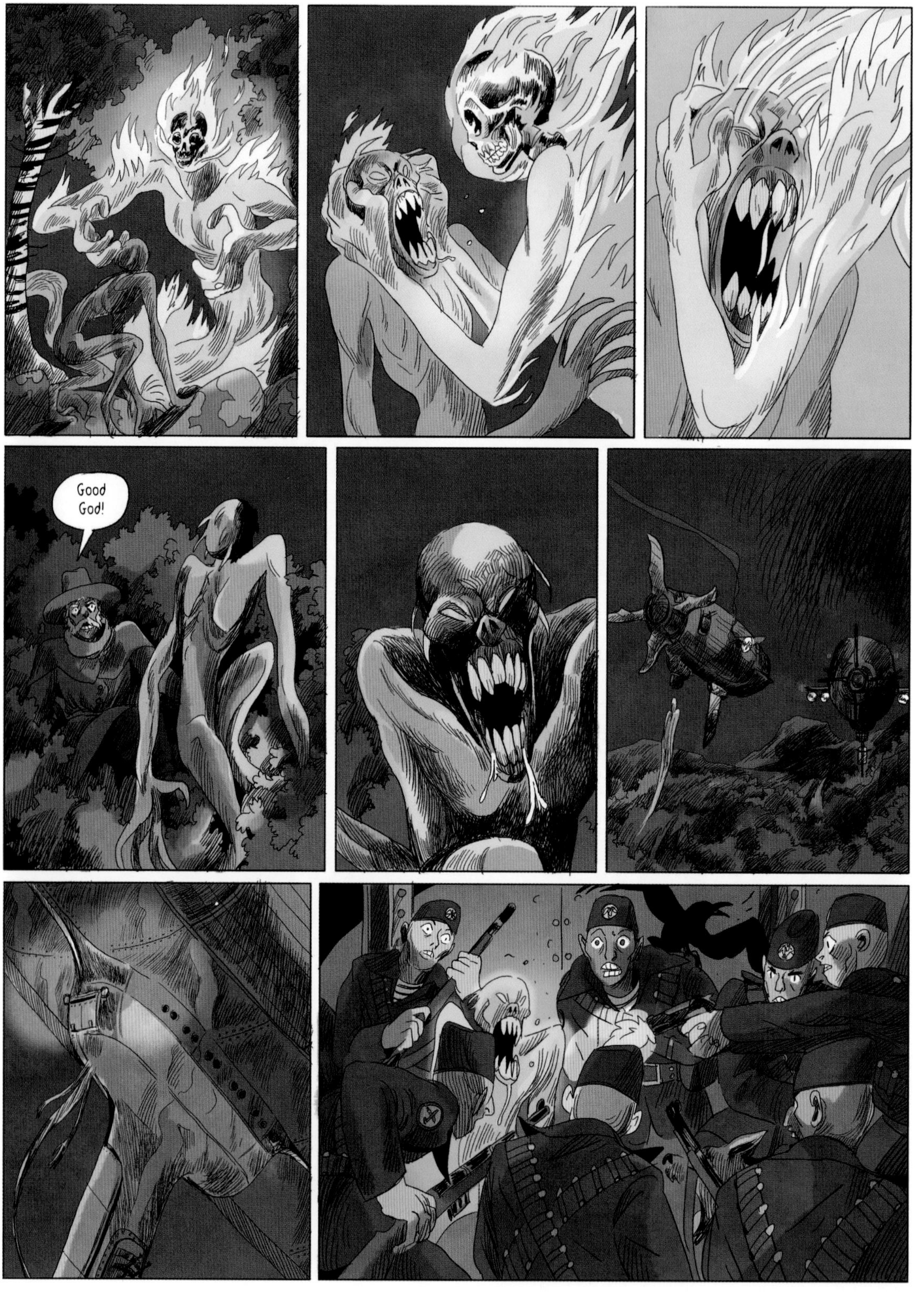
Good God!

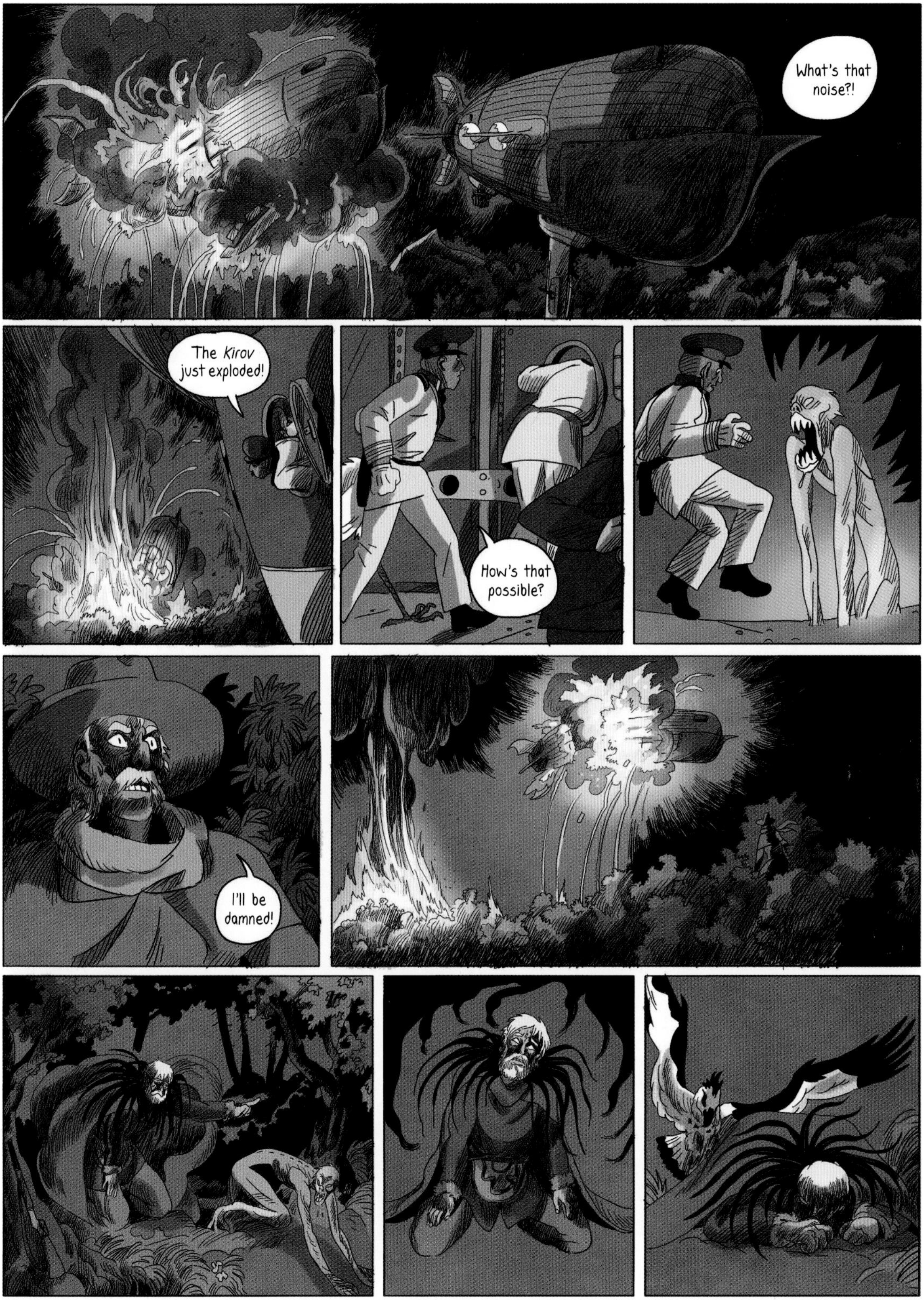
What's that noise?!
The *Kirov* just exploded!
How's that possible?
I'll be damned!

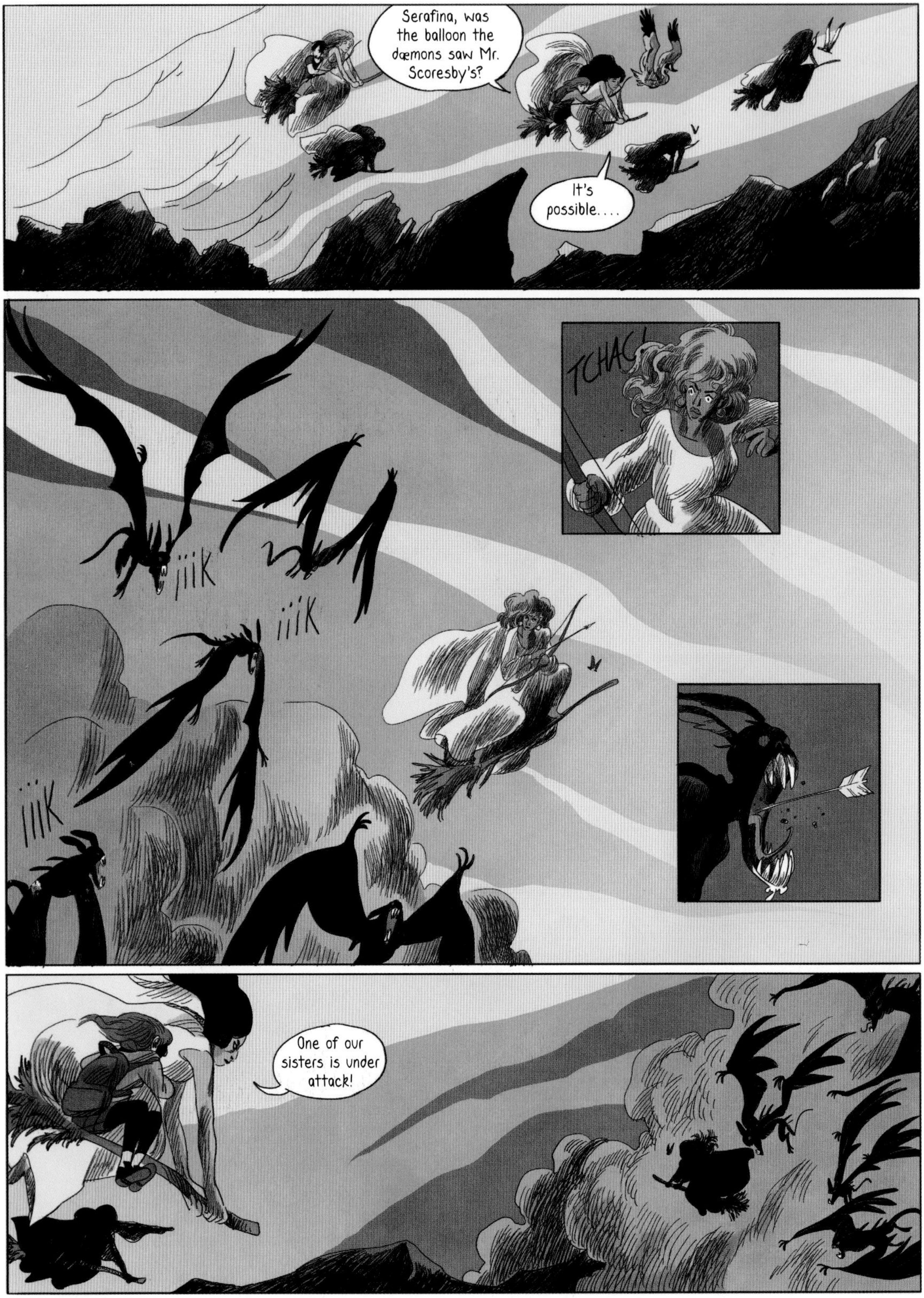

Serafina, was the balloon the dæmons saw Mr. Scoresby's?
It's possible....
TCHAC!
iiik
iiik
iiik
One of our sisters is under attack!

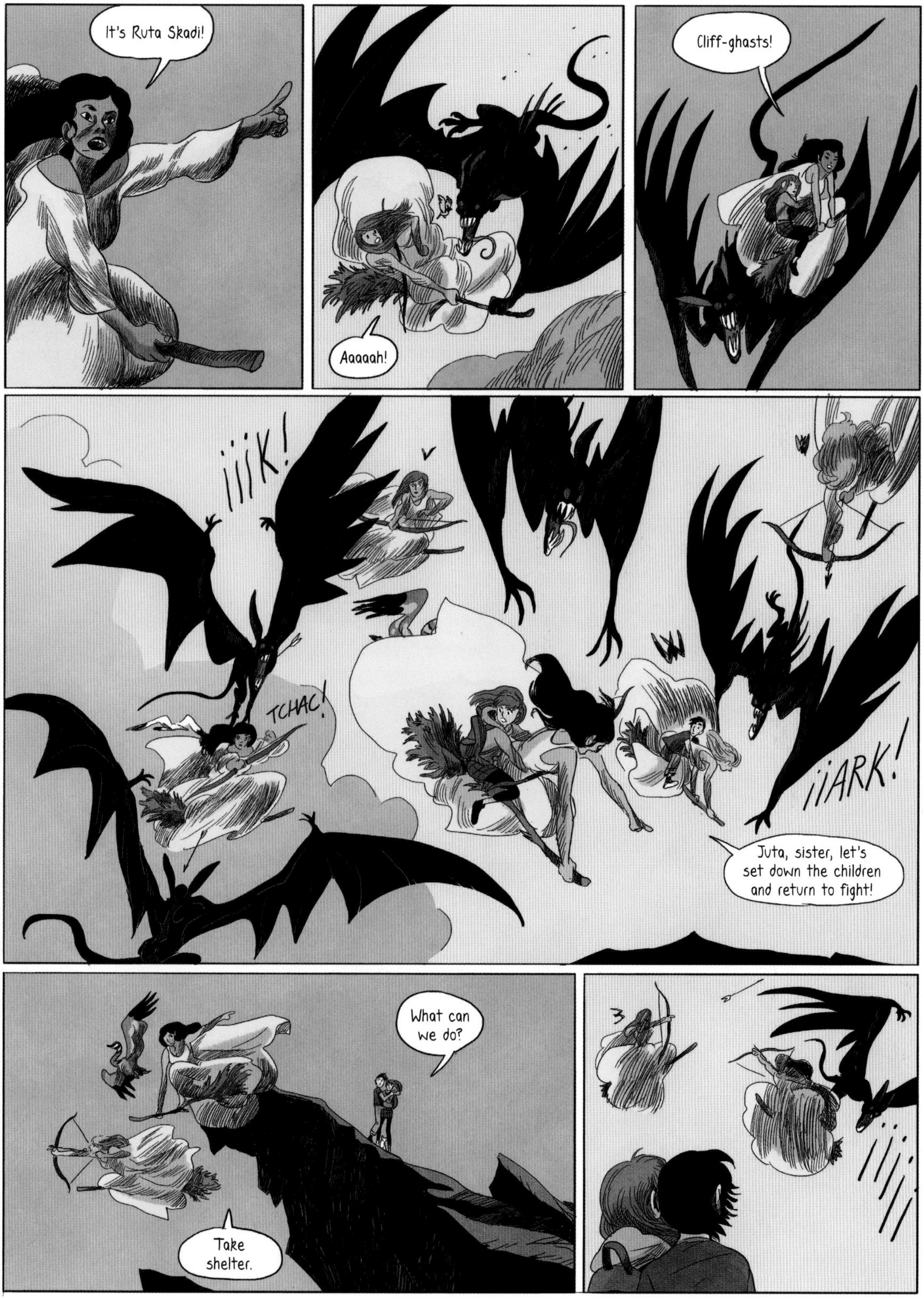

It's Ruta Skadi!
Aaaaah!
Cliff-ghasts!
¡¡¡K!
TCHAC!
¡¡ARK!
Juta, sister, let's set down the children and return to fight!
What can we do?
Take shelter.

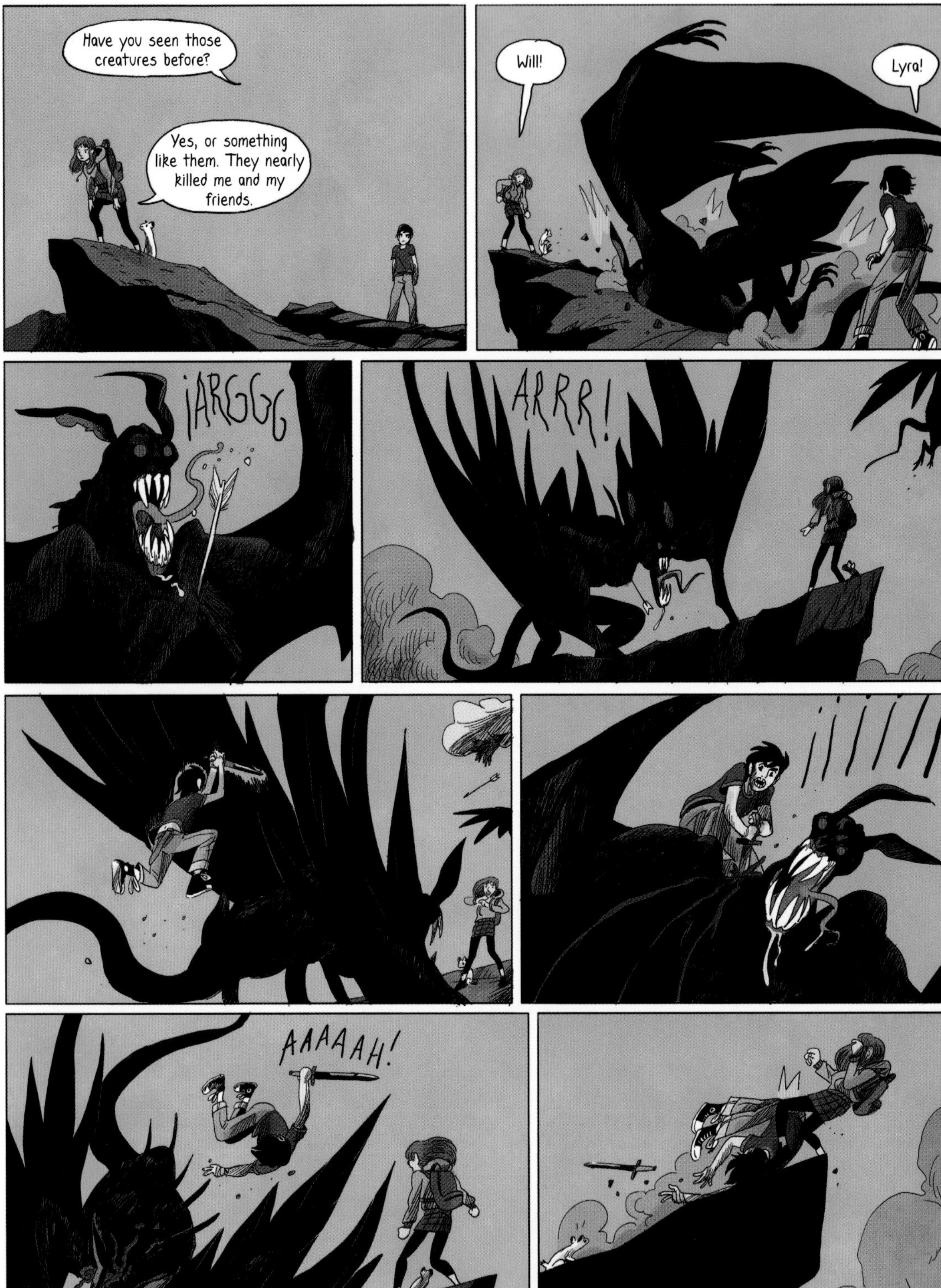
Have you seen those creatures before?
Yes, or something like them. They nearly killed me and my friends.
Will!
Lyra!
¡ARGGG
ARRR!
AAAAAH!

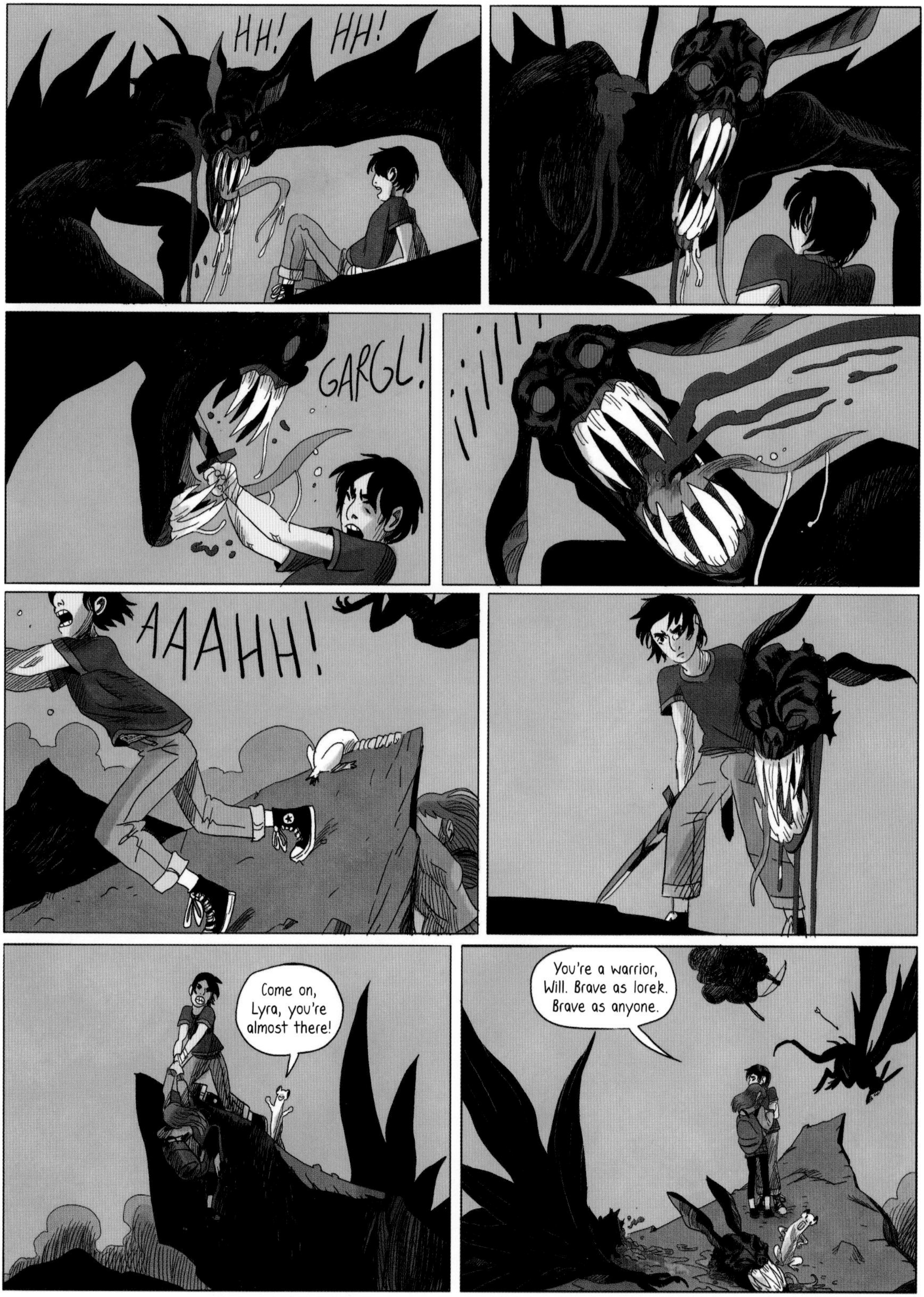
HH! HH!
GARGL!
AAAHH!
Come on, Lyra, you're almost there!
You're a warrior, Will. Brave as Iorek. Brave as anyone.

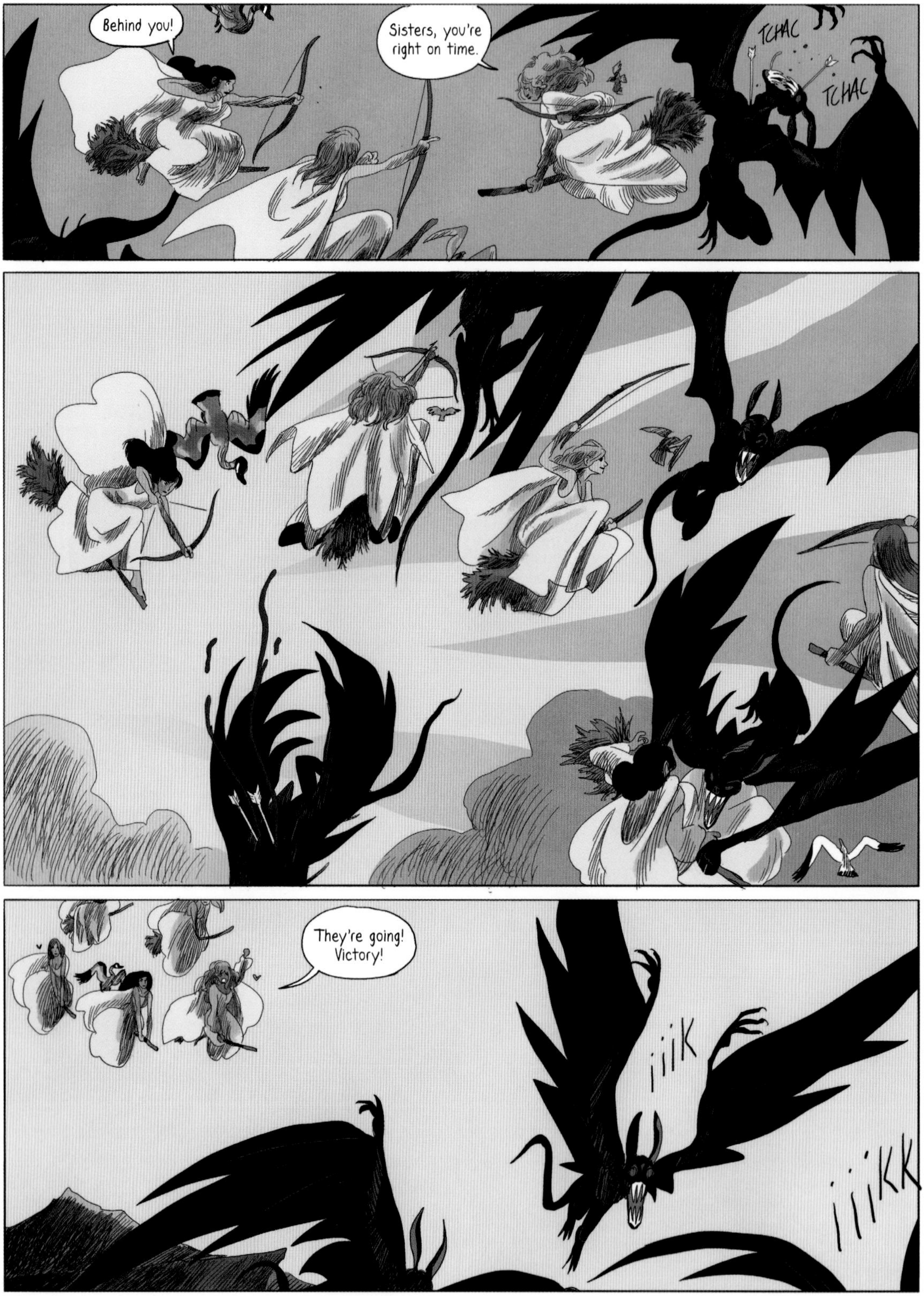
Behind you!
Sisters, you're right on time.
TCHAC
TCHAC
They're going! Victory!
iiiK
iiiKK

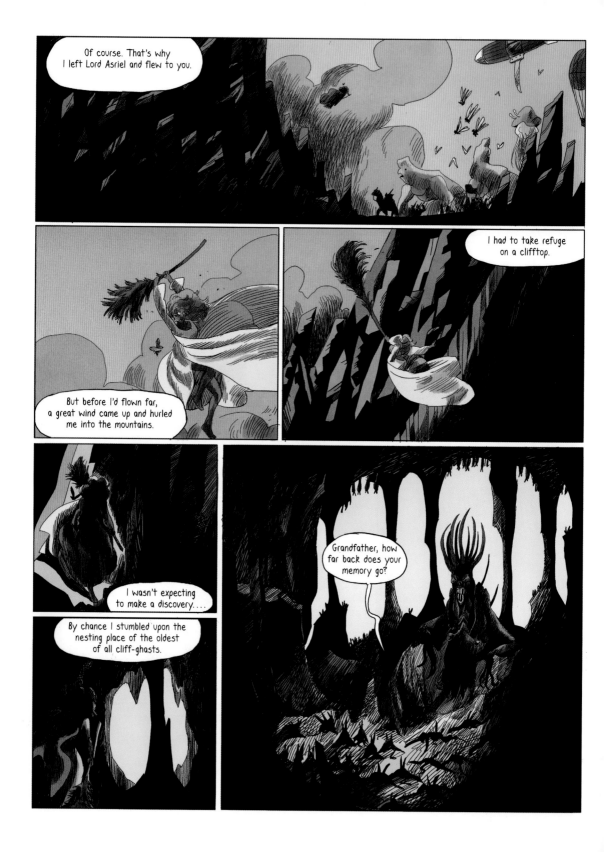

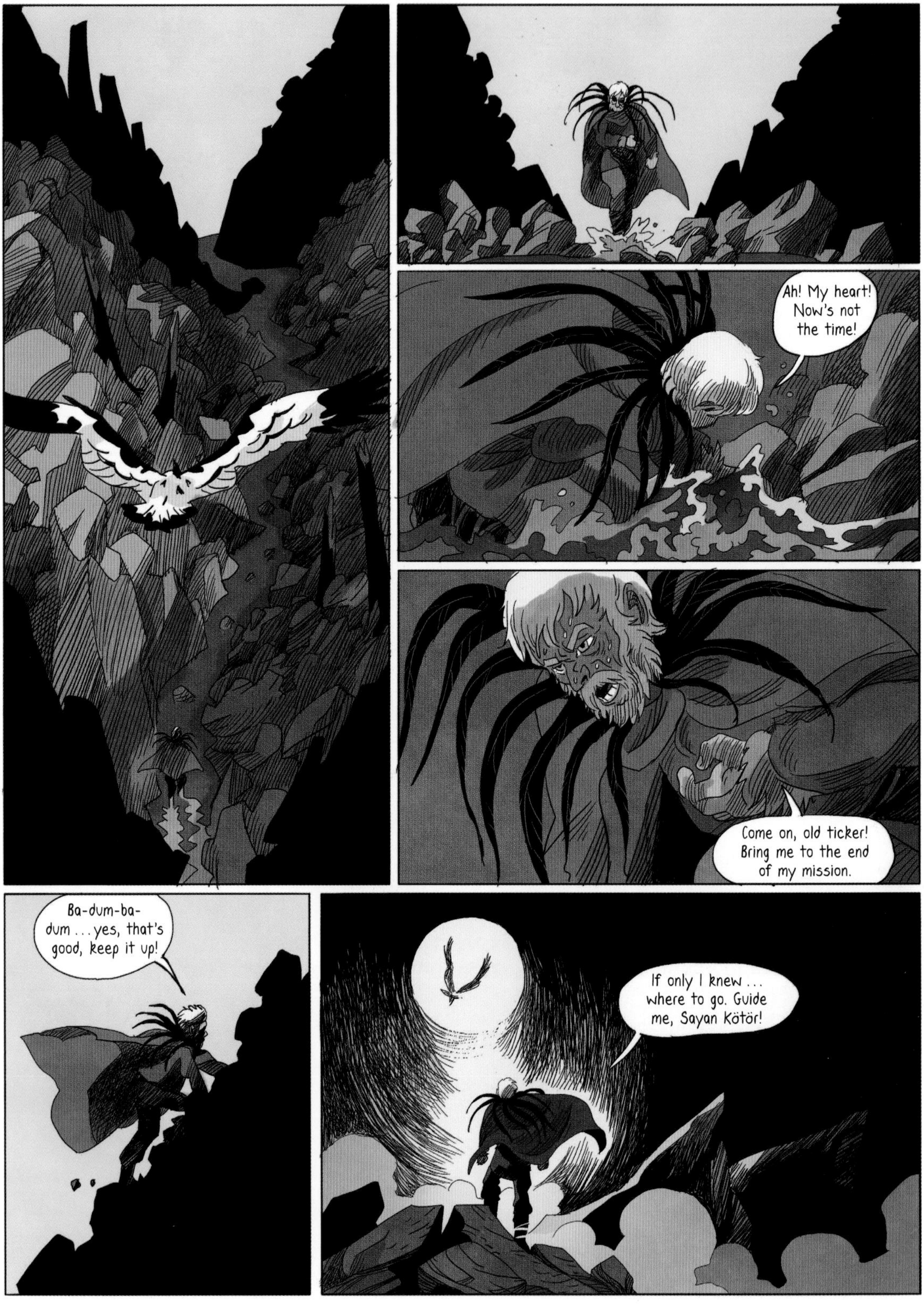
Ah! My heart! Now's not the time!
Come on, old ticker! Bring me to the end of my mission.
Ba-dum-ba-dum . . . yes, that's good, keep it up!
If only I knew . . . where to go. Guide me, Sayan Kötör!

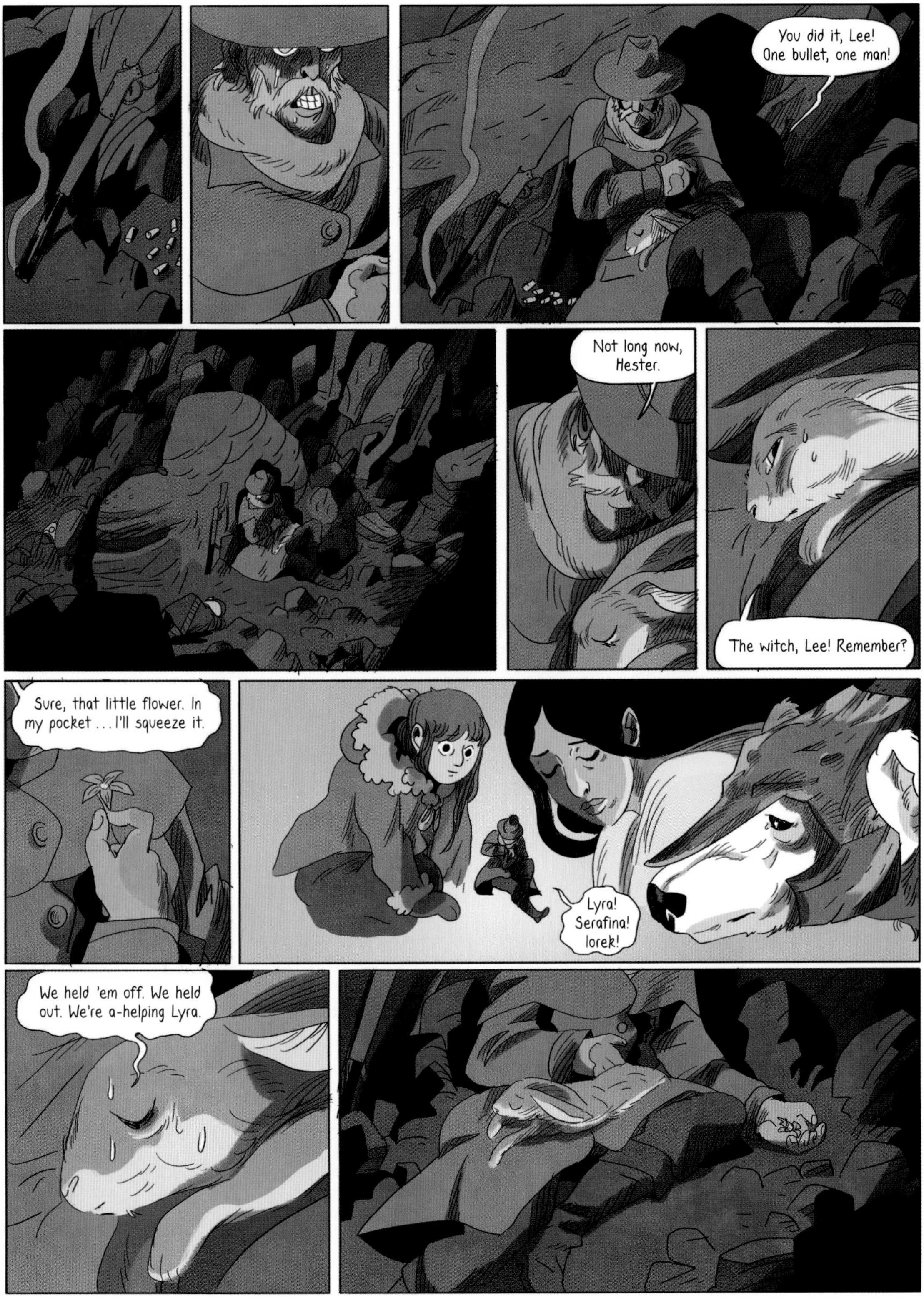
You did it, Lee! One bullet, one man!
Not long now, Hester.
The witch, Lee! Remember?
Sure, that little flower. In my pocket . . . I'll squeeze it.
Lyra! Serafina! Iorek!
We held 'em off. We held out. We're a-helping Lyra.

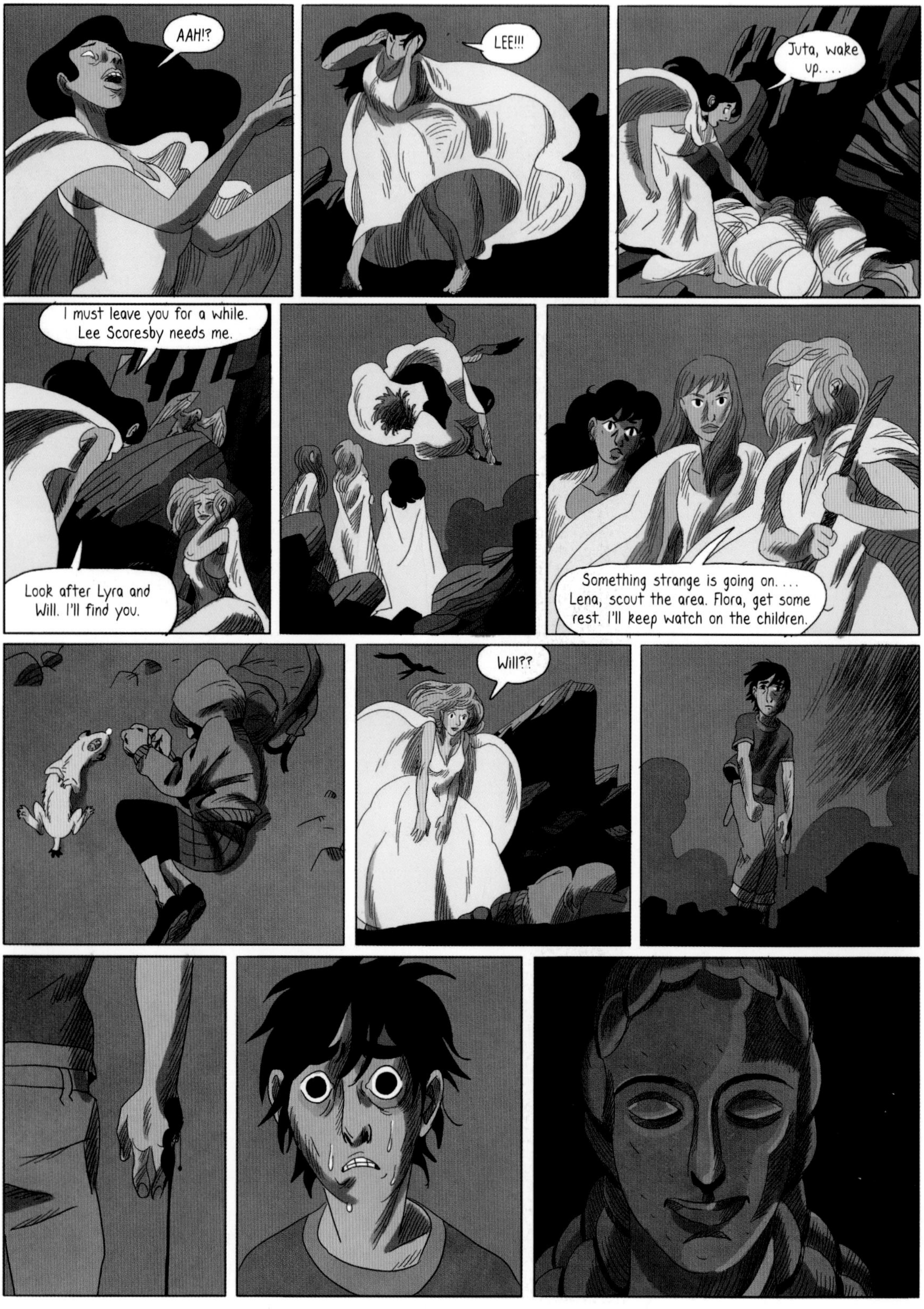
AAH!?
LEE!!!
Juta, wake up. . . .
I must leave you for a while. Lee Scoresby needs me.
Look after Lyra and Will. I'll find you.
Something strange is going on. . . . Lena, scout the area. Flora, get some rest. I'll keep watch on the children.
Will??

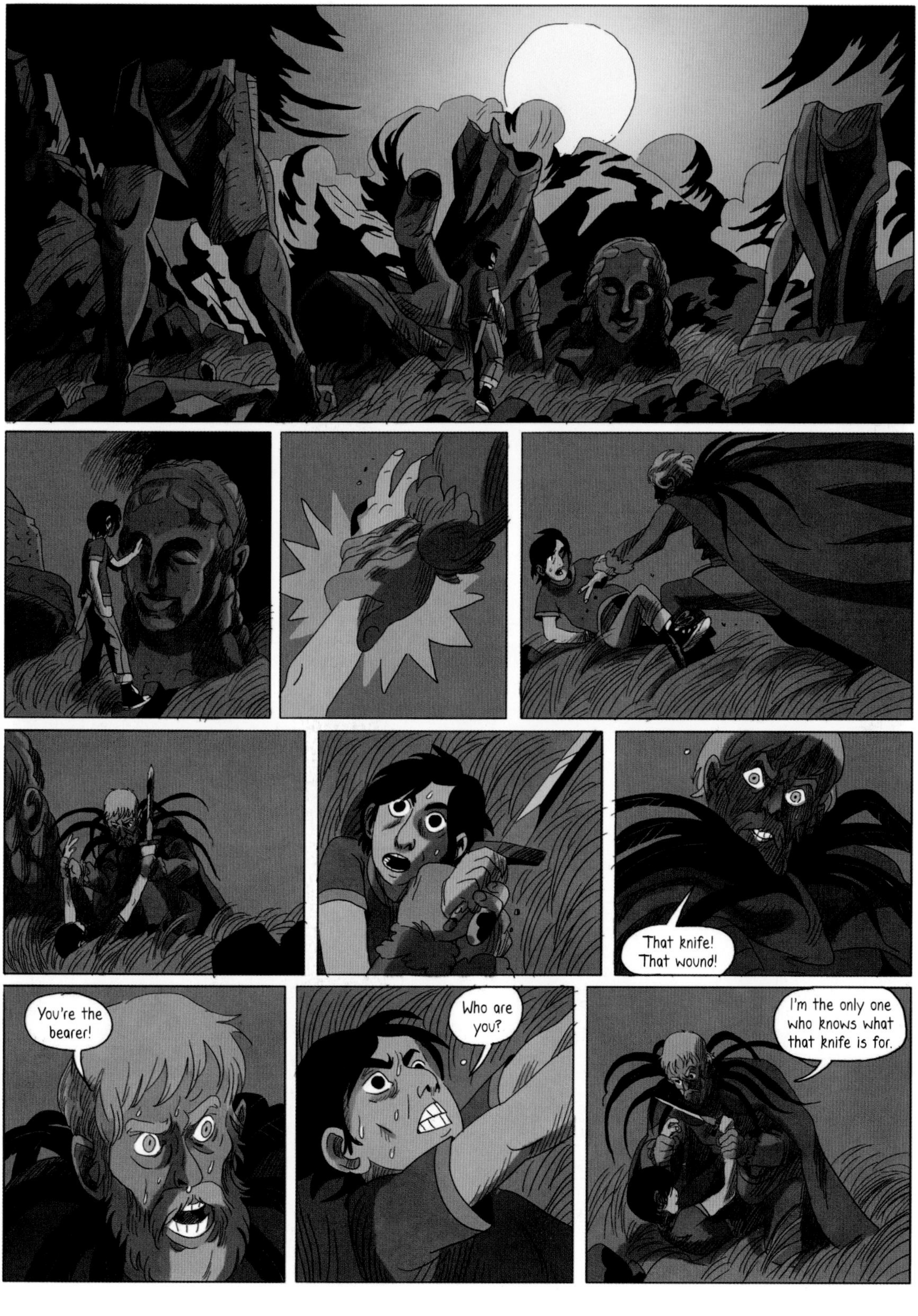
That knife!
That wound!
You're the bearer!
Who are you?
I'm the only one who knows what that knife is for.

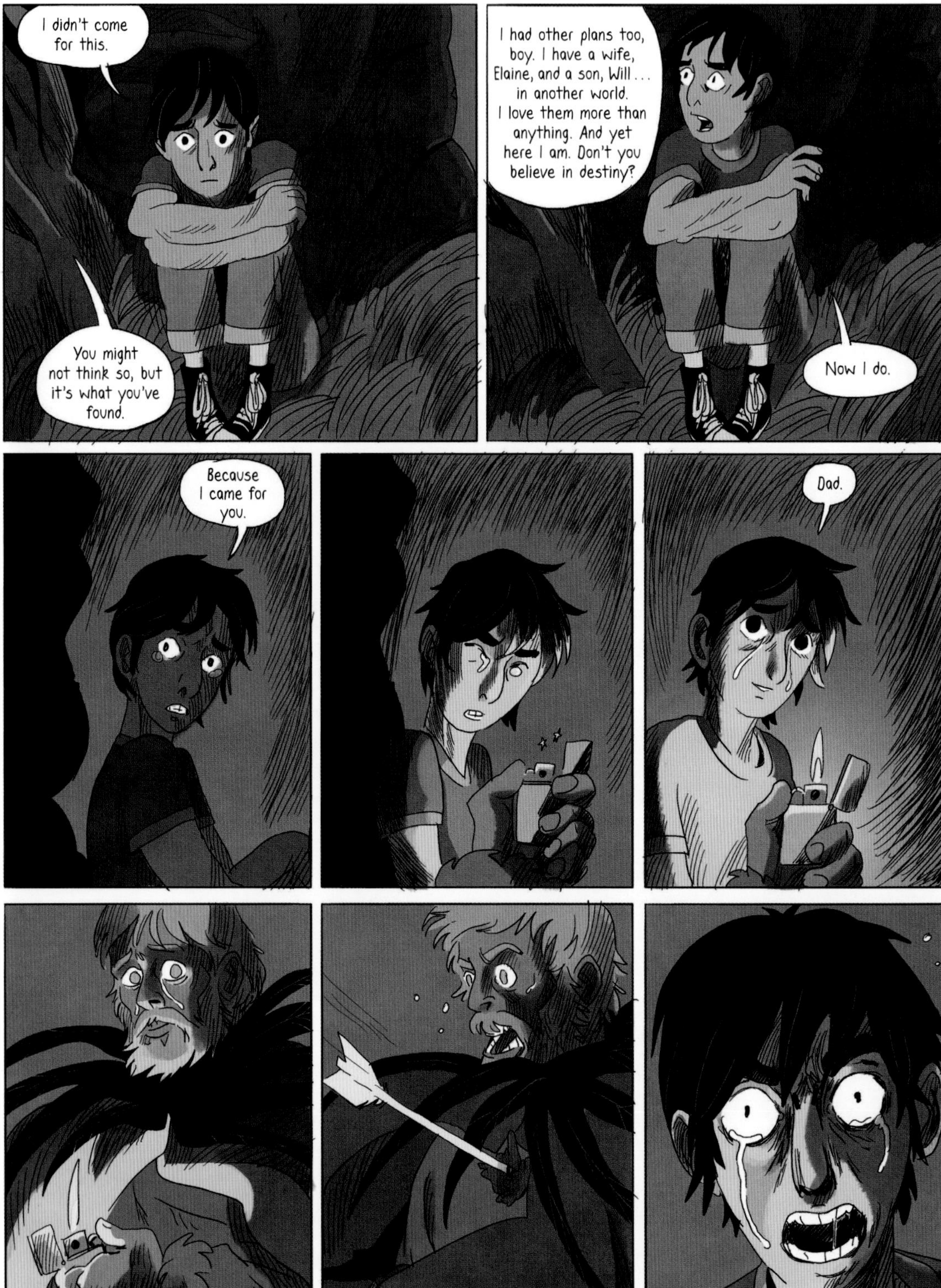
I didn't come for this.
You might not think so, but it's what you've found.
I had other plans too, boy. I have a wife, Elaine, and a son, Will . . . in another world. I love them more than anything. And yet here I am. Don't you believe in destiny?
Now I do.
Because I came for you.
Dad.

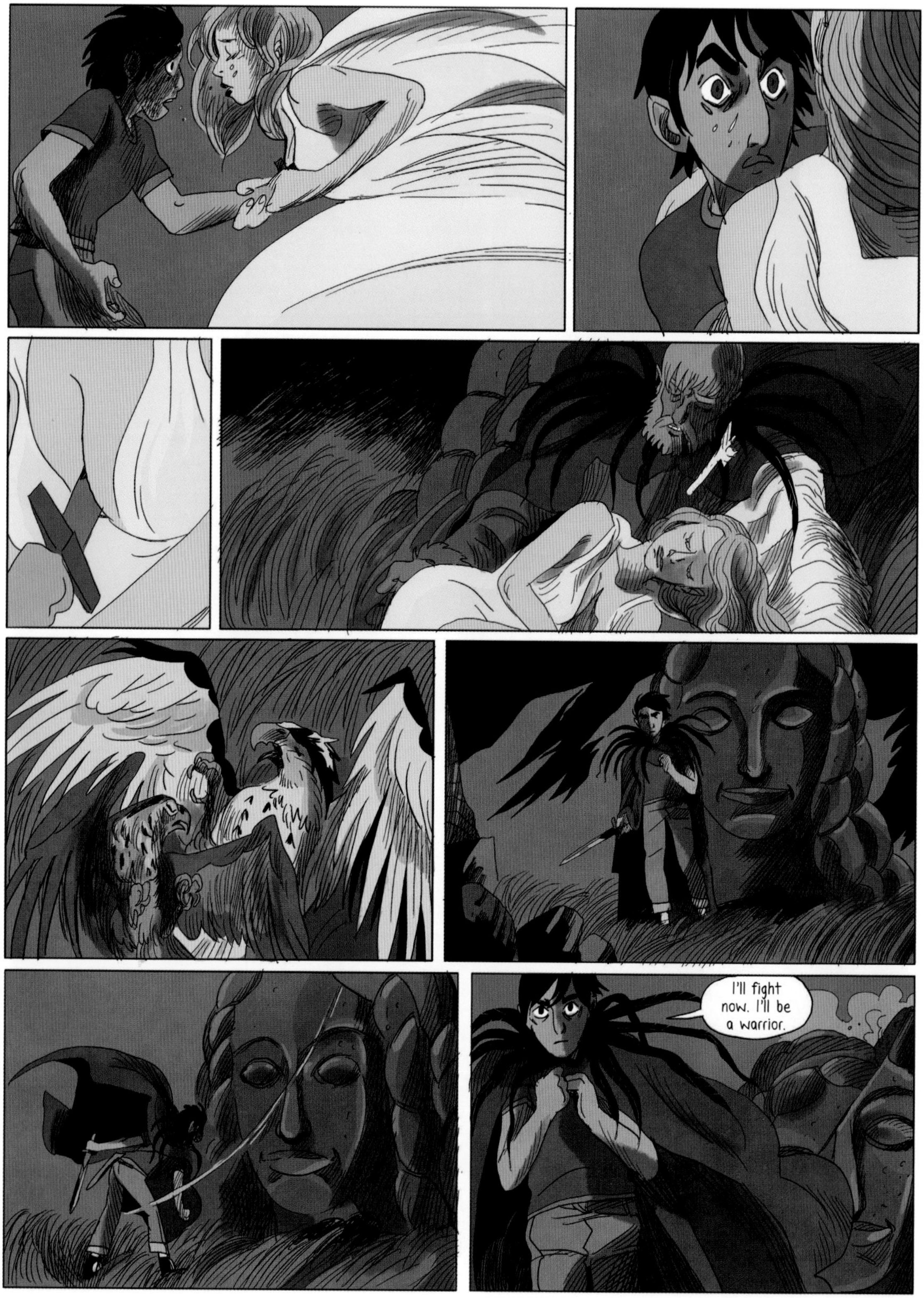
I'll fight now. I'll be a warrior.

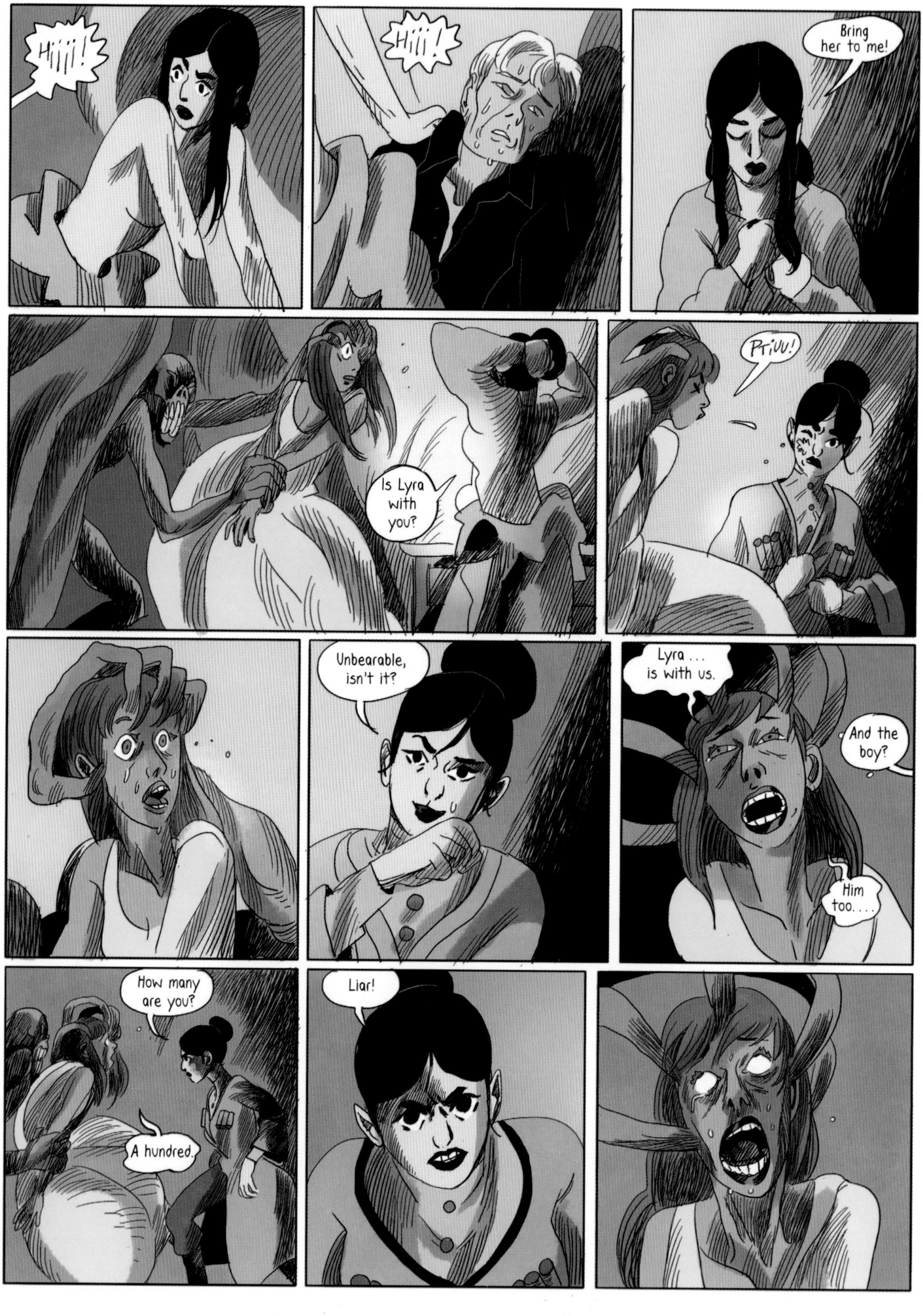
Hiiii!
Hiii!
Bring her to me!
Is Lyra with you?
Priuu!
Unbearable, isn't it?
Lyra . . . is with us.
And the boy?
Him too. . . .
How many are you?
A hundred.
Liar!

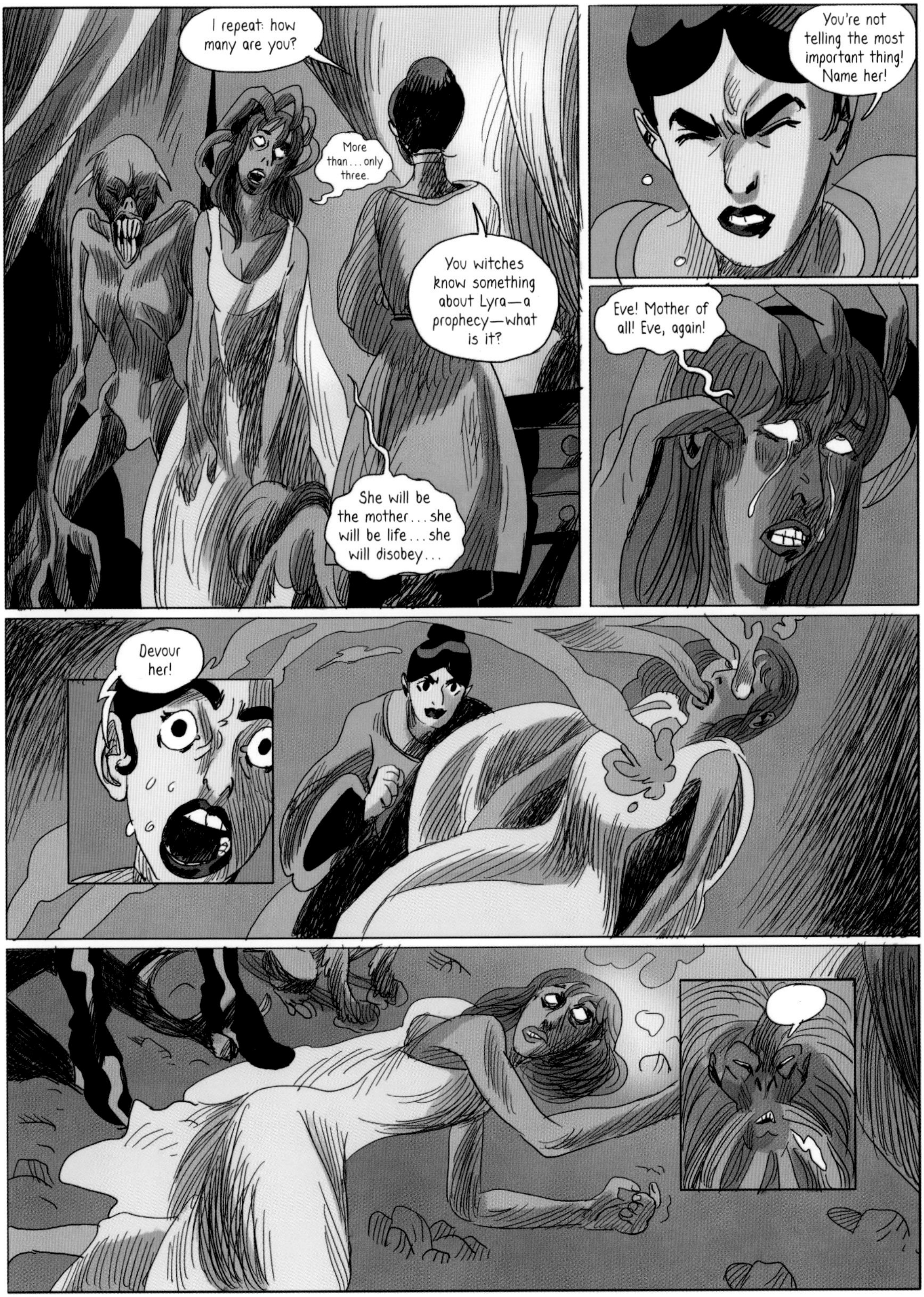
I repeat: how many are you?
More than . . . only three.
You witches know something about Lyra—a prophecy—what is it?
She will be the mother . . . she will be life . . . she will disobey . . .
You're not telling the most important thing! Name her!
Eve! Mother of all! Eve, again!
Devour her!

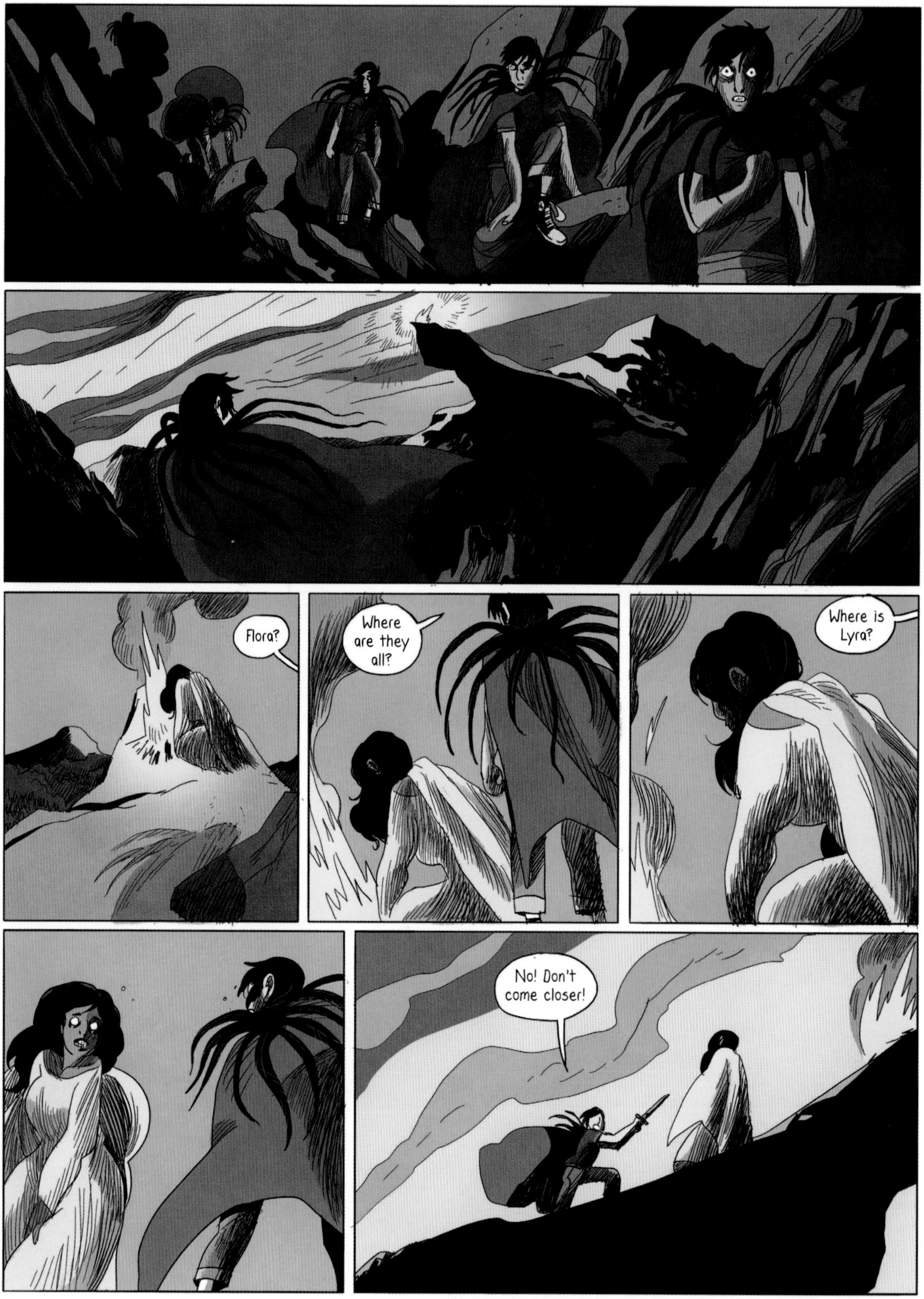
Flora?
Where are they all?
Where is Lyra?
No! Don't come closer!

HIS DARK MATERIALS

RETURN TO THE BEGINNING
OF LYRA'S JOURNEY IN:

Adapted from *The Golden Compass* © 1995 by Philip Pullman.

Excerpt text translation © 2015 by Annie Eaton, art © 2014 by Gallimard Jeunesse. Published by Alfred A. Knopf,

an imprint of Random House Children's Books, a division of Penguin Random House LLC, New York.

OXFORD

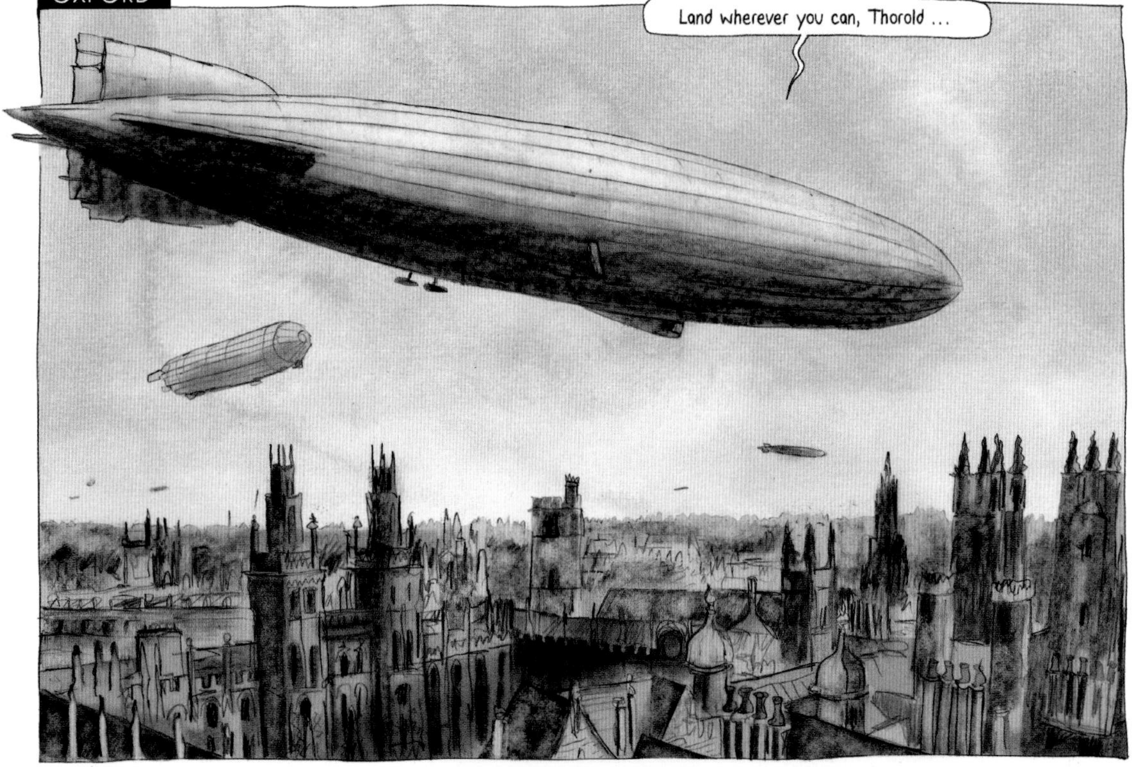
Land wherever you can, Thorold ...

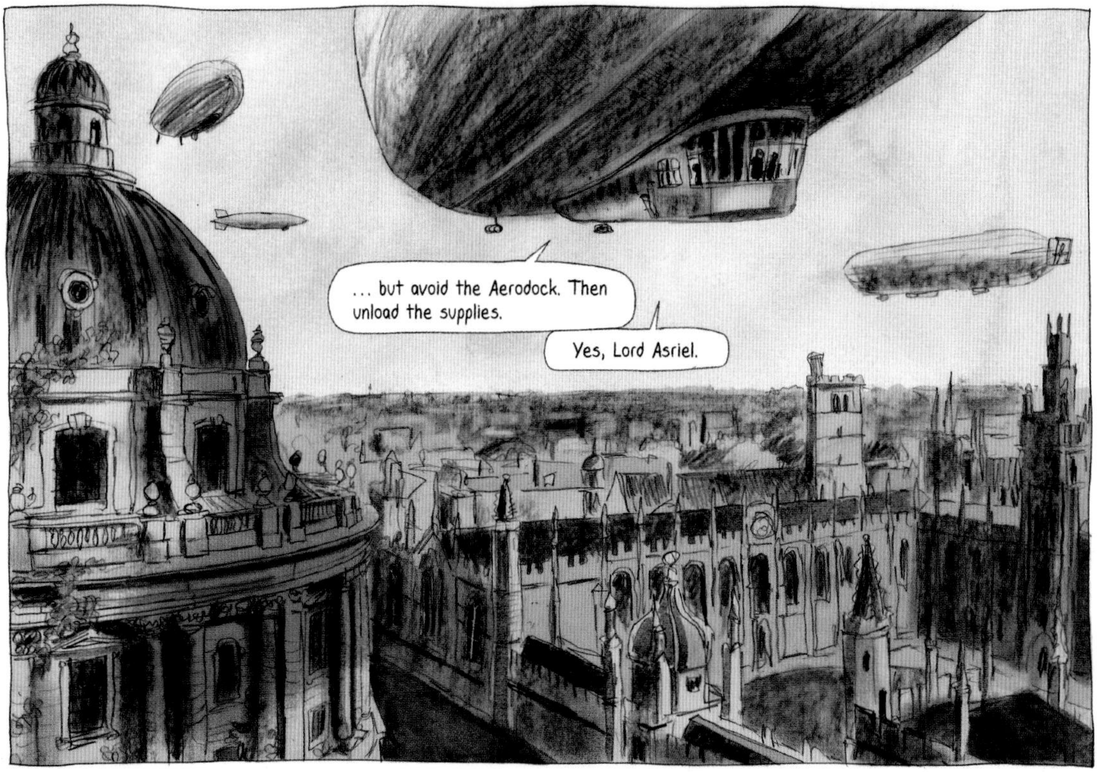
... but avoid the Aerodock. Then unload the supplies.
Yes, Lord Asriel.

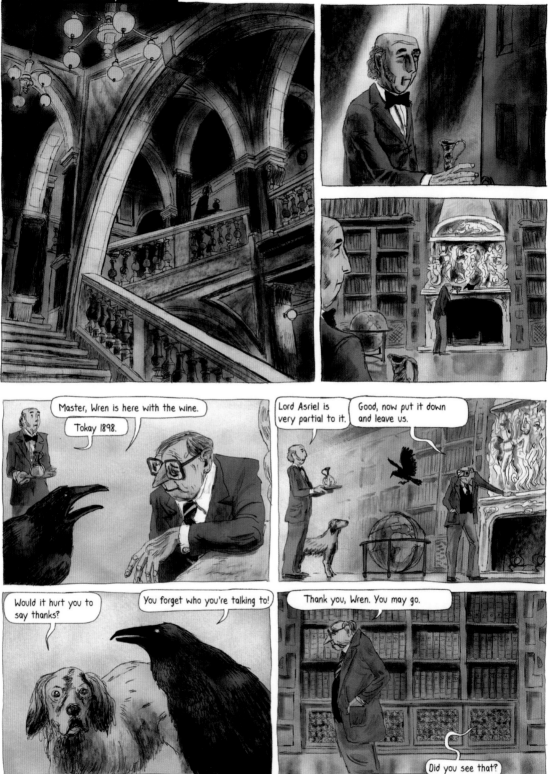